THE DODD, MEAD GALLERY OF HORROR

THE DODD, MEAD

Gallery of Horror

Edited by Charles L. Grant

DODD, MEAD & COMPANY · NEW YORK

Published by Dodd, Mead & Company, Inc.,
79 Madison Avenue, New York, N.Y. 10016

Distributed in Canada by
McClelland and Stewart Limited, Toronto

Manufactured in the United States of America

Designed by Judith Lerner

Library of Congress Cataloging in Publication Data
Main entry under title:

The Dodd, Mead gallery of horror.

    1. Horror tales, American.   2. Horror tales, English.
I. Grant, Charles L.   II. Dodd, Mead & Company.
PS648.H6D6   1983   813'.0872'08   82–24867
ISBN 0-396-08160-6; 0-396-08266-1 (pbk.)

CONTENTS

INTRODUCTION

MORE YEARS AGO than I care to remember, I used to spend every Saturday afternoon at the Lincoln Theater in Kearny, New Jersey, joining my friends in an escape from school, the weather, parents, homework, and anything (or anyone) else that tended to smack of childhood's worst Monster—being responsible (otherwise known as acting your age, or growing up). It was, at the time, quite natural to substitute for this Monster a delightful clutch of others— the werewolf, the vampire, the ghost, the banshee, the thing in the cellar, the thing in the attic. More often than not my friends and I would leave the theater laughing, walking stiff-legged or pretending we were wearing long black capes and fanging the girls walking by.

But as sure as cartoon follows first feature, there was also Saturday night. In bed. Alone. Sleeping the sleep of the innocent until *something* woke me up. Woke me up so hard, in fact, that I had a hard time going back to sleep; and often I would require the soothing services of my parents to assure me that I would, indeed, see the next dawn.

You would think that years of this would have cured me of Karloff and Lugosi and Zucco and all the others, but it didn't. And it didn't any of my friends, either, though no one would admit to the nightmares that followed the Saturday matinee. The only thing we did know was: they were fun. Not in the dreaming, but in the re-telling. After all, that's why we went to those films in the first place —to get scared then, and to get scared again later.

Since then the Monster has gotten me, for the most part. I have grown up, I have accepted some measure of responsibility here and there, and I do, on occasion, act my age (whatever the hell that means).

On the other hand, I also write and edit books like this, ones that if all goes well will give their readers a good dose of the chills, the shudders, and the outright shrieks now and then. After all, if the

9

truth be known, we haven't grown up all that much; the fears we have now aren't the same as they were when we were children, but they're fears just the same. They make our palms sweat, they give us nightmares, and they're sometimes powerful enough to alter our characters.

They are now, as they were then, *real*.

So why read about them?

Because this book you can put down, walk away from, close with a slam in the sure knowledge that all of the horrid things happening to the people in these pages can't happen to you. What's on these pages doesn't exist.

I still think they're fun to flirt with, however, to give in to now and again, and if they hit closer to home than they would have when we were kids, well, that's the nightmare risk, isn't it? That's where the fun comes in.

And to be sure that these writers haven't wasted their time, they ask only one thing of you (aside from a shadowy room and a cold wind and a pane that rattles unnervingly in the sash) : just as watching a film with two dozen graphic and full-color murders tends to numb the mind and produces little more than yawns, reading twenty or more stories at a clip is dulling, and ultimately disappointing. It doesn't make any difference to the authors gathered here how fast the traffic is going out on your street; all they ask is for a fair chance to do to you what you want them to—horrify, terrify, or just give you a dose of squirming anxiety.

These stories are variously graphic, quiet, oriented toward the supernatural, aimed at the psychological; some are bludgeons and some are razors; some will ask you for more work than others, and some will do their work more than once—like the shock of a virulent poison entering your system . . . and the aftertaste that lingers.

All, however, are in the business of recording nightmares.

And sooner or later you just might hit one of yours.

Of course, as long as the lights work, and as long as you don't really not for a minute believe in any of this stuff, it won't matter to you at all. That childhood Monster has gotten hold of you and transformed you, and you can handle most anything these days, especially stories that do nothing more than nibble a little at your imagination, tug a little at the shadows you were sure were banished when the sun came up.

Sure you can.

Sleep well.

CHARLES L. GRANT
Newton, New Jersey
January 1983

THE DODD, MEAD GALLERY OF HORROR

Something Nasty

BY WILLIAM F. NOLAN

*Adult seem to find wondrous delight in tormenting the young
to tears or to nightmares, primarily by aiming straight for
what they know will scare the young most. It may be a reaction to their own experiences before they "grew up," or it
may be something else, something worse—something basic.*

*William F. Nolan, a resident of California, has edited,
written, and co-authored dozens of books ranging from the
macabre to the thrills of sports car racing to his just-released
biography of Steve McQueen. He has also written screenplays
for television and film, among them* Burnt Offerings *and*
Trilogy Of Terror.

"HAVE you had your shower yet, Janey?"

Her mother's voice from below stairs, drifting smokily up to her,
barely audible where she lay in her bed.

Louder now; insistent. "Janey! Will you *answer* me!"

She got up, cat-stretched, walked into the hall, to the landing,
where her mother could hear her. "I've been reading."

"But I *told* you that Uncle Gus was coming over this afternoon."

"I hate him," said Janey softly.

"You're muttering. I can't understand you." Frustration. Anger
and frustration. "Come down here at once."

When Janey reached the bottom of the stairs her mother's image
was rippled. The little girl blinked rapidly, trying to clear her water-
ing eyes.

Janey's mother stood tall and ample-fleshed and fresh-smelling
above her in a satiny summer dress.

Mommy always looks nice when Uncle Gus is coming.

"Why are you crying?" Anger had given way to concern.

"Because," said Janey.

15

"Because why?"

"Because I don't want to talk to Uncle Gus."

"But he *adores* you! He comes over especially to see you."

"No, he doesn't," said Janey, scrubbing at her cheek with a small fist. "He doesn't adore me and he doesn't come specially to see me. He comes to get money from Daddy."

Her mother was shocked. "That's a terrible thing to say!"

"But it's true. *Isn't* it true?"

"Your Uncle Gus was hurt in the war. He can't hold down an ordinary job. We just do what we can to help him."

"He never liked me," said Janey. "He says I make too much noise. And he never lets me play with Whiskers when he's here."

"That's because cats bother him. He's not used to them. He doesn't like furry things." Her mother touched at Janey's hair. Soft gold. "Remember that mouse you got last Christmas, how nervous it made him. . . . Remember?"

"Pete was smart," said Janey. "He didn't like Uncle Gus, same as me."

"Mice neither like nor dislike people," Janey's mother told her. "They're not intelligent enough for that."

Janey shook her head stubbornly. "Pete was *very* intelligent. He could find cheese anywhere in my room, no matter where I hid it."

"That has to do with a basic sense of smell, not intelligence," her mother said. "But we're wasting time here, Janey. You run upstairs, take your shower and then put on your pretty new dress. The one with red polka dots."

"They're strawberries. It has little red strawberries on it."

"Fine. Now just do as I say. Gus will be here soon and I want my brother to be *proud* of his niece."

Blonde head down, her small heels dragging at the top of each step, Janey went back upstairs.

"I'm not going to report this to your father," Janey's mother was saying, her voice dimming as the little girl continued upward. "I'll just tell him you overslept."

"I don't care what you tell Daddy," murmured Janey. The words were smothered in hallway distance as she moved toward her room.

Daddy would believe anything Mommy told him. He always did.

16

Sometimes it was true, about oversleeping. It was hard to wake up from her afternoon nap. *Because I put off going to sleep. Because I hate it.* Along with eating broccoli, and taking colored vitamin pills in little animal shapes and seeing the dentist and going on roller coasters.

Uncle Gus had taken her on a high, scary roller coaster ride last summer at the park, and it had made her vomit. He liked to upset her, frighten her. Mommy didn't know about all the times Uncle Gus said scary things to her, or played mean tricks on her, or took her places she didn't want to go.

Mommy would leave her with him while she went shopping, and Janey absolutely *hated* being there in his dark old house. He knew the dark frightened her. He'd sit there in front of her with all the lights out, telling spooky stories, with sick, awful things in them, his voice oily and horrible. She'd get so scared, listening to him, that sometimes she'd cry.

And that made him smile.

"Gus. Always so *good* to see you!"

"Hi, Sis."

"C'mon inside. Jim's puttering around out back somewhere. I've fixed us a nice lunch. Sliced turkey. And I made some cornbread."

"So where's my favorite niece?"

"Janey's due down here any second. She'll be wearing her new dress—just for you."

"Well, now, isn't that nice."

She was watching from the top of the stairs, lying flat on her stomach so she wouldn't be seen. It made her sick, watching Mommy hug Uncle Gus that way, each time he came over, as if it had been *years* between visits. Why couldn't Mommy see how mean Uncle Gus was? All of her friends in class saw he was a bad person the first day he took her to school. Kids can tell right away about a person. Like that mean ole Mr. Kruger in geography, who made Janey stay after class when she forgot to do her homework. All the kids knew that Mr. Kruger was *awful*. Why does it take grownups so long to know things?

Janey slid backwards into the hall shadows. Stood up. Time to go downstairs. In her playclothes. Probably meant she'd get a spanking after Uncle Gus left, but it would be worth it not to have to put on her new dress for him. Spankings don't hurt *too* much. Worth it.

"Well, *here's* my little princess!" Uncle Gus was lifting her hard into the air, to make her dizzy. He knew how much she hated being swung around in the air. He set her down with a thump. Looked at her with his big cruel eyes. "And where's that pretty new dress your Mommy told me about?"

"It got torn," Janey said, staring at the carpet. "I can't wear it today."

Her mother was angry again. "That is *not* true, young lady, and you know it! I ironed that dress this morning and it is perfect." She pointed upward. "You march right back upstairs to your room and put on that dress!"

"No, Maggie." Gus shook his head. "Let the child stay as she is. She looks fine. Let's just have lunch." He prodded Janey in the stomach. "Bet that little tummy of yours is starved for some turkey."

And Uncle Gus pretended to laugh. Janey was never fooled; she knew real laughs from pretend laughs. But Mommy and Daddy never seemed to know the difference.

Janey's mother sighed and smiled at Gus. "All right, I'll let it go this time—but I really think you spoil her."

"Nonsense. Janey and I understand each other." He stared down at her. "Don't we, sweetie?"

Lunch was no fun. Janey couldn't finish her mashed potatoes, and she'd just nibbled at her turkey. She could never enjoy eating with her uncle there. As usual, her father barely noticed she was at the table. *He* didn't care if she wore her new dress or not. Mommy took care of her and Daddy took care of business, whatever that was. Janey could never figure out what he did, but he left every day for some office she's never seen and he made enough money there so that he always had some to give to Uncle Gus when Mommy asked him for a check.

Today was Sunday so Daddy was home with his big newspaper to read and the car to wax and the grass to trim. He did the same things every Sunday.

Does Daddy love me? I know that Mommy does, even though she spanks me sometimes. But she always hugs me after. Daddy never hugs me. He buys me ice cream, and he takes me to the movies on Saturday afternoon, but I don't think he loves me.

Which is why she could never tell him the truth about Uncle Gus. He'd never listen.

And Mommy just didn't understand.

After lunch, Uncle Gus grabbed Janey firmly by the hand and took her into the back yard. Then he sat her down next to him on the big wooden swing.

"I'll bet your new dress is *ugly*," he said in a cold voice.

"Is not. It's pretty!"

Her discomfort pleased him. He leaned over, close to her right ear. "Want to know a secret?"

Janey shook her head. "I want to go back with Mommy. I don't like being out here."

She started away, but he grabbed her, pulling her roughly back onto the swing. "You *listen* to me when I talk to you." His eyes glittered. "I'm going to tell you a secret. About yourself."

"Then tell me."

He grinned. "You've got something inside."

"What's that mean?"

"It means there's something deep down inside your rotten little belly. And it's *alive*!"

"Huh?" She blinked, beginning to get scared.

"A creature. That lives off what you eat and breathes the air you breathe and can see out of your eyes." He pulled her face close to his. "Open your mouth, Janey, so I can look in and see what's living down there!"

"No, I *won't*." She attempted to twist away, but he was too strong. "You're lying! You're just telling me an awful *lie*! You *are*!"

"Open wide." And he applied pressure to her jaw with the fingers of his right hand. Her mouth opened. "Ah, that's better. Let's have a look . . ." He peered into her mouth. "Yes, *there*. I can see it now."

She drew back, eyes wide, really alarmed. "What's it like?"

"Nasty! Horrid. With very sharp teeth. A *rat*, I'd say. Or something *like* a rat. Long and gray and plump."

19

"I don't have it! I don't!"

"Oh, but you do, Janey." His voice was oily. "I saw its red eyes shining and its long snaky tail. It's down there all right. Something nasty."

And he laughed. Real, this time. No pretend laugh. Uncle Gus was having himself some fun.

Janey knew he was just trying to scare her again—but she wasn't absolutely 100 percent sure about the thing inside. Maybe he *had* seen something.

"Do . . . any other people have . . . creatures . . . living in them?"

"Depends," said Uncle Gus. "Bad things live inside bad people. Nice little girls don't have them."

"I'm nice!"

"Well now, that's a matter of opinion, isn't it?" His voice was soft and unpleasant. "If you *were* nice, you wouldn't have something nasty living inside."

"I don't believe you," said Janey, breathing fast. "How could it be real?"

"Things are real when people believe in them." He lit a long black cigarette, drew in the smoke, exhaled it slowly. "Have you ever heard of voodoo, Janey?"

She shook her head.

"The way it works is—this witch doctor puts a curse on someone by making a doll and sticking a needle into the doll's heart. Then he leaves the doll at the house of the man he's cursed. When the man sees it he becomes very frightened. He makes the curse real by *believing* in it."

"And then what happens?"

"His heart stops and he dies."

Janey felt her own heart beating very rapidly.

"You're afraid, aren't you, Janey?"

"Maybe . . . a little."

"You're afraid, all right." He chuckled. "And you should be— with a thing like that inside you!"

"You're a very bad and wicked man!" she told him, tears misting her eyes.

And she ran swiftly back to the house.

That night, in her room, Janey sat rigid in bed, hugging Whiskers.

He liked to come in late after dark and curl up on the coverlet just under her feet and snooze there until dawn. He was an easy-going, gray-and-black housecat who never complained about anything and always delivered a small "meep" of contentment whenever Janey picked him up for some stroking. Then he would begin to purr.

Tonight Whiskers was not purring. He sensed the harsh vibrations in the room, sensed how upset Janey was. He quivered uneasily in her arms.

"Uncle Gus lied to me, didn't he, Whiskers?" The little girl's voice was strained, uncertain. "See . . ." She hugged the cat closer. "Nothing's down there, huh?"

And she yawned her mouth wide to show her friend that no rat-thing lived there. If one did, ole Whiskers would be sticking a paw inside to get it. But the cat didn't react. Just blinked slitted green eyes at her.

"I knew it," Janey said, vastly relieved. "If I just don't believe it's in there, then it *isn't*."

She slowly relaxed her tensed body muscles—and Whiskers, sensing a change, began to purr—a tiny, soothing motorized sound in the night.

Everything was all right now. No red-eyed creature existed in her tummy. Suddenly she felt exhausted. It was late, and she had school tomorrow.

Janey slid down under the covers and closed her eyes, releasing Whiskers, who padded to his usual spot on the bed.

She had a lot to tell her friends.

It was Thursday, a day Janey usually hated. Every other Thursday her mother went shopping and left her to have lunch with Uncle Gus in his big spooky house with the shutters closed tight against the sun and shadows filling every hallway.

But *this* Thursday would be all different, so Janey didn't mind when her mother drove off and left her alone with her uncle. *This* time, she told herself, she wouldn't be afraid. A giggle.

She might even have fun!

When Uncle Gus put Janey's soup plate in front of her he asked her how she was feeling.

"Fine," said Janey quietly, eyes down.

"Then you'll be able to appreciate the soup." He smiled, trying to look pleasant. "It's a special recipe. Try it."

She spooned some into her mouth.

"How does it taste?"

"Kinda sour."

Gus shook his head, trying some for himself. "Ummm . . . delicious." He paused. "Know what's in it?"

She shook her head.

He grinned, leaning toward her across the table. "It's owl-eye soup. Made from the dead eyes of an owl. All mashed up fresh, just for you."

She looked at him steadily. "You want me to upchuck, don't you, Uncle Gus?"

"My goodness no, Janey." There was oiled delight in his voice. "I just thought you'd like to know what you swallowed."

Janey pushed her plate away. "I'm not going to be sick because I don't believe you. And when you don't believe in something then it's not real."

Gus scowled at her, finishing his soup.

Janey knew he planned to tell her another awful spook story after lunch, but she wasn't upset about that. Because.

Because there wouldn't *be* any after lunch for Uncle Gus.

It was time for her surprise.

"I got something to tell you, Uncle Gus."

"So tell me." His voice was sharp and ugly.

"All my friends at school know about the thing inside. We talked about it a lot and now we all believe in it. It has red eyes and it's furry and it smells bad. And it's got lots of very sharp teeth."

"You *bet* it has," Gus said, brightening at her words. "And it's always hungry."

"But guess what," said Janey. "Surprise! It's not inside me, Uncle Gus . . . it's inside *you*!"

He glared at her. "That's not funny, you little bitch. Don't try to turn this around and pretend that ——"

He stopped in mid-sentence, spoon clattering to the floor as he stood up abruptly. His face was flushed. He made strangling sounds.

"It wants out," said Janey.

22

Gus doubled over the table, hands clawing at his stomach. "Call . . . call a . . . doctor!" he gasped.

"A doctor won't help," said Janey in satisfaction. "Nothing can stop it now."

Janey followed him calmly, munching on an apple. She watched him stagger and fall in the doorway, rolling over on his back, eyes wild with panic.

She stood over him, looking down at her uncle's stomach under the white shirt.

Something *bulged* there.

Gus screamed.

Late that night, alone in her room, Janey held Whiskers tight against her chest and whispered into her pet's quivering ear. "Mommy's been crying," she told the cat. "She's real upset about what happened to Uncle Gus. Are *you* upset, Whiskers?"

The cat yawned, revealing sharp white teeth.

"I didn't think so. That's because you didn't like Uncle Gus any more than me, did you?"

She hugged him. "Wanta hear a *secret*, Whiskers?"

The cat blinked lazily at her, beginning to purr.

"You know that mean ole Mr. Kruger at school. . . . Well, guess what?" She smiled. "Me an' the other kids are gonna talk to him tomorrow about something he's got inside him." Janey shuddered deliciously. "Something nasty!"

And she giggled.

Canavan's Back Yard

BY JOSEPH PAYNE BRENNAN

*The best Dark Fantasy deals, as does any good fiction, with
the real, the here and now, the world we all know; the difference, of course, is the twist the writer gives what we thought
we knew, what we thought we were comfortable with. That
twist doesn't have to be a jarring one; it just has to make
things look only slightly out of kilter.*

*Joseph Payne Brennan is one of the Masters of Dark Fan-
tasy, beyond all doubt. His short fiction has paved the way for
all of us working in the field today, and the following story
has withstood the test of time to rightfully be called a classic.*

I FIRST met Canavan over twenty years ago shortly after he had
emigrated from London. He was an antiquarian and a lover of old
books; so he quite naturally set up shop as a second-hand book
dealer after he settled in New Haven.

Since his small capital didn't permit him to rent premises in the
center of the city, he rented combined business and living quarters
in an isolated old house near the outskirts of town. The section was
sparsely settled, but since a good percentage of Canavan's business
was transacted by mail, it didn't particularly matter.

Quite often, after a morning spent at my typewriter, I walked out
to Canavan's shop and spent most of the afternoon browsing among
his old books. I found it a great pleasure, especially because Canavan
never resorted to high-pressure methods to make a sale. He was
aware of my precarious financial situation; he never frowned if I
walked away empty-handed.

In fact, he seemed to welcome me for my company alone. Only a
few book buyers called at his place with regularity, and I think he
was often lonely. Sometimes when business was slow, he would brew

25

a pot of English tea and the two of us would sit for hours, drinking tea and talking about books.

Canavan even looked like an antiquarian book dealer—or the popular caricature of one. He was small of frame, somewhat stoop-shouldered, and his blue eyes peered out from behind archaic spectacles with steel rims and square-cut lenses.

Although I doubt if his yearly income ever matched that of a good paperhanger, he managed to "get by" and he was content. Content, that is, until he began noticing his back yard.

Behind the ramshackle old house in which he lived and ran his shop, stretched a long, desolate yard overgrown with brambles and high brindle-colored grass. Several decayed apple trees, jagged and black with rot, added to the scene's dismal aspect. The broken wooden fences on both sides of the yard were all but swallowed up by the tangle of coarse grass. They appeared to be literally sinking into the ground. Altogether, the yard presented an unusually depressing picture, and I often wondered why Canavan didn't clean it up. But it was none of my business; I never mentioned it.

One afternoon when I visited the shop, Canavan was not in the front display room, so I walked down a narrow corridor to a rear storeroom where he sometimes worked, packing and unpacking book shipments. When I entered the storeroom, Canavan was standing at the window, looking out at the back yard.

I started to speak and then for some reason didn't. I think what stopped me was the look on Canavan's face. He was gazing out at the yard with a peculiar intense expression, as if he were completely absorbed by something he saw there. Varying, conflicting emotions showed on his strained features. He seemed both fascinated and fearful, attracted and repelled. When he finally noticed me, he almost jumped. He stared at me for a moment as if I were a total stranger.

Then his old easy smile came back, and his blue eyes twinkled behind the square spectacles. He shook his head. "That back yard of mine sure looks funny sometimes. You look at it long enough, you think it runs for miles!"

That was all he said at the time, and I soon forgot about it. I didn't know that was just the beginning of the horrible business.

26

After that, whenever I visited the shop, I found Canavan in the rear storeroom. Once in a while he was actually working, but most of the time he was simply standing at the window looking out at that dreary yard of his.

Sometimes he would stand there for minutes completely oblivious to my presence. Whatever he saw appeared to rivet his entire attention. His countenance at these times showed an expression of fright mingled with a queer kind of pleasurable expectancy. Usually it was necessary for me to cough loudly or shuffle my feet before he turned from the window.

Afterward, when he talked about books, he would seem to be his old self again, but I began to experience the disconcerting feeling that he was merely acting, that while he chatted about incunabula, his thoughts were actually still dwelling on that infernal back yard.

Several times I thought of questioning him about the yard, but whenever words were on the tip of my tongue, I was stopped by a sense of embarrassment. How can one admonish a man for looking out of a window at his own back yard? What does one say and how does one say it?

I kept silent. Later I regretted it bitterly.

Canavan's business, never really flourishing, began to diminish. Worse than than, he appeared to be failing physically. He grew more stooped and gaunt. Though his eyes never lost their sharp glint, I began to believe it was more the glitter of fever than the twinkle of healthy enthusiasm which animated them.

One afternoon when I entered the shop, Canavan was nowhere to be found. Thinking he might be just outside the back door engaged in some household chore, I leaned up against the rear window and looked out.

I didn't see Canavan, but as I gazed out over the yard I was swept with a sudden inexplicable sense of desolation which seemed to roll over me like the wave of an icy sea. My initial impulse was to pull away from the window, but something held me. As I stared out over that miserable tangle of briars and brindle grass, I experienced what for want of a better word I can only call *curiosity*. Perhaps some cool, analytical, dispassionate part of my brain simply wanted to discover what had caused my sudden feeling of acute depression. Or

27

possibly some feature of that wretched vista attracted me on a sub-conscious level which I had never permitted to crowd up into my sane and waking hours.

In any case, I remained at the window. The long dry brown grass wavered slightly in the wind. The rotted black trees reared motion-less. Not a single bird, not even a butterfly, hovered over that bleak expanse. There was nothing to be seen except the stalks of long brindle grass, the decayed trees, and scattered clumps of low-grow-ing briars.

Yet there was something about that particular isolated slice of landscape which I found intriguing. I think I had the feeling that it presented some kind of puzzle, and, that if I gazed at it long enough, the puzzle would resolve itself.

After I had stood looking out at it for a few minutes, I experi-enced the odd sensation that its perspective was subtly altering. Nei-ther the grass nor the trees changed, and yet the yard itself seemed to expand its dimensions. At first I merely reflected that the yard was actually much longer than I had previously believed. Then I had an idea that in reality it stretched for several acres. Finally, I became convinced that it continued for an interminable distance and that, if I entered it, I might walk for miles and miles before I came to the end.

I was seized by a sudden almost overpowering desire to rush out the back door, plunge into that sea of wavering brindle grass, and stride straight ahead until I had discovered for myself just how far it did extend. I was, in fact, on the point of doing so—when I saw Canavan.

He appeared abruptly out of the tangle of tall grass at the near end of the yard. For at least a minute he seemed to be completely lost. He looked at the back of his own house as if he had never in his life seen it before. He was disheveled and obviously excited. Briars clung to his trousers and jacket, and pieces of grass were stuck in the hooks of his old-fashioned shoes. His eyes roved around wildly; he seemed about to turn and bolt back into the tangle from which he had just emerged.

I rapped loudly on the window pane. He paused in a half turn, looked over his shoulder, and saw me. Gradually an expression of

28

normality returned to his agitated features. Walking in a weary slouch, he approached the house. I hurried to the door and let him in. He went straight to the front display room and sank down in a chair.

He looked up when I followed him into the room. "Frank," he said in a half whisper, "would you make some tea?"

I brewed tea, and he drank it scalding hot without saying a word. He looked utterly exhausted; I knew he was too tired to tell me what had happened.

"You had better stay indoors for a few days," I said as I left.

He nodded weakly, without looking up, and bade me good day.

When I returned to the shop the next afternoon, he appeared rested and refreshed but nevertheless moody and depressed. He made no mention of the previous day's episode. For a week or so it seemed as if he might forget about the yard.

But one day when I went into the shop, he was standing at the rear window, and I could see that he tore himself away only with the greatest reluctance. After that, the pattern began repeating itself with regularity. I knew that that weird tangle of brindle grass behind his house was becoming an obsession.

Because I feared for his business as well as for his fragile health, I finally remonstrated with him. I pointed out that he was losing customers; he had not issued a book catalogue in months. I told him that the time spent in gazing at that witch's half acre he called his back yard would be better spent in listing his books and filling his orders. I assured him that an obsession such as his was sure to undermine his health. And finally I pointed out the absurd and ridiculous aspects of the affair. If people knew he spent hours in staring out of his window at nothing more than a miniature jungle of grass and briars, they might think he was actually mad.

I ended by boldly asking him exactly what he had experienced that afternoon when I had seen him come out of the grass with a lost bewildered expression on his face.

He removed his square spectacles with a sigh. "Frank," he said, "I know you mean well. But there's something about that back yard— some secret—that I've got to find out. I don't know what it is exactly —something about distance and dimensions and perspectives, I think.

29

But whatever it is, I've come to consider it—well, a challenge. I've got to get to the root of it. If you think I'm crazy, I'm sorry. But I'll have no rest until I solve the riddle of that piece of ground."

He replaced his spectacles with a frown. "That afternoon," he went on, "when you were standing at the window, I had a strange and frightening experience out there. I had been watching at the window, and finally I felt myself drawn irresistibly outside. I plunged into the grass with a feeling of exhilaration, of adventure, of expectancy. As I advanced into the yard, my sense of elation quickly changed to a mood of black depression. I turned around, intending to come right out—but I couldn't. You won't believe this, I know—but I was lost! I simply lost all sense of direction and couldn't decide which way to turn. That grass is taller than it looks! When you get into it, you can't see anything beyond it.

"I know this sounds incredible—but I wandered out there for an hour. The yard seemed fantastically large—it almost seemed to alter its dimensions as I moved, so that a large expanse of it lay always in front of me. I must have walked in circles. I swear I trudged miles!"

He shook his head. "You don't have to believe me. I don't expect you to. But that's what happened. When I finally found my way out, it was by the sheerest accident. And the strangest part of it is that once I got out, I felt suddenly terrified without the tall grass all around me and I wanted to rush back in again! This in spite of the ghastly sense of desolation which the place aroused in me.

"But I've got to go back. I've got to figure the thing out. There's something out there that defies the laws of earthly nature as we know them. I mean to find out what it is. I think I have a plan and I mean to put it into practice."

His words stirred me strangely and when I uneasily recalled my own experience at the window that afternoon, I found it difficult to dismiss his story as sheer nonsense. I did—half-heartedly—try to dissuade him from entering the yard again, but I knew even as I spoke that I was wasting my breath.

I left the shop that afternoon with a feeling of oppression and foreboding which nothing could remove.

When I called several days later, my worst fears were realized—Canavan was missing. The front door of the shop was unlatched as usual, but Canavan was not in the house. I looked in every room.

Finally, with a feeling of infinite dread, I opened the back door and looked out toward the yard.

The long stalks of brown grass slid against each other in the slight breeze with dry sibilant whispers. The dead trees reared black and motionless. Although it was late summer, I could hear neither the chirp of a bird nor the chirr of a single insect. The yard itself seemed to be listening.

Feeling something against my foot, I glanced down and saw a thick twine stretching from inside the door, across the scant cleared space immediately adjacent to the house and thence into the wavering wall of grass. Instantly I recalled Canavan's mention of a "plan." His plan, I realized immediately, was to enter the yard trailing a stout cord behind him. No matter how he twisted and turned, he must have reasoned, he could always find his way out by following back along the cord.

It seemed like a workable scheme, so I felt relieved. Probably Canavan was still in the yard. I decided I would wait for him to come out. Perhaps if he were permitted to roam around in the yard long enough, without interruption, the place would lose its evil fascination for him, and he would forget about it.

I went back into the shop and browsed among the books. At the end of an hour I became uneasy again. I wondered how long Canavan had been in the yard. When I began reflecting on the old man's uncertain health, I felt a sense of responsibility.

I finally returned to the back door, saw that he was nowhere in sight, and called out his name. I experienced the disquieting sensation that my shout carried no further than the very edge of that whispering fringe of grass. It was as if the sound had been smothered, deadened, nullified as soon as the vibrations of it reached the border of that overgrown yard.

I called again and again, but there was no reply. At length I decided to go in after him. I would follow along the cord, I thought, and I would be sure to locate him. I told myself that the thick grass undoubtedly did stifle my shout and possibly, in any case, Canavan might be growing slightly deaf.

Just inside the door, the cord was tied securely around the leg of a heavy table. Taking hold of the twine, I crossed the cleared area back of the house and slipped into the rustling expanse of grass.

31

The going was easy at first, and I made good progress. As I advanced, however, the grass stems became thicker, and grew closer together, and I was forced to shove my way through them.

When I was no more than a few yards inside the tangle, I was overwhelmed with the same bottomless sense of desolation which I had experienced before. There was certainly something uncanny about the place. I felt as if I had suddenly veered into another world —a world of briars and brindle grass whose ceaseless half-heard whisperings were somehow alive with evil.

As I pushed along, the cord abruptly came to an end. Glancing down, I saw that it had caught against a thorn bush, abraded itself, and had subsequently broken. Although I bent down and poked in the area for several minutes, I was unable to locate the piece from which it had parted. Probably Canavan was unaware that the cord had broken and was now pulling it along with him.

I straightened up, cupped my hands to my mouth, and shouted. My shout seemed to be all but drowned in my throat by that dismal wall of grass. I felt as if I were down at the bottom of a well, shouting up.

Frowning with growing uneasiness, I tramped ahead. The grass stalks kept getting thicker and tougher, and at length I needed both hands to propel myself through the matted growth.

I began to sweat profusely; my head started to ache, and I imagined that my vision was beginning to blur. I felt the same tense, almost unbearable oppression which one experiences on a stifling summer's day when a storm is brewing and the atmosphere is charged with static electricity.

Also, I realized with a slight qualm of fear that I had got turned around and didn't know which part of the yard I was in. During an objective half-minute in which I reflected that I was actually worried about getting lost in someone's back yard, I almost laughed—almost. But there was something about the place that didn't permit laughter. I plodded ahead with a sober face.

Presently I began to feel that I was not alone. I had a sudden hair-raising conviction that someone—or something—was creeping along in the grass behind me. I cannot say with certainty that I heard anything, although I may have, but all at once I was firmly convinced that some creature was crawling or wriggling a short distance to the rear.

I felt that I was being watched and that the watcher was wholly malignant.

For a wild instant I considered headlong flight. Then, unaccountably, rage took possession of me. I was suddenly furious with Canavan, furious with the yard, furious with myself. All my pent-up tension exploded in a gust of rage which swept away fear. Now, I vowed, I would get to the root of the weird business. I would be tormented and frustrated by it no longer.

I whirled without warning and lunged into the grass where I believed my stealthy pursuer might be hiding.

I stopped abruptly; my savage anger melted into inexpressible horror.

In the faint but brassy sunlight which filtered down through the towering stalks, Canavan crouched on all fours like a beast about to spring. His glasses were gone, his clothes were in shreds and his mouth was twisted into an insane grimace, half smirk, half snarl.

I stood petrified, staring at him. His eyes, queerly out of focus, glared at me with concentrated hatred and without any glimmer of recognition. His gray hair was matted with grass and small sticks; his entire body, in fact, including the tattered remains of his clothing, was covered with them as if he had groveled or rolled on the ground like a wild animal.

After the first throat-freezing shock, I finally found my tongue.

"Canavan!" I screamed at him. "Canavan, for God's sake don't you know me?"

His answer was a low throaty snarl. His lips twisted back from his yellowish teeth, and his crouching body tensed for a spring.

Pure terror took possession of me. I leaped aside and flung myself into that infernal wall of grass an instant before he lunged.

The intensity of my terror must have given me added strength. I rammed headlong through those twisted stalks which before I had laboriously pulled aside. I could hear the grass and briar bushes crashing behind me, and I knew that I was running for my life.

I pounded on as in a nightmare. Grass stalks snapped against my face like whips, and thorns gashed me like razors, but I felt nothing.

33

All my physical and mental resources were concentrated in one fren-zied resolve: I must get out of that devil's field of grass and away from the monstrous thing which followed swiftly in my wake.

My breath began coming in great shuddering sobs. My legs felt weak and I seemed to be looking through spinning saucers of light. But I ran on.

The thing behind me was gaining. I could hear it growling, and I could feel it lunge against the earth only inches behind my flying feet. And all the time I had the maddening conviction that I was actually running in circles.

At last, when I felt that I must surely collapse in another second, I plunged through a final brindle thicket into the open sunlight. Ahead of me lay the cleared area at the rear of Canavan's shop. Just beyond was the house itself.

Gasping and fighting for breath, I dragged myself toward the door. For no reason that I could explain, then or afterwards, I felt absolutely certain that the horror at my heels would not venture into the open area. I didn't even turn around to make sure.

Inside the house I fell weakly into a chair. My strained breathing slowly returned to normal, but my mind remained caught up in a whirlwind of sheer horror and hideous conjecture.

Canavan, I realized, had gone completely mad. Some ghastly shock had turned him into a ravening bestial lunatic thirsting to savagely destroy any living thing that crossed his path. Remembering the oddly-focused eyes which had glared at me with a glaze of animal ferocity, I knew that his mind had not been merely unhinged—it was totally gone. Death could be the only possible release.

But Canavan was still at least the shell of a human being, and he had been my friend. I could not take the law into my own hands.

With many misgivings I called the police and an ambulance.

What followed was more madness, plus a session of questions and demands which left me in a state of near nervous collapse.

A half dozen burly policemen spent the better part of an hour tramping through that wavering brindle grass without locating any trace of Canavan. They came out cursing, rubbing their eyes and shaking their heads. They were flushed, furious—and ill at ease. They announced that they had seen nothing and heard nothing except some sneaking dog which stayed always out of sight and growled at them at intervals.

When they mentioned the growling dog, I opened my mouth to speak, but thought better of it and said nothing. They were already regarding me with open suspicion as if they believed my own mind might be breaking.

I repeated my story at least twenty times, and still they were not satisfied. They ransacked the entire house. They inspected Canavan's files. They even removed some loose boards in one of the rooms and searched underneath.

At length they grudgingly concluded that Canavan had suffered total loss of memory after experiencing some kind of shock and that he had wandered off the premises in a state of amnesia shortly after I had encountered him in the yard. My own description of his appearance and actions they discounted as lurid exaggeration. After warning me that I would probably be questioned further and that my own premises might be inspected, they reluctantly permitted me to leave.

Their subsequent searches and investigations revealed nothing new and Canavan was put down as a missing person, probably afflicted with acute amnesia.

But I was not satisfied, and I could not rest.

Six months of patient, painstaking, tedious research in the files and stacks of the local university library finally yielded something which I do not offer as an explanation, nor even as a definite clue, but only as a fantastic near-impossibility which I ask no one to believe.

One afternoon, after my extended research over a period of months had produced nothing of significance, the Keeper of Rare Books at the library triumphantly bore to my study niche a tiny, crumbling pamphlet which had been printed in New Haven in 1695. It mentioned no author and carried the stark title, *Deathe of Goodie Larkins, Witche*.

Several years before, it revealed, an ancient crone, one Goodie Larkins, had been accused by neighbors of turning a missing child into a wild dog. The Salem madness was raging at the time, and Goodie Larkins had been summarily condemned to death. Instead of

35

being burned, she had been driven into a marsh deep in the woods where seven savage dogs, starved for a fortnight, had been turned loose on her trail. Apparently her accusers felt that this was a touch of truly poetic justice.

As the ravening dogs closed in on her, she was heard by her retreating neighbors to utter a frightful curse:

"Let this lande I fall upon lye alle the way to Hell!" she had screamed. *"And they who tarry here be as these beastes that rende me dead!"*

A subsequent inspection of old maps and land deeds satisfied me that the marsh in which Goodie Larkins was torn to pieces by the dogs after uttering her awful curse—originally occupied the same lot or square which now enclosed Canavan's hellish back yard!

I say no more. I returned only once to that devilish spot. It was a cold desolate autumn day, and a keening wind rattled the brindle stalks. I cannot say what urged me back to that unholy area; perhaps it was some lingering feeling of loyalty toward the Canavan I had known. Perhaps it was even some last shred of hope. But as soon as I entered the cleared area behind Canavan's boarded-up house, I knew I had made a mistake.

As I stared at the stiff waving grass, the bare trees and the black ragged briars, I felt as if I, in turn, were being watched. I felt as if something alien and wholly evil were observing me, and though I was terrified, I experienced a perverse, insane impulse to rush headlong into that whispering expanse. Again I imagined I saw that monstrous landscape subtly alter its dimensions and perspective until I was staring at a stretch of blowing brindle grass and rotted trees which ran for miles. Something urged me to enter, to lose myself in the lovely grass, to roll and grovel at its roots, to rip off the foolish encumbrances of cloth which covered me and run howling and ravenous, on and on, on and on. . . .

Instead, I turned and rushed away. I ran through the windy autumn streets like a madman. I lurched into my rooms and bolted the door.

I have never gone back since. And I never shall.

The Conqueror Worm

BY STEPHEN R. DONALDSON

There are, of course, a fair number of fears that rely on things coming from out there, from the world of the supernatural that we, quite naturally, don't believe in—most of the time. There are, however, an equal number of things that do well enough frightening us, or making us cringe, without having to underscore them with things from the preternatural. People do, on occasion, fear each other, simply because they are afraid of giving so much of themselves that they reduce themselves to less than their self-image. Sometimes these problems are worked out. Sometimes they aren't.

Stephen R. Donaldson lives in New Mexico, and is the author of the worldwide bestselling fantasy series, The Chronicles of Thomas Covenant, the Unbeliever.

And anyone who lives in the Southwest will tell you quickly enough that the critter in this story is not an exaggeration.

And much of Madness, and more of Sin,
And Horror the soul of the plot.
—EDGAR ALLAN POE

BEFORE he realized what he was doing, he swung the knife.

(The home of Creel and Vi Sump. The livingroom.

(Her real name is Violet, but everyone calls her Vi. They've been married for two years now, and she isn't blooming.

(Their home is modest but comfortable: Creel has a good job with his company, but he isn't moving up. In the livingroom, some of the furnishings are better than the space they occupy. A good stereo contrasts with the state of the wallpaper. The arrangement of the furniture shows a certain amount of frustration: there's no way

37

to set the armchairs and sofa so that people who sit on them can't see the water-spots in the ceiling. The flowers in the vase on the end-table are real, but they look plastic. At night, the lights leave shadows at odd places around the room.)

They were out late at a large party where acquaintances, business associates, and strangers drank a lot. As Creel unlocked the front door and came into the livingroom ahead of Vi, he looked more than ever like a rumpled bear. Whisky made the usual dullness of his eyes seem baleful. Behind him, Vi resembled a flower in the process of becoming a wasp.

"I don't care," he said, moving directly to the sideboard to get himself another drink. "I wish you wouldn't do it."

She sat down on the sofa, took off her shoes. "God, I'm tired."

"If you aren't interested in anything else," he said, "think about me. I have to work with most of those people. Half of them can fire me if they want to. You're affecting my job."

"We've had this conversation before," she said. "We've had it eight times this month." A vague movement in one of the shadows across the room turned her head toward the corner. "What was *that?*"

"What was what?"

"I saw something move. Over there in the corner. Don't tell me we've got mice."

"I didn't see anything. We haven't got mice. And I don't care how many times we've had this conversation. I want you to stop."

She stared into the corner for a moment. Then she leaned back on the sofa. "I can't stop. I'm not *doing* anything."

"The hell you're not doing anything." He took a drink and re-filled his glass. "If you were after him any harder, you'd have your hand in his pants."

"That's not true."

"You think nobody sees what you're doing. You act like you're alone. But you're not. Everybody at that whole damn party was watching you. The way you flirt——"

"I wasn't flirting. I was just talking to him."

"The way you *flirt*, you ought to have the decency to be embarrassed."

38

"Oh, go to bed. I'm too tired for this."

"Is it because he's a vice-president? Do you think that's going to make him better in bed? Or do you just like the status of playing around with a vice-president?"

"I wasn't *flirting* with him. I swear to God, there's something the matter with you. We were just talking. You know—moving our mouths so that words could come out. He was a literature major in college. We have something in common. We've read the same books. Remember *books*? Those things with ideas and stories printed in them? All you ever talk about is football—and how somebody at the company has it in for you—and how the latest secretary doesn't wear a bra. Sometimes I think I'm the last literate person left alive."

She raised her head to look at him. Then she sighed, "Why do I even bother? You're not listening to me."

"You're right," he said. "There *is* something in the corner. I saw it move."

They both stared at the corner. After a moment, a centipede scuttled out into the light.

It looked slimy and malicious, and it waved its antennae hungrily. It was nearly ten inches long. Its thick legs seemed to ripple as it shot across the rug. Then it stopped to scan its surroundings. Creel and Vi could see its mandibles chewing expectantly as it flexed its poison claws. It had entered the house to escape the cold, dry night outside—and to hunt for food.

She wasn't the kind of woman who screamed easily; but she hopped up onto the sofa to get her bare feet away from the floor. "Good God," she whispered. "Creel, look at that. Don't let it come any closer."

He leaped at the centipede and tried to stamp one of his heavy shoes on it. But it moved so fast that he didn't come close to it. Neither of them saw where it went.

"It's under the sofa," he said. "Get off of there."

She obeyed without question. Wincing, she jumped out into the middle of the rug.

As soon as she was out of the way, he heaved the sofa onto its back.

The centipede wasn't there.

"The poison isn't fatal," Vi said. "One of the kids in the neigh-

39

borhood got stung last week. Her mother told me all about it. It's like getting a bad bee-sting."

Creel didn't listen to her. He lifted the entire sofa into the air so that he could see more of the floor. But the centipede was gone.

He dropped the sofa back onto its legs, knocking over the end-table, spilling the flowers. "Where did that bastard go?"

They hunted around the room for several minutes without leaving the protection of the light. Then he went and got himself another drink. His hands were shaking.

She said, "I wasn't flirting."

He looked at her. "Then it's something worse. You're already sleeping with him. You must've been making plans for the next time you get together."

"I'm going to bed," she said. "I don't have to put up with this. You're disgusting."

He finished his drink and refilled his glass from the nearest bottle.

(The Sumps' game-room.

(This room is the real reason why Creel bought this house over Vi's objections: he wanted a house with a game-room. The money that could have replaced the wallpaper and fixed the ceiling of the livingroom has been spent here. The room contains a full-size pool-table with all the trimmings, a long, imitation leather couch along one wall, and a wet-bar. But the light here isn't any better than in the livingroom because the fixtures are focused on the pooltable. Even the wet-bar is so ill lit that its users have to guess what they're doing.

(When he isn't working, traveling for his company, or watching football with his buddies, Creel spends a lot of time here.)

After Vi went to bed, Creel came into the game-room. First he went to the wet-bar and repaired the emptiness of his glass. Then he racked up the balls and broke so violently that the cueball sailed off the table. It made a dull, thudding noise as it bounced on the spongy linoleum.

"Fuck," he said, lumbering after the ball. The liquor he had con-

sumed showed in the way he moved but not in his speech. He
sounded sober.

Bracing himself with his custom-made cuestick, he bent to pick up
the ball. Before he put it back on the table, Vi entered the room.
She hadn't changed her clothes for bed. She had put her shoes back
on, however. She scrutinized the shadows around the floor and under
the table before she looked at Creel.

He said, "I thought you were going to bed."

"I can't leave it like this," she said tiredly. "It hurts too much."

"What do you want from me?" he said. "Approval?"

She glared at him.

He didn't stop. "That would be terrific for you. If I approved,
you wouldn't have anything else to worry about. The only problem
would be, most of the bastards I introduce you to are married. Their
wives might be a little more normal. They might give you some
trouble."

She bit her lip and went on glaring at him.

"But I don't see why you should worry about that. If those women
aren't as understanding as I am, that's their tough luck. As long as
I approve, right? There's no reason why you shouldn't screw anybody you want."

"Are you finished?"

"Hell, there's no reason why you shouldn't screw *all* of them. I
mean, as long as I approve. Why waste it?"

"Damn it, are you *finished*?"

"There's only one thing I don't understand. If you're so hot for
sex, how come you don't want to screw me?"

"That's not true."

He blinked at her through a haze of alcohol. "What's not true?
You're not hot for sex? Or you do want to screw me? Don't make
me laugh."

"Creel, what's the matter with you? I don't understand any of
this. You didn't used to be like this. You weren't like this when we
were dating. You weren't like this when we got married. What's
happened to you?"

For a minute, he didn't say anything. He went back to the edge of
the pooltable, where he'd left his drink. But with his cue in one hand

and the ball in the other, he didn't have a hand free. Carefully, he set his stick down on the table.

After he finished his drink, he said, "You changed."

"*I* changed? *You're* the one who's acting crazy. All I did was talk to some company vice-president about *books*."

"No, I'm not," he said. His knuckles were white around the cueball. "You think I'm stupid. Because I wasn't a literature major in college. Maybe that's what changed. When we got married, you didn't think I was stupid. But now you do. You think I'm too stupid to notice the difference."

"What difference is that?"

"You never want to have sex with me anymore."

"Oh, for God's sake," she said. "We had sex the day before yesterday."

He looked straight at her. "But you didn't want to. I can tell. You never *want* to."

"What do you mean, you can tell?"

"You make a lot of excuses."

"I do not."

"And when we do have sex, you don't pay any attention to me. You're always somewhere else. Thinking about something else. You're always thinking about somebody else."

"But that's *normal*," she said. "Everybody does it. Everybody fantasizes during sex. *You* fantasize during sex. That's what makes it fun."

At first, she didn't see the centipede as it wriggled out from under the pooltable, its antennae searching for her legs. But then she happened to glance downward.

"Creel!"

The centipede started toward her. She jumped back, out of the way.

Creel threw the cueball with all his strength. It made a dent in the linoleum beside the centipede, then crashed into the side of the wet-bar.

The centipede went for Vi. It was so fast that she couldn't get away from it. As its segments caught the light, they gleamed poisonously.

Creel snatched his cuestick off the table and hammered at the centipede. Again, he missed. But flying splinters of wood made the

42

centipede turn and shoot in the other direction. It disappeared under the couch.

"Get it," she panted.

He shook the pieces of his cue at her. "I'll tell you what I fantasize. I fantasize that you *like* having sex with me. You fantasize that I'm somebody else." Then he wrenched the couch away from the wall, brandishing his weapons.

"So would you," she retorted, "if you had to sleep with a sensitive, considerate, imaginative *animal* like you."

As she left the room, she slammed the door behind her.

Shoving the furniture bodily from side to side, he continued hunting for the centipede.

(The bedroom.

(This room expresses Vi as much as the limitations of the house permit. The bed is really too big for the space available, but at least it has an elaborate brass headstead and footboard. The sheets and pillowcases match the bedspread, which is decorated with white flowers on a blue background. Unfortunately, Creel's weight makes the bed sag. The closet doors are warped and can't be closed.

(There's an overhead light, but Vi never uses it. She relies on a pair of goosenecked Tiffany reading lamps. As a result, the bed seems to be surrounded by gloom in all directions.)

Creel sat on the bed and watched the bathroom door. His back was bowed. His right fist gripped the neck of a bottle of tequila, but he wasn't drinking.

The bathroom door was closed. He appeared to be staring at himself in the full-length mirror attached to it. But a strip of fluorescent light showed past the bottom of the door. He could see Vi's shadow as she moved around in the bathroom.

He stared at the door for several minutes, but she was taking her time. Finally, he shifted the bottle to his left hand.

"I never understand what you *do* in there."

Through the door, she said, "I'm waiting for you to pass out so I can go to sleep in peace."

He looked offended. "Well, I'm not going to pass out. I never pass out. You might as well give up."

Abruptly, the door opened. She snapped off the bathroom light and stood in the darkened doorway, facing him. She was dressed for bed in a nightie that would have made her look desirable if she had wished to look desirable.

"What do you want now?" she said. "Are you finished wrecking the game-room already?"

"I was trying to kill that centipede. The one that scared you so badly."

"I wasn't scared—just startled. It's only a centipede. Did you get it?"

"No."

"You're too slow. You'll have to call an exterminator."

"Damn the exterminator," he said slowly. "*Fuck* the exterminator. Fuck the centipede. I can take care of my own problems. Why did you call me that?"

"Call you what?"

He didn't look at her. "An animal." Then he did. "I've never lifted a finger to hurt you."

She moved past him to the bed and propped the pillows up against the brass bedstead. Sitting on the bed, she curled her legs under her and leaned back against the pillows.

"I know," she said. "I didn't mean it the way it sounded. I was just mad."

He frowned. "You didn't mean it the way it sounded. How nice. That makes me feel a whole lot better. What in hell *did* you mean?"

"I hope you realize you're not making this any easier."

"It isn't easy for *me*. Do you think I like sitting here begging my own wife to tell me why I'm not good enough for her?"

"Actually," she said, "I think you do like it. This way, you get to feel like a victim."

He raised his bottle until the tequila caught the light. He peered into the golden liquid for a moment, then transferred the bottle back to his right hand. But he didn't say anything.

"All right," she said after a while. "You treat me like you don't care what I think or how I feel."

"I do it the way I know how," he protested. "If it feels good for me, it's supposed to feel good for you."

"I'm not just talking about sex. I'm talking about the way you

44

treat me. The way you talk to me. The way you assume I have to like everything you like and can't like anything you don't like. The way you think my whole life is supposed to revolve around you."

"Then why did you marry me? Did it take you two years to find out you don't really want to be my wife?"

She stretched her legs out in front of her. Her nightie covered them to the knees. "I married you because I loved you. Not because I want to be treated like an object for the rest of my natural life. I need friends. People I can share things with. People who care what I'm thinking. I almost went to grad school because I wanted to study Baudelaire. We've been married for two years, and you still don't know who Baudelaire is. The only people I ever meet are your drinking buddies. Or the people who work for your company."

He started to say something, but she kept going. "And I need freedom. I need to make my own decisions—my own choices. I need to have my own life."

Again, he tried to say something.

"And I need to be cherished. You use me like I'm less interesting than your precious poolcue."

"It's broken," he said flatly.

"I know it's broken," she said. "I don't care. This is more important. I'm more important."

In the same tone, he said, "You said you loved me. You don't love me anymore."

"God, you're dense. *Think* about it. What on earth do you ever do to make me feel like *you* love *me*?"

He shifted the bottle to his left hand again. "You've been sleeping around. You probably screw every sonofabitch you can get into the sack. That's why you don't love me anymore. They probably do all kinds of dirty things to you I don't do. And you're hooked on it. You're bored with me because I'm just not exciting enough."

She dropped her arms onto the pillows beside her. "Creel, that's *sick*. You're *sick*."

Disturbed by her movement, the centipede crawled out between the pillows onto her left arm. It waved its poison claws while it tasted her skin with its antennae, looking for the best place to bite in.

45

This time, she did scream. Wildly, she flung up her arm. The centipede was thrown into the air.

It hit the ceiling and came down on her bare leg.

It was angry now. Its thick legs swarmed to take hold of her and attack.

With his free hand, he struck a backhand blow down the length of her leg that slapped the centipede off her.

As the centipede hit the wall, he pitched his bottle at it, trying to smash it. But it had already vanished into the gloom around the bed. A shower of glass and tequila covered the bedspread.

She bounced off the bed, hid behind him. "I can't take any more of this. I'm leaving."

"It's only a centipede," he panted as he wrenched the brass frame off the foot of the bed. Holding the frame in one hand for a club, he braced his other arm under the bed and heaved it off its legs. He looked strong enough to crush one centipede. "What're you afraid of?"

"I'm afraid of you. I'm afraid of the way your mind works."

As he turned the bed over, he knocked down one of the Tiffany lamps. The room became even darker. When he flipped on the overhead light, he couldn't see the centipede anywhere.

The whole room stank of tequila.

(The livingroom.

(The sofa sits where Creel left it. The endtable lies on its side, surrounded by wilting flowers. The water from the vase has left a stain that looks like another shadow on the rug. But in other ways the room is unchanged. The lights are on. Their brightness emphasizes all the places they don't reach.

(Creel and Vi are there. He sits in one of the armchairs and watches her while she rummages around in a large closet that opens into the room. She is hunting for things to take with her and a suitcase to carry them in. She is wearing a shapeless dress with no belt. For some reason, it makes her look younger. He seems more awkward than usual without a drink in his hands.)

"I get the impression you're enjoying this," he said.

"Of course," she said. "You've been right about everything else. Why shouldn't you be right now? I haven't had so much fun since I dislocated my knee in high school."

"How about our wedding night? That was one of the highlights of your life."

She stopped what she was doing to glare at him. "If you keep this up, I'm going to puke right here in front of you."

"You made me feel like a complete shit."

"Right again. You're absolutely brilliant tonight."

"Well, you look like you're enjoying yourself. I haven't seen you this excited for years. You've probably been hunting for a chance to do this ever since you first started sleeping around."

She threw a vanity case across the room and went on rummaging through the closet.

"I'm curious about that first time," he said. "Did he seduce you? I bet you're the one who seduced him. I bet you begged him into bed so he could teach you all the dirty tricks he knew."

"Shut up," she muttered from inside the closet. "Just shut up. I'm not listening."

"Then you found out he was too normal for you. All he wanted was a straight screw. So you dropped the poor bastard and went, looking for something fancier. By now, you must be pretty good at talking men into your panties."

She came out of the closet holding one of his old baseball bats. "Damn you, Creel. If you don't stop this, so help me God, I'm going to beat your putrid brains out."

He laughed humorlessly. "You can't do that. They don't punish infidelity. But they'll put you in jail for killing your husband."

Slamming the bat back into the closet, she returned to her search.

He couldn't take his eyes off her. Every time she came out of the closet, he studied everything she did. After a while, he said, "You shouldn't let a centipede upset you like this."

She ignored him.

"I can take care of it," he went on. "I've never let anything hurt you. I know I keep missing it. I've let you down. But I'll take care of it. I'll call an exterminator in the morning. Hell, I'll call ten exterminators. You don't have to go."

47

She continued ignoring him.

For a minute, he covered his face with his hands. Then he dropped them into his lap. His expression changed.

"Or we can keep it for a pet. We can train it to wake us up in the morning. Bring in the paper. Make coffee. We won't need an alarm clock anymore."

She lugged a large suitcase out of the closet. Swinging it onto the sofa, she opened it and began stuffing things into it.

He said, "We can call him Baudelaire."

She looked nauseated.

"Baudelaire the Butler. He can meet people at the door for us. Answer the phone. Make the beds. As long as we don't let him get the wrong idea, he can probably help you choose what you're going to wear.

"No, I've got a better idea. You can wear *him*. Put him around your neck and use him for a ruff. He'll be the latest thing in sexy clothes. Then you'll be able to get fucked as much as you want."

Biting her lip to keep from crying, Vi went back into the closet to get a sweater off one of the upper shelves.

When she pulled the sweater down from the shelf, the centipede landed on the top of her head.

Her instinctive flinch carried her out into the room. Creel had a perfect view of what was happening as the centipede dropped to her shoulder and squirmed inside the collar of her dress.

She froze. All the blood drained out of her face. Her eyes stared wildly.

"Creel," she breathed. "Oh my God. Help me."

The shape of the centipede showed through her dress as it crawled over her breasts.

"*Creel.*"

At the sight, he heaved himself out of his armchair and sprang toward her. Then he jerked to a stop.

"I can't hit it," he said. "It'll hurt you. It'll sting you. If I try to lift your dress to get at it, it might sting you."

She couldn't speak. The sensation of the centipede creeping across her skin paralyzed her.

For a moment, he looked completely helpless. "I don't know what to do." His hands were empty.

48

Suddenly, his face lit up.

"I'll get a knife."

Turning, he ran out of the room toward the kitchen.

Vi squeezed her eyes shut and clenched her fists. Whimpering sounds came between her lips, but she didn't move.

Slowly, the centipede crossed her belly. Its antennae explored her navel. All the rest of her body flinched, but she kept the muscles of her stomach rigid.

Then the centipede found the warm place between her legs.

For some reason, it didn't stop. It crawled onto her left thigh and continued downward.

She opened her eyes and watched as the centipede showed itself below the hem of her dress.

Searching her skin every inch of the way, the centipede crept down her shin to her ankle. There it stopped until she looked like she wasn't going to be able to keep herself from screaming. Then it moved again.

As soon as it reached the floor, she jumped away from it. She let herself scream, but she didn't let that slow her down. As fast as she could go, she dashed to the front door, threw it open, and left the house.

The centipede was in no hurry. It looked ready and confident as its thick legs carried it under the sofa.

A second later, Creel came back from the kitchen. He carried a carving knife with a long, wicked blade.

"Vi?" he shouted. "Vi?"

Then he saw the open door.

At once, a snarl twisted his face. "You bastard," he whispered. "Oh you *bastard*. Now you've done it to me."

He dropped into a crouch and searched the rug. He held the knife poised in front of him.

"I'm going to get you for this. I'm going to find you. You can bet I'm going to find you. And when I do, I'm going to cut you to pieces. I'm going to cut you into little, tiny pieces. I'm going to cut all your legs off, one at a time. Then I'm going to flush you down the disposal."

Stalking around behind the sofa, he reached the place where the endtable lay on its side, surrounded by dead flowers.

49

"You utter bastard. She was my wife."

But he didn't see the centipede. It was hiding in the dark water-stain beside the vase. He nearly stepped on it.

In a flash, it shot onto his shoe and disappeared up the leg of his pants.

He didn't know the centipede had him until he felt it climb over his knee.

Looking down, he saw the long bulge in his pants work its way toward his groin.

Before he realized what he was doing——

Death to the Easter Bunny!

BY ALAN RYAN

One of the more fascinating aspects of growing up is the convenient way adults manage to forget how terrifying all those wonderful holiday creatures can be to the young. In fact, adults tend to forget quite a bit about what it was really like to be a child, and when they are confronted with accurate memory, as opposed to a sort of revisionism, all the protestation in the world isn't going to change the fact that being older and wiser no longer means being less afraid.

Alan Ryan's latest novel is The Kill, *and his short stories continue to appear in all the major magazines and anthologies in the field. He is also a reviewer for* The Washington Post *and* The Cleveland Plain Dealer, *and does it all out of a book-lined apartment in the Bronx.*

WHEN Paul and I and the girls met the old man in the woods that day, we never thought we'd end up living here in the mountains. Of course, we never thought we'd have to kill the Easter Bunny either.

The four of us—that's Paul and Susanne, and Barbara and me—had been looking for some place we could go on weekends that wouldn't cost too much or be too far from New York. When we found Deacons Kill, about four hours north in the Catskills, we knew right away it was the kind of place we wanted. It's mostly dairy farms and wooded hills and plain, decent people. The town is nice too; it's small and everybody's pretty friendly and there's a great old hotel, called the Centennial Hotel, right on the village square. As soon as we discovered the Kill—that's what everybody calls the town—last winter, we started coming up all the time.

So there we were one day, the four of us walking along some backwoods road, just strolling because it was pretty cold and we didn't want to get too far away from where we'd left the car, and Susanne was complaining that she wasn't dressed warmly enough and Barbara was saying her new boots hurt her feet. Then Paul saw a small trail leading into the woods among the pine trees and he wanted to follow it a little way.

There was some discussion back and forth and finally we agreed to go a short distance, maybe five minutes' worth of walking, before turning back. Actually, I would have preferred to be back in our room at the Centennial Hotel with Barbara, just the two of us, but if I hadn't given in to Paul that time, we might never have met the old man and the Easter Bunny would still be running around and none of this would be happening.

We had gone only a little distance in among the pines when suddenly a voice called out and it was clearly yelling at us, no mistake about it.

"That's enough! Hold it right there!"

It wasn't so much the suddenness of it, or even the *sound* of it, that stopped us right in our tracks. It was really just the voice of an old man, rough and a little gravelly, but still just the voice of an old man. The thing that got to all of us as soon as we heard it, though, was the *tone*. It sounded like a lot of things all at once: angry, exasperated, determined, threatening. And frightened. It sounded frightened. The four of us stood rock still right where we were.

"What are you doing here? You don't belong here!"

I turned around to see where the voice was coming from and there was the old man. I'm not old enough to remember Gabby Hayes but I've seen pictures of him and this old man looked a little like that. Or maybe a little like the way we think of Rip Van Winkle. He had a beard that was gray and stringy, and his eyes were bright and had wrinkles all around them and his clothes were the color of the woods, gray and brown and no color in particular, and he was pointing a double-barreled rifle at the four of us.

"Holy shit!" Paul said behind me.

"What are you doing here?" the old man said again, and he panned the rifle back and forth like a movie camera. I could see his finger on the trigger.

"Hold on!" I said. "We're not doing anything. We were just taking a walk."

52

The old man stared at me pretty skeptically for a few seconds. I was thinking fast, or trying to, and wishing Paul would say something clever. Nobody had ever pointed a gun at me before. Mostly I was thinking that if the old guy really fired it, I'd be the first to get it, which I guess is a pretty selfish thought. But before I could think of what to say, the old man lowered the rifle and pointed it at the ground. That was when my knees started feeling weak and my heart started pounding. Behind me, I heard Barbara say, "Oh, my God," and I discovered that I had put one hand behind me to sort of protect her. She grabbed it and held it tight.

"What are you doing here?" the old man asked again, but he sounded less angry this time than he had before. I could almost have thought he sounded a little relieved.

I told him again that we had only been taking a walk, yes, in winter, we didn't mind the cold, we hoped we weren't trespassing, no, we weren't carrying guns, yes, we were planning on going right back out to the road, and so on and so on, with Paul helping out now with the answers, and finally the old man began to look like nothing more than just an old man who happened to be carrying a rifle.

It was Paul who asked the question, and, when he did, I could have kicked him for it.

"What are *you* doing here?" he said to the old man. "Do you own these woods?"

The old man looked at Paul very hard, then he looked at me, then at Barbara and Susanne, and then back at Paul again. You could almost see him making up his mind whether we were challenging him or not, or just asking, the way anybody might. I kept my eye on the rifle barrel but it stayed pointed at the ground.

The old man studied the four of us a little longer, then he said, "I own these woods as much as anybody does. Maybe more." There was a sort of stony grimness in the way he said it.

There was a kind of impasse at that point, him studying us and us studying him right back again. Then I could see his posture lose some of its tenseness and for the first time I knew we were really out of trouble.

I think it was Barbara who said something next, asked him a question maybe, and after that it was a fairly normal conversation, considering the circumstances. It wasn't exactly a prize-winning conversation or anything like that, like you might have in a good bar late at night, but we were all chatting more or less easily with him after a minute or so.

That first meeting seems even stranger now. I really don't know what we could have been talking about, and the others don't remember either (I guess we were still nervous from the way he'd scared us), except I know he said something about "intruders" a couple of times, meaning intruders into his woods. I do remember thinking that he sounded as if he might even get to be friendly after a while, even though we didn't learn anything about him at all. For all we found out that time, he might have lived in the trees. As it turned out, that wouldn't have been a bad guess.

When the conversation, if you can call it that, was starting to wear down, the old man said, and I do remember this part very clearly, "You can stop by again when you're this way." Then he added, more quietly, "I'll be here."

That's how it started.

Naturally we talked about the old man a lot that weekend and other times afterward. And of course we talked about it the next time the four of us went up there, which was a couple of weeks later.

We had only been in the hotel a little while on Friday evening. Barbara and I were still unpacking and putting clothes away and Barbara was upset because a blouse she wanted to wear to dinner on Saturday had gotten crushed in the suitcase. And we were fooling around a little too while we unpacked. There was a knock at the door and I opened it and Susanne and Paul came in.

Paul plopped himself down on one of the chairs by the window and Susanne sat on his knee and Paul said, "Let's go see that weird old guy in the woods."

"You have got to be kidding," I said right away, but the truth is, I'd been thinking about doing that myself but not saying anything because I thought the others would think I was crazy.

Paul was serious. "I am not kidding," he said. "I want to go see him. I think"—and here Paul got a really solemn and serious look on his face and the same kind of sound in his voice—"that it was nothing less than fate that brought us to him. Fate, I tell you. Kis-

54

met. We are *intended* to know the old coot and have all sorts of wonderful adventures with him." Paul teaches English, which explains a lot.

Well, we talked about it for a while and Barbara and Susanne and I all said we didn't want any part of it and the weather was too cold to go traipsing around in the woods anyway, but it turned out that none of us really meant it, so in the end we decided we'd go back and find that trail and see if the old man would actually be there again.

And so on Saturday we drove out to that same road and found the trail and started along it. We were all pretty nervous the farther we went, and we had to go a long way this time before anything happened—so far, in fact, that we were all starting to think that maybe we had imagined the old man in the first place or maybe he had only been a local farmer or a drifter who was having some fun at our expense. But of course just at the point when we were starting to talk about turning back toward the road, because it really was very cold that day, the old man stepped out from behind a tree—at least, that's what we thought when we talked about it later—and stood there on the path in front of us.

He didn't say anything right away this time, just looked at us. He still had the rifle but it was pointing at the ground.

I don't think any of us had actually believed that we'd see him again. But there he was, looking just the same as before.

The old man sort of nodded his head a little bit, which I took to be a greeting. Paul had been leading the way and was closest, so he was the first to speak.

"Hello," he said. "Bet you thought you'd never see us again." Which wasn't a very brilliant thing to say, but it suddenly made me realize for the first time that we had never learned the old man's name.

"Bet you thought you'd never see *me* again," the old man said. He wasn't smiling.

We shuffled around a little at that, because of course it was true. The next thing I remember is that we were talking with the old fellow again, the way we had the other time, easy and natural—talking about the woods, I guess, because I can't think what else it might have been. It's always happened that way, then and since, and

55

it always seems so weird later on: standing there in the woods, first in winter and later in spring and summer and so on, talking with him for a while but not remembering a word of what was said.

But I do remember clearly him saying, "Come home with me."

I know we followed him off the trail and deep into the woods and I know that we did some climbing up the hillsides (and I know that he had to lead us out to the path afterward), but I have no clear picture in my mind of how we got to his home, that first time or any of the other times.

When I think about it now, I have to admit that I don't understand either why we actually went with him in the first place. But we did. He led the way and we followed.

The old man lives way up high on a hill, in the very darkest and thickest part of the woods, the sort of place where you can almost imagine the Big Bad Wolf jumping out and attacking Little Red Riding Hood. The sort of place you dream about when you're a child . . . at least that's the best recollection of it I ever have. It's never really clear afterward, no more than it was that first time. It was as if a cloud or a mist surrounded the spot, hiding its details from us, while allowing us to glimpse just enough to make us think it was not-so-strange and not-so-scary. It might have been a shed or a cabin or a huge old mansion in the woods. It might have been a cave or a wooden structure in the treetops. It might have been none of those things. We didn't know then and we don't know now. But the old man somehow always made it all right.

Inside it was the same: vague, yet clear, real and unreal, not warm and not cold, odd and not-so-strange. That first time, the old man invited us to sit—there were things to sit on but I don't know what they were—and he gave us something to drink—something neither hot nor cold—but I don't know what it was.

And he talked. He talked about the hills and about the woods and rivers and streams and the trees and the rocks and the dirt, talked about the wildness of nature and its order, its beauty, its bestiality, about the air and the weather and about storms and rains and snows and winds.

We listened—that first time, as I remember, and every time since then—in thrall.

And he talked about the city, about how the city was different from the country and about how we had to learn the ways of the hills, and somehow we knew that he was right.

And after a while he led us out of the woods and we were back on the trail and then at the road and then at the car, and the four of us were looking at each other kind of funny, a little embarrassed, and none of us wanted to be the first to say that it had really happened or that it hadn't, but of course we knew it had.

"Holy shit!" Paul said softly when we were safely in the car.

Nobody said anything else just then, but we talked plenty when we got back to the Centennial. But that doesn't mean we knew what to make of it all, especially when the four of us realized that we had no clear idea of why we had gone with the old man or of how he had led us through the woods. Or of what his house—if it was a house—had looked like. Or of what we had talked about with him. None of it was clear, none of it made any logical kind of sense.

The one thing we knew for certain was that, after the first few seconds with the old man, we hadn't been afraid.

"He's some kind of sorcerer," Paul said, but he wouldn't look any of us in the eye as he said it.

"There's no such thing," Barbara said. "Don't be ridiculous." Barbara teaches physics and has no patience with stuff like that. She's a good sport, which is one of the things I like most about her, but she can be pretty sharp about things she considers dumb.

"Listen," Paul said, and he put on his most casual expression and turned to face Barbara because he knew she was the biggest skeptic among the four of us. "I'm not saying I believe what I just said, but I'm not saying I don't, either."

"That's a nice clear statement," Barbara said. I could see she was getting edgy.

"Come on, listen," Paul said. "Let's just examine this, okay? We meet a weird old guy in the woods. First he scares the hell out of us, sneaking up the way he did. Then he turns out to be all right. We talk with him for a while and——"

"——and after that we don't remember what happened," Barbara said quickly.

"I'm talking about the first time," Paul said.

"I'm talking about *both* times," Barbara answered.

Paul looked uncomfortable. "Well, okay, but that's part of it. I mean, the fact that we don't remember clearly what happened sort of suggests . . ." Paul hesitated, then grinned, then shrugged. "Maybe he put a spell on us."

"Oh God," Barbara said. "I don't believe this."

"It fits."

Barbara looked away from him.

"It fits," Paul said again.

"All this fresh country air is beginning to rot your brain," Barbara said, by which I knew she was beginning to give in.

"What do you think, Greg?" Susanne asked me. "You've been keeping pretty quiet."

I'd been keeping quiet because I'd been having the same sort of crazy ideas Paul was having, and I figured I'd let him be the one to put it into words. "I say it's as good an explanation as any. We'll just have to be sharp next time, maybe take notes or pictures or something, and then see what's going on."

The others nodded, and then suddenly we were all staring at each other and Barbara was squeezing my hand very tight. We hadn't talked about going back, hadn't said a word about it, but I'd just said "next time," and we all knew that we would.

That was in February and it was the beginning of March, about three weeks later, before we went back to Deacons Kill and saw the old man again.

Barbara had been playing basketball with the girls in her homeroom and had sprained her ankle so that she had to have it taped up for a couple of weeks. I went to the doctor with her when the bandages were taken off. The doctor said her ankle was fine now, and as soon as we were outside in the car, Barbara said, "Well, I'm ready," and I knew what she meant. I called Paul as soon as I got home and he said he'd tell Susanne—he didn't have far to go because I could hear her saying something in the background—and they'd be ready to roll on Friday. The only other thing we talked about was whether we'd take his car or mine.

Apart from that, we didn't say a single word about the old man the whole time we were back in the city.

*   *   *

It all happened just the same, except for one thing. This time, afterward, we remembered what the old man had talked to us about. At least, I did. I remembered it very clearly. The others didn't say so and I never said a word, not even to Barbara, but I could tell that they remembered too. We were all sort of avoiding each other's eyes and I could just tell.

He talked about intruders again, the way he had the first time we'd met him. He talked about how the world was filled with strange creatures, strange *beings*, living things that are alive in a way that's different from everything else in the world, and that therefore don't belong at all in the real world, don't fit into the human world, and how we have to get rid of them, how they pervert our minds and distort our view of reality. It made a lot of sense, the way he explained it. I can still hear his voice that time, low and soft but with a kind of hard tenseness in it. He knew what he was talking about. He said his life was devoted to ridding the world of these intruders. And he said that they were too much, too strong, for one old man alone and that he needed help to do it and that he had chosen us.

He didn't mention the Easter Bunny that time.

When he said he needed to see us again in a week, we all said together that we'd be there.

This was the time he first mentioned the Easter Bunny.

The four of us were sitting in the old man's . . . let's call it house, because by now we were able to see it more clearly than we had before. We were still vague about the route up the hill from the trail and the exact location of the house and what it looked like outside. But the inside was now clear enough for us to see it. The walls were very rough—maybe stone or some strange kind of logs—and there were no windows, but there were rugs or animal skins of some sort on the floor and plenty of places to sit, chairs and benches, although most often we just sat in a circle in the middle of a very big room, all five of us, while the old man talked.

Gradually, as we were there more and more often, we began asking questions, rather than just listening to him talk. He told us one time that he was very happy at having selected us and that he was glad we were getting into the spirit of it, glad that we were showing real progress and that we were beginning to understand the danger that threatened the world. That was what he called it: the danger that threatened the world.

He was very convincing when he spoke. I know he didn't pull any tricks on us, like hypnotism or something. I'm sure he did nothing of the sort. All I know is that he convinced us—and it seemed very clear, right from the start—that he had been waiting for us to come along and that . . . that we had been looking for him.

It's all very strange. After all, the four of us are just pretty ordinary people, like anybody else. We're not weird or anything, we don't belong to any crazy religious sects, we don't give a hoot about astrology or tarot cards or stuff like that, nothing crazy or freaky at all. We're all pretty bright, I guess, and pretty well educated, but that's certainly in our favor. At least, it makes it less likely that the old man could be playing any tricks on us, either then or now.

The simple fact was that everything he said made sense. It all made sense. And by the time he finished telling us about the Easter Bunny, we knew what he meant when he spoke about danger, danger that threatened the world.

Barbara was the one who said it first to the old man. "A lot of people," she said, keeping her voice very steady, "say the Easter Bunny is just imaginary."

The old man smiled patiently at her and then at the rest of us. "You see," he said softly. "You see what I mean. That's just the sort of thing I'm talking about. That monster comes out of hiding, tramps as free as you please all over the world, and yet he has people convinced that he doesn't even exist. It's amazing what these creatures can do to the human mind! Absolutely amazing! And terrifying." He leaned forward into the circle, his eyes sweeping slowly over the four of us as he spoke. "You do see, don't you? I know you do. Just think about it. If you asked anybody, anybody at all, they could tell you, I'm sure, what the Easter Bunny looks like, more or less. And of course, they all think he's very . . . well, they'd use words like *cute* and *cuddly* and *sweet*. Imagine! And yet, if you asked them whether or not he exists, they'd all say that he doesn't, that he's just a creature of myth or something. But children, small children, know perfectly well that he exists and they'll tell you so with no hesitation. Children are much closer to that sort of knowledge, they have an instinctive awareness of strange, primitive things like that. And if you stop to think about it, you know that there isn't a child in the world that would stand still and smile if he saw the Easter Bunny actually come around a corner and walk toward him. You know that child would run for its life. Well, children know these things and understand them. Oh yes, children know. It's only later on, as they grow older, that their minds become clouded, that they forget the most important things, the special kinds of instinctive knowledge they had when they were so young, before the world took hold of their minds. But they know. Children know. And they know enough to be afraid."

We were breathless at his speech, at the intensity of it, the fear in his voice, the determination to make us understand, to rip away the veil of adulthood that might cloud our eyes, to convince us of the need for action. It was a special moment and we were all frozen in silence when he finished speaking.

"How do you know?" Barbara said. Always the skeptic, from force of habit, but I could tell by the look on her face that she believed.

"I am different," the old man answered gently. "I am special. I can see clearer than others. And I can help you see."

We were nodding, convinced already. Barbara nodded too.

"When the time comes," the old man said, his voice barely a whisper because he was clearly exhausted from tension, "when the time comes, I will show you and you will know it for yourselves."

When he led us from the house to the trail later that day, the misty woods seemed alive with flitting spirits and shifting shadows.

We went to the woods every weekend after that.

Between trips, we never talked about it among ourselves. Talk like that was only for the forest, for the old man's house in the woods, and for the safety of his home and his presence.

The weather was still bad sometimes in March, but then at the beginning of April it began to get a little warmer, and here and there a little fresh green color began to appear at the edges of the roads in Deacons Kill. The woods themselves were still very dark and very bare, except for the firs, and damp because of the rain in April. When the old man led us up from the trail each weekend, we didn't even try to see the way. The woods were too frightening, too filled with malevolent spirits and creatures only half alive.

"The time is coming," the old man reminded us each week.

Easter Sunday would be at the end of April and we grew more and more tense as it approached.

Two weeks before it, the old man put us to work. He started by taking us outside his house for the first time. He surveyed the woods carefully—they were so thick, so strangely dense right there around the house, that it was impossible to see more than a few feet away. He chose several young trees and we cut them down and stripped them, all under his careful supervision, and brought the straight trunks inside. He instructed us in how to whittle the end down to a very sharp, very hard point, and how to trim the shaft to make a firm handhold. We prepared four of them for each of us, twenty in all. We worked at it for two weekends and then we were ready for Easter.

Since school was closed for the holiday, we got an early start on Good Friday. Our four-hour car trips up to Deacons Kill had grown very quiet in recent weeks, but this one was absolutely silent. The only sound we heard was the tires against the highway. We all knew what lay ahead and we were all, I'm sure, lost in our private thoughts. And our private fears.

The people at the hotel knew us by then, of course. They were always very friendly and had regarded us for a long time as "regulars," but they had also learned quickly that we didn't care to talk about where we went on Saturdays. I guess we looked especially tense that day because I remember that the woman just handed us our keys without saying a word. We had our regular rooms by then that they always kept ready for us on Friday. After we'd been going there a while, they had asked me one time if we'd be coming every weekend and I said yes and they gave us a special reduced rate. They're really good, generous people, decent people, and they have no idea of the danger that threatens them. It's because of people like them that we do what we do. It's the thought of people like them that gives us the strength and courage we need.

We ate dinner that night in the hotel's dining room—it's called

62

the Dining Room—and nobody spoke and I remember that it was very quiet because very few people go out to eat on Good Friday. We all ordered a good meal too, trying to build up our strength, I guess, although I'm sure the others had no better appetite for it than I did.

But we forced ourselves to eat and when we were done we went upstairs. Paul and Susanne went off to their room and Barbara and I went into ours without saying a word to them. None of us could talk, not about anything.

We didn't get much sleep. I stared at the ceiling most of the night and I know that Barbara tossed and turned beside me. I'm sure I must have dozed for a while but I think I was awake more than I was asleep. In the morning, Paul and Susanne looked tired and haggard too.

We didn't say a word as we got into the car and drove out to the woods to meet the old man. There was nothing to say.

It was different this time. Very different.

The old man said nothing, just brought us into the house. The sharpened stakes we had prepared the previous week were lined up against the wall. We shivered at the sight of them. It had been raining and chilly when we left the hotel and drove out to the trail to meet the old man, and that had us shivering too. I guess we wouldn't have given much for our chances just then.

The old man was obviously nervous himself. He couldn't keep his eyes away from the stakes against the wall, kept glancing at them, as if to reassure himself that they were still there. But he knew how we felt too and soon told us that we should get some rest, get as much sleep during the day as we could, because we would have to be out in the woods during the night, before the first light of dawn, and we knew what lay ahead of us.

Without any further talking, we lay down on the rugs and fell instantly asleep.

He woke us in the night, a little before dawn. I can still feel his bony fingers squeezing my shoulder.

I shivered and saw that the others were just waking up too.

In silence, the old man came to each of us and handed us four of the stakes we'd prepared. When I took mine, the wood felt cold in my hand.

Then we were outside.

The air was wet and cold and we all pulled our jackets tight around us. The old man turned to face us.

"Death to the Easter Bunny!" he whispered. His breath misted in the damp air.

Then he turned and walked slowly but determinedly into the darkest part of the forest, and we followed.

When we had been walking for some minutes, the air seemed to change around us. The mist itself changed and became more like an ordinary thin fog. Then it started raining lightly and we could see a little better, the details of trees and branches becoming clearer as our eyes grew accustomed to the woods. Also, very slowly, the air was getting lighter. The chill and dampness, as well as fear, kept us shivering but we did our best to fight it off. We learned very quickly that you can be frightened and yet be determined to do what you have to do.

We stayed very close together, and very silent, as we made our way through the woods, following the old man.

Finally he stopped and held out a hand as a signal to us. We came up close around him and saw that we were on the edge of a small natural clearing in the woods. Silently, the old man pointed and we could see, in the gradually brightening light, the faintest hint of a trail that entered the clearing on one side and left it on the other. This was where we would wait for the Easter Bunny.

Pointing in silence, the old man indicated where each of us was to hide. Except for the creak of branches overhead, the faint rustle of the pines, and the steady dripping of rain from the trees, the woods were silent around us in the slowly growing light.

Cold, wet, nervous, we settled down to wait.

It didn't take long.

I was sitting there on the ground, feeling the cold and the rain soaking through my clothes and trying not to think about what was happening. If I stretched my neck up just a little, I could see Barbara in her hiding place a few yards away. I could imagine what was going through her mind right now. She hadn't wanted to believe any of this, hadn't wanted it to be real. None of us did. But of course, we had no choice: the old man spelled it out and when a thing like that is shown to you, you can't just sit back and ignore it. And so here we were. I kept flexing my fingers around the shafts of my four spears. I was afraid that if I sat too still for too long, my fingers would freeze and I'd be at the beast's mercy.

From our hiding places, we could all see the nearly obscure trail that entered at the other side of the clearing. Our eyes were fixed on it as we waited.

And then suddenly I saw something.

Beyond the clearing, some distance away up that barely visible trail, I thought I saw a movement, thought I saw something white moving between the dark trees. I leaned forward, clutching the spears, and squinted into the fog. I thought I saw it again, something white, whiter than the fog itself, and then instantly it was gone. My heart was pounding, hammering at my chest, and I was short of breath. And then I saw it again.

I stretched upward a little, just enough to see Barbara, and I could tell from the angle and stiffness of her body that she had seen it too.

I held my breath.

And saw it again, closer this time.

It had just been a white blur at first, a patch of whiteness moving against the gray-white of the fog. But now it had a shape. It was upright, and tall. It seemed almost to float or drift between the trees, moving closer and closer to the clearing where we were hiding, but I still couldn't make out any details.

Off to my left, I heard a tiny, stifled choking sound from the old man and then I knew it was really coming.

I closed my eyes for a second, then opened them quickly and focused on the place where I had last seen it. There it was, moving toward us, its shape hidden for a second by the trees, then briefly visible through the thick, swirling fog, then hidden again. The mist and the gray light and my own fear made it appear so large, I thought. It couldn't be as big as it seemed.

It was a rabbit. A huge rabbit. Its thick fur was brilliant white, fuzzy and soft. I could see, as it came slowly closer, its long floppy ears, and thought I could even make out a touch of pink on the insides of them. It had short forepaws, short in relation to its overall size, but huge by any standard, and seemed to be holding them up close to its chest. It wasn't hopping, the way a real rabbit would hop, using its powerful hindquarters, but walking, I could see now, walking purposefully along the trail. There was no mistaking it. It was definitely walking upright in the most grotesque fashion.

I watched it, fascinated and horrified at the same time, as it grew and grew in size and slowly materialized, as it seemed, out of the mist. There was no denying it. I was looking at the Easter Bunny, and everything the old man had said was true.

It was real and unreal at the same time, a thing that moved in this world, the real world, and yet was not *of* this world. A monster.

It had to be killed.

"Death to the Easter Bunny!" I breathed, and carefully crouched, ready to spring at it. I was tense but no longer afraid. I knew what I had to do.

With some uncanny kind of communication that only takes place in moments of extreme crisis, I knew that the others were moving with me, ready to attack the beast the instant it came within range.

And then it was just beyond the clearing. A few steps would bring it into the open space where we could be on it. And, my God, it was enormous, perhaps twice my own height. I could see it now, see it really clearly for the first time. I could see its face, its pink nose, its horribly long white whiskers. And I could see what it was carrying in those paws it held up in front of it. There, brightly decorated with yellow and purple satin ribbons, was a woven straw Easter basket. I had to force myself from freezing at the sight.

The thing stepped into the clearing, almost filling it with its huge size.

And we were on it.

The old man was first. With a hoarse, wordless cry, he sprang from the trees right beside the Easter Bunny, leaped at it, and plunged a spear into the soft white fur of its neck. Taken by surprise, the Easter Bunny reeled back.

The other four of us were already moving, our spears aimed at the thing's heart, as the old man had taught us. I don't know if the others' spears struck home on that first mad thrust, but I know mine did.

I felt it strike, felt it sink into resisting flesh. Knowing it was in, I whirled away—the old man had taught us well—and took another of my spears and moved in again to jab at it. The technique was like that of the bull ring: get the first spears in to stick there and weaken and hamper the beast, then go at it with the rest of the spears. I saw blood staining the white fur bright red. Through it all, the beast never made a sound.

Now I could see the other spears in it, dangling from it, whipping around as the Bunny whirled, still confused from the sudden attack. There were several streams of red running through its fur. It was still desperately clutching the Easter basket to its chest, perhaps for protection from the thrusting spears, but that gave us yet another moment of advantage and we made good use of it. One of the flying spears—I think it was one of the old man's—struck it in the face and then one of its eyes was bleeding.

It let go of the basket and whirled around, dropping to all fours and desperately seeking a direction where it could spring to safety. Its mouth was open and blood-flecked foam sprayed out. Its pink eyes darted all around. But we were at it, spears jabbing, thrusting, from every direction, offering it no chance to escape.

The old man was closest in to the beast, almost on top of it, pounding and pounding with his spear. When the one he was using stuck in the monster's side and broke off, he used the remaining piece to poke at its eyes, drawing more blood. The thing crouched lower to the ground, turned, turned back, but we gave it no room to move. It was weakening now, and covered with blood. Then suddenly it rose up on its hindquarters, those powerfully muscled legs that could break a man's back with one kick. If it had a chance to give a single strong thrust, it might get away from us. I saw Paul dash in and drive his spear deep into the thing's belly. Barbara and Susanne were thrusting their points repeatedly at its face and it tried to raise those short forepaws up to protect itself and that's when the old man saw his opening and got in very close, almost directly under the thing where he could have been crushed if it had come down on him, and, using both hands for more power, drove the shaft of his spear directly into the monster's heart and sank it in right up to the place where he held it.

The thing shuddered violently, then was still for an instant, as if delicately balanced. Half a dozen spears protruded from its body. Brilliant red blood stained its white fur. Both eyes were bloody and sightless. The straw basket was trampled and shattered in the mud beneath its enormous feet. We leaped out of the way as it toppled over. The sound it made when it hit the ground seemed loud enough to shake the very floor of the forest and the bedrock of the mountain beneath.

We stood there, sweating, trembling, gasping for air, spears ready, prepared to leap at it again if a single muscle moved or even twitched.

We waited a long time, breathing hard, standing in a circle around its bleeding body, watching its blood soak into the earth, but the Easter Bunny never stirred again.

The four of us live in Deacons Kill now.

We finished out the school term in New York, but didn't sign contracts for another year. We all found jobs in the Kill and work here now. It doesn't really matter what we do, as long as we can support ourselves, and, besides, we live very simply. When we pooled all of our savings, we had enough to buy a house right on the edge of the old man's woods. The four of us live together here and we get along just fine.

Barbara and I were married in June. Susanne wanted to be a June bride too, so we made it a double ceremony. It's good to have friends you can count on, and to be close to them.

And of course we see the old man all the time now.

It's a nice house. It's small but we've made it very comfortable. The nicest part of it, we all agree, is the big fireplace. Once the weather got cool in October, we really appreciated it. None of us minded chopping firewood at all, because it's been so nice to keep a big fire roaring there in the evenings and keeping us warm at night.

But there's no fire in the fireplace tonight. Winters are very cold in the mountains and it's pretty cold in the house right now and the five of us are bundled up to keep warm. But we don't mind. We'll do what we have to do and we'll wait here in the cold and the dark as long as we have to.

Our work was only just started last April when we killed the Easter Bunny. That was only the beginning. Now we have more work to do, and we'll wait here as long as necessary by the fireplace and the chimney, because tonight is the night before Christmas and our stockings are hung and we're ready.

The Rubber Room

BY ROBERT BLOCH

A civilized person believes himself or herself capable of only civilized acts, deploring the rest but secretly fearing that he or she might, just might, one day be driven to some of them. It is, quite literally, a living nightmare that most of us manage to confine to the dark of our dreams. Best intentions, however, do not always produce the best results.

Robert Bloch is the author of dozens of novels and stories in the fields of Dark Fantasy, science fiction, suspense, and mystery. His latest novel is the bestselling Psycho II.

EMERY kept telling them he wasn't crazy, but they put him in the rubber room anyway.

Sorry, fella, they said. Only temporary, we got a space problem here, overcrowded, move you to another cell in a couple hours, they said. It's better than being in the tank with all them drunks, they said. Okay, so you had your call to the lawyer but just take it easy until he gets here, they said.

And the door went clang.

So there he was, stuck way down at the end of the cell-block in this little room all by himself. They'd taken his watch and his wallet, his keys and his belt, even his shoelaces, so there was no way he could harm himself unless he bit his own wrists. But that would be crazy, and Emery wasn't crazy.

Now all he could do was wait. There wasn't anything else, no choice, no options, no way, once you were here in the rubber room.

To begin with, it was small—six paces long and six paces wide. A reasonably active man could cover the distance between the walls in one jump but he'd need a running start. Not that there was any point in trying, because he'd just bounce harmlessly off the thick padding.

The windowless walls were padded everywhere from floor to ceiling and so was the door. The padding was seamless so it couldn't be torn or pried away. Even the floor was padded, except for a ten-inch square at the left far corner which was supposed to serve as a toilet facility.

Above him a tiny light bulb burned dimly behind its meshed enclosure, safely beyond reach from the floor below. The ceiling around it was padded too, probably to deaden sound.

Restraint room, that's what they said it was, but it used to be called a padded cell. Rubber room was just popular slang. And maybe the slang wouldn't be so popular if more people were exposed to the reality.

Before he knew what he was doing, Emery found himself pacing back and forth. Six paces forward, six paces back, over and over again, like an animal in a cage.

That's what this was, actually—not a room, just a cage. And if you stayed in a cage long enough you turned into an animal. Ripping and clawing and smashing your head against the walls, howling for release.

If you weren't crazy when you came in you'd go crazy before you got out. The trick, of course, was not to stay here too long.

But how long was too long? How long would it be before the lawyer arrived?

Six paces forward, six paces back. Grey spongy padding muffled his footsteps on the floor and absorbed the light from above, leaving the walls in shadow. Shadows could drive you crazy too. So could the silence, and being alone. Alone in shadows and silence, like he'd been when they found him there in the room—the other room, the one in the house.

It was like a bad dream. Maybe that's the way it feels when you're crazy, and if so he must have been crazy when it happened.

But Emery wasn't crazy now. He was perfectly sane, completely under control. And there was nothing here that could harm him. Silence can't harm you. What was the old saying? Violence is golden. No, not *violence*. Where had that come from? Freudian slip. To hell with Freud, what did he know? Nobody knew. And if he kept silent nobody ever would. Even though they'd found him they couldn't prove anything. Not if he kept silent, let his lawyer do the talking.

Silence was his friend. And the shadows were his friends too. Shadows hid everything. There had been shadows in the other room and no one could have seen clearly when they found him. You just *thought* you saw it, he'd tell them.

No, he'd forgotten—he mustn't tell them, just let the lawyer talk. What was the matter with him, *was* he going crazy here after all?

Six paces forward, six paces back. Keep walking, keep silent. Keep away from those shadows in the corners. They were getting darker now. Darker and thicker. Something seemed to be moving there in the far corner to the right.

Emery felt the muscles tightening in his throat and he couldn't control them; he knew that in a moment he was going to scream.

Then the door opened behind him and in the light from the corridor the shadow disappeared.

It was a good thing he hadn't screamed. They would have been sure he was crazy then, and that would spoil everything.

But now that the shadow was gone Emery relaxed. By the time they took him down the hall and into the visitor's room he was quite calm again.

His lawyer waited for him there, sitting on the other side of the grille barrier, and nobody was listening.

That's what the lawyer said. Nobody's listening, you can tell me all about it.

Emery shook his head and smiled because he knew better. Violence is golden and even the walls have ears. He wanted to warn his lawyer that they were spying on him but that would sound crazy. The sane thing to do was not to mention it, just be careful and say the right things instead.

He told the lawyer what everybody knew about himself. He was a decent man, he had a steady job, paid his bills, didn't smoke or drink or get out of line. Hardworking, dependable, neat, clean, no police record, not a troublemaker. Mother was always proud of her boy and she'd be proud of him today if she were still alive. He'd always looked after her and when she died he still looked after the house, kept it up, kept himself up, just the way she'd taught him to. So what was all this fuss about?

Suppose you tell me, the lawyer said.

That was the hard part, making him understand, but Emery knew everything depended on it. So he talked very slowly, choosing his words carefully, sticking to the facts.

World War II had happened before he'd been born, but that was a fact.

Emery knew a lot of facts about World War II because he used to read library books when Mother was alive. Improve your mind, she said. Reading is better than watching all that violence on the television, she said.

So at night when he couldn't sleep he read for hours sitting up in his room. People he worked with down at the shop called him a bookworm but he didn't care. There was no such thing as a bookworm, he knew that. There were worms that ate microorganisms in the soil and birds that ate worms and animals that ate birds and people who ate animals and microorganisms that ate people—like the ones that ate Mother until they killed her.

Everything—germs, plants, animals, people—kills other things to stay alive. This is a fact, a cruel fact. He could still remember the way Mother screamed.

After she died he read more. That's when he really got into history. The Greeks killed the Persians and the Romans killed the Greeks and the barbarians killed the Romans and the Christians killed the barbarians and the Moslems killed the Christians and the Hindus killed the Moslems. Blacks killed whites, whites killed Indians, Indians killed other Indians, orientals killed other orientals, Protestants killed Catholics, Catholics killed Jews, Jews killed Our Saviour on the Cross.

Love one another, Jesus said, and they killed him for it. If Our Saviour had lived, the gospel would have spread around the world and there'd be no violence. But the Jews killed Our Lord.

That's what Emery told the lawyer, but it didn't go down. Get to the point, the lawyer said.

Emery was used to that kind of reaction. He'd heard it before when he tried to explain things to girls he met after Mother died. Mother hadn't approved of him going with girls and he used to resent it. After she was gone the fellows at work told him it would do him good. Get out of your shell, they said. So he let them set up

74

some double-dates and that's when he found out that Mother was right. The girls just laughed at him when he talked facts.

It was better to stay in his shell, like a snail. Snails knew how to protect themselves in a world where everyone kills to live, and the Jews killed Our Saviour.

Facts, the lawyer said. Give me some facts.

So Emery told him about World War II. That's when the real killing began. Jewish international bankers financed the Napoleonic wars and World War I, but these were nothing compared to World War II. Hitler knew what the Jews were planning and he tried to prevent it—that's why he invaded those other countries, to get rid of the Jews, just as he did in Germany. They were plotting a war to destroy the world, so they could take over. But no one understood and in the end the Jew-financed armies won the war. The Jews killed Hitler just like they killed Our Saviour. History repeats itself, and that's a fact too.

Emery explained all this very quietly, using nothing except facts, but from the way his lawyer looked at him he could see it was no use.

So Emery went back into his shell. But this time he took his lawyer with him.

He told him what it was like, living alone in his house, which was really a big shell that protected him. Too big at first, and too empty, until Emery began to fill it up with books. Books about World War II, because of the facts. Only the more he read the more he realized that most of them didn't contain facts. The victors wrote the histories and now that the Jews had won they wrote lies. They lied about Hitler, they lied about the Nazi Party and its ideals.

Emery was one of the few people who could read between the lies and see the truth. Reminders of the truth could be found outside of books, so now he turned to them and started to collect them. The trappings and the banners, the iron helmets and the iron medals. Iron crosses were reminders too—the Jews had destroyed Our Saviour on a cross and now they were trying to destroy the crosses themselves.

That's when he began to realize what was happening, when he went to the antique shops where such things were sold.

75

There would be other people in these shops and they stared at him. Nobody said a word but they were watching. Sometimes he thought he could hear them whispering behind his back and he knew for a fact that they were taking notes.

It wasn't just his imagination because pretty soon some of the people down at work started asking him questions about his collection—the pictures of the party leaders and the swastika emblems and badges and the photographs of the little girls presenting flowers to the Führer at rallies and parades. Hard to believe these little girls were now fifty-year-old women. Sometimes he thought if he met one of those women he could settle down with her and be happy; at least she'd understand because she knew the facts. Once he almost decided to run an ad in the classified section, trying to locate such a woman, but then he realized it might be dangerous. Suppose the Jews were out to get her? They'd get him too. That was a fact.

Emery's lawyer shook his head. His face, behind the grille, was taking on an expression which Emery didn't like. It was the expression people wear when they're at the zoo, peering through the bars or the wire screens at the animals.

That's when Emery decided he'd have to tell his lawyer the rest. It was a risk, but if he wanted to be believed his lawyer must know all the facts.

So he told him about the conspiracy.

All these hijackings and kidnappings going on today were part of it. And these terrorists running around with ski-masks over their faces were part of the plan too.

In today's world, terror wears a ski-mask.

Sometimes they called themselves Arabs, but that was just to confuse people. They were the ones behind the bombings in Northern Ireland and the assassinations in South America. The international Jewish conspiracy was in back of it all and behind every ski-mask was a Jewish face.

They spread throughout the world, stirring up fear and confusion. And they were here too, plotting and scheming and spying on their enemies. Mother knew.

When he was just a little boy and did something naughty Mother used to tell him to behave. Behave yourself or the Jew-man will get you, Mother said. He used to think she was just trying to frighten

76

him but now he realized Mother was telling the truth. Like the time she caught him playing with himself and locked him in the closet. The Jew-man will get you, she said. And he was all alone in the dark and he could see the Jew-man coming through the walls and he screamed and she let him out just in time. Otherwise the Jew-man *would* have taken him. He knew now that this was the way they got their recruits—they took other peoples' children and brainwashed them, brought them up to be political terrorists in countries all over the world—Italy, Ireland, Indonesia, the Middle East—so that no one would suspect the real facts. The real facts, that the Jews were responsible, getting ready for another war. And when the other nations had destroyed themselves, Israel would take over the world.

Emery was talking louder now but he didn't realize it until the lawyer told him to hold it down. What makes you think these terrorists are after you, he asked. Did you ever see one?

No, Emery told him, they're too clever for that. But they have their spies, their agents are everywhere.

The lawyer's face was getting red and Emery noticed it. He told him why it was getting so hot here in the visitor's room—their agents were at work again.

Those people who saw Emery buying the flags and swastikas and iron crosses had been planted in the stores to spy on him. And the ones down at work who teased him about his collection, they were spies too, and they knew he'd found out the truth.

The terrorists had been after him for months now, planning to kill him. They tried to run him down with their cars when he crossed the street but he got away. Two weeks ago when he turned on the television there was an explosion. It seemed like a short-circuit but he knew better; they wanted to electrocute him only it didn't work. He was too smart to call a repairman because that's what they wanted—they'd send one of their assassins instead. The only people who still make house-calls today are the murderers.

So for two weeks he'd managed without electricity. That's when they must have put the machines in the walls. The terrorists had machines to make things heat up and at night he could hear a humming sound in the dark. He'd searched around, tapping the walls, and he couldn't find anything, but he knew the machines were there. Sometimes it got so hot he was soaked with sweat, but he didn't try

77

to turn down the furnace. He'd show them he could take it. And he wasn't about to go out of the house because he knew that's what they wanted. That was their plan, to force him out so they could get at him and kill him.

Emery was too smart for that. He had enough canned goods and stuff to get by and it was safer to stay put. When the phone rang he didn't answer; probably someone at the shop was calling to ask him why he didn't come to work. That's all he needed—come back to work so they could murder him on the way.

It was better to hole up right there in his bedroom with the iron crosses and the swastikas on the walls. The swastika is a very ancient symbol, a sacred symbol, and it protected him. So did the big picture of the Führer. Just knowing it was there was protection enough, even in the dark. Emery couldn't sleep any more because of the sounds in the walls—at first it had been humming, but gradually he could make out voices. He didn't understand Hebrew, and it was only gradually that he knew what they were saying. Come on out, you dirty Aryan, come out and be killed.

Every night they came, like vampires, wearing ski-masks to hide their faces. They came and they whispered, *come out, come out, wherever you are*. But he didn't come out.

Some history books said Hitler was crazy, and maybe that part was true. If so, Emery knew why. It was because he must have heard the voices too and known they were after him. No wonder he kept talking about the answer to the Jewish question. They were polluting the human race and he had to stop them. But they burned him in a bunker instead. They killed Our Saviour. Can't you understand that?

The lawyer said he couldn't understand and maybe Emery should talk to a doctor instead. But Emery didn't want to talk to a doctor. Those Jew doctors were part of the conspiracy. What he had to say now was in the strictest confidence.

Then for Christ's sake tell me, the lawyer said.

And Emery said yes, he'd tell him. For Christ's sake, for the sake of Our Lord.

Two days ago he'd run out of canned goods. He was hungry, very hungry, and if he didn't eat he'd die. The terrorists wanted to starve him to death but he was too smart for that.

So he decided to go to the store.

He peeked through all the windows first but he couldn't see any-one in a ski-mask. That didn't mean it was safe, of course, because they used ordinary people too. The only thing he could do was take a chance. And before he left he put one of the iron crosses around his neck on a chain. That would help protect him.

Then, at twilight, he went to the supermarket down the street. No sense trying to drive, because the terrorists might have planted a bomb in his car, so he walked all the way.

It felt strange being outside again and though Emery saw nothing suspicious he was shaking all over by the time he got to the store.

The supermarket had those big fluorescent lights and there were no shadows. He didn't see any of their spies or agents around either, but of course they'd be too clever to show themselves. Emery just hoped he could get back home before they made their move.

The customers in the store looked like ordinary people; the thing is, you can never be sure nowadays. Emery picked out his canned goods as fast as possible and he was glad to get through the line at the checkout counter without any trouble. The clerk gave him a funny look but maybe it was just because he hadn't shaved or changed clothes for so long. Anyway he managed, even though his head was starting to hurt.

It was dark when he came out of the store with his bag of grocer-ies, and there was nobody on the street. That's another thing the Jew terrorists have done—made us afraid to walk on the street alone. See what it's come to? Everyone's scared being out at night!

That's what the little girl told him.

She was standing there on the corner of the block when he saw her—cute little thing, maybe five years old, with big brown eyes and curly hair. And she was crying, scared to death.

I'm lost, she said. I'm lost, I want my Mommy.

Emery could understand that. Everybody's lost nowadays, wants someone to protect them. Only there's no protection any more, not with those terrorists around waiting for their chance, lurking in the shadows.

And there were shadows on the street, shadows outside his house. He wanted to help but he couldn't risk standing out here talking.

So he just went on, up the porch steps, and it wasn't until he opened the front door that he realized she had followed him. Little girl crying, saying please Mister, take me to my Mommy.

He wanted to go in and shut the door but he knew he had to do something.

How did you get lost, he asked.

She said she was waiting in the car outside the market while Mommy shopped but when Mommy didn't come back she got out to look for her in the store and she was gone. Then she thought she saw her down the street and she ran after her only it turned out to be another lady. Now she didn't know where she was and would he please take her home?

Emery knew he couldn't do that, but she was crying again, crying loud. If they were anywhere around they'd hear her, so he told her to come in.

The house smelled funny from not being aired out and it was very hot inside. Dark too with all the electricity turned off on account of the terrorists. He tried to explain but she only cried louder because the dark frightened her.

Don't be scared, Emery said. Tell me your Mommy's name and I'll phone her to come and get you.

So she told him the name—Mrs. Rubelsky, Sylvia Rubelsky—but she didn't know the address.

It was hard to hear because of the humming in the walls. He got hold of the flashlight he kept in the kitchen for emergencies and then he went into the hall to look up the name in the phone book.

There weren't any Rubelskys listed. He tried other spellings—Rubelski, Roubelsky, Rebelsky, Rabelsky—but there was nothing in the book. Are you sure, he asked.

Then she said they didn't have a phone.

That was funny; everybody has a phone. She said it didn't matter because if he just took her over to Sixth Street she could point out the house to him.

Emery wasn't about to go anywhere, let alone Sixth Street. That was a Jewish neighborhood. Come to think of it, Rubelsky was a Jewish name.

Are you Jewish, he asked her.

She stopped crying and stared at him and those big brown eyes got wider and wider. The way she stared made his head hurt more.

What are you looking at, he said.

That thing around your neck, she told him. That iron cross. It's like Nazis wear.

What do you know about Nazis, he asked.

They killed my Grandpa, she said. They killed him at Belsen. Mommy told me. Nazis are bad.

All at once it came to Emery in a flash, a flash that made his whole head throb.

She was one of *them*. They'd planted her on the street, knowing he'd let her into the house here. What did they want?

Why do you wear bad things, she said. Take it off.

Now she was reaching out towards the chain around his neck, the chain with the iron cross.

It was like that old movie he saw once long ago, the movie about the Golem. This big stone monster got loose in the Jewish ghetto, wearing the Star of David on its chest. A little girl pulled the star off and the Golem fell down dead.

That's why they sent her here, to pull off the iron cross and kill him.

No way, he said. And he slapped her, not hard, but she started to scream and he couldn't have that, so he put his hands around her neck just to stop the screaming and there was a kind of cracking sound and then——

What happened then, the lawyer asked.

I don't want to talk about it, Emery said.

But he couldn't stop, he *was* talking about it. At first, when he didn't find a pulse, he thought he'd killed her. But he hadn't squeezed that hard, so it must have happened when she touched the iron cross. That meant he'd guessed right, she was one of *them*.

But he couldn't tell anyone, he knew people would never believe that the terrorists had sent a little Jew-girl here to murder him. And he couldn't let her be found like this. What to do, that was the question. The Jewish question.

Then he remembered. Hitler had the answer. He knew what to do.

It was hot here and even hotter downstairs. That's where he carried her, downstairs, where the furnace was going. The gas furnace.

Oh my God, said the lawyer. Oh my God.

And then the lawyer stood up fast and went over to the door on the other side of the grille and called the guard.

Come back here, Emery said.

But he didn't listen, he kept whispering to the guard, and then other guards came up behind Emery on his side of the grille and grabbed his arms.

He yelled at them to let him go, not to listen to that Jew lawyer, didn't they understand he must be one of *them*?

Instead of paying attention they just marched him back down the hall to the rubber room and shoved him inside.

You promised you'd put me in another cell, Emery said. I don't want to stay here. I'm not crazy.

One of the guards said easy does it, the doctor is coming to give you something so you can sleep.

And the door went clang.

Emery was back in the rubber room, but this time he didn't pace and he didn't call out. It wouldn't do any good. Now he knew how Our Saviour had felt, betrayed and waiting for the crucifixion.

Emery had been betrayed too, betrayed by the Jew lawyer, and now all he could do was wait for the Jew doctor to come. Put him to sleep, the guard had said. That was how the conspiracy worked— they'd put him to sleep forever. Only he wouldn't let them, he'd stay awake, demand a fair trial.

But that was impossible. The police would tell about hearing the little girl scream and breaking into the house and finding him. They'd say he was a child-molester and a murderer. And the judge would sentence him to death. He'd believe the Jews just like Pontius Pilate did, just like the Allies did when they killed Our Führer.

Emery wasn't dead yet but there was no way out. No way out of the trial, no way out of the rubber room.

Or was there?

The answer came to him just like that.

He'd plead insanity.

Emery knew he wasn't crazy but he could fool them into believing

82

it. That was no disgrace—some people thought Jesus and the Führer were crazy too. All he had to do was pretend.

Yes, that was the answer. And just thinking about it made him feel better. Even if they shut him up in a rubber room like this he'd still be alive. He could walk and talk and eat and sleep and think. Think about how he'd tricked them, all those Jew terrorists who were out to get him.

Emery didn't have to be careful now. He didn't have to lie, the way he'd lied to the lawyer. He could admit the real truth.

Killing that little Jew-girl wasn't an accident, he knew what he was going to do the minute he got his hands around her throat. He squeezed just as hard as he could because that's what he'd always really wanted. To squeeze the necks of those girls who laughed at him, squeeze the guys at work who wouldn't listen when he told them about his collection and yes, say it, he wanted to squeeze Mother too because she'd always squeezed him, smothered him, strangled away his life. But most of all he squeezed the Jews, the dirty kike terrorists who were out to destroy him, destroy the world.

And that's what he had done. He hadn't cracked the little girl's neck, she wasn't dead when he carried her downstairs and opened the furnace door.

What he had really done was solve the Jewish question.

He'd solved it and they couldn't touch him. He was safe now, safe from all the terrorists and evil spirits out for revenge, safe forever here in the rubber room.

The only thing he didn't like was the shadows. He remembered how they'd been before, how the one in the far corner seemed to get darker and thicker.

And now it was happening again.

Don't look at it, he told himself. You're imagining things. Only crazy people see shadows moving. Moving and coiling like a cloud, a cloud of smoke from a gas furnace.

But he had to look because it was changing now, taking on a shape. Emery could see it standing in the corner, the figure of a man. A man in a black suit, with a black face.

And it was moving forward.

Emery backed away as the figure glided towards him softly and

83

silently across the padded floor, and he opened his mouth to scream.

But the scream wouldn't come, nothing was coming except the figure looming up before Emery as he pressed against the wall of the rubber room. He could see the black face quite clearly now—only it wasn't a face.

It was a ski-mask.

The figure's arms rose and the hands splayed out and he saw little black droplets oozing from the smoky wrists as the fingers curled around his throat. Emery struck out at the ski-mask, thrusting his fingers through the eye-holes, stabbing at the eyes behind them. But there was nothing under the mask, nothing at all.

It was then that Emery really went mad.

When they opened the door of the rubber room the shadow was gone. All they found was Emery and he was dead.

Apoplexy, they said. Heart failure. Better write up a medical report fast and close the case. Close the rubber room too while they were at it.

Just a coincidence of course, but people might get funny ideas if they found out. Two deaths in the same cell—Emery, and that other nut last week who bit open his own wrists, the crazy terrorist guy in the ski-mask.

Petey

BY T. E. D. KLEIN

Terror isn't always at its most effective when approached on the fast track; there are times when a certain amount of delib-*erate speed is required, a speed that allows you to see what's coming far enough in advance to be prepared—either to get out of the way or to defend yourself. The problem, however, is that you can do neither. You can only watch, and be help-less.*

    T.E.D. Klein lives in New York City, edits The Twilight Zone *magazine, and has written far less than his many fans would like. Though his settings are contemporary, his taste tends to the traditional—a taste he works to great and effective advantage.*

"LET'S face it, Doctor, if an inmate's suicidal there ain't a hell of a lot you can do. Sure, you can take away his shoes so he don't strangle himself with his shoelaces, and you take away his clothes for the same reason—I once seen a man hanging from the bars on his window by his T-shirt—and maybe just to be safe you take the cot out of his room, since last year we had a broad who slashed her wrists on the springs. . . .

"But you can't do everything. I mean, if they want to kill themselves they're gonna figure out a way to do it. We once had a guy who ran against the wall with his head. A nine-by-seven cell, that's all it was, so he couldn't build up much speed. . . . Still, he gave himself a pretty nice concussion. Put a nice dent in the plaster, too. Now, of course, we keep the place padded. And another one we had, I swear to God he just held his breath till he croaked. I mean it, if they've got the will they can do it.

"Now the guy you're gonna see, he had us fooled. We thought

85

we'd took every precaution with him, you know? But we should've used a straitjacket. Christ, the guy really tore hell out of his throat. With his bare hands yet."

"George, I've got to admit it: I'm jealous, I really am. This place is fantastic." Milton raised his glass. "Here's to you, you old son of a bitch! And to your new house."

He was about to down his Scotch, but Ellie stayed his hand. "Honey, wait. Let's let everybody in on it." She turned to the other guests, who were gathered in little clumps of conversation throughout the living room. "Hey, everybody! Can I have your attention, please? My husband has just proposed a toast to our charming host and hostess . . ." She waited for silence. "And to their bountiful kindness in letting us peasants——"

"Peons, Ellie, peons!" shouted Walter. Like the rest of them, he was already rather drunk.

"Yeah," echoed Harold, "us miserable peons!"

"Okay," Ellie laughed. "To their bountiful kindness in opening their new home——"

"Their *stately* new home."

"Their *mansion!*"

"For opening their mansion to us poor miserable downtrodden peons. And furthermore——"

"Hey," interrupted her husband, "I thought *I* was going to make the toast!" They all laughed. "I mean I've been practicing for this all week!" He turned to the rest, milking the joke. "I tell you, the old lady doesn't let me get a word in edgewise anymore!"

"Yeah, come on, El," shouted Walter, "give the poor guy a chance, and then you can put the muzzle back on!"

Everyone laughed except Walter's wife, Joyce, who whispered, "Really, honey, I sometimes think it's *you* that needs——"

"Ladies and gentlemen." Milton spoke with mock gravity. "I hereby propose a toast to our esteemed host——"

All eyes turned toward George, who grinned and made a low bow.

"——and to Phyllis, our *equally* esteemed hostess——"

"Gee, Ellie, you've really got him trained, haven't you!"

86

"I freely admit it," said Milton, placing the hand with the drink over his heart. "After twenty-eight years——"

"Twenty-seven."

"It just *feels* like twenty-eight!"

"Oh, Waltie, hush up."

"After twenty-seven years of wedded bliss, she's finally done it. She's even got me making my own bed!" He paused for the cheers and the groans, then turned toward Phyllis. "But as I was saying, I would like to pay tribute to that gracious, charming, ravishingly beautiful——"

Phyllis tittered.

"——stunningly coiffed——"

Self-consciously she patted the streaks in her new feathercut.

"——and delightfully sexy woman he calls his wife."

"I'll drink to that!"

"Hear hear!"

"You're allowed to drink to that too, Phyllis."

"Yeah, somebody mix Phyllis a drink."

"Oh, that's silly!" squealed Phyllis. "I'm not supposed to drink to myself."

"Nonsense, my dear." George handed her a vodka and tonic, then seized his own.

"And finally," continued Milton, raising his voice and his glass, "to the reason we're all gathered here tonight, the cause of all our celebration——"

"And jealousy," added his wife.

"To this beautiful, beautiful house, this rustic retreat nestled amidst the wilds of Connecticut, this find of a lifetime, which makes our own split-levels look like something out of Levittown——"

"You're laying it on a bit thick," said George. He winked at the others. "I think Milt missed his true calling. He should have been a poet, not a stockbroker."

"Or a real estate salesman!" cried Walter.

Milton continued undaunted. "This museum——"

"Museum?" George winced; all this congratulation embarrassed him. He could sense the envy in it, and the bitterness. "Mausoleum is more like it!"

87

"——containing room after room of the rarest antiquities——"

"Junk! Nothing but junk!"

"——this magnificent Colonial mansion——"

"Aw, come on, Milt! It's just an old *barn*, for Chrissake!"

"——in which George can play country squire and Phyllis lady of the manor, to their hearts' content——"

George laughed. "I've still got to drive to work every day!"

"——this baronial hall, this playground of the landed gentry, this irrefutable testament to the smartest real estate finagling this side of Manhattan Island——"

George's smile faded.

"——this glorious old homestead, now a *new* home for George and Phyllis, in the hope that their years are blessed with just as much luck as they've had in acquiring it."

There was a moment's uneasy silence.

"Are you done, Milt?" said George.

"That's right, old buddy." Milton downed his Scotch. The others followed with a round of applause, but it was a feeble one; George's embarrassment embarrassed them all. Then Walter yelled out, "And in the hope that you'll give lots more parties like this one! How about every weekend, for starters?" And that relaxed them into laughter, though a little too loud, a little too long.

"When are you gonna show us the rest of this place?" cried Sidney Gerdts.

"Yeah, when do we get a tour of the estate? That's what we came for!"

"Come on, Phyl, you promised."

"She's been talking about this place for the last six months!"

"Yeah, you really had us drooling."

"So what does she do now? Keeps us cooped up in this living room like a bunch of kids!"

"How about it, Phyl? What're you ashamed of?"

Phyllis smiled. "The tour starts when everybody gets here."

"Isn't everybody here?"

"Who's missing?"

"Herb and Tammie Rosenzweig haven't shown up yet," said George. "They told me they'd be able to make it. . . ."

"I think maybe they were having some trouble finding a sitter," said Doris, Sidney's wife. "I spoke to them this morning."

Harold made a face. "Aw, they're always late. It takes Tammie two hours to put on her makeup." He shuffled toward the bar and poured himself another whiskey and soda.

"Let's start without'em, then."

"Now, Sid, really," said Doris, taking him by the hand, "you know that wouldn't be fair. Come on, let's go over and look at these." She pulled him toward a wall of bookshelves. "Maybe you can reach the ones on the top. They're too high for me."

"Aw, gee, honey, they're just a lot of old books. Kid stuff, too, from the look of them. Fairy tales. Probably came with the house."

"But they look interesting, those big ones up there. Maybe they're worth a lot of money."

Grunting, he stood on tiptoe and removed one, a heavy volume shedding flakes of leather when he opened it, like a dead man's skin.

"Here, you take it. I can't read this stuff." He handed the book to his wife and turned away, bored.

Squinting at the text, Doris frowned in disappointment. "Oh, damn," she muttered, "wouldn't you just know it?"

George left off talking business with Fred Weingast and ambled over, glass in hand. "Having trouble, Dorie?"

She grimaced. "This really makes me feel my age. I used to be so good in French—even knew a word or two of Provençal, which I think this book is in—and now I don't remember a thing."

"Never could stand it, myself. All that masculine-feminine stuff, and those goddamn accents . . ." He took a sip of vodka. "Actually, I'd toss all these old books out, only they're a good investment."

Gerdts turned back to them. "Investment, did you say? You mean those things are really worth something?"

"Damn right. They're going up all the time." He nodded to the man who stood talking a few feet away. "Isn't that right, Fred?"

Weingast walked over, followed by Harold and another guest, Arthur Faschman. "Yeah, my accountant told me to get into books, especially with the market the way it is. But you've gotta have the room for'em." He shrugged. "Me, my apartment's much too small."

"Naw, that's not the problem," said Faschman. "The problem is keeping them cool and dry. Look at those things up there—they're probably full of mice and silverfish."

George laughed, a little uneasily. "Oh, I doubt there's any mice. We had the place fumigated before moving in. *Really* fumigated!" He took a sip of vodka. "But you know, you're right, those damned things do decay something awful, and when summer comes I bet they'll begin to smell. To tell you the truth, I've been thinking of selling the lot of them to some place down in New Haven. Maybe put in a nice hi-fi unit, or one of those new Betamax things."

"Yeah, that's a good idea," said Faschman. "I've been meaning to get one of those myself. And I'll tell you what you do then: you invest in stamps. They're a lot easier to keep."

Weingast nodded. "Stamps are okay," he said, "but my accountant says coins are even better. With gold prices going up, they're a pretty safe bet."

When George left them, the men were deep into high finance. He returned to the bar and refilled his glass.

Even with the Rosenzweigs' tardiness, and the absence of the Foglers and the Greens, and the fact that Bob Childs was sick and Evelyn Platt was away, it was a big housewarming party. The Brackmans were there, Milt and Ellie, and the Gerdtses, Sid and Doris, and Arthur and Judy Faschman, and Fred and Laura Weingast, and the Stanleys just back from Miami, Dennis and Sarah sporting their new suntans, and Harold and Frances Lazarus, and big Mike Carlinsky with his fiancée, whose name they all kept forgetting, and Phil and Mimi Katz, and the Chasens, Chuck and Cindy, and Walter Applebaum and his new wife, Joyce, and Steve and Janet Mulholland, and Jack and Irene Crystal, and the Fitzgeralds and the Goodhues, and Allen Goldberg and Paul Strauss and poor Cissy Hawkins, who was so homely Allen and Paul wouldn't talk to her, even though she was supposed to be fixed up with one of them.

Thirty-one people gathered in the Kurtzes' living room; and with the Rosenzweigs arriving now, amid much hugging and handshaking and cries of "At last!" and "It's about time!" and the inevitable wolf whistles at Tammie Rosenzweig's décolletage, that made thirty-three.

That was a lot of people, George decided. Too many, really, when one considered how many of them weren't even close friends. Why, he and Phyllis barely saw the Mulhollands from one year to the next. And as for the Goodhues, they didn't even know them; they'd been invited by the Fitzgeralds. Leaning back against the bar, George held the glass to his eye and surveyed his guests through a frost of vodka. At times like this it was hard to keep track of them: too many faces to smile at, too many names to remember. Sometimes they seemed almost interchangeable.

Still, it was nice to have a living room large enough to hold a crowd this size. And anyway, George reflected, he and Phyllis had vowed that as soon as they'd moved into the house they'd become great entertainers. A party like this was the perfect way to establish their new identities.

"George!" Phyllis broke into his reverie. "Come over here and take Tammie's coat." She looked up at Herb. "And as for you, I think you're a big enough boy to hang your own coat up. It's very informal tonight, we haven't really moved in yet. And you'll have to mix yourselves drinks, we don't even have a bartender!" She laughed, as if to suggest that, in the future, in this fine new house, bartenders would be routine.

Tammie was talking about how hard it was to find a decent sitter these days. "And so finally we decided the hell with it, and left her off at Herb's folks. They never go out anymore anyway." She smoothed her new dress.

"Lord, George, this place is swell!" said Herb, pumping George's hand. "I'm just sorry we didn't get here earlier, so we could see it by daylight. Bet those trees are beautiful this time of year. But God almighty, let me tell you, it's hard as hell to *find* this place!"

"Weren't Phyllis's directions good enough?"

"Oh sure, they were all right." Herb followed George to the coat closet. "But I mean, it gets so *dark* out here in the country. I'm just not used to it." He paused until George had found a spare hanger for Tammie's coat. "We took the Turnpike all the way up to New Haven—that part was fine, of course—and we got off at Clinton, just like we were supposed to . . . But once you're off 81 the road gets pretty bad. It's like they suddenly turned out the lights! No markers or anything." He shook his head. "You've got influence on

91

the State Highway Commission, don't you, George? I mean, you really ought to do something about it. It's a disgrace!"

"Yeah, the roads are a little tricky at night, till you get used to them."

"Tricky? They're a lot worse than tricky, let me tell you. I damn near *hit* something! Honest to God, I think it was a bear."

"Oh, come on, Herb!" George slapped him on the back. "You've been living in Yonkers too long. This is the country, sure, but it's not the middle of the *woods*, for Chrissake! This is Connecticut! There haven't been bears around here for hundreds of years."

"Well, whatever it was——"

"Probably some poor old sheep dog. All the farmers around here use 'em."

"Okay, okay, it was a sheep dog, then. Who knows? It was so dark . . . Anyway, I nearly hit the thing, and I would have if Tammie hadn't yelled. And then I got so rattled I missed the turnoff at, what is it, Death's Head?"

George laughed. "Brother, you've got some imagination! You Madison Avenue guys are all alike. The name of the town is Beth Head, dummy! *Beth* Head."

Herb laughed, too. "Anyway, I missed the place completely and ended up driving into the gates of some state park. Can you believe it? Tammie was having a fit! We're looking for your house and we end up in some damned *park!*"

"Yeah, that's Chatfield Hollow. I've done some fishing there. Very nice area."

"It must be, during the day. But it's not the kind of place I like to visit at night. Tammie thought she saw a light in the ranger's cabin—you know, the one by the gates—and I got out to ask directions. I mean, we hadn't even brought along a goddamned *map!*"

George grinned from ear to ear. "Poor Herb! You'll just never make a backwoodsman!"

"Damned right!" laughed Herb. "Tammie was fussing about her goddamned *dress* so much she didn't even think to . . . Well, anyway, I'm walking up to this godforsaken little cabin, and immediately I see that Tammie was wrong, there's no light in it, the place is boarded up for the season and all. . . . But just in case, I start pounding on the door, you know?, and yelling for the ranger. I mean, we were really *lost!*" He lowered his voice. "Besides, I knew Tammie would squawk if I didn't make sure it was really empty."

"And was it?"

"Of course it was! Who the hell would hang around a place like *that* all night?" He shook his head. "So there I am, pounding on this door and wondering if there's a pay phone around so maybe I could call you. . . . When I hear something lumbering through the bushes."

"Probably the ranger."

"I didn't wait to find out. You should have seen how fast I got back into that car and took off! Believe me, I was ready to head right back to New York, but Tammie wanted to show off her new dress." He paused. "And of course, I wanted to see this place."

"You tell Tammie what you heard?"

"Are you kidding? She'd make such fun of me I'd never hear the end of it. Listen, she thinks I'm a coward as it is. *She's* the tough one, she really is. I'd never have found this place if it weren't for her. She caught that last turnoff after I was half a mile past it. The damned thing's almost hidden by trees! You ought to cut a few of them down, for Chrissake!"

"I thought you were supposed to be the big conservationist."

Herb laughed. "Well, just because I send money to the Sierra Club doesn't mean I have to worship trees. I mean, someone's going to have an *accident* one of these days. Really, George, you ought to do something about it. Get them to put up some lights or something. You've got influence with the Highway Commission, don't you?"

"Not as much as people seem to think."

"Well, anyway, it's a safety hazard. I mean, that winding road, so goddamned narrow that I had to go about twenty miles an hour. . . . It's just a good thing there weren't any cars going the other way. As a matter of fact, there wasn't a single other car on the road. Pretty desolate for a place so close to New York."

"No pollution."

"Damn right! Hey, I *mean* it, old buddy. I may not be a nature freak, but I think it's great out here. Like to live here myself."

"Why not move, then? There must be a few homesteads for sale in these parts. I know there are a couple in the next county. I could even help you look. I mean, it gets a little lonely, sometimes. . . ."

"Hey, I thought you *liked* living way out here."

"Oh sure, of course I do. Wouldn't trade it for the world. I just mean, we don't have any friends in the area yet, and it'd be nice to have someone nearby."

"Aw, you make friends pretty quick, George. Besides, I could never afford a place like this. I mean, all this land!"

"No, really, it wasn't so bad. Didn't cost much."

"Come on, man! You've got room for a couple of good-sized golf courses out here. And that driveway of yours, it's as long as a country road. You know, I have to keep reminding myself how near we are to the city. There's so much land, I'll bet you could go hunting right on your own property. And probably get lost, too."

"Yeah, well, I guess we're really out in the sticks."

"But that's the best part! I mean it, that's just great! That's the whole point of living out here, I can see that now. The seclusion, the solitude . . . Boy, could I do with some solitude these days!"

"Business pretty rough, huh?"

"Boy, you know it! We're all tightening the belt. How about you?"

"Oh, pretty much the same, I guess."

"Aw, now don't be modest, George. You're always selling yourself short. This place must have cost a pretty penny."

George paused and cleared his throat. "Well to tell you the truth, it cost me almost nothing. Got it for a song. The owner went a little you-know-what." He tapped his head.

"Christ! Leave it to you to find the bargains!" They were back in the living room now. Herb gazed around him, taking in the furnishings, the sheer size of the room, the familiar faces of the other guests. "Oh well, I guess the rest of us will just have to get along with our little shacks in the suburbs!"

"Not me, man," Walter piped up. "I'm buying myself an estate just like this one." The others paused in conversation. Walter grinned. "Just as soon as the market picks up!"

"You'd better watch out, Walt," called Frances. "Someday somebody might just take you seriously. You'll run into some real estate

94

sharpie and wind up out in the street, walking around in a barrel!"

Milton moved toward them, staggering slightly, and put his arm around Walter's shoulder. He was very drunk. "If you wanna buy some land, you don't hafta wait till the market's better," he said. "You just gotta know the right people. Isn't that right, George?"

Under the weight of their curious stares, George managed to maintain his smile—but it was an effort. "Oh, you need a little patience, that's all. And you have to wait till the right deal comes along. I was just lucky, I guess." The look he gave Milton was not very pretty.

Phyllis stepped forward, not a moment too soon, and announced gaily, "Well, I don't know about you, but I'm just grateful to be living in a place like this. And now that Herb and Tammie are finally here, I'd like to show you just how lucky we are."

"Well, it's about time," said Ellie. She turned to the rest. "She's been keeping us in suspense."

"You mean at long last we'll get to see it?" asked Frances.

"That's right," replied Phyllis, all smiles. She fluttered her eyelids in parody of a Grand Duchess. "Madame Kurtz will now escort her guests around her palatial estate."

George managed an apologetic laugh. "It's just an old barn," he said. "Honest—nothing but a barn!"

"See, I got him trussed up pretty tight now. Won't catch me making the same mistake twice, no, sir!"

"Are you sure the straps aren't a little, um, too tight?"

"You kidding, Doc? If I loosened them things, he'd rip the bandages off in two seconds flat. No, sir, nothing doing."

The doctor stepped into the room. "Well, hello there," he said genially. "I'm sorry to find you like this. Hope you're not terribly uncomfortable. Just as soon as those lacerations heal, we'll remove those bandages . . . and then we'll see if we can't get you out of that jacket, okay? We believe in giving our patients here a second chance."

The man on the bed glared at him.

"And so I do hope that, um . . ." He turned to the orderly. "Can he hear what I'm saying?"

"Oh, yeah, he can hear you fine. But we think he must've done something to his vocal cords, you know? He don't seem able to speak." He smiled. "Just between you and me, I ain't so broken up about that. I mean, all that screaming, it was really getting to me. Always going on about feeding time . . . I mean, you'd think we never fed the guy!"

"It isn't fair. Honestly, it just isn't fair." Ellie gestured toward the bedroom. "Just look at that. That's exactly the kind of bed frame Milt and I have been looking all over New York for."

"I'll bet it's real brass, too," said Doris. "Hey, Frannie," she called over her shoulder, "do you think that bed frame's real brass?"

Frances emerged from the bathroom, Irene Crystal in tow. "I'm afraid so," she said. "God, I'm absolutely green with envy. And that quilt, did you ever *see* such a thing? It must have taken years! Don't you just love it?"

"Oh, I do," said Doris. "It's beautiful." She ran her hand down one of the gleaming bedposts.

"It's criminal, that's what I think," said Ellie. "Here I spend my whole life dreaming of a house in the country with a greenhouse and a pantry and a kitchen big enough to walk around in——"

"And a real library," said Doris.

"That's right, a real library, the kind they have in those Joan Fontaine movies, remember? With comfortable chairs and little tables next to them so you can sit and sip your sherry while you read . . . And who gets all this? The Kurtzes. I tell you, it's simply criminal. I mean, has anyone ever seen either of them so much as *open* a book?"

"Oh, George is a reader," said Frances. "I can tell."

"How?"

She grinned impishly. "There's a pile of *Sports Illustrated*s in the bathroom!"

"And how about that nursery?" said Doris. She enjoyed baiting Ellie.

"Yes, can you *imagine*? A separate nursery, and they don't even have children. It makes me so angry I could positively scream!"

"Oh, come on, El," said Frances, "don't get all worked up. Your

96

two kids aren't exactly toddlers anymore. Your oldest is already out of *college*, for God's sake!"

"Still, all I can think of is how nice this place would have been when Milt and I were just starting out. Damn it all, going home to Long Island's going to be such a letdown."

"You're not kidding," said Irene. "And the ride back's not going to be much fun either. Jack's been grumbling about it all night. We figure if we leave here at eleven—I mean, we've *got* to stay at least that late—we won't be home till past one."

"Well, my husband had a brilliant idea," said Frances. She seated herself on the bed. "He took one look at that guest room down the hall, the one with all those antique toys in it, and decided he wanted to spend the night here. He says if we hang around long enough, they'll have to ask us to stay the night."

"Hey, you little schemers in there!" They all looked up in guilty surprise, but it was only Mike Carlinsky standing tall and fat in the doorway, his fiancée on his arm. "I heard all that. You can hatch all the plots you want to about staying the night, but I warn you, Gail and I have dibs on this room." He strode inside, the wide plank floorboards creaking beneath his weight.

"Sorry, Mike, I'm afraid you're out of luck," said Frances. "This one's the master bedroom. See? Two dressers, two mirrors, and matching night tables."

Carlinsky grinned. "But just one bed, huh?" Its springs groaned as he seated himself heavily upon it. "Room enough for two, I'll admit, but still . . . didn't think old George had it in him anymore."

Fred Weingast poked his head into the room; other voices came from the hall behind him. "Michael, I do declare, you're getting as catty as the girls." He leaned against the doorway, still holding his half-filled cocktail glass. "I don't know about you people, but I'm not so sure I'd *want* to spend the night way out here. I'm a city boy, you know. Places like this make me nervous."

"Aw, what's the matter?" said Carlinsky. "Can't fall asleep without the sound of traffic?"

"He'll miss the roaches," said Ellie.

"Come on over and sit down with us." Carlinsky patted the bed beside him; there was just enough room for one more person.

Weingast looked doubtful. "Well, I don't think old George would be too happy if his bed collapsed . . . Think I'll go take a look at the attic, if I can make it up those stairs. I hear it's really something. Anyway, kids, you'd all better mind your manners. Our esteemed hostess is on her way upstairs——" He glanced back over his shoulder. "——accompanied, I do believe, by her royal entourage."

Indeed, the babble of voices grew louder; Phyllis was conducting her promised tour of the house.

Initially the company had trooped after her like a column of dutiful schoolchildren, gaping at the various rooms that formed the first floor: the parlor and the pantry, the library with its walls of closely packed bookshelves broken only by a set of windows, the kitchen with its original oaken beams and the cast-iron meat hooks still hanging from them, the dining area and the storerooms and the fragrant little potting shed that led into the greenhouse . . .

But thirty adults, inebriated at that, had proved a difficult group to keep together; they'd spilled over into the halls, getting sidetracked over old maps, lagging behind and returning to the living room to refill their glasses. At last she'd simply given up, and had encouraged them to wander wherever they pleased.

"Just make sure Walter doesn't trip down the stairs," she'd said, winking at him. "He looks drunk enough to break his neck! And oh, by the way, I know most of it's junk, but please try not to break anything at *this* early date. Wait till we've lived here a bit longer! Otherwise, you can have the run of the house and, I guess, the run of the grounds—if anyone feels like stepping outside in this weather." She glanced doubtfully toward the window.

"What's the matter," said Herb, "don't the bathrooms work?"

Phyllis laughed. "I just mean that if you're going to get sick, I'd rather you do it outside, all over the dead leaves, than on my nice new carpet!"

Most of the women had immediately gone back to the kitchen to exclaim once again over the maple breakfast table and the old wrought-iron gas range with the extra-deep compartment for baking bread. Others had gone ahead to the second floor, and a few of the men had made straight for the narrow stairway to the attic, vowing to "work from the top down."

Phyllis was now advancing along the upstairs hall, accompanied by the more faithful of her audience, including Cissy Hawkins, who followed her like a child afraid of getting lost.

"Wow," Cissy was saying, "the steps in these old houses are so *steep!*" She lingered near the top of the stairs, catching her breath. "How do you do it, Phyl?"

"Remember, I've been living here for six weeks now." She smiled down at the others still on the stairs; Janet Mulholland stood on the landing, panting softly and clutching the bannister for support. "Honestly, girls, it does wonders for the figure."

Janet glared at her with a touch of malevolence, then started up. "I had no idea how out of shape I was," she muttered. "I haven't been this winded since the elevator strike!"

But Phyllis was already walking down the hall to her bedroom, pointing out the wall hangings to Cissy and the others. "This one had to be repaired," she was saying. "See? Right here, in the corner, by the border. We had a little shop in New Haven do the reweaving. They're very cheap."

"Gosh, what *is* it?" asked Cissy. "I guess this green part is meant to be leaves, but what's that group in the center? Faces?"

"Animal faces, yes. But they're so faded I'm afraid you can hardly see them. The man in the shop said it was a Middle Eastern design." Phyllis turned and addressed the group in the hall. "You know, there are two kinds of tapestries: grotesque and arabesque. Arabesque just has leaves and flowers, but this one's a grotesque—there are animals mixed in."

Ellie stood in the doorway of the bedroom, then turned back to Frances. "Honestly, did you *ever?*" she whispered. "Listen to her, parading around her new knowledge to impress the masses."

"It's like the book, then, isn't it?" Cissy was saying. "*Tales of the Grotesque and Arabesque.*"

"Oh, really?" asked Phyllis. "What book?" She turned to the next tapestry; it had been hanging crookedly, and she adjusted it. "This one's in much better condition. See? It's a deer and a bear, I think. George is going to have it appraised."

Frances emerged from the bedroom. "Where is he, by the way?" she asked.

"Oh, probably downstairs."

99

"I saw him go in the bathroom at the end of the hall," said Weingast. He shambled toward the attic stairs, his drink sloshing in his glass. "The old boy looked a bit under the weather. Too much of this stuff." He held up his drink. "Anybody care to join me?"

"In the attic?" asked Carlinsky, getting up from the bed with a groan (and a little support from his fiancée). "Some of the guys are already up there prowling around, I think." He followed Weingast up the stairs, pulling his woman behind him.

"Gosh, Phyl, you mean you have two bathrooms up here?" asked Cissy.

Phyllis nodded modestly. "And two downstairs."

From behind them came a gasp. "Oh, this stuff's *lovely!*" Janet had made it up the stairs, and now stood examining the tiny figurines on a shelf by the guest room. "The expressions on these little things' faces are so *precious!* Bone china, aren't they?"

"I think so. Have you seen the ones inside the doorway?"

They followed her into the guest room, one wall of which was lined with ornamental shelves.

"Hey, this is some collection!"

Phyllis merely smiled.

"Good grief!" laughed Ellie. "What do you call this stuff—knick-knacks, gewgaws, thingamajigs, or um, let's see, how about what-nots?"

"Plain old bric-a-brac's good enough for me!"

"Gee, I haven't seen one of these in years." Ellie picked up a small glass globe with a winter scene inside: when she shook it, snow swirled in a miniature blizzard. The globe beside it held a shiny black beetle, and the one next to that a tiny bouquet of dried flowers —chrysanthemums, black-eyed Susans, cornflowers, even a tiny this-tle—all the colors of autumn.

Walter and Joyce Applebaum strolled in, arm in arm. While she joined the others by the shelves, he leaned back against the wall and closed his eyes, as if shutting out the room full of women. He was obviously quite drunk.

"This stuff must be worth a fortune," said Janet, examining the small figure of an elf carved in dark wood. "You just don't see things like this every day. And I'll bet the ones on the bottom"—she indicated a shelf of antique cast-iron banks, dogs, and elephants, a hunter and a bear, a clown and hoop—"would cost a couple of hundred dollars, at least in New York."

Phyllis shrugged. "Some of it's pretty valuable, all right, but a lot of it's just junk. George hasn't gotten around to throwing it out." She pushed aside two small stone sculptures—totemic heads of California basalt—and picked up a gray ceramic candle holder in the shape of a gargoyle, the black taper seeming to sprout from between the creature's wings. "This, for example. It looks old, doesn't it?"

"Medieval."

"Yes, but feel." She handed the thing to Janet. "See? Light as a feather. It's just some cheap plaster-of-Paris souvenir. From Paris, appropriately enough. We saw a lot of them when we were over last year. They sell them at Notre Dame for seven or eight francs."

Cissy looked disappointed. "Well, maybe it's not all exactly *priceless*," she said, "but you certainly have enough to open your own antique shop."

"Three antique shops!" said Frances.

Phyllis laughed. "This is nothing. Wait'll you see the attic!"

"What, *more*? Where'd you acquire all this stuff?"

"Don't forget, it wasn't us who acquired it. It was the man George bought this place from. That lunatic."

"Well, he may have been a lunatic, but he certainly had good taste," remarked Joyce, studying a group of prints on the wall by the window—a series of storybook illustrations by Doré, Rackham, and others; a Kirk pen-and-ink sketch showed what looked like the Notre Dame gargoyle, only the wings had been replaced by ropelike tentacles. "Eclectic, at least," she said. "What was he like?"

"I have no idea," said Phyllis. "I never met the man, thank God. George never wanted me to. I'm told he was highly unpleasant."

"What was the matter?" asked Frances. She was sliding open the drawer of a small end table; inside, the drawer was freshly dusted, and empty. "He keep raving about little green men?"

"He may have. He may very well have. All I know is, he had very unclean habits. This place stank like a sewer when I first saw it. And it wasn't fixed up like this, believe me. It was a mess."

"What, the whole house?"

"You could barely push your way through, for the junk."

"No, I mean the smell. All over?"

Phyllis paused to draw the curtains, holding back the night. "Every room. That's why we took so long to move in. First we tried to air the place out, but that didn't work, so then we had to have men in to fumigate. And believe me, those people charge an arm and a leg. George nearly had a fit."

"All I know is, it smells okay now," said Cissy a little too quickly. "Really, Phyl, you've done a marvelous job cleaning."

"Well, I don't really deserve the credit. There are people you can hire for jobs like that. Those fireplaces were the hardest, I'm told. Filled with dirt and ashes. I'm glad we won't have to depend on them when winter comes. Imagine, one in every room!"

"Even in the kitchen," sighed Joyce. "Oh, Waltie, if we could only have one built in our kitchen—even a fake one . . . Wouldn't that be nice?"

Her husband opened his eyes. They were bloodshot. "Yeah," he said, "we'd be the rage of Scarsdale." He looked away.

"Why don't you just settle for the hooks?" asked Frances.

"You mean those meat hooks on the ceiling?"

"Sure, they wouldn't cost much. And Walter could hang salami on them!"

"But we have no beams to put them in."

Phyllis intervened. "Obviously, then, the thing to do is to let George find you a house like this, beams and all."

"That's what I keep *tellin'* everybody," whined Walter.

She ignored him. "Come on, let me show you our bedroom. There's some more junk in there."

They followed her down the hall, and all the women who hadn't already seen the brass bed frame made the appropriate, and predictable, gasps of delight.

"Oh, where'd you *get* it?" Janet wanted to know. "You don't mean to tell me this came with the house, too."

Phyllis beamed. "Where else?"

"Boy, the previous owner must have lived a pretty good life here. What happened, his wife die and he go to pieces?"

"I'm sure I don't know," said Phyllis. "I doubt he was even married."

Janet's eyes widened. "You mean he lived here all alone? In this huge house?"

Phyllis shrugged. "I told you he was crazy. He may have had a dog or something to keep him company, I'm not sure. I think George said something about a pet."

The bedsprings groaned as Walter fell heavily onto the mattress. He lay back full length, careful nonetheless to keep his shoes off the patchwork quilt. "Well, I'd say he was one guy who knew how to live." Giving an extended yawn, he stretched as if ready for bed. "I mean, this is a comf'table place. A li'l drafty, but comf'table. An' this is a comf'table bed." He closed his eyes and appeared to doze.

Joyce looked an apology at her hostess. "He always gets like this when he's had a hard week. Anyone want to help me drag him out?"

"No-no-no, leave him be. Let him take a little nap. Like he said, it's a comfortable bed." Phyllis prided herself on her tact. "The weird thing is, the man we bought the house from didn't even use it. He slept on a cot."

"You're *kidding*!"

"Nothing but a cot?"

"That's all. I tell you, the way some bachelors live . . ." Phyllis shook her head. "George found this brass frame in the attic, underneath a pile of junk. We polished it up and bought a new mattress for it. But it's still not in such good condition. See?" She pointed toward the metal legs; they looked as if they'd been gnawed. "I'm afraid it got a bit battered up there."

From the hall came the sound of heavy feet on wood, and of loud voices. Herb peered into the doorway, blinking at the light. "Excuse me, ladies. Is my wife in here?"

"Tammie's downstairs."

"Hey, Walt! Walt!" Harold Lazarus burst into the room, pushing the others out of the doorway. "Wake up, boy, you've got to come up and see the attic." He began tugging at Walter's ankles.

"Honey, come on, leave him alone. He's taking a little nap." Frances put her arm around Harold's waist. "Let's go back downstairs. I want another seven-and-seven."

"Is it really nice up there?" asked Cissy.

"It's great!" said Harold, disengaging himself from his wife's arm. "There's stacks of magazines, some crazy old almanacs and star

103

charts, old knives, a barber chair, kids' toys . . . A lot of the stuff's
pretty rusted, but you ought to see the magazines. Almost a hundred
years old, some of them."

Phyllis frowned. "I nearly forgot about those things. When we
cleaned this place out, we put off doing the attic. We just stuck all
the junk up there, all the stuff we couldn't use. Someday we'll have
to go over the whole place—just as soon as it gets warm. As it is, it's
a firetrap, all that paper."

"Hey, don't throw those magazines away," said Harold. "They
might be worth something. A few bucks, at least."

Phyllis shook her head. "It's a real rats' nest up there. Like something out of the Collier brothers."

"That's for sure!" said Harold.

Fred Weingast entered the room, his glass now empty. "Hey,
that's a wild place you've got, Phyl. A lot of old toys, stuff in jars,
some old uniforms——Christ, I didn't think I'd ever seen one of
those Army jackets again, the kind with the snaps on the pockets
. . . There's even an old department store mannequin, way in the
corner, pretty chewed up now but scary as hell." He laughed. "I
mean, the thing was naked! Herb thought we'd found a body!"

"Come on, Frannie, let's go up." Harold tugged at his wife's arm.
I want to show you some of those old magazines. They've got ads
for women's clothes, and some of 'em are really a scream."

"Aw, honey, I'm too tired, and those steps look so steep. . . .
Couldn't you just bring a few down?" She turned to Phyllis for help.

"It's really not worth going up," agreed Phyllis. "It isn't insulated
up there, and the place really gets freezing this time of year. Especially at night."

"She's right, you know," said Weingast, shifting his empty glass
from hand to hand. "You could see your breath, even. Think I'll
head back down for a refill—something that'll really warm me up."
He turned to look down the hall. "Anyway, I think my wife's down
there."

Harold looked disappointed as the rest filed out behind Weingast.
He glanced at his friend; Walter lay sprawled on the bed, snoring
softly like some large hibernating animal. Harold gave him a few
ineffectual nudges, then said, "Ah, hell," and followed the others
downstairs.

*　　*　　*

George sat in the bathroom, crouching like some small hunted animal. He was acutely conscious of the muffled voices that penetrated the bathroom door, punctuated now and again by more boisterous ones when a couple strode past in the hall outside. He leaned forward, waiting for the cramps to subside. If he held his breath and strained to hear, he could pick out a few words. ". . . may take the option on it, but they don't . . ." That would be Faschman and, most likely, Sid Gerdts.

Silence for a while. Footsteps in the attic overhead. Then whispered voices, women's. "No, wait, don't go in."

"I just——"

"No, I think someone's in there."

The voices moved on.

George sighed and stared down at the tiles on the floor, wishing he had something to read. Against Phyllis's wishes he always left a few magazines in the bathroom near the stairs, but that had been occupied; and this one, right off the guest room, was still relatively bare, save for the black plastic shelves and soap dish, all glossy and sharp-edged, that his wife had put up this morning. Already the slab of soap lay melting like ice in a little puddle of greasy water. And little black guest towels, they were her idea, too, with stiff lace trim, to be left sopping on the floor or stuck awkwardly back on the rack. The house was not yet livable.

Yet any bareness was preferable to the squalor in which he'd found it. Of course, it was what he should have expected, after seeing the flecks of dried skin on the man's lips and the stain on those trousers. A recluse, they'd called him, using the polite word. Eyes like a sorcerer, they said. Perhaps the locals had thought him colorful. But George still recalled the socks on the dresser, the deposits under the sink, and the stench of rotting meat.

And the threats . . .

He felt his intestines churn, and winced; when would it stop? The tiles seemed to make some sort of pattern, but the pain made him impatient. Red rectangle at the upper left of each square, no, every other square, and in the next row the design was reversed, so that . . . Yet over near the door the pattern changed. Automatically he cursed the ancient, unknown builders of this house, then realized he himself had had the room retiled before moving in.

They'd kept all the original fixtures, though. It added to the atmosphere. The bathtub even had legs, like in the old pictures, reminding him of animal claws, thick and stubby. One, two, three . . . He lost count and started over. Yes, there were five fingers on each claw. They didn't make bathtubs like that anymore. Big enough for a whole family, too—not that the original owner had ever needed one that size. He'd smelled as if he hadn't bathed in years.

A woman's laughter echoed in the hall, and then the low, eager voice of a man, perhaps recounting a joke. Damn it, he'd miss the whole party this way! Searching for something to pass the time, he tugged out his wallet and began leafing through it. I.D. cards told him he was George W. Kurtz, credit cards listed restrictions in tiny blue print. . . . What a bore. He began counting his money.

"George?" Phyllis knocked on the door. "Are you in there?"

"Yeah," he grunted. "I'll be right out."

"Are you all right, honey?"

"Yeah, I'm okay. I'll be right out."

"Is there anything I can get you?"

"I said I was okay."

She seemed to go away for a moment, then returned; her voice came from just outside the door. "We're all going back downstairs. Walt's asleep on the bed, though. Don't wake him."

"Mmm."

"Did you say something, honey?" Holding his own breath, he could hear her breathing on the other side. She paused as if to say something else, then went away.

In the silence he wondered what was wrong with him. Something he'd eaten, perhaps. Those shrimp last night? But no, that had been two nights ago, and he'd barely had a thing all day. Maybe he could no longer hold his liquor.

Still, the ache felt like fear. He wondered what he was afraid of.

That was how it always worked: he'd feel the tension in the pit of his stomach, and only then would he attempt to choose the thoughts that had produced it. First the effect, then the cause—as if his mind held so many unexplored levels, mystery upon mystery, that he never knew the things it contained until his stomach told him.

Nerves, obviously, over the success of this party. The bane of all hosts, particularly at a big affair like this. Still, he hadn't realized he'd been so worried. . . .

An unsatisfying explanation—but abruptly the pain left him. He made himself ready and stepped into the hall, checking on Walter as he passed the bedroom; the face on the quilt looked red and puffy, like an infant's who'd gone to bed squawling. George fastened the door to the attic, sealing out the cold, and headed downstairs.

"I suppose pencil and paper are out of the question. . . ."

"Yeah, sure, I mean what do you expect? Give him a free hand and he'll go for them bandages. Give him a pencil and he'll poke his own eyes out. I don't put nothing past these people, not after what I seen."

The doctor sighed. "It's rather frustrating, you must admit. A perfect suicidal depressive, ripe for therapy, and he's incapable of speech." He stared at the man on the bed; the man on the bed stared back. "Perhaps when his throat heals, if we keep him in restraint. . . ."

"Sometimes he'll talk to me."

"Pardon? You say he speaks——"

"Well, no, not exactly. What I mean is, he taps his foot against the wall, see? Like when he wants me to turn him over."

The other shook his head. "I'm afraid that hardly constitutes real communication. A yes or-no response, perhaps, but quite useless for our needs. No, I think we'll simply have to wait a month or two, and then . . ."

"Oh, he don't just say yes or no. He taps out whole words. See, we got this code." He drew from his pocket a frayed scrap of paper. "A is one, B is two; it goes like that."

"And to say a word like 'zoo' would take all night. No, thanks." The doctor looked at his watch. "For the time being, some medication——"

"No, you don't understand. You see, Z is two taps, and then six. Twenty-six, get it? And O would be"—he studied the paper—"one, and then five. Pretty smart, huh?"

"It would still take all night, and I have thirty other patients to worry about." He looked again at his watch. "And rounds to make

before bedtime. No, I think we'll keep him on the Thorazine, and I'll prescribe twenty-five milligrams of Tofranil. We can try that for a while . . ." He walked down the hall, scribbling in his notebook.

The orderly remained in the doorway of the room, staring at the man on the bed. The man on the bed stared back.

In the living room Herb Rosenzweig was trying to organize a game. Faces turned as George entered.

"We missed you, George. Thought you'd fallen in!"

He grinned sheepishly and moved toward the bar, both flattered and annoyed that his absence had been noted. Couldn't these people fend for themselves? It wasn't as if they were all strangers to one another.

"Herb here thought you'd been eaten by a bear!"

"That's what I told'em, George."

George shrugged. "No such luck. I think it was what I ate!"

Amid their laughter Phyllis called, "Now, don't put ideas in their heads, or nobody'll finish the quiche. I spent all day making it." She pointed to the plates of hors d'oeuvres by the bar. "And you people aren't eating the sausages," she chided. "They'll just lie there in the refrigerator if no one eats them."

A few guests, cowed, shuffled toward the food. Cissy called to him from across the room. "We're going to tell our fortunes, George. You're just in time. Herb has a pack of cards."

"A Tarot deck," said Herb, pronouncing the final *t*. "I found it up in your attic, in one of the trunks." He held forth a green cardboard box decorated with line drawings and the words *Grand Etteilla*. Cellophane still clung to the sides. "I wanted to see what they looked like," he explained. "Hope you don't mind. I don't think the pack had ever been opened before."

"Do you know how to use them?"

"There's an instruction booklet inside. Only trouble is, it's in French."

"I'm a little rusty myself," George was saying, but Milton interrupted him.

"Ellie's a whiz at French. Christ, you should've seen her over there, last summer. They thought she was a native." He snatched the booklet from Herb's hand and gave it to his wife. "Go ahead, what's it say?"

"Oh, this is easy," she said. " '*Manière de Tirer le Grand Etteilla ou Tarots Egyptiens, Composé de Soixante-dix-huit Cartes Illustrées.*' Well, you can pick that up, can't you?"

"Something about Egyptian cards," said Frances.

"Does it say how to lay them out?" asked Herb.

Ellie flipped through the pages. "Hmm, there aren't any diagrams. Pretty cheap. There's something in the front, though. 'To use the cards, it is necessary first to strike the game by the person who . . .' " She paused in her reading. "Oh, I see. The person whose fortune's being told has to hit the cards with his left hand."

"Whose fortune's being told?" asked George, without much interest. Anything, though, to amuse the guests. . . .

Herb shrugged. "We can try Tammie's, if she wants. Does it say how to spread them?"

"I wish I could remember how Joan Blondell did them in *Nightmare Alley*," said Ellie. "All I remember is, she kept turning up the death card for Tyrone Power."

"The Hanged Man," said Cissy, with a nervous little laugh.

"Mmm, that's right. Well, let's see." Ellie squinted at the booklet. "Oh boy, this is so complicated. . . . I don't know if it's worth it. It'll take half an hour to set up."

"Aw, forget it then," said Herb, already casting about for new games to play.

Tammie put her arm around him. "From now on we'll stick to fortune cookies."

George watched the group begin falling away around him, dissolving into small clots of conversation, but Phyllis picked up her cue. "Why don't we do it the fast way? We'll all pick a card, and that'll be our fortune. Here, give me, I'll shuffle."

For tradition's sake she rapped once on the box, and the cards were duly passed among the guests until each held one. "I feel as though we're about to play bingo!" said Fred Weingast, puzzling over his card. "What is this, anyway? It's The Three of something, I can tell, but what are they? Dinner plates?"

Harold peered over his shoulder. "That's it—The Three of Dinner Plates!"

"They look like coins to me," said Weingast's wife.

Ellie was leafing through the booklet. "No," she said, "they're pentacles. See? A five-pointed star inside each circle."

109

"What's it supposed to mean?"

"Let's see. Okay, here we go." She looked up at Weingast and smiled mysteriously, then turned to the text. " 'A person noble and distinguished——' "

"Hey, that's me to a T!" shouted Weingast.

Ellie waited for the laughter to subside, then continued. "Sorry, people, but you've got it wrong. Listen. 'A person noble and distinguished has need of silver—uh, money—and you should lend it to him.' "

Immediately, and predictably, Harold scurried over and slapped him on the back. "Fred, old pal, how about it?"

There were several paragraphs of text still to read, but the gag had run its course. Ellie turned to the rest. "Okay, kids, who's next?" Ignoring the drunken cries of "Me-me-me-me," she reached for Frances' card. In smeary lithograph it depicted a small blond boy holding a gold chalice; the background was pastoral, with dark green hills and a waterfall. "Oh, a picture card," she said. "Maybe that means it's important." She squinted down at the text. "Apparently he's The Page of Cups. Sort of like The Jack of Diamonds, I guess. 'Have confidence absolute,' it says—absolute confidence—'in the young man blond that you offers . . . that offers you his services.' Gee, Frannie, who do you know who's blond?"

Harold answered for her. "Damn it, I'll bet it's that delivery boy!" He made a big show of being the cuckolded husband, which all but Frances found amusing.

"Do Phyllis next," suggested someone.

"Yeah, come on, do Phyllis." The others took up the chant.

Phyllis squirmed like a little girl asked to make a birthday speech. "No," she said, smiling nervously, "really, I don't want to hear mine. I always believe in fortunes, and they're always bad." She hid the card behind her back. "Do George's first."

Ellie shrugged. "Okay, then, let me see it." She held out her hand.

"But I haven't got a card," said George.

"Too busy playing the proper host," said Milton. He picked up the pile of cards. "Come on, there's more than half the pack left. Take one."

"Close your eyes first," added Herb.

George sighed. "Okay, okay. But I'm telling you, the guests are supposed to come first." He took the cards from Milton and shuffled through them, eyes shut. He lifted one from the middle of the deck and looked down at it. "Good God!" He slipped it back in the deck and continued to shuffle.

"Hey," cried Ellie, "I saw that. No fair. You cheated!"

"He's entitled," said Bernie. "I mean, it's his house, right?"

The other guests had lost interest in all fortunes but their own; some had wandered over to the bar. Ellie, however, wasn't mollified. "I'll bet he had The Hanged Man. Isn't that right, George? Just like in the movie?"

"Just like in the movie," said George, his eyes shut. "Here, give me a reading on this one." He drew forth a card and handed it to her.

"The Eight of Wands," she said. " 'Learning a trade or a profession. Employment or commission to come. Skill in affairs—in material affairs.' I'm afraid that's a pretty general one."

"Well, it's not so far off," said Milton. "George is skilled in material affairs."

Herb shrugged. "Yeah, but so are we all. I mean, this kind of stuff could apply to anyone here. It's really no better than that column in the *News*. You know, *The Stargazer's Prophecy*, or something like that. My secretary lives by it."

George had moved away from them. He stood by one of the windows, staring out at the night, trying to disguise the pain in his stomach. Because of the light inside it was impossible to see well, but he could hear the tapping of dead leaves against the glass. He heard, too, a few of the women squealing over Phyllis's card, The Lovers, and he thought of the one he had drawn forth, and had returned to the deck so hurriedly after the briefest glimpse—an amorphous mass of gray, like the back of some huge animal, illuminated as if by moonlight. It had seemed disturbingly familiar. Amid the babble of voices its memory was already beginning to fade, but not the uneasiness it had aroused, the vague, half-buried guilt. . . . With a start he noticed his own reflection in the window, and saw the savage twist of his mouth. He smoothed back his hair, smiled, and turned back to the company.

Entropy had set in. All but a few had tired of the game and had once again broken into smaller groups, those most bored drifting

III

toward the bar like sediment to the bottom of a pond. Sidney Gerdts was holding forth to the Goodhues and the Fitzgeralds—the fall of the dollar, or perhaps the rise of crime—and Phyllis was trying to get Paul Strauss to talk to poor Cissy Hawkins. Fred Weingast was making himself another drink. Over by the corner Herb and Milton sat on the couch comparing the achievements of their children. Others had wandered off to the kitchen and library. For the time being they all seemed occupied; he passed among them unnoticed, on his way back to the bathroom.

"I've never seen him like this," Herb was saying. "He's been so evasive. Usually he'll brag about a smart deal till you're sick of listening, but this time he played modest with me. I could tell something was funny the minute I came in."

"You mean that bit about 'just lucky, I guess'? Jesus, wasn't that something!" Milton shook his head.

"Yeah, all he'd say was the guy went a little ga-ga and sold him this place for a song."

"Is that what he told you?"

"That was it. But, well, you seem to know a bit more about what really went on."

Milton stared down into his glass, watching the ice cubes shrink and change shape. "Well, I don't know all that much."

"Aw, come on. I hear you've been riding him about it all night."

"Maybe I've sobered up a little since then."

"Aw, hell, you know I'll keep this to myself."

He studied Herb's face, and saw the endless cocktails of expense-account lunches, the daily betrayals disguised as good fellowship. Herb would make a good story out of this.

"How about it?"

"Well . . ." Milton watched George sidle through the room and head upstairs. "Okay, why not?"

In the room upstairs Walter slept fitfully. A floorboard groaned outside the door—George on his way up the hall—and was echoed by the huge limb of an elm beyond the window. Walter turned heavily onto his side, buried his face in the pillow, and slept on, one hand twisting a wrinkle of quilt as if clenched upon a steering wheel.

The women on the couch had begun talking about food costs, and Tammie was bored. It took parties like this to remind her that she preferred the company of men. "I'm sure they *are* better for you," Janet Mulholland was saying, "but the prices they charge in those health food stores are outrageous." Tammie looked around for her husband; he was in the corner by the window, talking with Milt Brackman. Pretty soon they'd be swapping dirty jokes.

A bridge table had been set up near the bar, piled high with paper plates and plastic forks. Big Mike Carlinsky was bent over it, showing something to his fiancée—what was her name? Gail.

"You want your fortune done?" He smiled up as Tammie strolled over; Gail looked at her coldly. "According to this, I'm gonna have five kids, but Gail's only gonna have two!" Laughing, he pointed to an open page in the booklet, but Tammie couldn't read a word of French. "You still got your card?"

The green box lay next to an empty hors-d'oeuvres platter, Tarot cards piled haphazardly beside it where guests had left them. The top card showed a stone tower crumbling as a bolt of lightning hit it. In the background the sea raged furiously.

"No, I put mine back in the box. There were just too many people ahead of me. But let's see, I think I can find it again." She began sorting through the deck, aware that Mike's eyes were on her; he was probably trying to decide if she was wearing a bra. "Hey, look at this," she said, producing the picture of a regal woman. "I like this one better than my own card! What's it mean?"

"The Queen of Swords," said Gail. "You're not allowed to choose, you know. You can't just pick the prettiest card and say you want it." She looked guardedly at her fiancé.

He was already flipping through the booklet. "Queen of Swords, huh? Sounds dangerous." He stopped and read to himself, lips moving. "Something about old age, I think." Tammie stiffened.

"Isn't '*vielle*' the word for old?" He saw she wasn't grinning, and his own grin faded. "But apparently it means one thing if you hold it one way and something else if it's upside down."

113

"It was right side up, wasn't it?" said Gail.

"The other way," he went on, "it means the woman tyrannizes her husband. Hhmm! Poor old Herb! And I always thought *he* wore the pants."

Tammie forced a laugh. "Oh, I let him think so, that's all!" She looked over at her husband, still deep in conversation with Milton. "Now I want to find the card I really picked."

She scanned the pack. Most of the cards were bare but for groups of symbols—seven cups, four pentagrams, a series of sticklike objects—reminding her of the canasta deck at home. But some of them bore full-color illustrations, archetypes even she could respond to. "This is nice. A chariot, I guess. Ugh! Here's Death." The skeleton leaned casually on his scythe. "I thought The Hanged Man was supposed to be the death card."

"I guess not," said Gail. "See? Here it is." She turned the card upside down, so that the figure stared at them. "And, see, he's smiling."

"What's this one?" asked Mike. "Looks like a phallic symbol, doesn't it!" He glanced at Tammie. The card showed an enormous hand emerging godlike from the clouds, clasping an upright stick.

"Thats the Ace of Wands," said Gail. And, in explanation: "I've got a paperback at home. I haven't bought the cards yet, though. I've seen much prettier decks than this. Remember, Mike? Down in the Village? But it seemed like a waste of money."

"Mmm." He turned over some cards that had been left face down. "Maybe I'll buy you a pack. For slow parties." He laughed guiltily. "What do you think this one's supposed to be?"

She took it from him and stared at it. It was a night scene, with a few stars low in the background. At the center was a gray liver-shaped thing; animal, apparently, though the head was turned away. "Gee, I don't think I've ever seen this kind before." She handed it back to him, not looking at it. "Of course, every set is different. I like the modern ones best. Like the deck we saw that time in the Village."

Tammie studied the card for a moment, then gave a tentative smile. "Reminds me of veal cutlet!" A moment later she joined Mike's laughter, laying the card face down on the table. "Do you think there are any of those cute little sausages left?"

"Well, the platter's gone, but I can look in the fridge." He put his hand on Gail's shoulder. "Be back in a second, honey."

The foot tapped against the wall, paused, then tapped eight times in succession. Seated at the foot of the bed, the orderly looked down at the paper. "Eighteen, that's . . . R."
The foot tapped twice, then once. U. Once, then four times.

"I got the story from Bart Cipriano," Milton was saying. "He works in Commissioner Brodsky's office at the capitol, and he's buddy-buddy with George. So's Brodsky. At first I was surprised they weren't here tonight, but then I realized they'd already been to this house—and often, I'll bet. Besides, George may be just a little ashamed of them."

"Why? Who is this Brodsky?"

"He's with the State Highway Commission."

"Oh yeah, I remember hearing that George had a bit of clout in that department. Not bad for a guy with an office in New York."

"But don't forget, he's lived here in Connecticut all his life. And until a few months ago he was living right down the block from Brodsky. Big poker players, both of them." He looked for signs of interest in the other's face. Herb's gaze never wavered. "Anyway, according to Cipriano, the state had been planning a big highway up here, to replace 81——"

"It's about time! The roads are so dark I damned near had an accident getting here."

"——and it was supposed to cut right through this property." He made a slicing motion. "Yep, that's right—all this land, this house, even, was right in the path of the highway. So some people were going to have to get out of the way. Not that many, of course. It's pretty underpopulated around here. Tobacco country, mainly, and a few small farms. I guess that's why they picked this place to run the road through."

"Jesus, you mean they're gonna demolish this place?"

Milton shook his head. "Not so fast. Just after the notices were sent out—you know, 'Dear Sir, You've got six months to find another house,' or something like that—the crooks in the governor's office cut back funds and the whole plan was canceled. No road after all. But thanks to the usual red tape—you know how these state governments are—they decided the cutback wouldn't be official till the end of the fiscal year. Which means that, all this time, Brodsky had a letter sitting on his desk junking the project, except that he wasn't supposed to tell anyone." He paused for effect. "Well, guess who he told."

"George?"

"Your friend and mine. I guess he knew that George was looking for a bigger place and, who knows?, maybe he owed him a favor. Let's not be naïve—this sort of thing goes on all the time. And maybe George had something on him, I don't know. Anyway, he gave George the go-ahead. He said, in effect, Pick yourself whatever house you like from Beth Head on up to Tylersville, and we'll get it for you." He took a sip of his drink. "I expect a little money may have changed hands."

"I don't understand. You mean he had free choice? Any place he wanted?"

"That's right. And he wanted this." He shrugged. "Who wouldn't? Just look around. I don't think George had ever seen the inside of this place, though, till he watched the state marshals break down the door. You see, the guy in here wouldn't get out. A bit of a crackpot, they say."

"And once George was in, you mean——"

"Exactly. They announced the highway wouldn't go through after all. And by then it was too late."

"But how about the guy they'd kicked out? Couldn't he sue, for Chrissake? I mean, he had a pretty good case for himself, and . . . Hell! He could bring'em all to court for a stunt like that."

"Nope, not where he is now. I told you he was a loony, didn't I?"

"You mean——"

"Uh-huh. They had him put away." Milton grinned. "Oh, that part was all aboveboard, nothing funny about that. From what I hear, he was a real straitjacket case. Kicked like a wild man when they took him away, biting and spitting . . . And calling for his son to come back and help him. 'Petey,' he kept screaming, 'Petey, Petey,' over and over. At least that's what it sounded like. I guess he thought his son would come to his rescue. Only——"

"Only what?"

"Only he didn't have a son."

"Tsk tsk tsk. Poor guy."

"Yeah, well, that's what I thought. But Cipriano says he wasn't too charming a character. He said the marshals had to literally hold their noses when they broke down the door, that's how bad it was. Like the lion house at the zoo, he said. Maybe the guy had pets and never cleaned up after them. Cost George a fortune to have the place fixed up." He stared into his drink; the ice had shrunk and lost its shape, floating on the surface like a jellyfish, evolution in reverse. "Still, he made a killing on this deal. He bought the house from the state, and got it for next to nothing."

"How about the other people they moved out? They put up a stink, too?"

"That supposed to be a pun?"

Herb guffawed. "Never thought of that!"

"You don't understand—they never *had* to move anybody else. They just held off till George was home free, and then Brodsky announced the cutback. The notices were rescinded, and everybody was happy."

"Oh, I get it." Herb looked disappointed. "So it's too late now, huh?"

"Too late for what?"

"To pick up a place like this for myself."

"R.U.N. *Run?*"

The man on the bed nodded. His foot tapped once, twice, and three times; once, twice, and five times.

"*Run away.*"

The man on the bed nodded.

Irene Crystal put her hand on Phyllis's. "Excuse me," she whispered, "we're going now, I just wanted to say good-bye."

Phyllis left Cissy to fend for herself. "Oh, what a shame!" she cried automatically. "Can't you stay just a little longer? It's so early yet."

"I'd love to, dear, believe me. But Jack's folks are coming over tomorrow morning, and if I know them"—she rolled her eyes comically—"they'll be ringing the bell at nine."

Phyllis kept Irene talking while ushering her toward the coat closet, anxious lest the sight of one early departure produce a mass exodus among the others. "Well, I certainly do hope you'll find the time to come out again real soon. It's not as far as it looks, really, once you know the way."

"Oh, no, honestly, it wasn't a bad trip at all." Jack was already standing by the coat closet. Phyllis looked nervously at the other guests. "It's just that his folks are coming down, otherwise we'd never think of leaving so soon."

Jack leaned toward her. "I wanted to thank George," he said solemnly, a small boy remembering his manners, "but he was in the bathroom. You will thank him for me, won't you?"

"God, is he in there *again*?" Phyllis grimaced. "Yes, of course I will."

"Tell him we think it's just the most fantastic place we've ever seen. The find of a lifetime."

A few of the people at the bar had noticed them. Fred Weingast glanced at his watch. "Yes, of course I will." Phyllis wished the two would hurry up and leave quietly.

"I'm still amazed about what you said upstairs."

"Pardon me?"

"Upstairs," Irene went on. "In your bedroom. About the man before you living here all alone."

Phyllis watched Weingast out of the corner of her eye. "Quite a character, wasn't he?"

"But why a nursery?"

"What? Oh, the nursery! Well, we tried to keep things the way we found them. It was like that when we came. Maybe we'll turn it into another guest room." She flashed a big grin at the Crystals. "That way you'll be able to come more often, without——"

"No," Irene persisted, "I mean, it was already here when you moved in, right? But you said that man never had any children."

Damn it! Now Arthur Faschman was looking at his watch. "I'm sure I don't know," she said hurriedly. "I guess it was here when *he* moved in."

"With all those toys? A lot of them looked used."

"Maybe he played with them himself. I told you he was crazy."

"Honey, we're going to have a long drive as it is," said Jack. "I don't want to get back too late." He moved into the front hall, buttoning his overcoat.

Phyllis held the door open for them. "Whew! These November nights are freezing out here! It's the open fields, George says—no wind resistance." She backed away from the blast of cold air. Then, as if by rote: "Just make sure you drive carefully and get home safe."

Irene smiled. "I only allowed him two drinks all night." She kissed Phyllis on the cheek. "Bye-bye, dear, and thanks."

"Be sure to thank George for us," said Jack as the door was closing.

"So you think you're gonna run away, huh?" The man on the bed shook his head. "No, sir! You ain't going nowhere, buster. Last time an inmate got out, we caught up with him in less than twelve hours, and that was before we installed the new alarm system. Uh-uh, no way!"

The man on the bed shook his head, more violently this time; his mouth twisted into a snarl.

"Oh, I get it, you want me *to run away?"*

More violently still. Then, quickly: eight, two, and one; one and four . . .

H. U. N. G. R. Y.

The voices from the living room were lost in the twistings of the corridor, and the library stood dark and deserted. The door had been left open, but Ellie lingered in the hall, reluctant to enter. Running her hand along the inside of the doorway and finding no switch, she inched toward one of the heavy floor lamps that stood beside a desk, the two forms outlined by moonlight. The rug felt thick and silent beneath her feet, like animal fur. There was something about the room that made one tiptoe, lest some presence be disturbed.

The lamp's sudden glare dazzled her, and in the instant before blindness she saw something rise from the desktop. A cry came from them both, but the other was first to speak.

"Who . . . ? Uh-oh, what time is it?"

"Doris! *God*, you gave me a fright! Who were you hiding from?"

"Sorry, I must have fallen asleep. I was in the middle of this story"—she indicated the book that lay open on the desk—"and I thought I'd take a little nap. It's such a long trip home, and if I know Sid he'll be in no condition to drive." She rubbed her eyes. "He's been looking for me?"

"I'm sorry to say you haven't even been missed."

"Why, what time is it?"

"Not yet eleven, I think."

"Well *that's* a relief. Still early, then. Sorry I scared you. I probably shouldn't have turned off the light."

"What were you reading?"

She slid the book toward her. "It's a translation of one in the living room. A children's book, I think. I'm amazed he'd buy two copies."

"I gather you were using it as a pillow."

Doris smiled. "Yes, I—— Oh my gosh, did I get print all over my cheek?" She tilted her face in the light for the other's inspection. "This makeup picks up more dirt and soot, especially in the city. . . ."

"You're okay. You may have smeared that picture a bit, though." She pointed to a small woodcut in the center of the lefthand page. "Good Lord, what is it?"

"Isn't he cute? He's called the Little Devil." She flipped back toward the beginning of the story. "See, the farmer plants this bean, and then he waters it every day"—she indicated the illustrations—"and when autumn comes, and harvest time, there he is, growing right out of the ground."

Ellie wrinkled up her nose. "Precious."

George snapped off the bathroom light and walked down the hall to the small door at the end. When he opened it a rush of chill air settled around him; climbing the steep wooden stairs, he made a mental note, for the dozenth time, to see about having the attic insulated. Otherwise they'd simply have to keep the door locked all winter.

Upstairs his breath turned to mist, but the cold sobered him; it came in pleasant contrast to the stuffy air below. Anyway, he'd only stay up here for a minute or two, just long enough to see if the memories matched.

He picked his way through the piles of magazines, some neatly bound with twine, the result of their housecleaning, others strewn about the floor. The junk had accumulated here at the top of the house like debris left after a flood. A shape in the corner caught his eye, something pink and vulnerable—the mannequin, with its ravaged head, lying pressed into the crevice where sloping roof met floorboards. Turning away toward the metal cabinets against the far wall, he felt uneasy knowing it was behind him. Someone had removed the old blanket he'd thrown over it, Herb or one of the others. He thought briefly of searching for another cloth, perhaps some dusty tarpaulin, but the cold had seeped through his thin cotton shirt and added to his growing sense of urgency. Outside a wind stirred the roof beams.

His way to the cabinets was blocked by the dilapidated wreck of a bureau and, propped against it, the shell of a medicine chest, its door sagging open, the mirror somehow intact. He avoided looking at his image as he stepped past it: an old fear, resurrected in the faint attic light, to see some other face looking back at him. Straining, he shoved the bureau aside and pulled on the door nearest him; it yielded grudgingly, metal grating on metal. Within, a rack was hung with children's clothes; others lay crumpled on the metal floor, gathering dust. All were wrinkled, as if stored here after having been soiled, and like a gym locker, the cabinet reeked of old sweat. He let the door hang open.

The next was lined with deep shelves, empty but for a few rusted tools that had rolled backward into the darkness, and the door to the third had been torn from its hinges; bent double, it was shoved lengthwise into the cabinet, leaving one jagged end that stuck out. The door on the end swung open more easily, but stopped part way, blocked by the bureau; he tugged, jostling the cabinet slightly, but it held fast. He stepped around the bureau and peered inside.

It was as he remembered it. The jars rattled against the metal as if responding to the chill, their liquid insides sloshing rhythmically. In the front row small wrinkled things floated serenely in formaldehyde, fetuses of dog and pig and man, their bulbous eyes closed as if in reverie, with only the labels to tell them apart. He shoved his hip against the bureau; the door opened a few inches more and the slash of light grew wider.

Reaching into the darkness, he succeeded in shoving one of the jars to the side. Below an adhesive labeled "Pig" a huddled figure

121

bobbed up and down. The opening was still too narrow, the jar too big to remove, but in the space behind it he could make out a second row of jars. Pulling one to the front, into a stray beam of light that passed through a crack in the door, he wiped away the thin film of dust that obscured its contents. The tape read "PD#14" in black ballpoint. Regretting that he'd never found out just what those letters stood for, he peeled the tape aside to get a closer look.

Yes, the memories matched. It was just like the thing on the card. But the decomposition was worse than he'd remembered, worse than in the other specimens, as if the thing had shrunk and lost shape. Half buried in sediment, the small gray lump rested on the bottom, turning lazily in the cloudy liquid. Once, on his first time here, he'd been tempted to scrape aside the wax that sealed the top, to unscrew the lid and pour the contents down the toilet like a piece of bad meat. But tonight he understood, if only from the faint odor that hung about the shelves, how easily the smell would sicken him. He slid it back into place, between jars labeled "PD #13" and "PD #15," where it clinked against a third row—and there was still another row behind that. The shelves were deep. There were twenty-two jars in all, he knew, and the specimens seemed to grow progressively larger with each number; he remembered one jar on the bottom, hidden way in the back, nearly filled with something whose rotting flesh hung off it in ribbons. It had been too unpleasant to look at closely.

He closed the cabinet and picked his way back to the stairs, stumbling once on the tiny arm or leg of some long-discarded doll. Descending the stairs, he wondered how much it would cost to have the whole place cleaned out. In some ways this house had proved more expensive than he'd bargained for.

The iron railing felt thin and cold in his grip, and gave slightly when he leaned on it; a strong man might easily have yanked it free. The repairs an old house required . . . he wished he were handier at such tasks. Once, long ago, he'd had the necessary skills, and had enjoyed working with his hands. He'd been a schoolboy then; the world had contained fewer secrets. Biology had been his special love; he had even dreamed, once, of medical school. How much he'd forgotten since then, and how mystifying the world had become.

Perhaps he could find a doctor in the area, some country G.P. he could trust. He'd have a lot of questions for him: about things that floated silently in jars, and what they fed upon. And how big they could grow.

"Oh, El, you're just an old fogey. Don't you like fairy tales?" Doris pointed to the woodcut. "See? The farmer dresses him up in a little suit, and tucks him in at night, and he has himself a little friend."

"I don't think I'd want that thing for a friend."

"Well, that's the whole point. That's why he's called the Little Devil. He's supposed to help the farmer tend the garden and clean the house, but he just causes mischief and eats up whatever's lying around. Including a few of the neighbors."

Ellie shrugged. "I'm afraid I don't approve of fairy tales, at least not for very young children. They're really quite frightening, and so many of them are unnecessarily violent, don't you think? Our two grew up quite nicely without them, thank God." She paused, then added, "Not that a steady diet of the Hardy Boys and Nancy Drew is so much better, of course."

"Oh, these stories wouldn't frighten anyone. They're all told with tongue in cheek. Typically French."

"French, huh? That reminds me—that's what I came in for, something French. What's this book called?" She turned to the title page, *Folk Tales from Provençe.* Hmm, no author listed, I see. How about the story?"

"None there, either. All I know is, it's called, 'The Little Devil.' I don't know what the title is in French." She closed the book with a thump; the sound seemed excessively loud in so silent a room.

The attic door slammed loudly; he hadn't counted on the wind pulling it closed. Bathed in the warmth of the hall, he turned the corner, and froze involuntarily at the figure in the doorway—though his brain had long since identified it.

"Sorry, Walt. I wake you?"

Walter stumbled back to the bed, his eyes puffy and half shut. Creases from the quilt were etched into the side of his face. "Jesus," he muttered, a slackness still about his lips, "it's a good thing you did. I was having one hell of a nightmare."

George followed him into the room and stood awkwardly by the bed; he wished that Walter had picked somewhere else to sleep. He had left a sour, liquory smell in the room.

"Boy, it'll take me a while to get over this one. It seemed so god-damned *real*."

George smiled. "They all do, that's the point."

The other was not comforted. "I can still picture the whole thing. It was night, I remember——"

"Are you sure you want to talk about it? You'll forget faster if you put it out of your mind." He was bored by other people's dreams.

"No, man, you've got it backwards. You're *supposed* to talk about your nightmares. Helps you get rid of 'em." Walter shook his head and eased himself back on the quilt, the bedsprings twanging with each shift of his body. "It was at night, you see, but early, just after the sun had gone down—don't ask me how I know—and I was driving home. The countryside was exactly like it is around here."

"Here? You mean this part of the state?"

"Yeah. Only it was around seven at night, a few hours ago, and Joyce wasn't with me. I was alone in the car, and I wanted to get home. And somehow—you know how it is in dreams—I knew I'd lost my way. All the roads began looking the same, and I remember being very conscious of the fact that it was getting darker and darker all the time, and that if it got too dark I'd never make it. I was driving on this road that led through a tobacco field, just like the one we passed tonight——"

"Right, it's a big crop around here. We've got plantations just down the road."

"Yeah, crazy-looking things, laid out so flat and regular. . . . But I could barely see the land. It was dark now, except for a little glow in the sky, and I was driving very, very slowly, trying to find my way. You know, kind of following the beams of my headlights . . . And then way off in the field I noticed a farmer or someone, one of the hired hands, way out there in the tobacco, so I pulled over to the side of the road and leaned across the front seat, you know, to ask directions. . . . And I'd unrolled the window and was yelling to him when the man turned and made this odd movement with his head, kind of nodding at me, only I couldn't see the face, and then he came toward the car and bent down and I could see that *it wasn't a man*."

George gave him a moment's silence, then asked, "So what was it, then?"

The other rubbed his eyes. "Oh, something pale, puffy, not completely formed. . . . I don't know, it was only a dream."

"But, God damn it, you were just saying how realistic it was!" He found himself glancing toward the window, the shadow of the elm, and was angry.

"Well, you know how quickly you forget dreams, once you tell 'em . . . I don't know, I don't want to think about it anymore. Let's go downstairs and have a drink."

George followed him down with the old ache building once again in his stomach, feeling betrayed by both the world and his own body.

"Something French, huh? Were you looking for anything special?" asked Doris. She slipped the storybook back onto the shelf.

Ellie grinned at her. "You sound like you own the place."

"Well . . . I like books. Unlike my husband."

"I'll tell you, then——" Ellie surveyed the room, hands on hips. "I'm really just looking for a French dictionary. Is there any order to this place? Anything approximating a reference section?"

"Right this way, madame."

While the books in the living room had been bound almost exclusively in leather, obviously chosen for their decorative quality, the collection in the library was strictly functional. Glossy new paperbacks stood pressed against ragged quartos whose titles had long since rotted away. A pocket-sized *Field Guide to the Mammals* was lost in the shadow of an Audubon portfolio, and odd sets of fantasy pulps leaned against a sturdy black row of Arkham House editions, the gold imprint on their spines fading next to the magazines' garish primaries.

The reference section was relatively small, as if the collector had realized that one learns but little from books that try to tell too much. There was, though, a French dictionary on the bottom shelf, side by side with something called, *The Book of Hidden Things*. "I just wanted to look up a word from that stupid little pamphlet,"

Ellie explained, flipping through the pages. "The one that came with those cards."

Doris watched her friend read. "Found it?"

"Yes, *écartée*. It means isolated, alienated."

"Was that from your card?"

She nodded. "That's me, I guess. The original alienated woman." She gave a short laugh. "Hey, look at this! Speak of the devil!" She pointed to the shelf a little above eye level, where three books on the Tarot stood huddled between a history of superstition and Gresham's *Nightmare Alley*. "I'll bring all three in," she decided; two were cheap paperbacks, the third a fat little volume with a brown paper cover. "Milt's probably dying to leave, but first I'd like to give somebody a proper reading."

"Hungry! Aw, for Chrissake, not that again. I tell you I'm sick of that shit, I really am. You was just fed, not more than———"

The man on the bed shook his head.

"Oh, so all of a sudden you're not hungry, huh? You'd damn well better *not be, because I'm leaving in just one second; I mean it. I don't have to stick around and listen to this shit." He paused, and made a big show of looking at his watch. "Okay, you're not hungry."*

A nod.

"Someone else *is hungry?"*

Another nod, more emphatic.

"Well, who the hell gives a——— Oh, all right, go ahead." The foot was tapping another word. One, then six. P. Five. E. Two, and then a noiseless tap. Twenty. T.

"All right, that's it." The orderly rose; the tapping continued, but he stuffed the paper into his pocket. "That's it, buster. I've wasted enough time on you as it is. You can knock the goddamn wall down for all I care!" He turned and strode down the hall, muttering to himself. "Goddamn animal lover . . ."

There was a Pyramid Spread and a Magic Seven Spread and a Wish Spread and a Life Spread and a Horoscope Spread and, according to one of the paperbacks, something called a "Sephiroth Spread," as well as a Kabala Spread and a Cross Spread—"covering," as Milton suggested, "damn near all the religions except a Star of David

Spread"—but the Brackmans were in a hurry to leave soon, others having left already, and Milton had passed them all up for a simple "Yes or No Spread" that used only five cards.

"The two on the right are your past, the two on the left are your future, and the one in the middle is you now. We turn that over first." Ellie read from one of the paperbacks; the clothbound volume had proved a disappointment, its author dampening their spirits at the outset by informing readers that the Tarot had been invented as recently as the 1400s—worse, by charlatans—and that the seventy-eight-card deck was in fact two decks mistakenly grafted together, the one consisting of fifty-six playing cards, the Minor Arcana, the other of twenty-two picture cards, the Major Arcana, illustrating various magical symbols. All fortune-telling properties, he maintained, were strictly illusory. By the time Ellie had so informed the company, reading extended passages verbatim, she'd lookd up to find that her audience had dwindled from more than a dozen to her husband, Sid and Doris Gerdts, and Paul Strauss. They were gathered around a bridge table set up near the front hallway.

"So you've had domestic illusions," Ellie was saying, "but now you've seen through them——"

"What the hell are 'domestic illusions'?" asked Paul.

"——and you've set your sights higher, on philosophical aspirations." She had both paperbacks propped open before her, and—like the medieval's unquestioning faith in both Christian and Classical cosmologies—she saw no discrepancies in the two sets of predictions, at odds though they often were.

Milton's fond husband-smile had never wavered throughout her performance. "So much for my past," he said. "Now for the present." He turned over the center card. "This is me now."

Gerdts chuckled. "Looks like you're a girl, Miltie!" Indeed, the card was The Queen of Pentacles; surrounded as she was by foliage, sitting in a meadow beneath a rosy trellis, she seemed the most feminine of all the queens.

Milton forced a laugh. "Ah, what do these cards know?" he said. He reached for the first of the future-cards.

"No, wait," said his wife, "I'm sure there's a reading for you in this. Remember, it's only a symbol." She looked from book to book. "See? Just listen: It's a symbol of fertility—" Milt's eyebrows rose.

"——and charity. It says you're of Libra temperament, whatever that is——"

"Oh, God," said Paul, "not astrology too!"

"——and therefore have a deep love of justice." She looked up; her eyes met Milton's. "That part's true, anyway."

"Yes."

"And now the future," said Gerdts. "Come on, Milt." The other reached for the card.

"Now hold on a second," said Ellie. "Remember, boys, this one's the near future, because it's next to the center. . . . And the last is the distant future."

"Got you." He turned over the first card.

"You've got it upside down," said Doris. "Here, let me——"

"No, leave it be," Ellie ordered. "The meaning changes if it's that way." She scanned the illustrations in the guidebook, then shrugged. "Nothing like that in here. This book's no damned good." She looked in the other, explaining, "All decks have basically the same idea, but the actual pictures can be different. Like chess sets, it says here. Sometimes a queen is a beautiful young woman: other times she's shown as an Egyptian goddess, or a nun, or a naked girl." Her eyes kept scanning the pages. "But I really don't see anything like that. And no reference number on the bottom; that makes it harder to identify. What's it look like to you?"

"Like something hanging from a tree," said Doris. "A bat or a sloth. You know, those things that get the fungus on them . . ." She turned the card around. "And right side up it looks like——" She frowned.

"A sloth on the ground," said Milton. "Seen from the rear."

"Like those prehistoric things," added Paul. "Giant ground sloths." There was, in fact, something ancient in the squat gray form, crawling along a road beneath a starry sky, its head no more than a bulge in the background.

"Is there a table of contents?" asked Milton. His wife nodded. "Look up The Sloth. Or better yet, The Beast."

"It reminds me of that Maine folk tale," said Gerdts. "The one about the hunter who shot the bear and skinned it, and went off with the hide, leaving his own coat behind. . . . He turns around and he sees the bear following him, wearing his coat. That's what it is, it's a skinned bear."

"Could it be the card for Death?" asked his wife. "It looks like Death to me."

Gerdts searched through the pack. "Afraid not, Dorie. This one's Old Mr. Death, see?" The skull's eyes stared sightlessly out at them.

"I've looked all through these"—Ellie laid aside the paperbacks—"and there's nothing like it." She began leafing through the third book. "Maybe it's from another deck."

Milton turned it over. Its back bore the same design as the other cards.

Ellie sighed. "This book's no good either. I may have to do this by process of elimination." Paul glanced surreptitiously at his watch. "I'll figure it out," she said. "Don't worry."

"I'm not worrying," said Milton.

"Looks like I'm gonna have to leave," said Paul. "Tell me how it all comes out." He looked around for the host and hostess.

"I'm sure it isn't a number card, or a royal card," said Ellie, "so that means it has to be one of the Trumps Major."

"Ah, I've got it," said Milton. "Satan."

"But it hardly looks like——"

"It must be. I've looked through the whole pack, and there's no Satan card."

"Well . . ." She looked down at the card in question. "Yes, maybe there is the hint of a horn, around the other side . . . but would Satan really be facing away?"

"Maybe displaying his rump for us to kiss," said Doris. She blushed.

"Last call for quiche," yelled Phyllis from across the room. "Get it while it's hot!"

The Goodhues and the Fitzgeralds had left, having spent the evening in conversation with no one but themselves, and Paul was putting on his coat. He paused for one final mouthful of quiche.

The Gerdtses drifted toward the food table, more out of obligation than hunger, and—after making sure his wife was "absolutely stuffed"—Milton joined them, leaving Ellie alone with the cards.

Yes, the gray shape probably represented Satan; the mystery was solved. Yet it was all rather exasperating, for Satan in one book was a Mosaic-looking deity with a flowing beard; in another, a black magician; and in the third, a sullen, goatlike figure officiating at the unholy matrimony of two disciples. The thing that shambled across the card resembled none of them; it was simply, as her husband had said, The Beast.

She was thinking of the Little Devil of the storybook—*le Petit Diable*, she supposed it must be called—when her hand, straying to the remaining card in Milton's spread, unthinkingly turned it face up, revealing Satan upon his throne, the two naked mortals joined in wedlock before him.

The Lazaruses had just left, and Janet Mulholland backed away from the cold blast of air that dropped toward her legs as the door swung shut. Her husband was helping her with her coat, and Mike Carlinsky was searching in the closet for his fiancée's gloves. Arthur Faschman was standing by the window with Herb, watching the exodus.

"Getting late," said Herb.

Faschman looked at his watch. "Wow, I'll say! Hey, Judy," he called, "do you have any idea what time it is?"

"After twelve. So what?"

"So I've gotta drive Andy down to the orthodontist tomorrow morning, that's what. Unless you want to do it." He turned back to Herb. "Listen to her. Last of the swingers. You ought to hear her the morning after. Better yet, you ought to *see* her!" He looked at his watch, more nervously this time. "Hey, how is it outside? Not raining or anything, I hope . . ." He peered out the window.

"It's cold out there," said Milton. "George said it may even snow. El and I were all set to go, but now we're thinking of staying over."

"I must say, he's carrying that gentleman farmer bit a little too far," said Faschman. "I mean, just look. Isn't that a scarecrow out there?"

"Where?" Milton rubbbed his first against the glass. The light in the living room was strong, and he could see little more than his own reflection. "Where, in the yard?"

"No, way the hell out there, over on the other side of the field." He tapped on part of the pane; it was smeared with condensation.

"See? Ah, too late, the moon's behind a cloud. You'll pass it when you leave. You really going to stay all night?"

"Sure, why not? Free breakfast."

"Yeah," said Judy Faschman, coming up behind them, "if you don't mind leftover quiche."

Carefully Ellie laid out the cards. The Sun, The Moon, The Star . . . Judgment, Temperance, and Justice . . . She'd been standing here half an hour, checking, and they were all there. The Emperor, The Hermit, The Hierophant . . . Strength, The World, and The Wheel of Fortune. All twenty-two of them, the Trumps Major, each with its message. Satan, and Death, and The Hanged Man . . . and even The Fool. (Why did she always associate that with poor George? He'd been so out of sorts tonight.)

All had been accounted for; she'd matched them all with the illustrations in the book. What, then, was this additional card? The green cardboard box said, "78 cartes." That, and the brand name, *Grand Etteilla*—derived, the book had said, from Alliette, the unsavory magician who'd introduced them to the French court—and below it the seal of the printer, B. P. Grimaud, of Marseilles. Nothing about an extra trump, a spare, a bonus, a joker . . .

She studied it again. She hadn't noticed before, but in places the picture was rather disturbingly detailed. She could make out the bulletlike contours of a head just about to turn in her direction, and an upraised front claw, shadowy against the night. Something in the configuration of the stars in the background reminded her of the sky outside the windows. . . .

Hastily she placed the cards back in the box, slipping the gray hunched thing well into the middle of the pack, as if to cage it. The twenty-third trump, she suspected, was no joker.

"And here I thought you were going to stay over," said Phyllis.

"Aw, Phyl, come on. Admit it, you're relieved to get us out of the way. One less bed to make in the morning." Milton leaned forward and kissed her on the cheek. "My wife says she's tired, and when my wife says she's tired that means it's home for us." The excuse sounded lame; Ellie's sudden decision to leave, without even the offer to help clean up, had been rude.

"You sure you don't want one more before you go?" asked George. (Where had he come from?) He jiggled his drink invitingly, but it looked like the drink he'd been sipping all night.

Milton shook his head, smiling sheepishly. "Honest, kids, I just want to say, before I hit the road, that if I got a little out of hand tonight, you know, if I said anything I shouldn't have, well, I never was much good at holding my liquor and——"

"It was a pleasure, old buddy, honest." George slapped him on the arm; he seemed to be rallying. "If you said anything nasty, I sure didn't hear it."

Relief showed in Milton's face. "Yeah, well, thanks a lot. I mean it. I love this place and I had a great time here tonight." He reached for George's hand. "And I just hope you and Phyl are——"

"Honey!" Ellie's voice came from the driveway. "I'm standing out here in the cold, and you've got the car keys."

"Christ, yeah, gotta run." He looked over his shoulder. "Sorry El's a little cranky, but you know these women. Can't keep 'em up past midnight!" Pulling up his collar, he flashed Phyllis a big grin. "She really had a great time, and you can bet that——"

"Honey!"

Milton shrugged. "Bye now." He leaned into the hall. "G'night, everybody. See you soon." Then, stepping outside: "Whoops, get away from the door, Phyl, you'll catch cold." His footsteps crunched on the gravel.

Silence lay on the room; conversation had sputtered and died. The men took George's yawn as a signal to depart, but they waited for their wives to finish helping Phyllis clean up, careful to make no acknowledgment of the late hour. Allen Goldberg sat smoking disconsolately on the couch, watching Cissy Hawkins fuss over the few remaining platters of canapés and fruit; as the only remaining bachelor, Paul Strauss having made his exit, Allen was expected to drive Cissy home. He glanced toward Joyce Applebaum, who marched toward the kitchen carrying two bowls of clam dip and the remains of a cheesecake. She was a lot more attractive than Cissy. Her husband lay sprawled in the big armchair, his face red from drink and fatigue; he'd slept through most of the party. "Come on, baby, hurry it up," he said. Baby. All the men remarked on that; Walter had only been married a few months.

When Cissy offered to scrub the kitchen floor, Phyllis had to dissuade her. "Or I can help dry dishes," the girl pleaded.

"Honestly, Cis, you've been a terrific help all evening and there's nothing left to do." She withdrew her hands from the sink and shook them free of suds. "Now go back in there and relax, and we'll make sure you have a ride home."

Relieved, Cissy returned to the living room, only to face the sullen stares of the men. Awkwardly she moved to the bridge table and began tidying up—then, to busy herself, opened the green cardboard box. The Six of Swords was on top, followed by The Tower. She would put them in order, she decided, just as, in her apartment, she'd spent hours arranging and rearranging her few dozen books. Swords in this pile, cups in that, picture cards over there . . .

The picture cards were prettiest, but she wasn't sure how to arrange them until she saw the tiny numerals at the bottom. Judgment, number 20, the naked people sprouting from their graves like corn —why, you could see the woman's nipples—and number 7, The Chariot, would be before it, a black sphinx and a white sphinx roped together, and then 10, The Wheel of Fortune, with the white sphinx (the same?) perched on top, and 12, The Hanged Man, with his knowing smirk, and then The Fool, inexplicably numbered with a zero—perhaps that was a mistake, and she put it aside—and 8, Strength, the girl with—what was that?—a lion, and then The Moon, 18, shedding its light onto the open field, dogs howling below it, and then a huge gray animal staring malevolently at something beyond the edge of the card; they'd left off the number and she put it aside with The Fool, and then Temperance, number 14, which made her smile because her grandmother had been in the WCTU . . . She wondered if, to some people, her own beliefs appeared as ridiculous, and continued counting: The World, The Lovers, and Death. . . . When would he ask her if she needed a ride?

Allen had made the mistake of watching her, and when she looked up his eyes met hers. As if on cue, he stubbed out his cigarette and got to his feet. "Uh, Cissy, do you need a lift home?"

133

When George came into the kitchen, his wife whispered, "So are they planning to stay all night?"

He shrugged. "You know Herb—last to come, last to leave. He has that look on him, too, that philosophical-discussion look." Phyllis sighed. "But you know, I wouldn't mind him staying awhile. I'm not really tired."

"Well Tammie is, and so am I. If you two want to talk all night that's up to you. I'll put out some things in the guest room for them, but after that I'm going straight to bed." She eyed him accusingly. "Of course you're not tired, you haven't been running around all day. You spent half the party hiding in the bathroom."

Back in the living room Herb greeted him with, "You know, George, what this place needs is a nice little fire. That really would have made the evening, to have a fire going."

"Yeah, but they're a lot of bother." For a minute he'd thought Herb had suggested burning the house down.

"But what's a fireplace for if you don't build a fire on a cold night?"

"To tell you the truth, I'm not even sure if this chimney works. I'll have to get somebody in to check the flue." The bare fireplace looked like an empty stage, a performer still waiting in the wings. "Besides, Phyllis threw out all the firewood, and if you want any more you've got to walk half a mile to the woodshed"—he gestured toward a window—"all the way around back."

Herb stood. "I'm game," he said. "Just tell me where it is."

Tammie came out of the downstairs bathroom, her hair patted back into shape, the tiredness around her eyes concealed. "And where do you think you're going?" she said.

"To get some firewood," said Herb. "Build us a fire."

"Herb here's trying to prove he's an outdoorsman," explained George. "I made fun of him earlier tonight—I mean, when you two got lost on the way here—so now he's out to show me up."

Tammie pouted. "Really, honey, everyone's tired and ready for bed . . . And all of a sudden you have to build a fire?"

"*I'm* not tired," said Herb, on the defensive. "Anyway, a stack of lumber by the andirons would brighten up the living room. Add some atmosphere."

"Fine," said George, in no mood to argue. "You're hired. You're out new interior decorator. Now go through the kitchen, out the door to the greenhouse, but before you reach it turn right, go down the steps, and you'll see a path by the back of the house. Follow that around the garage and you'll see the woodshed, out near the hedges. I'm pretty sure it's unlocked."

"Better put a coat on, honey."

"I don't need it." Herb strode toward the kitchen.

"How'd you like Mike's fiancée?" asked Tammie when they were alone. She reached for a cigarette. "Think she's right for him?"

"Oh, I'd met her before. She's okay. It was Ellie who introduced them, you know."

"No kidding! Where, at the beach last summer?"

"Yeah."

"And what did you think of *her* tonight, lecturing out of that book?"

"Oh, she just gets a little carried away with the sound of her own voice, that's all." He noticed the books she'd left on the bridge table, and went to get them. They belonged in the library; only leather-bound books for the living room. "Ellie's a strong-minded woman."

"I'll say. Did you see how she bosses Milt around? When she decided it was time to leave, that was it, he had to go. Just like——" She looked toward the window. "Well, here comes Herb with the firewood."

"What, already? No, he must have gotten lost. Wonder why he's coming round the front." Taking a deep breath, he opened the green box. The cards spilled out onto the table.

Phyllis entered the room, wiping her hands on a dish towel.

He turned over several minor trumps, then a picture card, The Tower. Lightning flashed, stone walls crumbled, and beyond them raged the sea. He pushed it to one side. Somehow he wished that Herb had not gone out. "Hey honey, did you lock the back door?"

"Not yet. Why?" She went to the front window and drew the curtains. "Anybody ready for bed? I'll get some clean linen out."

"Now you're sure it's no bother?" asked Tammie. She stood. "Herb and I can make do with these couches, you know." They heard the crunch of gravel outside.

"Nonsense! We'll go upstairs and get the room ready, and by the time we come down the men'll have a fire going." George didn't

135

look up; he was absorbed in sorting through the cards, searching for one card in particular. "And we'll all have some hot chocolate. Won't that be nice?"

From outside came a high-pitched whistling; something thudded against the door. Tammie, who was closest, walked into the front hall. As her hand fastened on the doorknob, George gave a little gasp; he staggered back, dropping the card and what glared from it, and as she swung open the door he screamed, "No, Tammie, no!" But it was already too late; a gray shape filled the doorway, blotting out the night—and now, just as in the card, it turned to face him.

Out of Sorts

BY BERNARD TAYLOR

There is a certain grimness even to the brightest of days if one chooses to look for it; and there is a certain brightness to the grim, to be fair. What is required sometimes, then, is a mixture of both, one seeming to be the other to such a degree that what appears to be, isn't. Maybe. It's a time when playing "Let's Pretend" nudges you into something more than just a game.

Bernard Taylor is the author of Sweetheart, Sweetheart *(the best contemporary ghost story, bar none). He lives in London, where he also works as an actor and screenwriter.*

"OH, *not* the *twenty-first!*" Paul Gunn said. "Whatever made you choose *that* date?"

"I didn't *choose* it. That's the day the meeting falls—third Friday in the month." Sylvia shook her head. "There was nothing I could do about it."

"You could have arranged to hold the bloody thing somewhere else, couldn't you? Does it have to be here?"

"It's *my turn,*" Sylvia said with a sigh. "Besides, I'm president.— And apart from that I just wasn't thinking, I suppose. I can't be expected to remember *everything.*"

"No, but I do expect you to remember the *important* things." He made a sound of exasperation. "Can't you change it? It's bad enough at the best of times, but when the bloody house is filled with people——"

"It's only three days away," Sylvia said reasonably. "We planned it weeks ago and it's too late to alter it now." She looked at him entreatingly. "Oh, please don't be angry. You'll be all right. No one will bother you."

He refused to be entreated or pacified, though, and she watched as he angrily snatched up his newspaper, opened it unnecessarily roughly and submerged himself in its contents. End of conversation, as always.

His large, tanned hands looked very dark against the white of the paper. It was the hair on them. Thick and black, it made his hands look larger than they were. It was probably a turn-on to some women, she thought. Not to herself, though; not now—if it had ever been . . .

It *was* to Norma Russell, though, she was quite certain. Norma, with her model's 35 × 25 × 36 figure, her high cheek bones and sleek blonde hair. Paul's hirsute body would be just the thing to appeal to *her*.

If it came to looks, she reflected, it was quite obvious that she herself couldn't compete with anyone like Norma. Oh, once she'd been pretty in a vague, mousey kind of way, but not for years now. Well, she hadn't made any effort, had she? And why should she try, now, when there was no point?

And there *was* no point anymore. More than that, in her eyes it would have seemed the height of stupidity to go to the bother of dressing up when practically the only man who ever looked at you was your husband—and even when he *did* he didn't even see you. Yes, pointless, to say the least.

Paul, on the other hand, seemed to have grown sleeker and better looking in an over-fed kind of way over the years. Success showed clearly on him; in his clothes and his body—and his women. Yes, he did look better. That, she supposed, was what contentment and complacency did. She shot him a look of hatred as he lounged, protected by the shield of his paper. Then she turned and went upstairs.

This place, too, was a sign of his success. Set apart in this tiny Yorkshire village of Tallowford, the house was huge and rambling, exquisitely furnished; further testimony to the years of effort he'd put into his engineering company, now one of the most profitable small businesses in nearby Bradford.

In her study Sylvia sat down at her elegant desk, Louis XIV, genuine. Opening her diary she looked again at the date of the meeting. The 21st. No mistake. Then she checked over the Women's Circle committee list. There would be six of them. On the past two occasions there'd been only five—herself, Pamela Horley, Jill Marks, Janet True, and Mary Drewett. This time, though, there'd be six again. A replacement had been found for Lilly Sloane who had moved away—a replacement proposed by herself and voted in unanimously by the others: Norma Russell.

Norma, of course, had so eagerly accepted the offered place on the committee. "Well, if you really want me and you think I can be of help," she'd said. But she hadn't fooled Sylvia for one minute. Sylvia knew quite well that Norma's eagerness stemmed from the fact that as every third meeting was held in the Gunns' house it could only lead to more encounters between herself and Paul. . . .

Methodically Sylvia went through the list, telephoning the members to check that each was okay for the 21st. All except Norma. *Her* number was engaged. Not that Sylvia needed to worry; if there was one member she knew she could count on, that one was Norma.

Pushing her papers away from her she turned in her chair and looked around her. No expense had been spared in this room. The rest of the furniture was as elegant as the desk on which her elbow rested, as elegant as that in the bedroom next door—the bedroom in which she slept alone—except on those nights when Paul would come to her and use her for the release of frustrations. . . .

That's how it had gone on. That's how it *would* go on—unless something was done to stop it. Oh, she was safe enough, she knew; secure enough in the continuing of her material comforts. As much as Paul would like to see the back of her he'd never divorce her—or even leave her. He knew which side his bread was buttered, all right. Hence the comfort in which he kept her. And that, surely, was partly the reason for his resentment of her—the fact that he knew they were irrevocably tied—in sickness and in health, for as long as they both should live—for his dependence upon her.

Why, she sometimes asked herself, didn't *she* leave *him*? But what would she do if she did? Paul wouldn't support her, and she'd been trained for no particular occupation. For the past twenty-five years she'd known only this life—marriage to a man whose gratitude for her understanding had in no time worn threadbare . . .

But for all that, she thought, she could have put up with it—had it not been for his affairs. One after the other they had punctuated the years of their married life. And for that *she* was resentful—not just because of his infidelity and his rejection of herself, but because he gave to those *other* women what he never gave, never *had* given, to herself—not after the first few months of their courtship, anyway. *They* were allowed to see only the *best* side of him; the cheerfulness, the gentlemanliness, the solicitousness. She, through her near-total acceptance of the real person, was doomed to live with it, warts and all.

She got up from the desk and stood there in the silent room. It couldn't go on, though. And it *wouldn't*. No; after the 21st it wouldn't be the same. Come the 21st there'd be some changes made. Norma Russell would be the last, she'd make sure of that. After Norma there wouldn't be any more affairs.

When she got downstairs she found Paul on the phone. He started slightly when she suddenly appeared before him and said shakily into the receiver, voice thick with guile and not a little guilt:

"Well, Frank, I think we ought to leave it until our meeting next week. . . . we can discuss it fully then . . ." And Sylvia smiled to herself as she went by him, realizing why Norma's telephone had been engaged, and at the realization that *they* thought she was so easily fooled. Not she. *Frank*, indeed. She was a lot smarter than they dreamed. Certainly a damn sight smarter than that vacuous, simpering Norma with her Gucci shoes, Charlie perfume, and Dior sunglasses. Norma Russell, with her sophisticated approach and smug, know-it-all manner didn't know it all by any means.

Not yet. She would in time.

Paul left his office early that Friday, came into the house and flopped down onto the sofa saying he had a headache. Sylvia guessed well enough how he was feeling, but any sympathy she once might have felt for him had long ago vanished.

They ate an early dinner and as soon as it was over he went upstairs to the attic. Sylvia followed after a while, quietly opened the door and looked in. He was sound asleep. Backing out again, she turned the key and pushed home the bolts. For a second she listened but no sound came to her through the heavy oak door. She turned and went back downstairs to get ready for the meeting.

The women all arrived within a few minutes of each other around eight o'clock, and with the coffee already made they got down fairly quickly to the business of the evening. That business was the forthcoming summer fête and the Women's Circle's part in it. The discussion went smoothly, and so it should have, for each of them—with the exception of Norma—had helped organise a dozen similar events in the past.

Finally it was all sorted out and Sylvia summed up the results of their discussion.

"All right, then," she said, "I think that's it. So you, Pam, and you, Janet, will get together and organise the refreshments and the baking competition. And you, Jill and Mary, will work on the jumble." Smiling at Norma—who returned the smile—she went on: "And that leaves Norma and me to take care of the Fancy Goods and the white elephant stall. Is that okay?"

The next forty minutes were spent in drinking more coffee and generally talking over the finer points of their various tasks. There was much talk of "willing hands" and "helpers" and "generous donors"; various names were bandied about, and there were the endlessly expressed hopes that on the day the weather would be kind to them. Sylvia began to get the feeling that the meeting would never end; never before had the conversation of her friends seemed quite so meaningless. But there, never before had she herself had quite such serious matters on her mind.

At last, though, it was nine-forty-five. The meeting was over. As they all got up to go, chattering their goodnights, Sylvia caught at Norma's sleeve, saying, "Oh, Norma—are you in a particular hurry to get away——?"

"No, why?" Norma's expression of eagerness-to-please didn't fool Sylvia for one moment. Now she was like a cat that had found the cream; not only had she been voted onto the committee but she had furthermore been chosen to work closely with Sylvia. From now on she'd have a cast-iron excuse for phoning or calling at the house at practically any time.

Sylvia smiled as sweetly and as naturally as she could under the circumstances. "I was just wondering whether you'd care to stay behind for a little while so that we can go over—in more detail—a few of the things you and I will be looking after . . ."

141

"Of course. I'd be *glad* to. Anytime at all, Sylvia—you just let me know." She'd picked up her bag but now she set it down again at the side of the sofa.

When the other members had all gone out into the night Sylvia came back into the sitting room. As she sat down Norma said to her:

"I suppose Paul hates being around when these—these hen parties are in session, doesn't he?"

Sylvia nodded. "Loathes it, my dear. Absolutely."

"Does he—er—er get back late. . . .?"

Oh, thought Sylvia, so obviously Norma had told Paul that she'd be coming to the meeting—and it was equally obvious that he'd told her he'd be out somewhere. Well, that was understandable. "I'm sorry?" Sylvia said, "——what did you ask me?"

"Paul—does he usually stay out late when you have your meetings?"

"Oh, yes, usually he does. Not tonight, though . . ." And that, she thought, should get her going. It did.

"Oh," said Norma, "——is there something different about tonight?" She sounded very casual.

"Yes, the poor dear didn't go out. He can't. He's just not up to it." Sylvia watched, hiding the pleasure she felt as a look of concern flashed into Norma's green eyes.

"Is he *ill?*" Norma asked.

"No, no—just a little out of sorts."

"Oh, what a shame. Perhaps you should have phoned and cancelled the meeting. Won't he have been disturbed by all our chatter down here?"

Sylvia shook her head. "No, he won't have heard a thing. He's up in the attic. In his den, as he calls it. He's got a bed up there—well away from it all. It's much the best place for him at a time like this, when he's not himself. Anyway——" she pulled her note pad towards her as if to signify that it was time for them to get on with their work. Then, suddenly, with a look of dismay, she dropped her pencil and clapped her hand to her mouth. "Oh, my God!" she said.

"What's the matter?" Norma stared at her in surpise. Her concern looked genuine.

"I think I'm losing my mind," Sylvia said. "It's going, I swear it's going. My *mem*ory. Oh, dear!"

"What's up?"

"I promised faithfully that I'd drop a few little things over to Mrs Harrison this afternoon. She can't get out, what with her leg, and she's got her daughter coming for lunch tomorrow. I did all her shopping for her this afternoon—and it's still out there in the kitchen." She glanced at the clock. "Just ten o'clock. I'll bet she's been expecting me all day. How dreadful." She sat as if pondering for a moment then said: "I know she doesn't go to bed till quite late. . . . I think I'll just give her a ring and then take the stuff round. I shan't get a chance in the morning, I know . . ."

Even as she finished speaking Sylvia was opening her address book and looking up Mrs Harrison's number. She dialled it and Mrs Harrison answered almost immediately. She sounded so pleased to hear Sylvia's voice. No, she said, she hadn't been in bed; she was watching the telly darts championship—adding with a little giggle that she quite liked big men. Refusing to take no for an answer Sylvia then said that she was going to get straight on her bike and bring the groceries round. After all, it was only two miles and no one ever came to harm in Tallowford.

Sylvia had put on her coat and was picking up the basket before she seemed to remember that Norma was still there.

"Oh, Norma, my dear," she said. "After asking you to stay behind I now go rushing off like this. I do apologise. Whatever must you think of me?"

"I think you're a very kind person," Norma simpered. "That's what I think."

And Sylvia, in spite of her loathing for the creature, found herself thinking, How true.

She hitched the handle of the basket more securely over her arm. "My bike's just round the side," she said. "Would you be an angel and make sure that I've turned off the gas under the kettle and that there are no cigarettes burning anywhere. . . . Oh, and if Paul *should* by any chance call out just tell him I'll be back in about an hour or a little longer. Would you mind?" She moved to the door. "You can let yourself out, can't you?"

Hardly hearing Norma's reply, Sylvia opened the front door and went to her bicycle. Then, after carefully securing the basket she got on and pedalled away. The night was so bright as she sped down the

143

lonely country road that she really had hardly any need of her bicycle lamp at all.

From the window Norma watched the red glow of Sylvia's tail light till it disappeared. Then she made a lightning check of the gas taps and the ashtrays. Everything was fine.

Yes, everything was fine. Everything was perfect.

In the hall she stood quite still and looked up the stairs. Then, after a second or two, she began to climb. She didn't put on the lights; she couldn't take the chance of being seen through a window by some passing villager.

He was in the attic, Sylvia had said. Norma went up the stairs, past the first floor and on up the next flight—narrower now and turning. At the top she came to a stop, hesitated a moment and then softly called out:

"Paul———?"

Silence. And then she heard a sound. It came from the door a few yards to her right. Moving towards it she saw to her horror that it was locked and bolted! Sylvia had locked him in! How *could* she?!

The key, though, was in the lock. She turned it, then pulled back the bolts. Then, turning the handle, she opened the door and stepped inside.

"Paul———?" She stood with her back to the closed door and whispered his name into the darkness.

"Paul? Paul, are you there? It's me—Norma. I've come to pay you a little surprise visit. . . ."

The room was swallowed up in shadow. She could see nothing. She could *hear* something, though. Breathing.

"———Paul, is that you?" It didn't sound like him. "Sylvia said you weren't quite yourself tonight—so I've come to cheer you up a bit—if I can!" She laughed nervously into the dark. The sound of the breathing was growing a little louder, coming a little nearer.

"Paul," she said, "———is that you there———? Come on, now—don't fool about. . . ."

Suddenly the moon, the full moon, was no longer obscured by the clouds. Suddenly the room was bathed in light. She saw the bars at the window—thick, metal bars. She noticed, too, the complete absence of furniture. There was only straw on the floor. She became

144

aware, too, of the strong animal smell that permeated the air around her.

And then she saw Paul coming towards her.

In the brilliant silver light of the full moon he lunged towards her and she felt him reach out with one huge clawed paw, felt herself wrenched forward, towards the great snout, the great fangs that opened, dripping in anticipation. She heard the guttural sound from deep in his throat.

The sound that came from her own throat, a small, pleading cry of terror, was cut off before she'd hardly had a chance to utter it.

At Mrs Harrison's Sylvia looked at her watch. It was almost eleven. She put down her cup, got to her feet and took up the empty basket. It had been so nice, she said, but she really *must* get back. There'd be a lot of cleaning up to do. Besides, Paul might wake up and start to worry about her. He never did, usually, but he could get very funny when he was out of sorts.

"It's probably the full moon," Mrs Harrison said, giggling. "Did you notice there's a full moon tonight? I swear it makes a difference to some people. You might not believe this, but I'm sure it used to affect my husband. He used to go right off his food. Wouldn't eat a thing."

Sylvia looked out of the window at the moon's big, white face. "Oh, well," she said with a little smile, "I can't say it takes Paul like that. He gets absolutely ravenous."

The Sunshine Club

BY RAMSEY CAMPBELL

Life, some would have us believe, would be awfully simple if only we were free to express our emotions more openly, put aside constraint and confront ourselves and our neighbors with honesty and truth. The problem with this, however, lies in the definitions of "truth" and "honesty" and "simple." Who decides what the proper definitions are? And who, by the same token, can really judge whether truth is staring us down? It has occurred to a few that it isn't always profitable to know everything another is thinking.

Ramsey Campbell has won the World and British fantasy awards for his short fiction, has been nominated for same for his novels (the latest of which is The Nameless), *and is also a superb editor. He lives in England with his wife Jenny and a growing family, and is at his best when he's at his darkest.*

"WILL this be the last session?" Bent asked.

I closed his file on my desk and glanced at him to detect impatience or a plea, but his eyes had filled with the sunset as with blood. He was intent on the cat outside the window, waiting huddled on the balcony as the spider's cocoon like a soft white marble in one corner of the pane boiled with minute hectic birth. Bent gripped my desk and glared at the cat, which had edged along the balcony from the next office. "It'll kill them, won't it?" Bent demanded. "How can it be so calm?"

"You have an affinity for spiders," I suggested. Of course, I already knew.

"I suppose that ties in with the raw meat."

"As a matter of fact, it does. Yes, to pick up your question, this may well be the last session. I want to take you through what you gave me under hypnosis."

147

"About the garlic?"

"The garlic, yes, and the crosses."

He winced and managed to catch hold of a smile. "You tell me, then," he said.

"Please sit down for a moment," I said, moving around my desk and intervening between him and the cat. "How was your day?"

"I couldn't work," he muttered. "I stayed awake but I kept think-ing of how it'd be in the canteen. All those swines of women laugh-ing and pointing. That's what you've got to get rid of."

"Be assured, I will." I'll have you back at the conveyor belt before you know, I thought: but there are more important fulfilments.

"But they all saw me!" he cried. "Now they'll all look!"

"My dear Mr Bent—no, Clive, may I?—you must remember, Clive, that odder dishes than raw meat are ordered every day in can-teens. You could always tell them it was a hangover cure."

"When I don't know why myself? I don't want that meat," he said intensely. "*I* didn't want it."

"Well, at least you came to see me. Perhaps we can find you an alternative to raw meat."

"Yes, yes," he said hopelessly. I waited, staring for a pause at the walls of my office, planed flat by pale green paint. Briefly I felt enclosed with his obsession, and forced myself to remember why. When I looked down I found that the pen in my hand was hurrying lines of crosses across the blotter, and I flipped the blotter onto its face. For a moment I feared a relapse. "Lie down," I suggested, "if it'll put you at your ease."

"I'll try not to fall asleep," he said, and more hopefully, "It's nearly dark." When he'd aligned himself on the couch he glanced down at his hands on his chest. Discovered, they flew apart.

"Relax as completely as you can," I said, "don't worry about how," and watched as his hands crept comfortingly together on his chest. His sleeves dragged at his elbows, and he got up to unbutton his jacket. He'd removed his hat when he entered my office, though with its wide black brim and his gloves and high collar he warded off the sting of sunshine from his shrinking flesh. I'd coaxed his body out of its blackness and his mind was following, probing timidly forth from the defences which had closed around it. "Ready," he called as if we were playing hide and seek.

148

I placed myself between the couch and the window in order to read his face. "All right, Clive," I said. "Last time you told me about a restaurant where your parents had an argument. Do you remember?"

His face shifted like troubled water. Behind his eyelids he was silent. "Tell me about your parents," I said eventually.

"But you know," said his compressed face. "My father was good to me. Until he couldn't stand the arguments."

"And your mother?"

"She wouldn't let him be!" his face cried blindly. "All those Bibles she knew he didn't want, making out he should be going to church with her when she knew he was afraid——"

"But there was nothing to be afraid of, was there?"

"Nothing. You know that."

"So you see, he was weak. Remember that. Now, why did they fight in the restaurant?"

"I don't know, I can't remember. Tell me! Why won't you tell me?"

"Because it's important that you tell me. At least you can remember the restaurant. Go on, Clive, what was above your head?"

"Chandeliers," he said wearily. A bar of sunset was rising past his eyes.

"What else can you see?"

"Those buckets of ice with bottles in."

"You can't see very much?"

"No, it's too dim. Candles——" His voice hung transfixed.

"Now you can see, Clive! Why?"

"Flames! F—— The flames of hell!"

"You don't believe in hell, Clive. You told me that when you didn't know yourself. Let's try again. Flames?"

"They were—inside them—a man's face on fire, melting! I could see it coming but nobody was looking——"

"Why didn't they look?"

His shuddering head pressed back into the couch. "Because it was meant for me!"

"No, Clive, not at all. Because they knew what it was."

But he wouldn't ask. I waited, glancing at the window so that he would call me back; the minute spiders stirred like uneasy caviar.

149

"Well, tell me," he said coyly, dismally.

"If you were to go into any of a dozen restaurants you'd see your man on fire. Now do you begin to see why you've turned your back on everything your parents took for granted? How old were you then?"

"Nine."

"Is it coming clear?"

"You know I don't understand these things. Help me! I'm paying you!"

"I am, and we're almost there. You haven't even started eating yet."

"I don't want to."

"Of course you do."

"Don't! Not——"

"Not——"

Outside the window, against the tiger-striped blurred sky, the cat tensed to leap. "Not when my father can't," Bent whispered harshly.

"Go on, go on, Clive! Why can't he?"

"Because they won't serve the meat the way he likes."

"And your mother? What is she doing?"

"She's laughing. She says she'll eat anyway. She's watching him as they bring her, oh——" His head jerked.

"Yes?"

"Meat——"

"Yes?"

It might have been a choke or a sob. "Guh! Guh! Garlic!' he cried, and shook.

"Your father? What does he do?"

"He's standing up. Sit down! Don't! She says it all again, how it's sacrilegious to eat blood—— He's, oh, he's pulling the cloth off the table, everything falls on me, everybody's looking, she comes at him, he's got her hair, she bites him then she screams, he smiles, he's smiling, I hate him!" Bent shook and collapsed in the shadows.

"Open your eyes," I said.

They opened wide, trustful, protected by the twilight. "Let me tell you what I see," I said.

"I think I understand some things," he whispered.

"Just listen. Why do you fear garlic and crosses? Because your mother destroyed your father with them. Why do you want and yet not want raw meat? To be like your father who you really knew was weak, to make yourself stronger than the man who was destroyed. But now you know he was weak, you know you are stronger. Stronger than the women who taunt you because they know you're strong. And if you still have a taste for bloody meat, there are places that will serve it to you. The sunlight which you fear? That's the man on fire, who terrified you because you thought your father was destined for hell."

"I know," Bent said. "He was just a waiter cooking."

I switched on the desk-lamp. "Exactly. Do you feel better?"

Perhaps he was feeling his mind to discover whether anything was broken. "Yes, I think so," he said at last.

"You will. Won't you?"

"Yes."

"No hesitation. That's right. But Clive, I don't want you hesitating when you leave this office. Wait a minute." I took out my wallet. "Here's a card for a club downtown, the Sunshine Club. Say I sent you. You'll find that many of the members have been through something similar to what you've been through. It will help."

"All right," he said, frowning at the card.

"Promise me you'll go."

"I will," he promised. "You know best."

He buttoned his coat. "Will you keep the hat? No, don't keep it. Throw it away," he said with some bravado. At the door he turned and peered past me. "You never explained the spiders."

"Oh, those? Just blood."

I watched his head bob down the nine flights of stairs. Perhaps eventually he would sleep at night and go forth in the daytime, but the important adjustments had been made: he was on the way to accepting what he was. Once again I gave thanks for night shifts. I went back to my desk and tidied Bent's file. Later I might look in at the Sunshine Club, reacquaint myself with Bent and a few faces.

Then, for a moment, I felt sour fear. Bent might encounter Mullen at the club. Mullen was another who had approached me to be cured, not knowing that the only cure was death. As I recalled that Mullen had gone to Greece months before, I relaxed—for I had relieved Mullen of his fears with the same story, the raw meat and the garlic, the parents battling over the Bible. In fact it hadn't happened that way at all—my mother had caused the scene at the dining-room table and there had been a cross—but by now I was more familiar with the working version.

The cat scraped at the window. As I moved toward it, the cat's eyes slitted darkly and it tensed. I waited and then threw the window open. The cat howled and fell. Nine storeys: even a cat could scarcely survive. I stood above the lights of the city, lights clustering toward the dark horizon, and the tiny struggling red spiders streamed out from the window on threads, only to drift back and settle softly, like a rain of blood, on my face.

Down Among the Dead Men

BY GARDNER DOZOIS and JACK DANN

The inherent horrors of this setting are obvious enough; to think they could be compounded by a touch of Dark Fantasy, and by a recognition of what a human being can (and will) do when presented with the right opportunities at the right times, is not simply adding acid to the burn. This is a horror story in every sense of the word.

Gardner Dozois lives in Philadelphia, is the author of the acclaimed novel Strangers, *and has edited, with Jack Dann as well as on his own, the cream of anthologies published over the past decade. Jack Dann lives in Binghamton, New York, and is the author of such highly regarded works as* Junction *and* Timetripping; *he writes seldom, but with a power as gentle as a hammer.*

BRUCKMAN first discovered that Wernecke was a vampire when they went to the quarry that morning.

He was bending down to pick up a large rock when he thought he heard something in the gully nearby. He looked around and saw Wernecke huddled over a *Musselmann*, one of the walking dead, a new man who had not been able to wake up to the terrible reality of the camp.

"Do you need any help?" Bruckman asked Wernecke in a low voice.

Wernecke looked up, startled, and covered his mouth with his hand, as if he were signing to Bruckman to be quiet.

But Bruckman was certain that he had glimpsed blood smeared on Wernecke's mouth. "The *Musselmann*, is he alive?" Wernecke had often risked his own life to save one or another of the men in his barracks. But to risk one's life for a *Musselmann*? "What's wrong?"

"Get away."

All right, Bruckman thought. Best to leave him alone. He looked pale, perhaps it was typhus. The guards were working him hard enough, and Wernecke was older than the rest of the men in the work-gang. Let him sit for a moment and rest. But what about that blood . . . ?

"Hey, you, what are you doing?" one of the young SS guards shouted to Bruckman.

Bruckman picked up the rock and, as if he had not heard the guard, began to walk away from the gully, toward the rusty brown cart on the tracks that led back to the barbed-wire fence of the camp. He would try to draw the guard's attention away from Wernecke.

But the guard shouted at him to halt. "Were you taking a little rest, is that it?" he asked, and Bruckman tensed, ready for a beating. This guard was new, neatly and cleanly dressed—and an unknown quantity. He walked over to the gully and, seeing Wernecke and the *Musselmann*, said, "Aha, so your friend is taking care of the sick." He motioned Bruckman to follow him into the gully.

Bruckman had done the unpardonable—he had brought it on Wernecke. He swore at himself. He had been in this camp long enough to know to keep his mouth shut.

The guard kicked Wernecke sharply in the ribs. "I want you to put the *Musselmann* in the cart. Now!" He kicked Wernecke again, as if as an afterthought. Wernecke groaned, but got to his feet. "Help him put the *Musselmann* in the cart," the guard said to Bruckman; then he smiled and drew a circle in the air—the sign of smoke, the smoke which rose from the tall grey chimneys behind them. This *Musselmann* would be in the oven within an hour, his ashes soon to be floating in the hot, stale air, as if they were the very particles of his soul.

Wernecke kicked the *Musselmann*, and the guard chuckled, waved to another guard who had been watching, and stepped back a few feet. He stood with his hands on his hips. "Come on, dead man, get up or you're going to die in the oven," Wernecke whispered as he tried to pull the man to his feet. Bruckman supported the unsteady *Musselmann*, who began to wail softly. Wernecke slapped him hard. "Do you want to live, *Musselmann*? Do you want to see your family again, feel the touch of a woman, smell grass after it's been mowed?

154

Then *move.*" The *Musselmann* shambled forward between Wernecke and Bruckman. "You're dead, aren't you, *Musselmann,*" goaded Wernecke. "As dead as your father and mother, as dead as your sweet wife, if you ever had one, aren't you? Dead!"

The *Musselmann* groaned, shook his head, and whispered, "Not dead, my wife. . . ."

"Ah, it talks," Wernecke said, loud enough so the guard walking a step behind them could hear. "Do you have a name, corpse?"

"Josef, and I'm not a *Musselmann.*"

"The corpse says he's alive," Wernecke said, again loud enough for the SS guard to hear. Then in a whisper, he said, "Josef, if you're not a *Musselmann,* then you must work now, do you understand?" Josef tripped, and Bruckman caught him. "Let him be," said Wernecke. "Let him walk to the cart himself."

"Not the cart," Josef mumbled. "Not to die, not——"

"Then get down and pick up stones, show the fart-eating guard you can work."

"Can't. I'm sick, I'm. . . ."

"Musselmann!"

Josef bent down, fell to his knees, but took hold of a stone and stood up with it.

"You see," Wernecke said to the guard, "it's not dead yet. It can still work."

"I told you to carry him to the cart, didn't I," the guard said petulantly.

"Show him you can work," Wernecke said to Josef, "or you'll surely be smoke."

And Josef stumbled away from Wernecke and Bruckman, leaning forward, as if following the rock he was carrying.

"Bring him *back!*" shouted the guard, but his attention was distracted from Josef by some other prisoners, who, sensing the trouble, began to mill about. One of the other guards began to shout and kick at the men on the periphery, and the new guard joined him. For the moment, he had forgotten about Josef.

"Let's get to work, lest they notice us again," Wernecke said.

"I'm sorry that I——"

Wernecke laughed and made a fluttering gesture with his hand—

smoke rising. "It's all hazard, my friend. All luck." Again the laugh. "It was a venial sin," and his face seemed to darken. "Never do it again, though, lest I think of you as bad luck."

"Carl, are you all right?" Bruckman asked. "I noticed some blood when——"

"Do the sores on your feet bleed in the morning?" Wernecke countered angrily. Bruckman nodded, feeling foolish and embarrassed. "And so it is with my gums, now go away, unlucky one, and let me live."

They separated, and Bruckman tried to make himself invisible, tried to think himself into the rocks and sand and grit, into the choking air. He used to play this game as a child; he would close his eyes, and since *he* couldn't see anybody, he would pretend that nobody could see him. And so it was again. Pretending the guards couldn't see him was as good a way of staying alive as any.

He owed Wernecke another apology, which could not be made. He shouldn't have asked about Wernecke's sickness. It was bad luck to talk about such things. Wernecke had told him that when he, Bruckman, had first come to the barracks. If it weren't for Wernecke, who had shared his rations with Bruckman, he might well have become a *Musselmann* himself. Or dead, which was the same thing.

The day turned blisteringly hot, and guards as well as prisoners were coughing. The air was foul, the sun a smear in the heavy yellow sky. The colors were all wrong: the ash from the ovens changed the light, and they were all slowly choking on the ashes of dead friends, wives, and parents. The guards stood together quietly, talking in low voices, watching the prisoners, and there was the sense of a perverse freedom—as if both guards and prisoners had fallen out of time, as if they were all parts of the same fleshy machine.

At dusk, the guards broke the hypnosis of lifting and grunting and sweating and formed the prisoners into ranks. They marched back to the camp through the fields, beside the railroad tracks, the electrified wire, conical towers, and into the main gate of the camp.

Bruckman tried to block out a dangerous stray thought of his wife. He remembered her as if he were hallucinating: She was in his arms. The boxcar stank of sweat and feces and urine, but he had been inside it for so long that he was used to the smells. Miriam had been sleeping. Suddenly he discovered that she was dead. As he screamed, the smells of the car overpowered him, the smells of death.

Wernecke touched his arm, as if he knew, as if he could see through Bruckman's eyes. And Bruckman knew what Wernecke's eyes were saying: "Another day. We're alive. Against all the odds. We conquered death." Josef walked beside them, but he kept stumbling, as he was once again slipping back into death, becoming a *Musselmann*. Wernecke helped him walk, pushed him along. "We should let this man become dead," Wernecke said to Bruckman.

Bruckman only nodded, but he felt a chill sweep over his sweating back. He was seeing Wernecke's face again as it was for that instant in the morning. Smeared with blood.

Yes, Bruckman thought, we should let the *Musselmann* become dead. We should all be dead. . . .

Wernecke served up the lukewarm water with bits of spoiled turnip floating on the top, what passed as soup for the prisoners. Everyone sat or kneeled on the rough-planked floor, as there were no chairs.

Bruckman ate his portion, counting the sips and bites, forcing himself to take his time. Later, he would take a very small bite of the bread he had in his pocket. He always saved a small morsel of food for later—in the endless world of the camp, he had learned to give himself things to look forward to. Better to dream of bread than to get lost in the present. That was the fate of the *Musselmanner*.

But he always dreamed of food. Hunger was with him every momnt of the day and night. Those times when he actually ate were in a way the most difficult, for there was never enough to satisfy him. There was the taste of softness in his mouth, and then in an instant it was gone. The emptiness took the form of pain—it *hurt* to eat. For bread, he thought, he would have killed his father, or his wife. God forgive me, and he watched Wernecke—Wernecke, who had shared his bread with him, who had died a little so he could live. He's a better man than me, Bruckman thought.

It was dim inside the barracks. A bare lightbulb hung from the ceiling and cast sharp shadows across the cavernous rooms. Two tiers of five-foot-deep shelves ran around the room on three sides, bare wooden shelves where the men slept without blankets or mattresses.

Set high in the northern wall was a slatted window, which let in the stark white light of the kliegs. Outside, the lights turned the grounds into a deathly imitation of day; only inside the barracks was it night.

"Do you know what tonight is, my friends?" Wernecke asked. He sat in the far corner of the room with Josef, who, hour by hour, was reverting back into a *Musselmann*. Wernecke's face looked hollow and drawn in the light from the window and the lightbulb; his eyes were deep-set and his face was long with deep creases running from his nose to the corners of his thin mouth. His hair was black, and even since Bruckman had known him, quite a bit of it had fallen out. He was a very tall man, almost six foot four, and that made him stand out in a crowd, which was dangerous in a deathcamp. But Wernecke had his own secret ways of blending with the crowd, of making himself invisible.

"No, tell us what tonight is," crazy old Bohme said. That men such as Bohme could survive was a miracle—or, as Bruckman thought—a testament to men such as Wernecke who somehow found the strength to help the others live.

"It's Passover," Wernecke said.

"How does he know that?" someone mumbled, but it didn't matter how Wernecke knew because he *knew*—even if it really wasn't Passover by the calendar. In this dimly lit barracks, it *was* Passover, the feast of freedom, the time of thanksgiving.

"But how can we have Passover without a *seder?*" asked Bohme. "We don't even have any *matzoh*," he whined.

"Nor do we have candles, or a silver cup for Elijah, or the shankbone, or *haroset*—nor would I make a seder over the *traif* the Nazis are so generous in giving us," replied Wernecke with a smile. "But we can pray, can't we? And when we all get out of here, when we're in our own homes in the coming year with God's help, then we'll have twice as much food—two *afikomens*, a bottle of wine for Elijah, and the *haggadahs* that our fathers and our fathers' fathers used."

It *was* Passover.

"Isadore, do you remember the four questions?" Wernecke asked Bruckman.

And Bruckman heard himself speaking. He was twelve years old again at the long table beside his father, who sat in the seat of honor.

To sit next to him was itself an honor. "How does this night differ from all other nights? On all other nights we eat bread and *matzoh*; why on this night do we eat only *matzoh*?

"*M'a nisht'ana halylah hazeah....*"

Sleep would not come to Bruckman that night, although he was so tired that he felt as if the marrow of his bones had been limned away and replaced with lead.

He lay there in the semi-darkness, feeling his muscles ache, feeling the acid biting of his hunger. Usually he was numb enough with exhaustion that he could empty his mind, close himself down, and fall rapidly into oblivion, but not tonight. Tonight he was noticing things again, his surroundings were getting through to him again, in a way that they had not since he had been new in the camp. It was smotheringly hot, and the air was filled with the stinks of death and sweat and fever, of stale urine and drying blood. The sleepers thrashed and turned, as though they fought with sleep, and as they slept, many of them talked or muttered or screamed aloud; they lived other lives in their dreams, intensely compressed lives dreamed quickly, for soon it would be dawn, and once more they would be thrust into hell. Cramped in the midst of them, sleepers squeezed in all around him, it suddenly seemed to Bruckman that these pallid white bodies were already dead, that he was sleeping in a graveyard. Suddenly it was the boxcar again. And his wife Miriam was dead again, dead and rotting unburied....

Resolutely, Bruckman emptied his mind. He felt feverish and shaky, and wondered if the typhus were coming back, but he couldn't afford to worry about it. Those who couldn't sleep couldn't survive. Regulate your breathing, force your muscles to relax, don't think. Don't think.

For some reason, after he had managed to banish even the memory of his dead wife, he couldn't shake the image of the blood on Wernecke's mouth.

There were other images mixed in with it, Wernecke's uplifted arms and upturned face as he led them in prayer, the pale strained face of the stumbling *Musselmann*, Wernecke looking up, startled, as he crouched over Josef . . . but it was the blood to which Bruckman's feverish thoughts returned, and he pictured it again and again

159

as he lay in the rustling, fart-smelling darkness: the watery sheen of blood over Wernecke's lips, the tarry trickle of blood in the corner of his mouth, like a tiny scarlet worm. . . .

Just then a shadow crossed in front of the window, silhouetted blackly for an instant against the harsh white glare, and Bruckman knew from the shadow's height and its curious forward stoop that it was Wernecke.

Where could he be going? Sometimes a prisoner would be unable to wait until morning, when the Germans would let them out to visit the slit-trench latrine again, and would slink shamefacedly into a far corner to piss against a wall, but surely Wernecke was too much of an old hand for that. . . . Most of the prisoners slept on the sleeping platforms, especially during the cold nights when they would huddle together for warmth, but sometimes, during the hot weather, people would drift away and sleep on the floor instead; Bruckman himself had been thinking of doing that, as the jostling bodies of the sleepers around him helped to keep him from sleep. Perhaps Wernecke, who always had trouble fitting into the cramped sleeping niches, was merely looking for a place where he could lie down and stretch his legs. . . .

Then Bruckman remembered that Josef had fallen asleep in the corner of the room where Wernecke had sat and prayed, and that they had left him there alone.

Without knowing why, Bruckman found himself on his feet. As silently as the ghost he sometimes felt he was becoming, he walked across the room in the direction Wernecke had gone, not understanding what he was doing nor why he was doing it. The face of the *Musselmann*, Josef, seemed to float behind his eyes. Bruckman's feet hurt, and he knew, without looking, that they were bleeding, leaving faint tracks behind him. It was dimmer here in the far corner, away from the window, but Bruckman knew that he must be near the wall by now, and he stopped to let his eyes readjust.

When his eyes had adapted to the dimmer light, he saw Josef sitting on the floor, propped up against the wall. Wernecke was hunched over the *Musselmann*. Kissing him. One of Josef's hands was tangled in Wernecke's thinning hair.

Before Bruckman could react—such things had been known to happen once or twice before, although it shocked him deeply that

160

Wernecke would be involved in such filth—Josef released his grip on Wernecke's hair. Josef's upraised arm fell limply to the side, his hand hitting the floor with a muffled but solid impact that should have been painful—but Josef made no sound.

Wernecke straightened up and turned around. Stronger light from the high window caught him as he straightened to his full height, momentarily illuminating his face.

Wernecke's mouth was smeared with blood.

"My God!" Bruckman cried.

Startled, Wernecke flinched, then took two quick steps forward and seized Bruckman by the arm. "Quiet!" Wernecke hissed. His fingers were cold and hard.

At that moment, as though Wernecke's sudden movement were a cue, Josef began to slip down sideways along the wall. As Wernecke and Bruckman watched, both momentarily riveted by the sight, Josef toppled over to the floor, his head striking against the floorboards with a sound such as a dropped melon might make. He had made no attempt to break his fall or cushion his head, and lay now unmoving.

"My God," Bruckman said again.

"Quiet, I'll explain," Wernecke said, his lips still glazed with the *Musselmann*'s blood. "Do you want to ruin us all? For the love of God, be *quiet*."

But Bruckman had shaken free of Wernecke's grip and crossed to kneel by Josef, leaning over him as Wernecke had done, placing a hand flat on Josef's chest for a moment, then touching the side of Josef's neck. Bruckman looked slowly up at Wernecke. "He's dead," Bruckman said, more quietly.

Wernecke squatted on the other side of Josef's body, and the rest of their conversation was carried out in whispers over Josef's chest, like friends conversing at the sickbed of another friend who has finally fallen into a fitful doze.

"Yes, he's dead," Wernecke said. "He was dead yesterday, wasn't he? Today he has just stopped walking." His eyes were hidden here, in the deeper shadow nearer to the floor, but there was still enough light for Bruckman to see that Wernecke had wiped his lips clean. Or licked them clean, Bruckman thought, and felt a spasm of nausea go through him.

"But *you*," Bruckman said, haltingly. "You were. . . ."

161

"Drinking his blood?" Wernecke said. "Yes, I was drinking his blood."

Bruckman's mind was numb. He couldn't deal with this, he couldn't understand it at all. "But *why*, Eduard? Why?"

"To live, of course. Why do any of us do anything here? If I am to live, I must have blood. Without it, I'd face a death even more certain than that doled out by the Nazis."

Bruckman opened and closed his mouth, but no sound came out, as if the words he wished to speak were too jagged to fit through his throat. At last he managed to croak, "A vampire? You're a vampire? Like in the old stories?"

Wernecke said calmly, "Men would call me that." He paused, then nodded. "Yes, that's what men would call me. . . . As though they can understand something simply by giving it a name."

"But Eduard," Bruckman said weakly, almost petulantly. "The *Musselmann*. . . ."

"Remember that he *was* a *Musselmann*," Wernecke said, leaning forward and speaking more fiercely. "His strength was going, he was sinking. He would have been dead by morning, anyway. I took from him something that he no longer needed, but that I needed in order to live. Does it matter? Starving men in lifeboats have eaten the bodies of their dead companions in order to live. Is what I've done any worse than that?"

"But he didn't just die. You *killed* him. . . ."

Wernecke was silent for a moment, and then said, quietly, "What better thing could I have done for him? I won't apologize for what I do, Isadore; I do what I have to do to live. Usually I take only a little blood from a number of men, just enough to survive. And that's fair, isn't it? Haven't I given food to others, to help them survive? To *you*, Isadore? Only very rarely do I take more than a minimum from any one man, although I'm weak and hungry all the time, believe me. And never have I drained the life from someone who wished to live. Instead I've helped them fight for survival in every way I can, you know that."

He reached out as though to touch Bruckman, then thought better of it and put his hand back on his own knee. He shook his head. "But these *Musselmanner*, the ones who have given up on life, the walking dead—it is a favor to them to take them, to give them the solace of death. Can you honestly say that it is not, *here*? That it is better for them to walk around while they are dead, being beaten and abused by the Nazis until their bodies cannot go on, and then to be thrown into the ovens and burned like trash? Can you say that? Would *they* say that, if they knew what was going on? Or would they thank me?"

Wernecke suddenly stood up, and Bruckman stood up with him. As Wernecke's face came again into the stronger light, Bruckman could see that his eyes had filled with tears. "You have lived under the Nazis," Wernecke said. "Can you really call *me* a monster? Aren't I still a Jew, whatever else I might be? Aren't I *here*, in a deathcamp? Aren't I being persecuted too, as much as any other? Aren't I in as much danger as anyone else? If I'm not a Jew, then tell the Nazis—they seem to think so." He paused for a moment, and then smiled wryly. "And forget your superstitious boogey-tales. I'm no night-spirit. If I could turn myself into a bat and fly away from here, I would have done it long before now, believe me."

Bruckman smiled reflexively, then grimaced. The two men avoided each other's eyes, Bruckman looking at the floor, and there was an uneasy silence, punctuated only by the sighing and moaning of the sleepers on the other side of the cabin. Then, without looking up, in tacit surrender, Bruckman said, "What about *him*? The Nazis will find the body and cause trouble. . . ."

"Don't worry," Wernecke said. "There are no obvious marks. And nobody performs autopsies in a death camp. To the Nazis, he'll be just another Jew who has died of the heat, or from starvation or sickness, or from a broken heart."

Bruckman raised his head then and they stared eye to eye for a moment. Even knowing what he knew, Bruckman found it hard to see Wernecke as anything other than what he appeared to be: an aging, balding Jew, stooping and thin, with sad eyes and a tired, compassionate face.

"Well, then, Isadore," Wernecke said at last, matter-of-factly. "My life is in your hands. I will not be indelicate enough to remind you of how many times your life has been in mine."

Then he was gone, walking back toward the sleeping platforms, a shadow soon lost among other shadows.

Bruckman stood by himself in the gloom for a long time, and then

163

followed him. It took all of his will not to look back over his shoulder at the corner where Josef lay, and even so Bruckman imagined that he could feel Josef's dead eyes watching him reproachfully as he walked away, abandoning Josef to the cold and isolate company of the dead.

Bruckman got no more sleep that night, and in the morning, when the Nazis shattered the gray pre-dawn stillness by bursting into the shack with shouts and shrilling whistles and barking police dogs, he felt as if he were a thousand years old.

They were formed into two lines, shivering in the raw morning air, and marched off to the quarry. The clammy dawn mist had yet to burn off, and, marching through it, through a white shadowless void, with only the back of the man in front of him dimly visible, Bruckman felt more than ever like a ghost, suspended bodiless in some limbo between Heaven and Earth. Only the bite of pebbles and cinders into his raw, bleeding feet kept him anchored to the world, and he clung to the pain as a lifeline, fighting to shake off a feeling of numbness and unreality. However strange, however *outré*, the events of the previous night had *happened*. To doubt it, to wonder now if it had all been a feverish dream brought on by starvation and exhaustion, was to take the first step on the road to becoming a *Musselmann*.

Wernecke is a vampire, he told himself. That was the harsh, unyielding reality that, like the reality of the camp itself, must be faced. Was it any more surreal, any more impossible, than the nightmare around them? He must forget the tales his old grandmother had told him as a boy, "boogey-tales" as Wernecke himself had called them, half-remembered tales that turned his knees to water whenever he thought of the blood smeared on Wernecke's mouth, whenever he thought of Wernecke's eyes watching him in the dark. . . .

"Wake up, Jew!" the guard alongside him snarled, whacking him lightly on the arm with his rifle-butt. Bruckman stumbled, managed to stay upright and keep going. Yes, he thought, wake up. Wake up to the reality of this, just as you once had to wake up to the reality of the camp. It was just one more unpleasant fact he would have to adapt to, learn to deal with. . . .

164

Deal with how? he thought, and shivered.

By the time they reached the quarry, the mist had burned off, swirling past them in rags and tatters, and it was already beginning to get hot. There was Wernecke, his balding head gleaming dully in the harsh morning light. He didn't dissolve in the sunlight, there was one boogey-tale disproved. . . .

They set to work, like golems, like ragtag clockwork automatons.

Lack of sleep had drained what small reserves of strength Bruckman had, and the work was very hard for him that day. He had learned long ago all the tricks of timing and misdirection, the safe ways to snatch short moments of rest, the ways to do a minimum of work with the maximum display of effort, the ways to keep the guards from noticing you, to fade into the faceless crowd of prisoners and not be singled out, but today his head was muzzy and slow, and none of the tricks seemed to work.

His body felt like a sheet of glass, fragile, ready to shatter into dust, and the painful, arthritic slowness of his movements got him first shouted at, and then knocked down. The guard kicked him twice for good measure before he could get up.

When Bruckman had climbed back to his feet again, he saw that Wernecke was watching him, face blank, eyes expressionless, a look that could have meant anything at all.

Bruckman felt the blood trickling from the corner of his mouth and thought, *the blood . . . he's watching the blood . . .* and once again he shivered.

Somehow, Bruckman forced himself to work faster, and although his muscles blazed with pain, he wasn't hit again, and the day passed.

When they formed up to go back to the camp, Bruckman, almost unconsciously, made sure that he was in a different line from Wernecke's.

That night in the cabin, Bruckman watched as Wernecke talked with the other men, here trying to help a new man adjust to the dreadful reality of the camp, there exhorting someone who was slipping into despair to live and spite his tormentors, joking with old hands in the flat, black, bitter way that passed for humor among them, eliciting a wan smile or occasionally even a laugh from them, finally leading them all in prayer again, his strong, calm voice raised in the ancient words, giving meaning to those words again. . . .

He keeps us together, Bruckman thought, he keeps us going. Without him we wouldn't last a week. Surely that's worth a little blood, a bit from each man, not even enough to hurt. . . . Surely they wouldn't even begrudge him it, if they knew and really understood. . . . No, he *is* a good man, better than the rest of us, in spite of his terrible affliction.

Bruckman had been avoiding Wernecke's eyes, hadn't spoken to him at all that day, and suddenly he felt a wave of shame go through him at the thought of how shabbily he had been treating his friend. Yes, his friend, regardless, the man who had saved his life. . . . Deliberately, he caught Wernecke's eyes, and nodded, and then, somewhat sheepishly, smiled. After a moment, Wernecke smiled back, and Bruckman felt a spreading warmth and relief uncoil his guts. Everything was going to be all right, as all right as it could be, here. . . .

Nevertheless, as soon as the inside lights clicked off that night, and Bruckman found himself lying alone in the darkness, his flesh began to crawl.

He had been unable to keep his eyes open a moment before, but now, in the sudden darkness, he found himself tensely and tickingly awake. Where was Wernecke? What was he doing, who was he visiting tonight? Was he out there in the darkness even now, creeping closer, creeping nearer . . . ? Stop it, Bruckman told himself uneasily, forget the boogey-tales. This is your friend, a good man, not a monster. . . . But he couldn't control the fear that made the small hairs on his arms stand bristlingly erect, couldn't stop the grisly images from coming. . . .

Wernecke's eyes, gleaming in the darkness. . . . Was the blood already glistening on Wernecke's lips, as he drank . . . ? The thought of the blood staining Wernecke's yellowing teeth made Bruckman cold and nauseous, but the image that he couldn't get out of his mind tonight was an image of Josef toppling over in that sinisterly boneless way, striking his head against the floor. . . . Bruckman had seen people die in many more gruesome ways during his time at the camp, seen people shot, beaten to death, seen them die in convulsions from high fevers or cough their lungs up in bloody tatters from pneumonia, seen them hanging like charred-black scarecrows from

166

the electrified fences, seen them torn apart by dogs . . . but somehow it was Josef's soft, passive, almost restful slumping into death that bothered him. That, and the obscene limpness of Josef's limbs as he sprawled there like a discarded rag-doll, his pale and haggard face gleaming reproachfully in the dark. . . .

When Bruckman could stand it no longer, he got shakily to his feet and moved off through the shadows, once again not knowing where he was going or what he was going to do, but drawn forward by some obscure instinct he himself did not understand. This time he went cautiously, feeling his way and trying to be silent, expecting every second to see Wernecke's coal-black shadow rise up before him.

He paused, a faint noise scratching at his ears, then went on again, even more cautiously, crouching low, almost crawling across the grimy floor.

Whatever instinct had guided him—sounds heard and interpreted subliminally, perhaps?—it had timed his arrival well. Wernecke had someone down on the floor there, perhaps someone he had seized and dragged away from the huddled mass of sleepers on one of the sleeping platforms, someone from the outer edge of bodies whose presence would not be missed, or perhaps someone who had gone to sleep on the floor, seeking solitude or greater comfort.

Whoever he was, he struggled in Wernecke's grip, but Wernecke handled him easily, almost negligently, in a manner that spoke of great physical power. Bruckman could hear the man trying to scream, but Wernecke had one hand on his throat, half-throttling him, and all that would come out was a sort of whistling gasp. The man thrashed in Wernecke's hands like a kite in a child's hands flapping in the wind, and, moving deliberately, Wernecke smoothed him out like a kite, pressing him slowly flat on the floor.

Then Wernecke bent over him, and lowered his mouth to his throat.

Bruckman watched in horror, knowing that he should shout, scream, try to rouse the other prisoners, but somehow unable to move, unable to make his mouth open, his lungs pump. He was paralyzed by fear, like a rabbit in the presence of a predator, a terror sharper and more intense than any he'd ever known.

The man's struggles were growing weaker, and Wernecke must have eased up some on the throttling pressure of his hand, because the man moaned "Don't . . . please don't . . ." in a weak, slurred voice. The man had been drumming his fists against Wernecke's back and sides, but now the tempo of the drumming slowed, slowed, and then stopped, the man's arms falling laxly to the floor. "Don't . . ." the man whispered; he groaned and muttered incomprehensibly for a moment or two longer, then became silent. The silence stretched out for a minute, two, three, and Wernecke still crouched over his victim, who was now not moving at all. . . .

Wernecke stirred, a kind of shudder going through him, like a cat stretching. He stood up. His face became visible as he straightened up into the full light from the window, and there was blood on it, glistening black under the harsh glare of the kliegs. As Bruckman watched, Wernecke began to lick his lips clean, his tongue, also black in this light, sliding like some sort of sinuous ebony snake around the rim of his mouth, darting and probing for the last lingering drops. . . .

How smug he looks, Bruckman thought, like a cat who has found the cream, and the anger that flashed through him at the thought enabled him to move and speak again. "Wernecke," he said harshly.

Wernecke glanced casually in his direction. "You again, Isadore?" Wernecke said. "Don't you ever sleep?" Wernecke spoke lazily, quizically, without surprise, and Bruckman wondered if Wernecke had known all along that he was there. "Or do you just enjoy watching me?"

"Lies," Bruckman said. "You told me nothing but lies. Why did you bother?"

"You were excited," Wernecke said. "You had surprised me. It seemed best to tell you what you wanted to hear. If it satisfied you, then that was an easy solution to the problem."

" 'Never have I drained the life from someone who wanted to live,' " Bruckman said bitterly, mimicking Wernecke. " 'Only a little from each man.' My God—and I believed you! I even felt sorry for you!"

Wernecke shrugged. "Most of it *was* true. Usually I only take a little from each man, softly and carefully, so that they never know, so that in the morning they are only a little weaker than they would have been anyway. . . ."

"Like Josef?" Bruckman said angrily. "Like the poor devil you killed tonight?"

Wernecke shrugged again. "I have been careless the last few nights, I admit. But I need to build up my strength again." His eyes gleamed in the darkness. "Events are coming to a head here. Can't you feel it, Isadore, can't you sense it? Soon the war will be over, everyone knows that. Before then, this camp will be shut down, and the Nazis will move us back into the interior—either that, or kill us. I have grown weak here, and I will soon need all my strength to survive, to take whatever opportunity presents itself to escape. I *must* be ready. And so I have let myself drink deeply again, drink my fill for the first time in months. . . ." Wernecke licked his lips again, perhaps unconsciously, then smiled bleakly at Bruckman. "You don't appreciate my restraint, Isadore. You don't understand how hard it has been for me to hold back, to take only a little each night. You don't understand how much that restraint has cost me. . . ."

"You are gracious," Bruckman sneered.

Wernecke laughed. "No, but I am a rational man; I pride myself on that. You other prisoners were my only source of food, and I have had to be very careful to make sure that you would last. I have no access to the Nazis, after all. I *am* trapped here, a prisoner just like you, whatever else you may believe—and I have not only had to find ways to survive here in the camp, I have had to procure my own food as well! No shepherd has ever watched over his flock more tenderly than I."

"Is that all we are to you—sheep? Animals to be slaughtered?"

Wernecke smiled. "Precisely."

When he could control his voice enough to speak, Bruckman said, "You're worse than the Nazis."

"I hardly think so," Wernecke said quietly, and for a moment he looked tired, as though something unimaginably old and unutterly weary had looked out through his eyes. "This camp was built by the Nazis—it wasn't *my* doing. The Nazis sent you here—not I. The Nazis have tried to kill you every day since, in one way or another—and I have tried to keep you alive, even at some risk to myself. No one has more of a vested interest in the survival of his livestock than the farmer, after all, even if he does occasionally slaughter an inferior animal. I have given you food——"

"Food you had no use for yourself! You sacrificed nothing!"

"That's true, of course. But *you* needed it, remember that. Whatever my motives, I have helped you to survive here—you and many others. By doing so I also acted in my own self-interest, of course, but can you have experienced this camp and still believe in things like altruism? What difference does it make what my reason for helping was—I still helped you, didn't I?"

"Sophistries!" Bruckman said. "Rationalizations! You twist words to justify yourself, but you can't disguise what you really are—a monster!"

Wernecke smiled gently, as though Bruckman's words amused him, and made as if to pass by, but Bruckman raised an arm to bar his way. They did not touch each other, but Wernecke stopped short, and a new and quivering kind of tension sprang into existence in the air between them.

"I'll stop you," Bruckman said. "Somehow I'll stop you, I'll keep you from doing this terrible thing——"

"You'll do nothing," Wernecke said. His voice was hard and cold and flat, like a rock speaking. "What can you do? Tell the other prisoners? Who would believe you? They'd think you'd gone insane. Tell the *Nazis*, then?" Wernecke laughed harshly. "They'd think you'd gone crazy too, and they'd take you to the hospital—and I don't have to tell you what your chances of getting out of there alive are, do I? No, you'll do *nothing*."

Wernecke took a step forward; his eyes were shiny and blank and hard, like ice, like the pitiless eyes of a predatory bird, and Bruckman felt a sick rush of fear cut through his anger. Bruckman gave way, stepping backward involuntarily, and Wernecke pushed past him, seeming to brush him aside without touching him.

Once past, Wernecke turned to stare at Bruckman, and Bruckman had to summon up all the defiance that remained in him not to look uneasily away from Wernecke's agate-hard eyes. "You are the strongest and cleverest of all the other animals, Isadore," Wernecke said in a calm, conversational, almost ruminative voice. "You have been useful to me. Every shepherd needs a good sheepdog. I still need you, to help me manage the others, and to help me keep them going long enough to serve my needs. This is the reason why I have taken so much time with you, instead of just killing you outright." He shrugged. "So let us both be rational about this—you leave me alone, Isadore, and I will leave you alone also. We will stay away from each other and look after our own affairs. Yes?"

"The others. . . ." Bruckman said weakly.

"They must look after themselves," Wernecke said. He smiled, a thin and almost invisible motion of his lips. "What did I teach you, Isadore? Here everyone must look after themselves. What difference does it make what happens to the others? In a few weeks almost all of them will be dead anyway."

"You *are* a monster," Bruckman said.

"I'm not much different from you, Isadore. The strong survive, whatever the cost."

"I am *nothing* like you," Bruckman said, with loathing.

"No?" Wernecke asked, ironically, and moved away; within a few paces he was hobbling and stooping, vanishing into the shadows, once more the harmless old Jew.

Bruckman stood motionless for a moment, and then, moving slowly and reluctantly, he stepped across to where Wernecke's victim lay.

It was one of the new men Wernecke had been talking to earlier in the evening, and, of course, he was quite dead.

Shame and guilt took Bruckman then, emotions he thought he had forgotten—black and strong and bitter, they shook him by the throat the way Wernecke had shaken the new man.

Bruckman couldn't remember returning across the room to his sleeping platform, but suddenly he was there, lying on his back and staring into the stifling darkness, surrounded by the moaning, thrashing, stinking mass of sleepers. His hands were clasped protectively over his throat, although he couldn't remember putting them there, and he was shivering convulsively. How many mornings had he awoken with a dull ache in his neck, thinking it no more than the habitual body-aches and strained muscles they had all learned to take for granted? How many nights had Wernecke fed on *him*?

Every time Bruckman closed his eyes he would see Wernecke's face floating there in the luminous darkness behind his eyelids . . .

171

Wernecke with his eyes half-closed, his face vulpine and cruel and satiated . . . Wernecke's face moving closer and closer to him, his eyes opening like black pits, his lips smiling back from his teeth . . . Wernecke's lips, sticky and red with blood . . . and then Bruckman would seem to feel the wet touch of Wernecke's lips on *his* throat, feel Wernecke's teeth biting into *his* flesh, and Bruckman's eyes would fly open again. Staring into the darkness. Nothing there. Nothing there *yet*. . . .

Dawn was a dirty gray imminence against the cabin window before Bruckman could force himself to lower his shielding arms from his throat, and once again he had not slept at all.

That day's work was a nightmare of pain and exhaustion for Bruckman, harder than anything he had known since his first few days at the camp. Somehow he forced himself to get up, somehow he stumbled outside and up the path to the quarry, seeming to float along high off the ground, his head a bloated balloon, his feet a thousand miles away at the end of boneless beanstalk legs he could barely control at all. Twice he fell, and was kicked several times before he could drag himself back to his feet and lurch forward again. The sun was coming up in front of them, a hard red disk in a sickly yellow sky, and to Bruckman it seemed to be a glazed and lidless eye staring dispassionately into the world to watch them flail and struggle and die, like the eye of a scientist peering into a laboratory maze.

He watched the disk of the sun as he stumbled toward it; it seemed to bob and shimmer with every painful step, expanding, swelling and bloating until it swallowed the sky. . . .

Then he was picking up a rock, moaning with the effort, feeling the rough stone tear his hands. . . .

Reality began to slide away from Bruckman. There were long periods when the world was blank, and he would come slowly back to himself as if from a great distance, and hear his own voice speaking words that he could not understand, or keening mindlessly, or grunting in a hoarse, animalistic way, and he would find that his body was working mechanically, stooping and lifting and carrying, all without volition. . . .

A *Musselmann*, Bruckman thought, I'm becoming a *Musselmann*

. . . and felt a chill of fear sweep through him. He fought to hold onto the world, afraid that the next time he slipped away from himself he would not come back, deliberately banging his hands into the rocks, cutting himself, clearing his head with pain.

The world steadied around him. A guard shouted a hoarse admonishment at him and slapped his rifle-butt, and Bruckman forced himself to work faster, although he could not keep himself from weeping silently with the pain his movements cost him.

He discovered that Wernecke was watching him, and stared back defiantly, the bitter tears still runneling his dirty cheeks, thinking, *I won't become a* Musselmann *for you, I won't make it easy for you, I won't provide another helpless victim for you*. . . . Wernecke met Bruckman's gaze for a moment, and then shrugged and turned away.

Bruckman bent for another stone, feeling the muscles in his back crack and the pain drive in like knives. What had Wernecke been thinking, behind the blankness of his expressionless face? Had Wernecke, sensing weakness, marked Bruckman for his next victim? Had Wernecke been disappointed or dismayed by the strength of Bruckman's will to survive? Would Wernecke now settle upon someone else?

The morning passed, and Bruckman grew feverish again. He could feel the fever in his face, making his eyes feel sandy and hot, pulling the skin taut over his cheekbones, and he wondered how long he could manage to stay on his feet. To falter, to grow weak and insensible, was certain death; if the Nazis didn't kill him, Wernecke would. . . . Wernecke was out of sight now, on the other side of the quarry, but it seemed to Bruckman that Wernecke's hard and flinty eyes were everywhere, floating in the air around him, looking out momentarily from the back of a Nazi soldier's head, watching him from the dulled iron side of a quarry cart, peering at him from a dozen different angles. He bent ponderously for another rock, and when he had pried it up from the earth he found Wernecke's eyes beneath it, staring unblinkingly up at him from the damp and pallid soil. . . .

That afternoon there were great flashes of light on the eastern horizon, out across the endless flat expanse of the steppe, flares in rapid sequence that lit up the sullen gray sky, all without sound. The

Nazi guards had gathered together in a group, looking to the east and talking in subdued voices, ignoring the prisoners for the moment. For the first time Bruckman noticed how disheveled and unshaven the guards had become in the last few days, as though they had given up, as though they no longer cared. Their faces were strained and tight, and more than one of them seemed to be fascinated by the leaping fires on the distant edge of the world.

Melnick said that it was only a thunderstorm, but old Bohme said that it was an artillery battle being fought, and that that meant that the Russians were coming, that soon they would all be liberated.

Bohme grew so excited at the thought that he began shouting, "The Russians! It's the Russians! The Russians are coming to free us!" Dichstein and Melnick tried to hush him, but Bohme continued to caper and shout—doing a grotesque kind of jig while he yelled and flapped his arms—until he had attracted the attention of the guards. Infuriated, two of the guards fell upon Bohme and beat him severely, striking him with their rifle-butts with more than usual force, knocking him to the ground, continuing to flail at him and kick him while he was down, Bohme writhing like an injured worm under their stamping boots. They probably would have beaten Bohme to death on the spot, but Wernecke organized a distraction among some of the other prisoners, and when the guards moved away to deal with it, Wernecke helped Bohme to stand up and hobble away to the other side of the quarry, where the rest of the prisoners shielded him from sight with their bodies as best they could for the rest of the afternoon.

Something about the way Wernecke urged Bohme to his feet and helped him to limp and lurch away, something about the protective, possessive curve of Wernecke's arm around Bohme's shoulders, told Bruckman that Wernecke had selected his next victim.

That night Bruckman vomited up the meager and rancid meal that they were allowed, his stomach convulsing uncontrollably after the first few bites. Trembling with hunger and exhaustion and fever, he leaned against the wall and watched as Wernecke fussed over Bohme, nursing him as a man might nurse a sick child, talking gently to him, wiping away some of the blood that still oozed from the corner of Bohme's mouth, coaxing Bohme to drink a few sips of soup,

174

finally arranging that Bohme should stretch out on the floor away from the sleeping platforms, where he would not be jostled by the others. . . .

As soon as the interior lights went out that night, Bruckman got up, crossed the floor quickly and unhesitatingly, and lay down in the shadows near the spot where Bohme muttered and twitched and groaned.

Shivering, Bruckman lay in the darkness, the strong smell of earth in his nostrils, waiting for Wernecke to come. . . .

In Bruckman's hand, held close to his chest, was a spoon that had been sharpened to a jagged needle point, a spoon he had stolen and begun to sharpen while he was still in a civilian prison in Cologne, so long ago that he almost couldn't remember, scraping it back and forth against the stone wall of his cell every night for hours, managing to keep it hidden on his person during the nightmarish ride in the sweltering boxcar, the first few terrible days at the camp, telling no one about it, not even Wernecke during the months when he'd thought of Wernecke as a kind of saint, keeping it hidden long after the possibility of escape had become too remote even to fantasize about, retaining it then more as a tangible link with the daydream country of his past than as a tool he ever actually hoped to employ, cherishing it almost as a holy relic, as a remnant of a vanished world that he otherwise might almost believe had never existed at all. . . .

And now that it was time to use it at last, he was almost reluctant to do so, to soil it with another man's blood. . . .

He fingered the spoon compulsively, turning it over and over; it was hard and smooth and cold, and he clenched it as tightly as he could, trying to ignore the fine tremoring of his hands.

He had to kill Wernecke. . . .

Nausea and an odd feeling of panic flashed through Bruckman at the thought, but there was no other choice, there was no other way. . . . He couldn't go on like this, his strength was failing; Wernecke was killing him, as surely as he had killed the others, just by keeping him from sleeping. . . . And as long as Wernecke lived, he would never be safe, always there would be the chance that Wernecke would strike as soon as his guard was down. . . . Would Wernecke scruple for a second to kill *him*, after all, if he thought that he could do it safely . . . ? No, of course not. . . . Given the chance, Wernecke would kill him without a moment's further thought. . . . No, he must strike *first*. . . .

Bruckman licked his lips uneasily. Tonight. He had to kill Wernecke *tonight*. . . .

There was a stirring, a rustling: someone was getting up, working his way free from the mass of sleepers on one of the platforms. A shadowy figure crossed the room toward Bruckman, and Bruckman tensed, reflexively running his thumb along the jagged end of the spoon, readying himself to rise, to strike—but at the last second, the figure veered aside and stumbled toward another corner. There was a sound like rain drumming on cloth; the man swayed there for a moment, mumbling, and then slowly returned to his pallet, dragging his feet, as if he had pissed his very life away against the wall. It was not Wernecke.

Bruckman eased himself back down to the floor, his heart seeming to shake his wasted body back and forth with the force of its beating. His hand was damp with sweat. He wiped it against his tattered pants, and then clutched the spoon again. . . .

Time seemed to stop. Bruckman waited, stretched out along the hard floorboards, the raw wood rasping his skin, dust clogging his mouth and nose, feeling as though he were already dead, a corpse laid out in a rough pine coffin, feeling eternity pile up on his chest like heavy clots of wet black earth. . . . Outside the hut, the kliegs blazed, banishing night, abolishing it, but here inside the hut it was night, here night survived, perhaps the only pocket of night remaining on a klieg-lit planet, the shafts of light that came in through the slatted window only serving to accentuate the surrounding darkness, to make it greater and more puissant by comparison. . . . Here in the darkness, nothing ever changed . . . there was only the smothering heat, and the weight of eternal darkness, and the changeless moments that could not pass because there was nothing to differentiate them one from the other. . . .

Many times as he waited Bruckman's eyes would grow heavy and slowly close, but each time his eyes would spring open again at once, and he would find himself staring into the shadows for Wernecke. Sleep would no longer have him, it was a kingdom closed to him

176

now; it spat him out each time he tried to enter it, just as his stomach now spat out the food he placed in it. . . .

The thought of food brought Bruckman to a sharper awareness, and there in the darkness he huddled around his hunger, momentarily forgetting everything else. Never had he been so hungry. . . . He thought of the food he had wasted earlier in the evening, and only the last few shreds of his self-control kept him from moaning aloud.

Bohme did moan aloud then, as though unease were contagious. As Bruckman glanced at him, Bohme said "Anya," in a clear calm voice; he mumbled a little, and then, a bit more loudly, said, "Tseitel, have you set the table yet?" and Bruckman realized that Bohme was no longer in the camp, that Bohme was back in Dusseldorf in the tiny apartment with his fat wife and his four healthy children, and Bruckman felt a pang of envy go through him, for Bohme, who had escaped.

It was at that moment that Bruckman realized that Wernecke was standing there, just beyond Bohme.

There had been no movement that Bruckman had seen. Wernecke had seemed to slowly materialize from the darkness, atom by atom, bit by incremental bit, until at some point he had been solid enough for his presence to register on Bruckman's consciousness, so that what had been only a shadow a moment before was now suddenly and unmistakably Wernecke as well, however much a shadow it remained.

Bruckman's mouth went dry with terror, and it almost seemed that he could hear the voice of his dead grandmother whispering in his ears. Boogey-tales. . . . Wernecke had said *I'm no night-spirit.* Remember that he had said that. . . .

Wernecke was almost close enough to touch. He was staring down at Bohme; his face, lit by a dusty shaft of light from the window, was cold and remote, only the total lack of expression hinting at the passion that strained and quivered behind the mask. Slowly, lingeringly, Wernecke stooped over Bohme. "Anya," Bohme said again, caressingly, and then Wernecke's mouth was on his throat.

Let him feed, said a cold remorseless voice in Bruckman's mind. It will be easier to take him when he's nearly sated, when he's fully

177

preoccupied and growing lethargic and logy . . . growing *full*. . . .

Slowly, with infinite caution, Bruckman gathered himself to spring, watching in horror and fascination as Wernecke fed. He could hear Wernecke sucking the juice out of Bohme, as if there was not enough blood in the foolish old man to satiate him, as if there were not enough blood in the whole camp. . . . Or perhaps the whole world. . . . And now Bohme was ceasing his feeble struggling, was becoming still. . . .

Bruckman flung himself upon Wernecke, stabbing him twice in the back before his weight bowled them both over. There was a moment of confusion as they rolled and struggled together, all without sound, and then Bruckman found himself sitting atop Wernecke, Wernecke's white face turned up to him. Bruckman drove his weapon into Wernecke again, the shock of the blow jarring Bruckman's arm to the shoulder. Wernecke made no outcry; his eyes were already glazing, but they looked at Bruckman with recognition, with cold anger, with bitter irony, and, oddly, with what might have been resignation or relief, with what might almost have been pity. . . . Bruckman stabbed again and again, driving the blows home with hysterical strength, panting, rocking atop his victim, feeling Wernecke's blood spatter against his face, wrapped in the heat and steam that rose from Wernecke's torn-open body like a smothering black cloud, coughing and choking on it for a moment, feeling the steam seep in through his pores and sink deep into the marrow of his bones, feeling the world seem to pulse and simmer and change around him, as though he were suddenly seeing through new eyes, as though something had been born anew inside him, and then abruptly he was *smelling* Wernecke's blood, the hot organic reek of it, leaning closer to drink in that sudden overpowering smell, better than the smell of freshly baked bread, better than anything he could remember, rich and heady and strong beyond imagining.

There was a moment of revulsion and horror, and he had time to wonder how long the ancient contamination had been passing from man to man to man, how far into the past the chain of lives stretched, how Wernecke himself had been trapped, and then his parched lips touched wetness, and he was drinking, drinking deeply and greedily, and his mouth was filled with the strong clean taste of copper.

The Crazy Chinaman

BY JOHN COYNE

Regrets about things we've done that we ought not to have done can, if not handled properly, turn into incredible displays of breast-beating and self-pity. Guilt, whether justified or not, can be either cleansing or destructive. Both can be deadly when the object of our regret, rationally or not, doesn't want us to forget what we've done. It's one problem we couldn't run away from even if we wanted to. Especially if we wanted to.

John Coyne, one of the most gifted and literary writers among us, is the author of the bestselling novels The Piercing, The Searing, *and, most recently,* Hobgoblin. *He lives in New York, and his next novel will be called* The Shroud.

AFTERWARDS Pete wished they had never said anything to him, but of course it was too late. They had been pitching pennies at the base of the water tower when he came up, and Joe, the bigger of the two, looked around and said,

"Hi, Chinaman! Why aren't you smiling?"

Pete, the other kid, who was skinnier than the first caddy and smaller, laughed. It was a big joke among the kids.

"Why do you always call me a Chinaman?" the man asked. "I am a Filipino. Before the war my family were important people."

As he spoke, his small body trembled. He was a man in his late twenties, but the exact year was hard to determine for his face was boyish, soft looking, and the color of copper.

The two boys stared at him and then the older one said, laughing,

"Well, if you're such a big shot in the Philippines why don't you go home, 'cause you ain't nobody here."

The caddy was right. The Filipino wasn't anyone. He worked at the Club too, during the summer months when he was out of college.

179

He worked in the kitchen at night, cleaning the dishes and stoves.

The boys had seen him many times as they did today, walking alone in the late afternoon. He was always dressed in white, always walking slowly with his hand stuck in his back pockets, his face passive, his eyes down.

As the caddies kept pitching, the Filipino came over and stood for a moment watching. Then he said to Joe,

"What have I done to hurt you?"

The boy kept pitching and answered without looking at the man,

"You ain't done nothing. What are you asking a screwy question like that for?"

"Because you more than any caddy want to hurt me."

"You're crazy," Joe said. He had lost four successive times while lagging, and turning to the Filipino added, "Come on, Chinaman, leave me alone. You're bringing me bad luck."

"I am not Chinese. I am a Filipino. Now you tell me why you dislike me."

"Okay, Chinaman; I'll tell you. My old man was getting your job see, but the manager said, no we got to save it for our little Filipino. Now he ain't got no fuckin' job 'count of you."

The Filipino was silent for a moment. He stood still, his body leaning forward, staring at the ground, his hands stuck in his back pockets. Then he said,

"That is the reason?"

"Why don't you stay in your own fuckin' country?"

The Filipino did not reply, but he kept looking at the young boy. His face stayed passive. His eyes, which were small and dark, blurred briefly with tears. Then he said to the caddy, almost apologetically,

"You tell your father he can take my job. I am finished with it." He turned away from the caddies and walked toward the main country club road.

The caddies did not say anything until he was out of hearing.

"Hey, Joe," the smaller boy asked, "what's the matter with him?"

"How in the fuck should I know? That Chinaman is crazy anyway. Come on, pitch!"

The Filipino walked all the way down to the main road, then

turned and came back, and began to climb the water tower. It was only then that the two caddies again paid attention to him.

"Hey, Chinaman, whatcha doing?" Joe asked. He had stopped lagging to watch the Filipino. The man did not answer, but kept climbing, one rung at a time.

Down below, the smaller caddy asked,

"What's he gonna do, Joe?"

"How the fuck should I know?" Then to the Filipino he shouted, "Hey, Chinaman, you're going to kill yourself."

"I betcha he's gonna jump, Joe. I betcha!"

"Shut the shit up, will ya? He ain't gonna jump. Come on, pitch."

"No, I wanta see." The boy moved back from the base of the tower for a better view.

The Filipino had reached the top leg and pulled himself through the small hole in the platform that surrounded the white water tank. He stood up on the platform and looked over the rail of the hundred-foot-high tower.

The caddies noticed the sharp contrast his dark face and hands made against his white clothes and the white tank. It was when he began to walk slowly around the tank, looking out into the distance, that Joe said,

"I told you he was just lookin' around. Come on, let's go home."

"I ain't goin' anywhere, Joe, until I see if he's gonna jump."

"What difference is it of yours if some crazy Chinaman jumps? He ain't your friend."

"He'll kill himself."

"What the fuck do you care?"

The Filipino had come around to their side of the tower and was standing directly above them.

"Hey, Chinaman!" Joe yelled to him. "What are you gonna do—jump?"

The Filipino did not answer. He was leaning against the railing, his face turned upward. Everything was white, the clouds, the tank, his clothes. His tanned face and hands were the only dark splotches in the picture. Slowly he swung his left leg over the rail, and then, sitting on the rail, pulled his other leg over so that both caddies could see his legs dangling over the side.

"I told you, Joe; I told you he'd jump!" Pete was yelling, not looking away from the figure perched on the high rail. "It's your damn fault, Joe; it's your goddam fault."

"It ain't my fuckin' fault!"

"You called him a Chinaman."

"So did you, so did everyone. Don't go blaming me, man."

"Yeah, but you started it. Come on, we got to get somebody."

"Hold it; we ain't gettin' no help," Joe answered. "That's what the fuckin' Chinaman wants. As soon as we leave he'll come down. We'll get fired if we bring everyone running down here and the Chinaman is alive. That fucker!"

"You think so, Joe?"

Joe did not answer, but called out to the Filipino,

"All right, Chinaman, jump. I'll catch you. Come on. What's the matter, Chinaman, you scared?" He held out his arms.

It was then, while Joe was holding out his arms, that the figure pushed itself off, and the black and part of the white ripped from the picture, fell gracefully, slowly, arms and legs outstretched.

For a moment both caddies were stunned, then Pete jumped away and ran. It was Joe who couldn't move. His hands outstretched, he kept waiting for the falling white figure. Then at the last moment, he turned away, frightened to look, and the body hit the ground, bounced up again higher than him, and hit a second time, jerking once, and lay still.

Pete was screaming: "I told you he'd jump! I told you!"

Joe stared at the body, at the way the blood pumped from the Filipino's gaping mouth, then he ran to the man, yelling at him,

"Why did you jump? Why did you jump, you crazy Chinaman?"

The Filipino did not answer. He only rolled to his feet and climbed the tower again.

Pete screamed.

Joe stayed where he was, arms helplessly outstretched.

The Filipino jumped, and Joe missed again. And a third time, a fourth, until Pete broke and raced away, not wanting to be there when Joe finally caught him.

Gravid Babies

BY MICHAEL BISHOP

A Novel of Horrific Menace
in Considerable Synopsis

One of the most difficult feats in writing horror/terror stories is producing the desired results while, at the same time, producing a smile on the reader's face; there is, in less skilled hands than Bishop's, a tendency for the reader to walk off without realizing he's bleeding to death. A moment or two of reflection, however, is usually enough to correct that, when you realize that what you thought was funny, or amusing, is something else again.

Michael Bishop has written, in Transfigurations *and "The White Otters of Childhood," some of the most telling science fiction of the past twenty years; he has also exhibited a fondness for the macabre, with a skill that puts most of his colleagues to shame.*

CARRION CITY, COLORADO, once a boisterous gold-mining town guyed to a windy upland meadow in the Sangre de Christo Mountains, is today a ramshackle shadow of its former self. Two cafés, a feed store, a garage, a grocery, an elementary school, and three or four businesses catering to the seasonal tourist trade provide jobs for some of the locals, but since its founding in 1934, at the height of the Great Depression, the Helen Hidalgo Hutton Hospital for Advanced Lycanthropic Hebephrenia has kept Carrion City from becoming just another ghost town. Employing twenty-two of the town's residents (nearly a fifth of the entire population), this forbidding prisonlike structure attracts patients and sightseers from the world over. By late 1981, for instance, three émigré former victims

183

of LH had achieved such spectacular cures that they were permitted to meet their monthly checkups on an outpatient basis, one of them commuting all the way from Silistra, Bulgaria. Another twelve patients live right on the premises, padding the flagstone corridors barefoot, curling up together to sleep, and, during thunderstorms or blizzards, raising their eerie voices in plangent harmony with the wind. Although an important state official elected on Ronald Reagan's coattails repeatedly points out that the staff of this facility outnumbers the patients, the hospital weathers these fashionable political attacks because the contributions of cured alumni (many of whom are titled Europeans of awesome longevity and no little wealth) make it virtually self-supporting. Besides, no one—not even the perfervid Reaganite—really wants to extinguish the final *raison d'être* of Carrion City.

Mary Smithson, née Sylvester, works the night-shift at the hospital as chief psychiatric resident, a position to which she rose in only eight years. A product of Carrion City elementary, between 1968 and 1972 Mary Sylvester attended a semiprestigious medical college and psychiatric institute in Denver on a full scholarship furnished by the Helen Hidalgo Hutton Benevolent Foundation. The terms of this grant demanded that she intersperse her professional studies with a close textual scrutiny of all thirty-seven of Mrs. Hutton's published novels, at the rate of approximately a novel a month (excluding summers and preholiday examination periods). Afterward, of course, Mary was required to work at the hospital for no less than four years and to spend her free time diligently promoting the Hutton canon among the literate citizenry of the American Southwest. This latter stipulation did not fret or demoralize Mary because with the exception of *My Friend Freckles*, a maudlin dog story, she *liked* the novels —most of them nape-tickling gothics or suspenseful romances, all with a strong regional flavor—of her deceased benefactress. Her favorites, which she read over and over, were *Rebecca Random Remembers* and *The Wolves of West Elk Springs*. Although the terms of her scholarship caused her to be graduated in the lower tenth of her class, no particular stigma attached to this poor showing, as her rapid and well-deserved rise at the hospital itself vividly attests.

Russell Smithson, Mary's husband, is another case. Mary met Russell in Denver, not at school but in a grim counter-culture bistro nestled beneath a noisy overpass of I-25. This solitary young man was poring over a paperback book by candlelight, heedless of the honky-tonk plonking of a piano and the unsyncopated caterwauling of the bearded musician diddling it. Taking full advantage of the new interpersonal permissiveness, Mary sat down at the loner's table. (The book in front of Russell turned out to be Erich Segal's *Love Story*. Mary herself was carrying copies of *The Pathologic Basis of Disease* and the original 1922 edition of *The Allegiance of Alamosa Allie*.) Soon these two people, strangers only a moment past, were engaged in spirited debates about the war in Southeast Asia, abortion, the legalization of marijuana, nuclear disarmament, and the poetry of Rod McKuen. Disagreeing on almost everything, they struck sparks off each other. That Russell was an aspiring writer bowled Mary over. It excused not only his tastes in contemporary literature but also an inbred bourgeois sensibility that seemed to harken back to Calvin Coolidge. As a kind of test, Mary loaned him *The Allegiance of Alamosa Allie*, Mrs. Hutton's most impassioned feminist tract in novel form; indeed, her only one. When the couple met again a week later, Russell expressed a qualified but unquestionably sincere regard for the old gal's prose style and narrative skills. Even the "suffragettist rant and deck-stacking"—his harshest criticism of the book—had not really put him off. This news relieved and delighted Mary. Three months later they were wed, and the sacramental photographs taken in Red Rocks amphitheatre show the happy couple clad from head to foot in hand-stitched leather and Indian beads.

Today, in Carrion City, Russell is a househusband. Eighteen-month-old Tiffany, whose gestation and birth did not long remove Mary from her duties as psychiatric resident at the hospital, occupies most of Russell's time, particularly since she sleeps during the day when Mary sleeps. Russell must adhere to this same schedule or else rely on cat naps and interstitial snoozes to purge his system of the poisons of wakefulness. At night while Mary works and Tiffany toddles about the Smithsons' tiny stucco house, Russell prepares his daughter's special soybean-based formula, washes diapers, dusts and vacuums, plays with the child, and plans that day's principal meal, which the Smithsons will eat when nearly everyone else in Carrion City is sitting down to breakfast. This arrangement does not displease Russell for the telling reason that it gives him an excuse—an excuse unavailable to him between 1972 and 1980—for the conspicuous unsuccessfulness of his writing career. Moreover, it keeps him indoors sleeping when most of the inhabitants of Carrion City are maliciously abroad, ready to spring upon him, should he chance their way, a host of excruciating questions about his perennial lack of "gainful employment." Even the derelict old men and callow make-believe prospectors at the feed store have chided him about his idleness, able-bodied buck that he is. Tiffany, bless her, has put a stop to their insufferable ragging. She has allayed Russell's guilt without yet forcing him to renounce the last of his writerly hopes. The pursuit of literary riches, after all, is not finally incommensurate with the mundane responsibilties of househusbandry.

For the past eight months Russell has been taking a correspondence course from the Wealthy Ghostwriters School, Inc., of Baltimore, Maryland. (Ads for this curriculum, featuring endorsements from sought-after mercenaries who have ghosted the life stories of Hollywood celebrities, indicted politicians, and famous role-model drug addicts, regularly appear as inserts in women's magazines and weekly TV viewing guides.) Between his many household chores Russell manfully squeezes in time to work on his assignments from the school. His reading list includes the autobiographies of Benvenuto Cellini, Benjamin Franklin, Ulysses S. Grant, Vera Brittain, and Malcolm X. According to the prospectus supplied with his introductory assignments packet, the essence of good ghostwriting is the *convincing* simulation of genuine autobiography. In fact, his first task as a correspondent student required him to copy out in painstaking longhand three chapters from Rousseau's *Confessions*. Later he must pretend to be, and frame an appropriate style for, popular personalities as diverse as Mickey Mouse, Mickey Spillane, David Stockman, Yogi Berra, Paul "Bear" Bryant, Anita Bryant, Ron Ely, Ronald McDonald, and so on and so on. This is not easy. On two or three occasions Mary has come home to find Russell neglecting the preparation of dinner or even Tiffany's unchanged diaper in a manic attempt to complete one of these infuriating assignments. Understanding her husband's motivations and needs, Mary does not rebuke him. However, it pains her to discover that Russell is not above plagiarizing from *Rolling Stone* or *The National Enquirer*

186

when a deadline draws near and one of these unhappy tabloids contains material marginally applicable to his purposes. What a bounder he sometimes is.

To be truthful, though, Mary's mind is usually on her own work. The night-shift personnel at the Hutton Hospital bear an extremely taxing responsibility. As even casual students of the disease must know, victims of lycanthropic hebephrenia—especially those in its later stages—almost invariably succumb to their most radical transmogrifications between twelve midnight and an hour or so before dawn. Physicians, orderlies, nurses, and custodial help working these critical hours must frequently confront in actual fact that dread aspect of LH so persistently, and inaccurately, exploited by film makers, novelists, and the popular press. Mary Smithson has been eyeball to eyeball with the reality. As a result, she understands that, exactly like persons susceptible to epileptic seizures or hives, the victims of Chaney's Syndrome (as it is sometimes called in the literature) have a capacity for life, vocational fulfillment, and spiritual growth equal to that of any nonafflicted human being. Sensationalized images of hirsute men and women, slavering like beasts as they lope along on all fours under a full or a grossly gibbous moon, do not reflect the reality of the disease or improve the prognosis for its unfortunate sufferers. Instead such images reinforce scientifically discredited prejudices and destroy the self-esteem of the victim at a time when high self-esteem may lead to a complete recovery. Contrariwise, a poor self-image may cause an irreversible descent into a lycanthropy with no psychological dimension whatsoever. True werewolves are made rather than born, Mary often tells visiting medical personnel, and it is the greed and insensitivity of society at large that makes them. Lycanthropy in its hebephrenic manifestations, meanwhile, responds exceptionally well to professional treatment.

Mary has proof of this observation in the person of Amadeus Howell, a young Englishman who has resided in the hospital since its founding. (Records on file in the administrative offices indicate that Howell was born in London, England, on August 12, 1914, but in his human guise, to which he nowadays clings with cheering tenacity, he still looks no older than twenty.) Perhaps twice a month sudden physical lapses testify to Howell's continuing thralldom to the disease; further, his behavior in periods relatively free of lupine shapeshifting still displays a frivolous or juvenile quality owing to the persistence of his hebephrenia. Nevertheless, Mary is hopeful that judicious doses of sulfur, asafetida (vulgarly known as devil's dung), castor, and hypericum (St.-John's-wort), along with sympathetic nightly counseling, will soon enable young Howell to take advantage of the hospital's outpatient program. That he has stopped asking fatuous questions like "Can't you use a child-proof bottle cap as a contraceptive?" and "Isn't Morley Safer?" in favor of such formidable quodlibets as "Whence does evil come?" and "Wouldn't it be better for the world not to exist than for one innocent child to suffer?" strikes Mary as undeniable evidence of Howell's release-oriented improvement. That he frames these puzzlers while sniffing the gum stuck to his heel or playing a game of Donkey Kong on the Curtis Mathes in the third-floor dayroom, she reflects, simply underscores the need for a concentrated staff effort to exorcise the last vestiges of his lingering puerility. They are very close, though. Mary can almost taste their impending triumph.

In March, snow resting like cake icing on the hospital's turrets and crenelations, Russell informs Mary that the Wealthy Ghostwriters School, Inc., wants two chapters of "the autobiography of an unforgettable character"—he shows her this phrase on the assignment sheet—by the end of April. Students who fail to submit at least ten thousand words of acceptable material risk either outright termination or a tuition increase, probably the latter. The Smithsons cannot afford another jump in Russell's tuition. His most recent correspondence work has prompted not only riotous blue-penciling from the graders in Baltimore but also a deluge of interdelineated sarcasm. Russell has tried to console himself with the fact that worst hit by these criticisms are the passages cribbed verbatim from tabloids, but his morale continues to sink and Mary fears for his mental and emotional stability. "How am I going to do *this* assignment when even finger exercises like impersonating Alexander Haig throw me for a loop?" Russell wants to know. A *loup-garou*, thinks Mary, unable to divorce her husband's tiresome crisis from her own professional considerations; this thought, in turn, brings to mind the case and countenance of Amadeus Howell. When Russell asks, "Where am I going to find an unforgettable character whose autobiography I can ghost?" Mary cannot prevent herself from suggesting her premier patient as a likely subject. Russell oozes gratitude and enthusiasm in approximately equal measures. Like Studs Terkel, he intends to tape-record his subject's testimony. Then he will conscientiously transcribe Asmodeus's story for immediate mailing to Baltimore. Once again, he confesses, his wife has saved him from almost certain failure. "It's not Asmodeus," she replies, nervously second-guessing herself. "It's Amadeus."

The interviews at the hospital begin well enough. While Mary selflessly diverts her energies to other patients, Amadeus speaks into her husband's recorder at encouraging length. Unfortunately, Mary has neglected to tell Russell that Amadeus suffers not only from Chaney's Syndrome but also from a variety of sporadic alexithymia that sometimes renders his verbal narratives tedious in the extreme; where other people would color their recountings of formative episodes with remembered angst or joy, Amadeus merely enumerates and drones. One night, in fact, he avoids any discussion of his past to relate in painful, repetitive detail the plot of a Helen Hidalgo Hutton novel entitled *The Valiant Vargamors of Tall Pine Valley*, the book in which Mrs. Hutton found a cathartic outlet for some of her own recurring experiences with LH. Russell squirms. Mary has always circumvented the problem of young Howell's alexithymia by recourse to insult-confrontation techniques, but, ignorant of these, Russell later accuses her of attempting to sabotage his correspondence work by setting him up with a congenital bore. Worse, he must take Tiffany along to the interviews, and the child is growing increasingly restive sitting on the flagstones stacking her plastic doughnuts on their plastic obelisk. Mary soothes her husband with explanations and a heartfelt appeal to try again. Two nights later, while pacing back and forth reciting the utterly fascinating particulars of his early years in Soho, Amadeus begins to undergo the startling change quintessentially characteristic of Chaney's Syndrome. Hollywood special effects cannot hold a candle to the sweat-inducing actuality of this transformation. Tiffany's eyes bulge like burn blisters, and Russell hurriedly scribbles notes even as he attempts to watch every evanescent flicker of this rare anatomical phenomenon. Tonight the physical as well as the psychic dam has burst, and Russell believes that *The Autobiography of Amadeus Howell* is going to catapult him to the very top of his correspondence class.

"Nice doggy," says Tiffany as Amadeus strides past her stack of plastic doughnuts. The werewolf is mouthing what Russell assumes to be a continuation of his life story. Whines and vaguely quizzical growls must now carry the major burden of this account, however, and these are pretty much unintelligible. "Nice doggy," Tiff reiterates, touching the man-animal's silver-gray shoulder. Amadeus does indeed appear to be a nice doggy; the movements of his svelte but powerful body reassure rather than threaten, and the caterpillar patches of shocking white fur above his opalescent eyes give him a look of comical bewilderment, rather like a scholarly gentleman with his eyebrows raised. (His clothes lie in rumpled piles about the room. How he shed them without rending them or revealing a delinquent patch of human skin Russell does not know.) As Amadeus playfully nuzzles Tiffany, Russell shuts off the tape recorder to watch. Apparently the hebephrenic aspects of the disease become more pronounced in its manifest lupine phase, for the man-animal has begun to leap about like a puppy. He snatches up one of Tiffany's plastic doughnuts and flings it high into the air. For some unaccountable reason this trick so distresses the child that when her playmate lunges to seize another of her toys, she takes two handsful of his luxuriant fur and administers a vicious bite to his flank. (Even two floors away Mary can hear Amadeus howl.) The werewolf spins, nips Tiff on the bottom lip, and rushes toward Russell as if to knock him to the floor. Instead he bolts down the corridor and into the concealing bowels of the building, the child's outraged wail pursuing him like one of the Eumenides. Mary, stricken with contradictory varieties of remorse, puts an end to Russell's visitation privileges. At least, she consoles herself, their baby's werewolf bite is nothing much to remark, a mere pale hickey.

Successive events crowd and jostle one another. Russell sequesters himself away from wife and daughter and completes his make-or-break assignment in an angry forty-eight-hour burst. Then, on Sunday night, he declares that from now on he is going to adopt a more conventional schedule; to accommodate it, Tiff must begin attending Willa Clanahan's Lucy van Pelt Day Nursery for Precious Preschoolers, a low-budget neighborhood institution with an enrollment of (plus or minus) eight. If the graders in Baltimore flag the first two chapters of *The Autobiography of Amadeus Howell*, he intends to abandon the quest for literary notoriety and to dip into their meager savings to open a gun shop in Jim Rawley's moribund Timberline Café. Mary, hoping against hope that his graders maintain their cynically high standards, acquiesces. That Russell has threatened to embark upon a nine-to-five business career, even the operation of a gun shop, cheers her long-suffering soul. Although she could write a horror novel about the decade over which she has lent him her emotional or financial support, Russell probably could not. Postcards ordinarily exaust his talent as well as his stamina, his recent creative binge notwithstanding. Her own talent and stamina, meanwhile, must go toward rescuing Amadeus Howell from the disastrous setback occasioned by Russell and Tiffany's joint presence in his room. Since the incident he has grown snappish, remote, and even sillier than usual; indeed, over the weekend he has suffered two more lupine metamorphoses, and on her Monday shift Mary finds him wearing a flea collar along with the designer choke chain that another staff member gave him for Christmas. So virulent is the residual frivolity plaguing him that each time Mary questions him, he responds with a snippet of ungrammatical lyrics from a mid-1960s hit by Sam the Sham and the Pharaohs. Later, on her coffee break, she must struggle to keep from crying.

Tiffany's first week at Willa Clanahan's does not go well, either. She has had no experience playing with other children, and the toddlers at the Lucy van Pelt Day Nursery compose an aggressive, headstrong lot. Russell, ensconced before the game shows and soap operas on the television set, takes a string of telephone calls from Mrs. Clanahan about his daughter's bossiness, selfishness, and highhanded refusals to compromise with her other "babies," whose seniority Tiffany has no inclination to acknowledge much less respect. "Tie her to a chair in the kitchen," Russell advises Mrs. Clanahan. "I will not," the put-upon woman declares, ringing off. But she calls back late in the afternoon to report that Tiff has inaugurated the vile strategy of going from child to child and biting each one on his or her dimpled thigh or elbow, whichever anatomical target is more accessible. After inflicting these wounds, she throws back her head and howls rather sweetly at the Tiffany lamp in the den. "I thought I'd tie her to a chair in the kitchen," Mrs. Clanahan admits. Russell replies, "Go right ahead." On Friday, this drastic precautionary measure carried over, reluctantly, from the previous afternoon, Mrs. Clanahan telephones to discuss Tiff's anomalous behavior at lunch; the child will not drink her milk or eat her chicken sandwich, insisting instead on such exotic fare as Ovaltine-laced sarsaparilla and leftover three-bean salad. "Is it okay to give her such things?" Mrs. Clanahan inquires. "Go right ahead," Russell replies. "So long as it isn't poisoned coyote bait, I don't give a damn *what* you feed her." Mrs. Clanahan disapproves of this crass sentiment, but she generously indulges Tiffany's whim. Kids are her principal kick in life.

On Saturday morning the child is dreadfully ill. Russell imputes responsibility to Mrs. Clanahan, but Mary, just home from another bad night at the hospital, carefully examines her daughter and identifies the trouble as, dear God, morning sickness. For a moment both parents stand tremulously aghast before the heartstopping monstrousness of this possibility. What a perverse, repugnant, thoroughly evil and unthinkable contingency. "It's Jim Rawley's little boy, Sean," Russell eventually blurts. "I've *never* trusted that sneaky kid, but, mark my words, I'm going to see that he does the honorable thing!" Mary, another suspicion in mind, prevents her husband from pursuing this course by suggesting that they take Tiff to the hospital for more conclusive tests. The rabbit dies. Home again, they make their daughter as comfortable as possible and find themselves confronting a bizarre set of uniformly odious options. (Parenting in the final fifth of the twentieth century poses challenges altogether unimaginable to mothers and fathers of previous generations.) A little over a week later, however, the Smithsons have company in their misery, for Mrs. Clanahan, something of an expert on pregnancy and childbirth, has independently deduced that four of Tiffany's little classmates undoubtedly share her delicate condition. In Carrion City news of this spectacular sort gets around fast. And when Mary confides in her husband that Amadeus Howell may be directly, albeit inadvertently, responsible for Tiff's present troubles, and therefore indirectly answerable for the epidemic at the Lucy van Pelt Day Nursery, Russell gleefully spreads this word, too, with the result that soon the entire town is ablaze with talk of a werewolfing attack on the Helen Hidalgo Hutton Hospital for Advanced Lycanthropic Hebephrenia. That the daughters of men may suffer no further indignity, monsters must die. . . .

In the lovely April evening that Russell Smithson, Jim Rawley, and their many macho cohorts assemble their front-wheel-drive pickups at Sam Kelsall's feed store, here to load their shotguns, check out their spotlights, and bolster one another's fidgety courage, Mary carries Tiffany to the hospital to warn Amadeus Howell and the other inmates to escape. She also places a long-distance call to the highway-patrol headquarters in Pueblo, Colorado, three hours away on the sagebrush-punctuated western periphery of the Great Plains. Will representatives of the patrol arrive in time to beard the male townsfolk at their ill-organized vigilantism? No. But by the time of the actual assault every last one of the bewildered hebephrenics has already fled. Amadeus, honorary president of their Fenris Society, leads the other patients up into the snow-mantled peaks of the Sangre de Cristo range. (Slavering like beasts, they lope along on all fours under a gibbous moon.) Meanwhile, Russell and his revengeful henchmen, unaware that Mary and Tiffany are huddling inside the building, blast away at the walls with buckshot and mull the various methods by which they might be able to burn the hospital to the ground. They know in their bones that at this point in the proceedings a conflagration is obligatory, but no one has yet determined how to set the bleak, imposing structure afire. Burnt-out matches litter the roadside, and the aroma of randomly splashed gasohol emanates in waves from the building's foundations. Mrs. Hutton's institution will not catch. Finally, sirens screaming, four state patrol cars come hot-rodding into Carrion City. Almost simultaneously Mary appears on the battlements with Tiffany in her arms, an Ophelia-esque madonna high above the shameful anarchy of the townsfolk. Abashed by this brave and melancholy show, Russell borrows a bullhorn and begins to talk Mary down by reciting from long-repressed memory the entire first part of Allen Ginsberg's "Howl." Twenty minutes before he has finished, the state troopers and Russell's colleagues-in-arms have all departed for home. The siege is over. The Smithsons are reunited. But at what cost?

Patientless, the hospital must temporarily close its doors and release its staff. Mary, more fortunate than most, receives an interim appoinment (salaried) to the board of the Helen Hidalgo Hutton Benevolent Foundation. Soon thereafter Russell learns that on the basis of his first two chapters an agent of the Wealthy Ghostwriters

School, Inc. has negotiated a six-figure advance from a reputable New York publishing house for *The Autobiography of Amadeus Howell*, which will be marketed as a novel. He has eighteen months in which to deliver the finished manuscript. Mary disguises her chagrin as best she can. Elated but calculating, Russell hires a light aircraft and the services of an experienced bush pilot to help him find the absconded patients, among whom resides the only living being who can bring his incomplete narrative to a fitting and truthful end. During the third week of Russell's absence (his search has not gone well at all), Tiffany is delivered of three tiny malamute puppies with endearing cream-colored eyebrows. Struggling to preserve her optimism, Mary reflects that at least she and Russell will not have to buy the child a dog. A week later Tiffany's four playmates from Mrs. Clanahan's undergo equally unnerving parturitions, and in the best pioneer tradition neighbor rallies around neighbor to reassure and console. (There is some discreet but sanguine speculation that perhaps one day these canine children will repopulate the hospital.) Russell eventually limps home without having found Amadeus or any other member of the Fenris Society. Mary can tell that he is going to be a lousy grandfather. He begins talking about using the pups as sled-dogs, once they acquire sufficient weight and strength to aid him in his pursuit of their absent sire. Snarling, the bravest of the pups bites Russell on the ankle. Mary intervenes to save her grandchild's hide. Later that night she lies beside her unsuspecting husband thinking of Amadeus Howell and his lairlike hideaway on the icy steeps. Certain passages in *The Wolves of West Elk Springs* seem to have prefigured this portentous moment. There is a flutter in her stomach. It is terrifyingly difficult not to giggle. . . .

The Chair

BY DENNIS ETCHISON

*It isn't always necessary (or always right) to use the bound-
aries of Dark Fantasy to exercise one's fear; there is certainly
enough of it to go around in the so-called real world—that
one there, outside your door. It's the easy way out, however,
to spend time on a mass murderer or a psychotic sniper, or a
suddenly snapped veteran of one war or another; it's much
more difficult to use an ordinary person—like you, for example—and explore the very real possibility that no one, not any
one, is permanently rational. Think about it—there are a lot
of people out there, smiling.*

*Dennis Etchison is the premier short story writer in Dark
Fantasy, and his first collection has just been published. He
lives in California, and is the winner of the 1982 British Fantasy Award.*

"MARTY," she said, "I need you."

He studied the lips. The air was opalescent with cigarette smoke,
the lights too far away to make it easy. Her complexion was smooth
and taut; a faint bloom of perspiration glittered in the shadows below her cheekbones. It was impossible, of course. And yet . . .

"*Christy?*" he said, incredulous.

He wanted to reach out and touch her to be sure. At the same time
he was seized by a desperate impulse to leave his chair and run:
between tables to the bar, even to the dance floor where faces he
seemed to know had been grafted onto bodies he would never recognize, bodies that now gyrated feverishly to music he thought he had
forgotten long ago.

"I've been looking for you all night," she said. "I——I was afraid
you wouldn't come." He heard her voice masked by the noise, as
though through a wind tunnel. "Can we go somewhere? We can't
talk here."

Martin rose uncertainly and followed. The crowd surged. Her

form grew smaller and was lost to him. He threaded a path between abandoned chairs, his arm brushing a table, upsetting a half-finished glass of wine. A red blot spread across the white linen. He righted the empty glass and tried to move on.

A powerful hand stopped his wrist.

"Didn't think you'd get away that easy, did you?"

Martin looked up. A smudged copy of a face from his childhood towered over him. Around the eyes grainy skin crinkled in amusement, emphasizing preternaturally blue contact lenses.

"Bill Crabbe," said the tall man expectantly.

Martin gaped. It was true. Crabbe, the baseball star from high school. Martin shook his hand.

"How ya doin', buddy?" Crabbe pumped his arm. "My gosh, Jerry Marber! You're sure lookin' good. What you been doin' with yourself all these years?"

Martin realized he had been mistaken for someone else.

He considered correcting the tall man. At that moment there was a pause in the music and hyperventilating couples pressed back between the wooden pillars to their banquet tables. An intoxicating cloud of hair spray and cologne blew over him. He gazed through the crowd to the polished walls and round windows, searching for Christy's face. He cleared his throat.

"Excuse me, Jer," said Crabbe abruptly, "but there's Wayne Fuller. I gotta say hi. My gosh, look at him. He hasn't changed a bit, has he? Old Wayne. Hey, over here!"

Crabbe moved on, paddling against the throng with his big pitcher's hand outstretched.

Martin spotted an exit. Christy or someone very much like her was leaning against the lacquered door, trying to light a cigarette while her eyes grew whiter, sweeping the ballroom.

For me, he thought. She's waiting for me, even after so many years. I should have known. I should have kept the faith. Well, maybe I have without realizing it.

We'll find out now, won't we?

Couples swept past in a frenzied rush. The room seemed to tilt as bodies hurried to one side. The backs of men with polyester suits and indeterminate waistlines bobbed six deep in front of the cash bar. Martin took a deep breath. He felt drunk. He steadied himself against a chair and aimed for the other side.

"Jimmy!" called a booming voice.

He pressed on through louvers of crepe paper strung from the bandstand, a wall of voices closing in. Heads streaked with graying sideburns and permanent wave curls blocked his way. When they moved aside, he noticed that Christy was gone from the doorway.

"Jimmy Madden! Knew it was you!"

The gravel voice of a bull-necked football coach boomed again. This time it jarred him to a standstill.

Martin turned and was confronted by a short-sleeved sport shirt, the same print he remembered from school. He scrutinized the face above and nodded, smiling impatiently.

What was the coach's name?

Then he realized it was not the coach's face, after all. It was War-rick. Mark Warrick, once star lineman for the Greenworth Buck-skins. He had made it to the state play-offs, if Martin remembered correctly.

"Nice to see you, Mark," said Martin reflexively. "Only I'm not . . ."

A sweet-smelling woman disengaged from the pack and took pos-session of Martin's left arm. He felt her breast push into his side.

"Gail!" said Warrick. His lantern jaw dropped open and uneven teeth shone there wetly. "Are you still with Bob? I mean——"

"Not for a year-and-a-half," announced Gail. She kneaded Mar-tin's forearm as if measuring it. "And how are you, Joe?"

The man in the sport shirt plowed ahead. "Guess what, Gail? I'm Head Coach at GHS now. Did you hear? Uh, are you, I mean, did you come alone?"

She said, "Don't I see your wife, Mark? That sweet little thing over there in the corner, waiting for someone to ask her to dance? What *was* her name?"

Martin was aware of the underwiring of her bra prying his ribs apart. She turned on him again, inches away, and blinked into his eyes from beneath lids heavy with raccoon mascara.

"Joe Ivy. Did you know that I used to have the most humongous crush on you?"

"Yes," said Martin hurriedly. "No. I didn't. I don't. That is, it isn't me. I'm not really here."

He disembraced and tripped forward, wrinkling someone's satin. The exit still appeared the length of a football field away, as if seen through the small end of a telescope. He jostled wrists and left ice cubes clinking thickly in plastic cocktail tumblers, and made a final run for the deck and the night outside.

He was chilled by the sudden touch of a harbor breeze on his neck.

He did not slow until he had gone all the way astern on the Promenade Deck, where he leaned back on his elbows and allowed the image of the Windsor Room to recede into a frame of brass portholes and freshly painted guardrails.

The doorway to the ballroom remained open, throwing a rectangle of yellow light onto the boards below the main mast. Through the doorway he made out a hand-lettered streamer of bunting on the aft wall, above the bar. WELCOME GREENWORTH HIGH SCHOOL CLASS OF '62, it read, 20 YEAR REUNION.

She stepped in front of him, eying him in the old way. Behind her head a warm glow caught her hair. He tried to read her expression, but in the backlight there was no clue. He sought for the right way to begin again. He straightened, his body inching involuntarily closer to her, and the spill of warmth diminished to a sliver and faded as the exit door whispered shut. A round of whooping applause rose up inside as a toast was made onstage, and then the door sealed and there was only the rhythm of a drumroll to blend with the lapping of dark waters that rocked the bulkhead almost imperceptibly beneath his feet.

He wanted to make up for so much lost time, to force her to a confrontation so long in the coming, to send bolts of blue fire shimmering over her and down her throat. Instead he said, "Christy."

She dropped her cigarette, and a wind swirled it away in a vortex of sparks.

"I want to know," he said, "how it's been for you. I want to know it all. Or whatever you want to tell. If you can tell me. You know you can. Christy." He held out his hand.

She lowered her eyes and fumbled for another cigarette.

"I'm glad everything worked out for you and Sherman," he lied.

He almost gagged on the name. It was the first time he had said it or even allowed himself to think it for perhaps fifteen years. Sherman the loser, the guy who never had any friends. Till Martin came along and tried to help. In the end, Martin learned about helping too much. . . .

Your move, he thought, afraid to think any further. Tell me that it's dead between you, that it always was. Tell me that you haven't changed, and make me believe that I haven't, either. Do it. Do it now, or stay out of the rest of my life.

She was suddenly shy, unable to look at him. "I don't know how to——"

"Begin anywhere."

He waited.

A solitary pleasure craft passed in the bay, its running lights obscured for seconds at a time by the massive rigging of the deck upon which he and Christy stood.

"You always hated him, didn't you." She said it oddly, as if to reassure herself. As if the idea gave her some kind of satisfaction.

"What does it matter?"

"I think it does. That's why I came."

That's why? he thought, growing more disoriented by the minute. Well, if she wants to explain, she's certainly taken her time about it.

As if I care. As if it makes any difference now.

I was never angry at her. Hurt, yes. And confused. *I would have married you myself, did you know that?* But angry? I could never let myself feel that, and now it's part of another life, what happened then. One thing is certain: she can't speak for him, Iago in a crew-neck sweater. She couldn't then and she can't now. He had a chance, once, to face me. He didn't. And now it's too late.

"Forget it," he said. "Things happen. Even among friends. Especially among the best of friends."

Her eyes lifted and glared, pinwheels in the centers.

"You were always so damned forgiving. Do me a favor, Marty. Stop being so understanding! You know you hate him. Admit it."

Was she daring him? He could not imagine why. What would be the point?

"Christy, I meant what I said. I want to know that you're happy. That's all. If you don't believe that, then you never really knew me."

"But I do know you. That's why, Marty. That's why I need you now."

Her voice softened and the years disappeared like wildflowers over the hills. He remembered or imagined her, he did not know which, sprawled across his lap, curled against his chest. So many nights . . .

"Marty."

Then, just as unexpectedly, he was snapped back to the present as her tone tightened again in a rising glissando of barely suppressed emotion.

He began to doubt himself. Had it been his fault, then? Some incident he had conveniently forgotten all this time which had sent her packing and into Sherman's arms? Had he somehow misremembered for so long what happened that night? Was that possible?

Marty. Only she had ever called him that. Perhaps no one else ever would, no matter how many more years were left to him.

She moved her body until they were close enough to touch, and yet they were not touching. He was aware of the heat radiating from her skin, trembling the taut membrane of his clothing. The scent of her burned his nostrils. He forced himself to breathe.

"Marty," she said. A single strand of hair, invisible as a spider's web, touched his cheek. "Do I have to beg? *I need you.*"

She told him it was five minutes away. Whether it was more or less than that he did not notice.

Behind them the Queen Mary's raked funnels, piped in red and black and towering like the truncated stacks of a nuclear power plant, gave the converted liner an illusion of movement, as if the ship had docked there only temporarily and was even now pulling up anchor to pace the car out of the old Naval Yard and around the misty intersections of the coastline.

She looked at him once as a blurred refinery passed outside, but she was not seeing him. The plume of an endless fire licked the sky, the natural gas burnoff of a pipeline to the center of the earth. She was seeing through him, a translucent X-ray of his flesh and bones in position there against the glass where she had arranged for it to be.

A sign with the words DE LUXE APARTMENTS swam into view.

She turned past it, again, then fine-tuned the wheel at the end of a cul-de-sac behind the building and parked beneath power lines that crackled as if underwater.

It was one of those courtyard blocks that dead-end at the ocean, where accelerated disrepair is rationalized as quaint because there is nowhere left to move once one has reached the edge of the continent.

The headlights clicked off and the fog stopped swirling. A steady corona encircled a streetlamp like a halo around the moon. The pulse of the motor was replaced by the breathing of an unseen tide.

She leaned across him. Against his will his fingers curved to receive her.

"Wait," she said. "We're almost there. God, I've waited so long for this. You don't know."

She retrieved her purse from behind the seat, put away her keys and swung out of the car.

Their footsteps clacked on the sidewalk. A rusty tricycle like a twisted spider littered a shadowy yard. Somewhere television voices were muffled by flickering blue window shades. A cat cried from a hidden place with the voice of a human baby. They climbed steps to the second floor. The corroded screen door creaked with the sound of a fingernail on a blackboard. A deadbolt lock glistened under the scratchings of her key.

"Here. We won't need the lights."

She led him into darkness. A soft cushion met the backs of his legs.

The room took on dim form. Gradually black oblongs of furniture appeared around him, only to dissolve when looked at too closely. Through a doorway, in the cavern of another room, the constant eye of a pilot flame burned coolly beneath a gas appliance of unknown shape.

Seconds passed.

Stray light began to creep in from the courtyard outside, so that the indistinct plane of slatted window blinds cast the suggestion of bars over his hands.

He smelled an old perfume, and then she was gliding down and down next to him in the overstuffed chair. He heard the whisper of her stockings, her body as it moved in her clothing.

201

"Christy . . ."

She stopped his mouth with cold fingers. He saw the glint of her eyes as they focused past him.

"What?" he asked.

"Shh."

He followed her gaze across the room.

A thin strip of light glowed beneath a door at the end of a hallway.

Was someone else here?

Not *him*. Surely she wouldn't have——

A child, then. Why not?

Of course there would have been a child for them. It was only natural. Why hadn't he expected it?

Still the thought took him by surprise, even unnerved him. How old? he wondered. How long after she left him had——?

But no. He put that possibility from his mind.

He touched her awkwardly, unsure of the moment.

She moved her head from side to side, and her lips brushed his. They were, he thought, as cool and dry as desert flowers.

"No," she said hoarsely. "Later. I promise. But first there's something you have to do."

"Wait," he said, realizing where he was and what he was doing. "You've got me wrong. I didn't come here to . . ."

"Didn't you?" She blinked at him. Was she mocking him? She was, he decided. She was.

She rose, pulling him out of the chair. In spite of himself his body strained after her.

An afterimage of her crossed the room.

He heard a knocking.

She was standing at the end of the hall, in front of the closed door.

He followed as, on the other side, a shadow passed across the crack of light.

Something moved. Something heavy.

There was a jangling of keys, and the door opened.

Martin was momentarily blinded by a flood of light. When his eyes were able to adjust, he saw the figure of a man before him.

"Honey," she said, "I——I've brought someone home for you."

The figure stood so stiffly for so long that Martin began to wonder if it might be a manikin. Finally he detected movement in the eyes, tiny dots peering out of tunneled sockets. Then the shoulders slumped, the low bulk shuffling aside, the thinning spikes of uncombed hair vibrating in the flare of a dozen or more high-intensity light bulbs which were plugged into every corner of the small room.

She fidgeted, her tone winding up like a violin string again.

"You remember Jack, don't you?"

Her eyes darted nervously between them. The irises were closed down to pinpoints. He could not help but notice now a fine webbing of lines etched around her eyes, radiating outward, imprinted there as if by years of squinting under a merciless sun The pupils were washed out like a faded photograph.

"Don't you, Sherm?" she said.

Martin stared at her.

What the hell is she doing? he thought. What kind of sick game is this?

The man in the bedroom smoothed his hair and rubbed his soft hands over his white face, and straightened.

Martin had no choice. He stepped over the threshold.

There was a closeness in the air, a sickly-sweet incense that was a mixture of old clothes and unchanged bedding and slow currents of exhaled air circulating and recirculating above overheated lamps. The man made an effort to draw himself up to his full height, and Martin was overcome with disbelief.

He remembered Sherman as several inches taller, his own height exactly, in fact. But it was as if the frame had contracted with time, the spine settling, the posture folding in on itself to support so much sagging flesh. Martin tried to believe his eyes.

Often lately he had found himself wondering what a man his own age was supposed to look like. As a point of reference he had hoped to identify at least one passing on the streets. But he had never been sure.

Now he knew.

A shudder crept up his spine and over his scalp.

And then something which had once seemed so important left him with an inner shrugging that was like a sea change, a great burden lifting and departing in a flash. His eyes stung.

He glanced back and saw that Christy was no longer there.

"Jack," said Sherman tightly. It was Sherman, all right. "Jack Martin. We have a lot to talk about. We must have. Sit down. Won't you. Jack."

The son of a bitch, thought Martin. The poor, tired, worn-out, sorry son of a bitch. The years with her, years that were supposed to have been mine, and look, just look what they've done for him.

And, thinking that, so much hate went—somewhere. Anywhere. Receding into the white light, going, and gone. All at once he felt himself very old, like everyone else a victim of unforeseeable circumstance. Like the ones back on the hotel liner, the rest of his classmates. They were no longer so very strange, were they? And neither was this man. This old friend. It was true, wasn't it?

It was. And there was nothing he could do about it.

He sat.

"I reckon you heard. About me and Chris getting married."

"Yes," said Martin.

Sherman lowered himself gingerly into a straight-backed chair.

Martin noted that the room was nearly bare, with no concessions to comfort. Everything in sight had been painted in blacks and whites. There was a collection of FBI "wanted" posters framed plainly on the walls; he recognized the faces of a kidnapped heiress and a famous Black radical teacher; another, that of a square-jawed young man with rimless glasses and a doomed, defiant expression, eluded him. Somewhere a simple electric clock ground through its endless cycle.

"So. How the hell are you, Jack?"

Spare me, he thought. Spare us both. And yet how else to get through this conversation?

"Can't complain." Quickly Martin acted to forestall the inevitable personal histories. "Say, what's with all the lights?" It was a reasonable enough question. He really did want to know. "Not running scared of the dark in your old age, are you, man?"

It was also at least half a joke, but that part of it didn't work.

Sherman regarded him with detachment, jingling an oversized key-ring. On a shelf behind him two miniature armies of historical foot-soldiers collected dust on a board, eternally poised to relive some long-forgotten battle.

"Yeah, well. Guess you could say I got my fill of dark places in the Corps, know what I mean?"

At some point down the years Martin had allowed a single bit of information about Sherman to enter his consciousness: that he had served in some branch of the armed forces. Enlisted, he seemed to recall.

"Marines?" he asked.

"Army Corps of Engineers. They had me doing field work in New Mexico. You know what a spelunker is, Jack?" He said it with a trace of pride.

"I think so." Martin racked his brain. "You mean you made maps of caves, that sort of thing?"

Sherman nodded. "Carlsbad was blacker'n the place where the Devil throws his old razor blades."

"Ah." That explained it, then. After a fashion. He guessed. "So. What have you been up to since?"

"Well, there was Chris to consider, of course." Of course. "I needed something with, you know, more of an opportunity for advancement."

"Right."

What's a former spelunker to do? wondered Martin. It seemed absurd. But then what did not? For the life of him he could not think of an appropriate follow-up occupation. Indeed he could not even imagine making a living by crawling around caves with a flash-light and a notebook.

It takes all kinds, he thought. And, really, was it any more ridiculous than the way he himself had found? Yes, he thought, it takes all kinds. Any way is good enough to make what people mean when they point at something and call it a life. Who am I to judge?

"So," Sherman was saying, "I went into a career in law enforcement."

What else? thought Martin. Why not? For those who like that sort of thing, well, I'd have to say that's more or less just the sort of thing they would like. Right?

"After I graduated from Texas A & M, a buddy of mine got me an in with the Department of Corrections. I had it all planned out. I was going to work my way up through the system—they start you out as a jailer no matter where you train—and then transfer back here. It was as good a place as any to start."

"Beats Terminal Island, eh?" He didn't know what else to say.

"Yeah. That was what I thought. Till those bastards got hold of me."

Martin drew a blank.

Sherman sat forward on his chair, his eyes bulging. "They took thirteen hostages."

"They did?"

"Yeah. When it was over, two of us got out alive."

Martin shook his head. "I'm sorry," was all he could come up with. "I didn't know."

I still don't, he thought. Some kind of prison riot, was that what Sherman was talking about? There had been the one at Attica, others. Quite a few others. He couldn't remember the names of the institutions. He didn't want to ask.

"You know what those bastards did?"

Martin held up his hand. "No, I don't, but . . ."

"They did *things* to us." Sherman was shaking with rage. "Things that shouldn't happen to any man."

He was not talking it out. He was reliving it.

Martin wondered if it would ever be over for him. The answer was clear enough. It was written there in the man's twisted face.

Martin wanted to help but for some reason resisted the impulse. Besides, he asked himself, what was there to do?

"I'm not the man I was, Jack. Not the man she married. I'm just not the same. You know?"

Martin nodded, embarrassed.

"I wanted to go back in and get every one of them. With my bare hands. The State swore they'd do it for me. But they didn't do the job right."

Martin squirmed. The heavy wooden chair was beginning to wear through the seat of his pants. It certainly had not been designed for extended use.

206

"Things have changed a lot since then," Sherman was saying.

Martin was developing a splitting headache. The small, severe room with its pounding lights was becoming oppressive. He wished for Christy to return and lead him out. He had done what she asked. He had faced Sherman, or had allowed Sherman to face him, for whatever it was worth.

"I'll make it right again, Jack. What we're going to have is another kind of revolution in this country. And it starts right here."

"Let it go, man," said Martin gently. His throat was dry. He swallowed wih pain. "Life's too short."

"Yeah." Sherman jerked his pale hand to indicate a neat stack of books next to the toy soldiers. "That's why I'm ready."

Martin sat forward, eager for an excuse to shift his weight from the punishing seat. He shielded his eyes. The titles on the nearest spines shimmered into legibility. *Crime and Punishment in America. A New Handbook of Hanging. History of the Guillotine. Executions USA.*

"They'll be out in a few years," said Sherman, "if they aren't already. I know they'll find me. They always have. And when they come for me this time, I'll be waiting."

The nearest light bulb sang with current, electrifying the air.

Martin became aware of a feeling he had suppressed all night. It was that tingling you begin to register when you know something is terribly wrong but you don't quite know what it is yet. It was here, not only inside him but all around him, prickling his legs like pins and needles. That he could not name it made it no less real. He could ignore it no longer.

He saw the other man as if for the first time.

Martin flexed his legs and started out of the chair.

The pale man was on his feet. In one quick step he was standing over Martin.

He reached around the chair.

Martin looked down.

A strap dropped from under the armrest and buckled over his wrist, cinching it to the chair. First one wrist, then the other. He watched. It might have been happening to someone else.

Sherman swayed over him, his breath sour, light coruscating

through the filaments of his hair. Then he doubled over in a bowing motion. Martin heard the ringing of another buckle, another as straps closed over his ankles.

"What . . . ?" he began.

"You want to know what this is, Jack? Look over there."

The framed face of the sullen young man wavered on the wall alongside the other posters. The thick bifocals, the defiant sneer, the 'fifties haircut . . .

"That," said Sherman, "is the Bantam Red Head himself. Old Dead Eye, they called him. One of the worst bastards who ever lived. He blew away eleven people before they got him. But they got him good, didn't they? June 25th, 1959, the basement of the Nebraska State Penitentiary. It was painted white. Just for him. Charlie Starkweather. You've heard the name?"

Martin listened to Sherman's flat, expressionless voice as the blood pounded in his ears.

"And this is what they used. That buddy of mine, he let me know when they retired it. Had it shipped out piece by piece, just for me." Sherman patted the high backrest proudly. "Charlie Starkweather's chair. The same one, by God. And now it's mine."

Martin felt himself trapped in a nightmare from which he could not awaken.

"Why?"

Sherman's face split in a tortured smile. "Twenty-two hundred volts, that's why. I had to wire this room special. Still, if I don't turn off these lights, every fuse in the building will blow."

He wagged his head with satisfaction.

"I read everything there is to know about it. First the body turns red, then black. If you leave it on long enough. The brain cooks hard as an egg and the blood burns down to charcoal. Never fails. It never has yet, and they used it twelve times. Fast and clean, you know. It does the job right—takes care of a lot of paying back. In less than sixty seconds."

With a casual motion Sherman turned off the first light.

"But *why*?" said Martin. "Why are you doing this?"

Sherman shuffled to the next light.

"Who knows why anything ends up the way it does, Jack? If I'd

208

never met you. If I'd never met Chris. If I'd never gone to work where I did. A whole lot of ifs. If you hadn't treated her like you did."

He switched off another lamp.

"If you hadn't let me marry her."

Click.

Martin strained against the straps. The leather cut into his wrists.

Click.

"You might say those are the mystery parts, I guess. But I know one thing. I'm going to start living in my own house justified. And that's a fact."

Click.

A growing darkness spread as Sherman spoke from the shrinking, impenetrable depths of the room. Martin was nearly blind, the ghosts of the lamps burned into the backs of his eyes. He arched his body and slammed his head into the backboard. But the straps held.

Sherman hesitated by the last lamp. His silhouette blazed in bas-relief.

Then he reached into a fuse box by the door.

Martin's heart was ready to burst out of his chest.

Sherman lowered his hand. He relaxed and slumped against the white wall. His eyes twinkled out of the shadows.

"Anyway. You get the picture. That's the way it'll happen. When it happens."

He wheezed, his body rocking with compressed laughter.

"See how easy it is? No matter what time of the day or night they come for me, I won't have anything to worry about. Will I, Jack?"

He lumbered back toward Martin.

With a flick of his fingers he released Martin's arms. As he knelt before the chair and unstrapped the legs, he raised his chalky face.

"Well," he asked, "what do you think of my little demonstration?"

Slowly, very slowly Martin raised himself. Though his legs would not work properly, he dragged himself to the door. He said nothing. There was nothing to say.

One by one Sherman switched the lights back on. The bulbs shivered to life with a faint high-frequency whine.

Martin swung one foot over the threshold behind him, into the waiting blackness of the hallway.

Sherman collapsed wearily into the big chair. It was larger than Martin had realized, made of heavy boards bolted together in a grotesque, inhuman design. The weight of it, the edges and the extreme angles gave it the appearance of a malevolent throne.

Sherman rested easily in it. As if his body had molded itself to the rigid contours, the unyielding angles with years of practice. As if he belonged there.

"Anyway," he said. "It was nice to see you. Jack."

Already his voice was withdrawing, slipping away.

"Stop by again. Anytime. Bring a friend. I don't go out much anymore. Inside, outside. What's the difference? It's all the same. Isn't it."

He sighed, his cracking voice barely audible.

"They should have finished me off," he added, "when they had the chance."

On the wall, close to the door jamb, was the power box. The cover was open, a gleaming switch inside waiting to be thrown. Martin measured its proximity to his hand.

Maybe I'd be doing him a favor, he thought. Maybe I'd be doing us all a favor. I couldn't have known that until I saw. For one shining moment I actually thought that I could forgive him and everything would be all right. But now that's asking too much. How can there be forgiveness for the unforgiving? His judgment will have to come from someone stronger than myself.

There was a movement behind him.

"*You can do it.*"

The words were whispered directly into his ear by a voice at least as detached and bloodless as Sherman's.

"You know you can!" she hissed. "You've always hated him. Admit it! It will make you free. It will make us both free. You'll see! It will——"

Her tone was seductive, excessively reasonable. The sound of it was almost cruel. The words were almost kind.

Martin met her eyes.

Her face was no more than an inch away. It glimmered there, half in darkness and half in the synthetic light, a film of excitement giving off an unnatural redolence. Her breath was hot, passionate at last. A rising pulse raced through the vein at her throat.

It was, he decided, a face he no longer knew.

"I——I can't do it myself. I'm not strong enough. But you! You can. You know you can. And then——"

He lurched past her and plunged into total darkness.

As Martin stepped out of the cab, an enclosed boarding ramp pointed the way up to the Queen Mary Hilton's foredecks and tiered rooms like a tunnel leading him back into the heart of a sleeping juggernaut.

Despite the hour, the parking lot contained the cars of several hundred late visitors, scattered in irregular rows beneath the mercury vapor security lamps. Surely at least some of the cars belonged to diehard members of the reunion party.

He mounted the ramp and headed for the escalators.

The Windsor Room was deserted, the celebration's tattered paper decorations fluttering in the updraft of an unseen air conditioner. The foyer was still furnished with a makeshift horseshoe of card tables draped in white linen and marked by hand-drawn arrows and directions for registration. On the table table labeled "J thru N," a stack of unclaimed name badges reclined among pencils and straight pins, already gathering dust.

A reflection of the bay outside rippled across the ornate ceiling, creating an impression that the entire deck lay submerged beneath the waters of the harbor. At the end of one of the connecting corridors an electric floor polisher whirred on through the night; the sound seemed to be coming from more than one direction at once.

Martin walked through the hall to the damp Promenade Deck, but there was no one in sight.

He turned up his collar and left the area.

He searched long passageways of locked staterooms from which no sound could be heard. An occasional room service tray blocked his path, littered with half-eaten snacks or the remains of party setups. Once he saw a cart loaded with dirty glasses and buckets of drained champagne bottles. He hesitated by the door. There was a DO NOT DISTURB warning hung on the knob and no light or movement was detectable within, only the low drone of a fitful snoring.

He moved on.

As he approached the lounge at the end of the ship, he heard the cacophony of cheap disco music overlaid with raucous voices and the chiming of glasses raised in desperate celebration.

He rounded the last corner and stood watching. Inside, men in wrinkle-proof suits and women in stiff gowns and uncomfortable shoes lifted a last round under the patient eyes of a half-dozen weary cocktail waitresses.

He came to the carpeted entrance.

"I'm sorry, sir," said a young woman, "but we've already had last call. The coffee shop is still open if you'd care to——"

"Hey, Macklin!"

"Thats fine," said Martin. "It's all right. I'm looking for some-one."

"Jim Macklin!" A man with a loose tie tipped his glass from a table by the window.

"Excuse me," Martin told the waitress. "I think I see him now."

He dodged barstools. As he neared the window, a hand from an adjoining table clamped over his wrist.

"Where you goin', Jer?" It was Crabbe, the baseball star. "Take a load off and pull up a chair."

"Thanks, I . . ."

"Bill, I think you've had one too many," said a woman with a beehive hairdo. "This here's Dave McClay. I'd know him anywhere."

The man at the window table leaned close. "Aren't you Jim Mack-lin? I could've sworn——"

"What are you talking about?" said a man with thinning hair. "I'd know my old friend Marston anywhere! Remember how we used to go toolin' around at night, up by the graveyard where——"

"Hello," said Martin. "I don't mean to intrude on your party."

A waitress appeared carrying the bar tab on a platter.

"What you drinkin'?" asked Crabbe.

"Sorry, folks, the bar's closed."

"Boo!"

"What time is it? It can't be that——"

"Come up to my room," said the man at the window table. "I got a suite for the weekend. Had to fly all the way from Salt Lake City and——"

"And boy are your arms tired!" said the woman with the beehive hairdo.

They all had a good laugh over that.

On the way out, Martin said to the baseball player, "Do you remember a guy in our class named Sherman?"

"Sherman," said Crabbe. He navigated the barstools uncertainly. "Oh, sure! That jack-off? Everybody on the team hated his guts. Aw, is he here tonight?"

"Not exactly," said Martin.

They arrived at the elevator.

"Let's have a *real* party," said one of the women. She tried to punch the call button and missed.

"Old Sherman," said Crabbe thoughtfully. "Christ, the only party he ever got invited to was on April Fool's Day." He shook his head. "What a dork!"

"Where?' said the woman.

"He couldn't make it tonight," said Martin.

The elevator opened and the others maneuvered to find places inside. Martin took Crabbe's arm and held him aside.

"He wanted to come," said Martin, "but he's got a bit of a problem. At home. You know? I was thinking. You might be able to do something for him. Kind of lend him a hand, so to speak."

"That creep." Crabbe spat on the floor. "I always wanted to kick that son of a bitch's ass around the corner."

"Believe me," said Martin, "I know what you mean."

The elevator door was closing.

"Are you guys coming with us or not?" asked the drunken woman.

"We'll be up later," said Martin, "to celebrate."

"Don't start without me!" yelled Crabbe.

He was too far gone to resist. Martin steered him toward the lobby, measuring his words.

"It's not far," he said. "I stopped by myself a little while ago."

They were coming up on the main exit, the ramp to the parking lot and the profound darkness outside.

"He's just the same as he used to be," Martin was saying, "only worse. If you know what I mean."

They stood together on the doormat and the panels slid away before them onto the waiting night.

"Say, listen, Bill. I really think you might be able to do him a big favor. Not to mention me. And yourself. If you've got a few minutes. I can show you the way."

A line of cabs hovered at the curb.

"I was wondering. Do you feel like driving? Or," suggested Martin, "would it be quicker to take a cab?"

Crabbe regained his footing and weaver forward, allowing Martin to let him continue.

A moment later they were speeding away, red taillights disappearing in the mist, and the fog settled like rain all around where they had been, closing over the lot and the ship and the rest of the world.

The Typewriter

BY DAVID MORRELL

There have been lots of stories about the machine, and there will probably be lots more as writers try to figure out why and how they do what they do. A touch of humor is added to this one, but it's only a camouflage for what lies beneath—much like walking across a room whose floor is covered with balloons, but balloons filled with rusty razors. It might also be said that the profession involved here does not have to be writing.

David Morrell, a professor at the University of Iowa, is the author of The Totem, First Blood, *and, most recently,* Blood Oath. *He is known not only for his perceptions of fear, but also for his admirable ability to suit style to story.*

ERIC tingled as if he'd touched a faulty lightswitch or stepped on a snake. His spine felt cold. He shuddered.

He'd been looking for a kitchen chair. His old one—and the adjective was accurate—in fact, his *only* kitchen chair had been destroyed last night, crushed to splinters by a drunken hefty poetess who'd lost her balance and collapsed. In candor, "poetess" was far too kind a word for her. Disgustingly commercial, she'd insulted Eric's Greenwich Village party guests with verses about cats and rain and harbor lights—"I hear your sights. I see your sounds."—a female Rod McKuen. *Dreadful*, Eric had concluded, cringing with embarrassment.

His literary parties set a standard, after all; he had his reputation to protect. The Subway Press had just released his latest book of stories, *After Birth*. The title's punning resonance had seemed pure genius to him. Then too, he wrote his monthly column for the *Village Mind*, reviewing metafiction and post-modern surreal prose. So when this poetaster had arrived without an invitation to his party,

Eric almost had instructed her to leave. The obese editor from *Village Mind* had brought her, though, and Eric sacrificed his standards for the sake of tact and the continuation of his column. In the strained dry coughing that resulted from her reading, Eric had majestically arisen from his tattered cushion on the floor and salvaged the occasion by reciting his story, "Bird Dung." But when he later gaped in horror at the wreckage of his only kitchen chair, he realized how wrong he'd been to go against his principles.

The junk shop was a block away, below the Square and near the College. "Junk" described it perfectly. The students bought their beds and tables from the wizened man who owned the place. But sometimes, lost among the junk, there were some bargains, and, more crucial, he didn't have much choice. In truth, his stories earned him next to nothing. He survived by selling T-shirts outside movies and by handouts from his mother.

From the glaring humid sunlight, Eric stepped inside the junk shop.

"Something for you?" the wrinkled owner asked.

Sweating, he said aloofly, "Maybe. I'm just browsing."

"Suit yourself, my friend." The old man sucked a quarter-inch of cigarette. His yellow fingernails needed clipping. He squinted at a race-track form.

The room was long and narrow, cluttered maze-like with the detritus of poor sad people's failure. Here, a shattered mirror on a bureau. There, a musty mattress. While the sunlight fought to reach the room's back reaches, Eric groped to find his way.

He touched a grimy coffee table with its legs splayed. It sat on a sofa split obscenely down the middle. Dirty foam bulged, powdery, disintegrating. Pungent odors flared his nostrils.

Kitchen tables. Even one stained kitchen sink. But he found no kitchen chair.

He braved the farthest corners of the maze. Tripping over a lamp cord, he fell hard against a listing dresser. As he rubbed his aching side and felt the shroud-like cobwebs tickling his cheeks, he faced a mouldy pile of *Liberty*, *Colliers*, and *Post* and saw a low squat bulky object almost hidden in the shadows. That was when he shuddered, as if he'd touched a spider's nest or heard a skeleton's rattle.

The thing was worse than ugly. It revolted him. All those knobs and ridges, curlicues and levers. What use could they serve? They were a grotesque demonstration of bad taste, as if its owner had decided that the basic model needed decoration and had welded all this extra metal onto it. A crazed machinist's imitation of kinetic art. Abysmal, he thought. The thing must weigh two hundred pounds. Who'd ever want to type on such a monster?

But his mind began associating. Baudelaire. *Les Fleurs du Mal.* And Oscar Wilde, and Aubrey Beardsley. Yes, *The Yellow Book*!

He suddenly felt inspired. An ugly typewriter. He grinned despite the icy shiver down his spine. Deliciously, he savored what his friends would say if he displayed it. He'd tell them he'd decided to continue Baudelaire's tradition. He'd be decadent. He'd be outrageous. Evil stories from an evil typewriter. He'd maybe even start a trend.

"How much for this monstrosity?" he asked casually.

"Eh? What?" the junk man said.

"This clunker here. This mutilated typewriter."

"Oh, that," the old man said. His skin was sallow; his hair looked like the cobwebs Eric stood among. "You mean that priceless irreplaceable antique."

"No. I mean this contorted piece of garbage."

The old man considered him, then nodded grimly. "Forty bucks."

"But that's outrageous! Ten at most!"

"No, forty. And it's not outrageous, pal. It's business. That fool thing's been on my hands for over twenty years. I never should have bought it, but it came with lots of good stuff, and the owners wouldn't split the package. Twenty bucks. Two bucks a year for taking space. I'm being generous. I ought to charge a hundred. Lord, I hate that damn fool thing."

"Then you should pay me just to get it out of here."

"And I should go on welfare. But I don't. The price is forty. Just today. For you. A steal. Tomorrow it goes up to fifty."

Pulling out a creaky battered drawer, the old man reached in his desk and lit another quarter-inch of cigarette.

Though Eric was tall and good-looking, he was also quite thin. An artist ought to look ascetic, he told himself, though in truth he didn't have much choice. His emaciation wasn't only for effect. It was also his penance, the result of starvation. Art paid little, he'd discovered. If you told the truth, you weren't rewarded. How could he expect the System to encourage deviant opinions?

His apartment was only a block away, but it seemed a mile. He struggled with his purchase. His thin body ached as he zig-zagged, gasping. Knobs jabbed his ribs, and levers poked his armpits. His knees bent. His wrists strained at their sockets. God Almighty, he thought, why did I buy this thing? It doesn't weigh two hundred pounds. It weighs a ton.

And ugly! Oh, good Lord, the thing was ugly! In the harsh cruel glare of day, it looked even worse than he'd imagined. If that junk man turned his lights on for a change, his customers could see what they were buying. What a fool I've been, he thought. I ought to go back and make him refund my money. But behind the old man's counter, there'd been a sign. The old man had emphatically read it: ALL SALES FINAL.

He sweated up the bird-dunged steps to his apartment building. "Tenement" was more accurate. The cracked front door had a broken lock. Inside, plaster dangled from the ceiling; paint peeled from the walls. The floor heaved; the stairway sagged; the bannister listed. What a dump, he thought. The cabbage smell overwhelmed him; onions, and a more pervasive odor that reminded him of urine.

He trudged up the stairs. The old boards creaked and bent. He feared they'd snap from the weight he carried. He'd fall through. The whole debilitated building might topple on him. Three flights. Four. Mount Everest was probably easier. Four juvenile delinquents —rapists, car thieves, muggers, he suspected—snickered at him as they left an apartment. One of the old winos on the stairs shook his head at him, dismayed.

At last he lurched up to the seventh floor but nearly fell back down. He fought for balance as he struggled down the hall, his thin legs wobbling. He groaned, not just from his painful burden but as well from what he saw.

A man was pounding angrily on Eric's door: the landlord, "Hard-ass" Simmons, though the nickname wasn't apt because his rear looked like two massive globs of Jello quivering when he walked. He had a beer gut and a whisker-stubbled face. His lips looked like two worms.

As Eric stopped, surprised, he nearly lost his grip on the ugly awkward typewriter. He cringed and turned to go back down the stairs.

But Simmons pounded on the door again. Pivoting his beefy hips disgustedly, he saw his quarry in the hall. "So there you are." He aimed a finger, gunlike.

"Mr. Simmons. Why, how nice to see you."

"Crap. Believe me, it's not mutual. I want to see your money."

Eric mouthed the word as if he didn't know what "money" meant.

"The rent," the landlord said. "What you forget to pay me every month. The dough. The cash. The bucks."

"Oh, that. But I already gave it to you."

Simmons glowered. "In the Stone Age. I don't run a charity. You owe me three months rent."

"My mother's awfully sick. I had to give her money for the doctor bills."

"Don't hand me that. The only time you see your mother is when you go crawling to beg her for a loan. If I was you, I'd find a way to make a living."

"Mr. Simmons, please, I'll get the money."

"When?"

"Two weeks. I only need two weeks. I've got some *Star Wars* T-shirts I can sell."

"You'd better, or you'll know what outer space is. It's the street. I'll sacrifice the three months rent you owe me for the pleasure of evicting you."

"I promise. I've got a paycheck coming for the column I write."

Simmons snorted. "Writer. That's a laugh. If you're so hot a writer, explain to me why you're not rich. And what's that ugly thing you're holding? Jesus, I hate to look at it. You must've found it in the garbage."

"No, I bought it." He straightened, proud, indignant. Then the thing seemed twice as heavy, and he stooped. "I needed a new typewriter."

"You're dumber than I thought. You mean you bought that piece of junk instead of paying me the rent? I ought to kick you out of here right now. Two weeks. You'd better have the money, or you'll do your typing in the gutter."

Simmons waddled past. He lumbered down the creaky stairs. "A writer. What a joke. And I'm the King of England. Arthur Hailey. He's a writer. Harold Robbins. *He's* a writer. Judith Krantz and Sidney Sheldon. *You*, my friend, you're just a bum."

As Eric listened to the booming laughter gradually go dimmer down the creaky stairs, he chose between a clever answer and the need to set his burden down. His aching arms were more persuasive. Angry, he unlocked the door. Embarrassed, he stared at his purchase. Well, I can't just leave it in the hall, he thought. He nearly sprained his back to lift the thing. He trundled in and kicked the door shut. He surveyed his living room. The dingy furniture reminded him of where he'd bought the stuff—that junk shop. What a mess I'm in, he told himself. He didn't know where he could get the rent. He doubted his mother would lend him further money. Last time, at her penthouse on Fifth Avenue, she'd been angry with him.

"Your impractical romantic image of the struggling starving artist. . . . Eric, how did I go wrong?" she'd asked. "I spoiled you. That must be it. I gave you everything. You're not a youngster now. You're thirty-five. You've got to be responsible. You've got to find a job."

"And be *exploited*?" he had replied, aghast. "*Debased*? The capitalistic system is *degenerate*."

She'd shaken her head and tisk-tisk-tisked in disappointment. "But that system is the source of what I lend you. If your father came back from that boardroom in the sky and saw how you've turned out, he'd drop dead from another heart attack. I've not been fair. My analyst says I'm restricting your development. The fledgling has to learn to fly, he says. I've got to force you from the nest. You'll get no further money."

He sighed now as he lugged the grotesque massive typewriter across the living room and set it on the chipped discolored kitchen counter. He'd have set it on the table, but he knew the table would collapse from all the weight. Even so, the counter groaned, and he held his breath. When the counter stopped protesting, he exhaled.

He watched the drip-drip-drip of water from the rusty kitchen tap. He glanced up at the noisy kitchen clock which, though he frequently reset it, always was half an hour fast. Subtracting from the time on the clock, he guessed at half past one. A little early for a drink, but I've got a good excuse, he told himself. A *lot* of good excuses. Bourbon, ice, and water. Fattening, but better than beer. He drank it in three swallows, gasping from the warmth that surged toward his complaining empty stomach.

Well, there's nothing here to eat, he told himself and poured another drink. This albatross took all the money I'd saved for food. He felt like kicking it, but since it wasn't on the floor, instead he slammed it with his hand. And nearly broke his fingers. Dancing around the room, clutching his hand, he winced and cursed. To calm himself, he poured more bourbon.

Christ, my column's due tomorrow, and I haven't even started it. If I don't meet my deadline, I'll lose the only steady job I've got.

Exasperated, he hurried toward the living room where his old, faithful, manual Olympia waited on its desk-like altar opposite the door, the first thing people saw when they came in. This morning he'd tried to start the column, but distracted by his broken kitchen chair, he hadn't been able to find the words. Indeed, distraction from his work was common with him.

Now again he faced the blank page staring up at him. Again his mind blocked, and no words came. He sweated more profusely, straining to think. Another drink would help. He went back to the kitchen for his glass. He tensely lit a cigarette. No words. That's always been my problem. Desperately he gulped the bourbon. Art was painful. If he didn't suffer, then his work would have no value. Joyce had suffered. Kafka. Mann. The agony of greatness.

In the kitchen, he felt the liquor start to work on him. The light dimmed, and the room appeared to tilt. His cheeks felt numb. He rubbed his awkward fingers through his thick blond neck-long hair and peered disgustedly at the thing on the kitchen counter. "You," he said. "I'll bet your keys don't even work." He grabbed a sheet of paper. "There." He turned the roller, and surprisingly it fed the paper smoothly. "Well, at least you're not an absolute disaster." He drank more bourbon, lit another cigarette.

His column didn't interest him. No matter how he tried, he couldn't think of any theories about modern fiction. He could think only about his situation, what would happen in two weeks when Simmons came to get the rent. "It isn't fair. The System's against me."

Suddenly he felt inspired. He'd write a story. He'd tell the world exactly what he thought about it. He already knew the title. Just four letters. And he typed them: *Scum*.

The keys moved easier than he'd expected. Smoothly. Slickly. But as gratified as he felt, he was also distinctly puzzled—for the keys typed longer than was necessary.

His lips felt thick. His tongue felt sluggish from the bourbon as he leaned down to see what kind of imprint the old ribbon had made. He blinked. He leaned much closer. He'd typed *Scum*, but what he read was *Fletcher's Cove*.

He frowned, astonished. Had he drunk so much he couldn't control his typing? Were his bourbon-awkward fingers hitting keys merely at random? No, for if he typed at random, he ought to be reading gibberish, and *Fletcher's Cove*, though the words weren't what he'd intended, wasn't gibberish.

My mind, he told himself, it's playing tricks. I think I'm typing one thing, but unconsciously I'm typing something else. The bourbon's confusing me.

To test his theory, he concentrated to uncloud his mind and make his fingers more alert. Certain he'd be typing what he wanted, he hit several keys. The letters clattered toward the paper, taking the exact amount of time they should have. He'd meant to type *a story*, but as he breathed quickly, frowning toward the paper, what he read was something else: *a novel*.

He gaped. He knew he hadn't written that. Besides, he'd always written stories. He'd never tried—he didn't have the discipline—to write a novel. What the hell was going on? In frustration, he quickly typed, *The quick brown fox jumped over the lazy dog*.

But this is what he read: *The town of Fletcher's Cove had managed to survive, as it had always managed to survive, the fierce Atlantic winter.*

He felt that awful tingle again. Like ice against his spine, it made him shiver. This is crazy, he thought. I've never heard of Fletcher's Cove, and that redundant clause, it's horrible. It's decoration, gingerbread.

Appalled, he struck the keys repeatedly, at frenzied random, hoping to read nonsense, praying he hadn't lost his mind.

Instead of nonsense, though, he saw these words: *The townsfolk*

222

were as rugged as the harsh New England coastline. They had char-
acters of granite, able to withstand the punishments of nature, as if
they had learned the techniques of survival from the sturdy rocks
along the shore, impervious to tidal onslaughts.

He flinched. He knew he hadn't typed those words. What's more,
he never could have *forced* himself to type them. They were terrible.
Redundancy was everywhere, and Lord, those strained commercial
images. The sentences were hack work, typical of gushy hideous
bestsellers.

Anger seized him. He typed frantically, determined to discover
what was happening. His writer's block had disappeared. The no-
tion of bestsellers had inspired him to write a column, scorning the
outrageous decadence of fiction that was cynically designed to pan-
der to the basest common taste.

But what he read was something different. *Deep December snows*
enshrouded Fletcher's Cove. The land lay dormant, frozen. January.
February. The townsfolk huddled, imprisoned near the stove and
hearth inside their homes. They scanned the too-familiar faces of
their forced companions. While the savage wind howled past their
bedroom windows, wives and husbands soon grew bored with one
another. March came with its early thaw. Then April, and the land
became alive again. But as the warm spring air rekindled nature, so
within the citizens of Fletcher's Cove, strong passions smoldered.

Eric stumbled toward the bourbon. This time he ignored the glass
and drank straight from the bottle. He shook, feeling nauseous. He
felt scared to death.

The tasteless bourbon dribbled from his numb dense lips. His
mind spun. He clutched the kitchen counter for support. In his de-
lirium, he thought of only three conclusions. One, he'd gone insane.
Two, he was so drunk that, like the wino on the stairs, he was hallucinating. Three, the hardest to accept, this wasn't an ordinary typewriter.

The way it looks should tell you that.

Good God.

The telephone's harsh ring jolted him. He nearly slipped from the
counter. Fighting for balance, he teetered toward the living room.
The phone was one more thing he would soon lose, he thought. For

two months, he'd failed to pay the phone bill. The way his life was going, he suspected that this call was from the company, telling him it was canceling his service.

Eric fumbled to pick up the phone. He hesitantly said, "Hello," but those two syllables slurred, combining as one. ". . . Lo," he said and then repeated in confusion. ". . . Lo?"

"Is that you, Eric?" a man's loud nasal voice told him. "You sound different. Are you sick? You've got a cold?" The editor of *Village Mind*.

"No, I was working on my column," Eric said, attempting to control the drunken thickness in his voice. "The phone surprised me."

"On your column? Eric, I could break this to you gently, but I know you're strong enough to take it on the chin. Forget about your column. I won't need it."

"What? You're canceling my——" Startled, Eric felt his heart skip. He abruptly turned cold sober.

"Hey, not just your column. Everything. The *Village Mind* is folding. It's kaput. It's bankrupt. Hell, why beat around the bush? It's broke."

His editor's cliches had always bothered Eric, but now he felt too stunned to be offended. "Broke?" Stark terror flooded through him.

"Absolutely busted. See, the IRS won't let me write the magazine off. They insist it's a tax dodge, not a business."

"Fascists!"

"To be honest, Eric, they're right. It *is* a tax dodge. You should see the way I juggle my accounts."

Now he was completely certain he'd gone insane. He couldn't actually be hearing this. The *Village Mind* a fraud, a con game? "You can't be serious!"

"Hey, Eric, look, don't take this hard, huh? Nothing personal. It's business. You can find another magazine. I've got to run, pal. See you sometime."

He heard the sudden drone of the dial tone. Its dull monotony amplified inside his head. His stomach churned. The System. Once again, the System had attacked him. Was there nothing sacred, even Art?

He dropped the phone back on its cradle. Hopelessly, he rubbed his throbbing forehead. If he didn't get his check tomorrow, he couldn't even buy a loaf of bread. His phone would be disconnected. He'd be dragged from his apartment. The police would find his starved emaciated body in the gutter. Either that or—he cringed—he'd have to find a steady—here he swallowed with great difficulty—job.

He panicked. Could he borrow money from his friends? He heard their scornful laughter. Could he beg more money from his mother? He imagined her disowning him.

It wasn't fair! He'd pledged his life to Art, and he was starving while those hacks churned out their trashy popular bestsellers and were millionaires! There wasn't any justice!

He felt a gleam light his eyes. He heard a click. A trashy popular bestseller? Something those hacks churned out? Well, in his kitchen, waiting on the counter, was a hideous contraption that a while ago had churned like crazy.

That horrific word again. Like crazy? Yes, and *he* was crazy. To believe that what had happened in his drunken fit was more than an illusion.

Better see a shrink, he told himself.

And how am I supposed to pay him?

Totally discouraged, Eric tottered toward the bourbon in the kitchen. Might as well get blotto. Nothing else will help.

He sipped the lukewarm bourbon, staring at the grotesque typewriter and the words on the paper. Though the letters were now blurred by alcohol, they nonetheless were readable, and more important, they seemed actual. He swigged more bourbon, tapping at keys in stupefaction, randomly, no longer startled when the gushy words made sense. It was a sign of his insanity, he told himself, that he could stand here at this kitchen counter, hitting any keys he wanted, and not be surprised by the result. No matter what the cause or explanation, he apparently was automatically composing the outrageous saga of the passions and perversions of the folks in Fletcher's Cove.

"Yes, Johnny," Eric told the television personality and smiled with humble candor. "*Fletcher's Cove* burst out of me in one enormous flash of inspiration. Frankly the experience was scary. I'd been waiting all my life to tell that story, but I wasn't sure I had the talent.

225

Then one day I took a chance. I sat down at my faithful battered typewriter. I bought it in a junk shop, Johnny. That's how poor I was. And Fate or Luck or something was on *my* side for a change. My fingers seemed to dance across the keys. The story leapt out from me toward the page. A day doesn't go by that I don't thank the Lord for how he's blessed me."

Johnny tapped a pencil on his desk with practiced ease. The studio lights blazed. Eric sweated underneath his thousand-dollar sharkskin suit. His hundred-dollar designer haircut felt stiff from hairspray. In the glare, he squinted from the set but couldn't see the audience, though he sensed their firm approval of his rags-to-riches wonderful success. America was validated. One day, there'd be a shrine to honor its most cherished saint: Horatio Alger.

"Eric, you're too modest. I'm told you're not just our country's most admired novelist. You're also a respected critic, and a short story of yours won a prestigious literary prize."

Prestigious? Eric thought, inwardly frowning. Hey, be careful, Johnny. With a word that big, you'll lose our audience. I've got a book to sell.

"Yes," Eric said, admiring his host's sophisticated light gray hair. "The heyday of the *Village Mind*. The good old days in Greenwich Village. That's a disadvantage of success. I miss the gang down at the Square. I miss the coffee houses and the nights when we'd get together, reading stories to each other, testing new ideas, talking till after dawn."

Like hell I miss them, he thought. That dump I lived in. And that fat-assed Simmons. He can have his cockroach colony and those winos on the stairs. The *Village Mind?* A more descriptive title would have been the *Village Idiot*. And literary prize? The Subway Press awarded prizes every month. Sure, with the prizes and a quarter, you could buy a cup of coffee.

"You'll admit success has its advantages, however," Johnny said.

Eric shrugged disarmingly. "A few more creature comforts."

"You're a wealthy man."

You bet I'm wealthy, he thought. A million bucks for the hardback. Three million for the paperback. Two million for the movie, and a quarter million from the book club. Then the British rights, the other foreign rights in twenty countries. Thirteen million was the

226

total. Ten percent went to his agent. Ten percent went to his business manager. Another five percent to his publicity director. After that, the IRS held out its hand for half. But Eric had been clever. Oil and cattle, real estate—he coveted tax shelters. His three trips to Europe he wrote off as research. He'd incorporated. His estate, his jet, his yacht, he wrote off as expenses. After all, a man in his position needed privacy to write, to earn more money for the government. When everything was said and done, he pocketed five million dollars. Not bad for a forty-buck investment, though to hedge against inflation Eric wished he'd found a way to keep a few more million. Well, I can't complain.

"But Johnny, money isn't everything. Oh, sure, if someone wants to give it to me, I won't throw the money in the Hudson River," Eric said and laughed and heard the audience respond in kind. Their laughter was good-natured. You can bet they wouldn't turn down money either. "No, the thing is, Johnny, the reward I most enjoy comes when I read the letters from my fans. The pleasure they've received from *Fletcher's Cove* is more important than material success. It's what this business is about. The reading public."

Eric paused. The interview had gone too smoothly. Smoothness didn't sell his book. What people wanted was a controversy.

Beneath the blazing lights, his underarms sweated in profusion. He feared he'd stain his sharkskin suit and ruin it, but then he realized he could always buy another one.

"I know what Truman Capote says, that *Fletcher's Cove* is hardly writing—it's mere typing. But he's used that comment several times before, and if you want to know what I think, he's done several *other* things too many times before."

The audience began to laugh, but this time cruelly.

"Johnny, I'm still waiting for that novel he keeps promising. I'm glad I didn't hold my breath."

The audience laughed more derisively. If Truman had been present, they'd have stoned him.

"To be honest, Johnny, I think Truman's lost his touch with that great readership out there. The middle of America. I've tasted modern fiction, and it makes me gag. What people want are bulging stories filled with glamor, romance, action, and suspense. The kind of thing Dickens wrote."

The audience exploded with approval.

"Eric," Johnny said, "you mentioned Dickens. But a different writer comes to mind. A man whose work was popular back in the fifties. Winston Davis. If I hadn't known that you wrote *Fletcher's Cove*, I'd have sworn it was something new by Davis. But of course, that isn't possible. The man is dead—a tragic boating accident when he was only forty-eight. Just off Long Island, I believe."

"I'm flattered you thought of him," Eric said. "In fact, you're not the only reader who's noticed the comparison. He's an example of the kind of author I admire. His enormous love of character and plot. Those small towns in New England he immortalized. The richness of his prose. I've studied everything Davis wrote. I'm trying to continue his tradition. People want true, honest, human stories."

Eric thought what Winston Davis wrote was dreadful. Wretched. He hadn't even *heard* of Winston Davis till fans began comparing his book with Davis's. Puzzled, he'd gone to the New York Public Library and squirmed with keen discomfort as he'd tried to struggle through a half dozen books by Davis. He couldn't finish *any* of them. Tasteless dreck. Mind-numbing trash. The prose was deadening, but Eric recognized it. The comparison was valid. *Fletcher's Cove* was like a book by Winston Davis. Eric had been frowning as he'd left the Public Library. He'd felt that apprehensive tingle again. Despite their manifold appearance throughout *Flecher's Cove*, he'd never liked coincidences.

"One last question," Johnny said. "Your fans are anxious for another novel. Can you tell us what the new one's about?"

"I'd like to, but I'm superstitious, Johnny. I'm afraid to talk about a work while it's in progress. I can tell you this, though." Eric glanced around suspiciously as if he feared that spies from rival publishers were lurking in the studio. He shrugged and laughed. "I guess I can say it. After all who'd steal a title after several million people heard me stake a claim to it. The new book is called *Parson's Grove*." He heard a sigh of rapture from the audience. "It takes place in a small town in Vermont, and—well, I'd better not go any further. When the book is published, everyone can read it."

"Totally fantastic," his agent said. His name was Jason Epstein. He was in his thirties, but his hair was gray and thin from worry.

He frowned constantly. His stomach gave him trouble, and his motions were so hurried that he seemed to be on speed. "Fantastic. What you said about Capote—guaranteed to sell another hundred thousand copies of your book."

"I figured," he said. Outside the studio, he climbed in the limousine and waited for his agent. "Jason, you're not happy, though."

The chauffeur drove them through the evening fog in Burbank.

"We've got problems," Jason agreed.

"I don't see what. Here, have a drink to calm your nerves."

"And wreck my stomach? Thanks, but no thanks. Eric, listen to me. I've been talking to your business manager."

"I hear it coming. You both worry too damn much."

"But Eric, you've been spending money like you're printing it. That jet, that yacht, that big estate. You can't afford them."

"Hey, I've got five million bucks. Let me live a little."

"No, you don't."

Eric stared. "I beg your pardon."

"No, you haven't got five million dollars. All those trips to Europe. And that beach house here in Malibu, the place in Bimini."

"I've got investments. Oil and cattle."

"But the wells went dry. The cattle died from hoof-and-mouth disease."

"You're kidding me."

"My stomach isn't kidding. Eric, you've got mortgages on those estates. That fifty-thousand-buck Ferrari—it's not paid for. And the Learjet isn't paid for either. You're flat broke."

"All right, I've been extravagant, I'll grant you."

Jason gaped. "Extravagant?" he said. "*Extravagant?* You've lost your mind is what you've done."

"Hey, you're my agent. Make another deal for me."

"I did already. What's the matter with you? Have you lost your memory with your mind? A week from now, your publisher expects a brand new book from you. He's got two million dollars for the hardback rights. I let him have the book. He lets me have the money. That's the way the contract was arranged. Have you forgotten?"

"What's the matter then? Two million bucks will pay my bills."

"But Eric, where's the book? You don't get any money if you don't deliver that new book."

229

"I'm working on it."

Jason moaned. "Dear God, you mean it isn't finished yet? I asked you, Eric. No, I pleaded with you. Please stop partying. Get busy. Write the book, and then have all the parties you want. What is it, Eric? All those women, did they sap your strength, your brains, or what?"

"You'll have the book a week from now."

"Oh, Eric, I wish I had your confidence. You think writing's like turning on a tap? Hey, it's work. Suppose you get a block. Suppose you get the flu or something. How can anybody write a novel in a week?"

"You'll have the book. I promise, Jason. Anyway, if I'm a little late, it doesn't matter. I'm worth money to the publisher. He'll just extend the deadline."

"Eric, you don't listen. Everything depends on timing. The publicity is set to start. The printer's ready, waiting. If you don't deliver, the publisher will think you've made a fool of him. The movie tie-in will collapse. The book club will get angry. They're depending on you, Eric, you don't understand. Big business. You don't disappoint big business."

"Not to worry, Jason." Eric smiled to reassure him. "Everything's taken care of. I intend to start tonight."

"God help you, Eric. Hit those keys, man. Hit those keys."

The Lear soared away from L.A. International. Above the city, Eric peered down toward the grids of streetlights and gleaming freeways in the darkness. Glancing west toward the ocean's rim that he was leaving, he saw a hint of crimson on the far horizon.

Might as well get started, he decided with reluctance.

As the engine's muffled roar came through the fuselage, he reached inside a cabinet and lifted the enormous grotesque typewriter. He took it everywhere with him, afraid of fire or theft if it was unattended.

Struggling, Eric set it on a table. He'd given orders to the pilot not to come back to the passenger compartment. A thick bulkhead separated Eric from the pilot. Here, as at his mansion up the Hudson, Eric did his typing in strict secrecy.

The work was boring, really. Toward the end of *Fletcher's Cove*, he hadn't even faced the keyboard. He'd watched a week of television while he let his fingers tap whatever letters they by chance selected. After all, it didn't make a difference what he typed. The strange machine did the composing. At the very end of every television program, he'd read the last page the machine had typed, hoping to see *The End*. And one day, finally, those closing words appeared before him.

After the success of *Fletcher's Cove*, he'd started typing again. He'd read the title *Parson's Grove* and worked patiently for twenty pages. Unenthusiastically. What he'd learned from his experience was that he'd never liked writing, that instead he liked to talk about it and be called a writer, but the pain of work did not appeal to him. And this way, when his mind was not engaged, the work was even less appealing. To be absolutely honest, he thought, I should have been a prince.

He'd put off typing *Parson's Grove* as long as possible. The money came so easily Eric didn't want to suffer even the one week he'd calculated would be necessary to complete the manuscript.

But Jason had alarmed him. There's no money? Then I'd better go back to the gold mine for some more. The goose that laid the golden egg. Or what was it a writer's helper once was called? Amanuensis. Sure, that's what I'll call you, Eric told his weird machine. From now on, you'll be my amanuensis. He couldn't believe he was actually a millionaire—at least on paper—flying in his own Learjet, en route to New York, the *Today* show, the *Tomorrow* show, and then *Good Morning, America*. This can't be really happening.

It was, though. And if he wanted to continue his fine life, he'd better type like hell for one week to produce his second book.

The jet streaked through the night. He shoved a sheet of paper into his amanuensis. Bored, he sipped a glass of bourbon. He selected a cassette of *Halloween* and put it in his Beta player. Watching television where some kid stabbed his big sister, Eric started typing.

Chapter Three. . . . Ramona felt a rapture. She had never known such pleasure. Not her husband, not her lover, had produced such ecstasy within her. Yes, the milkman . . .

Eric yawned. He watched a nut escape from an asylum. He watched some crazy doctor try to find the nut. A babysitter screamed a lot. The nut got killed a half dozen times but still survived because apparently he was the boogey man.

Without once looking at the keyboard, Eric typed. The stack of pages grew beside him. He finished drinking his fifth glass of bourbon. *Halloween* ended. He watched *Alien* and an arousing woman in her underwear who'd trapped herself inside a shuttle with a monster. Somewhere over Colorado—Eric later calculated where and when it happened—he glanced at a sheet of paper he'd just typed and gasped when he discovered the prose was totally nonsensical.

He fumbled through the stack of paper, realizing that for half an hour he'd been typing gibberish.

He paled. He gaped. He nearly vomited.

"Good God, what's happened?"

He typed madly, *Little Bo Peep has lost her sheep.*

Those words were what he read.

He typed, *The quick brown fox.*

And *that* was what he read.

He scrambled at the keyboard, and the scramble faced him on the paper.

By the time he reached New York's La Guardia, he had a two-inch stack of frantic gibberish beside him, and, to make things worse, the typewriter abruptly jammed. He heard a nauseating crunch inside it, and the keys froze solidly. He couldn't make them manufacture even gibberish. It's got a block, he thought and moaned. Dear God, it's broken, busted, wrecked.

We both are.

He tried slamming it to free the keys, but all he did was hurt his hands. He suddenly feared he'd break more parts inside it. Drunkenly, he set a blanket over it and struggled from the jet to put it in the limousine that waited for him. He wasn't due at the television interviews till tomorrow. As the sun glared blindingly on New York, he rubbed his haggard whisker-stubbled face and in panic told the chauffeur, "Take me to Manhattan. Find a shop that fixes typewriters."

The errand took two hours through stalled trucks, accidents, and detours. Finally, the limousine double-parked on Fifty-Second Street, and he stumbled with his burden toward a store with Olivettis in the window.

"I can't fix this," the young serviceman informed him.

Eric moaned, "*You've got to.*"

"See this brace inside. It's cracked. I don't have any parts for something strange like this." The serviceman was horrified by the sheer ugliness of the machine. "I'd have to weld the brace. But buddy, look, a piece of junk this old, it's like a worn-out shirt. You patch an elbow, and the shirt tears at the patch. You patch the new hole, and the shirt tears at the new patch. When you're through, you haven't got a shirt. You've just got patches. If I weld this brace, the heat'll weaken this old metal, and the brace'll crack in other places. You'll keep coming back till you've got more welds than metal. Anyway, a weird design like this, I wouldn't want to fool with it. Believe me, buddy, I don't understand this thing. You'd better find the guy who built it. Maybe *he* can fix it. Maybe he's got extra parts. Say, don't I know you?"

Eric frowned. "I beg your pardon?"

"Aren't you famous? Weren't you on the Carson show?"

"No, you're mistaken," Eric told him furtively. He glanced down at his eighteen-karat Rolex watch and saw it was almost noon. Good God, he'd lost the morning. "I've got to hurry."

Eric grabbed the broken typewriter and tottered from the building toward the limousine. The traffic's blare unnerved him.

"Greenwich Village," he blurted to the bored chauffeur. "As fast as you can get there."

"In this traffic? Sir, it's noon. The rush hour."

His stomach burned. He trembled, sweating. When the driver reached the Village, Eric gave directions in a frenzy. He kept glancing at his watch. At almost twenty after one, he had a sudden fearful thought. Oh, God, suppose the place is closed. Suppose the old guy's dead or out of business.

He cringed. But then he squinted through the windshield, seeing the dusty windows of the junk shop down the street. He scrambled from the limousine before it completely stopped. He grabbed the massive typewriter, and though adrenaline spurred him, his knees wobbled as he fumbled at the creaky junk shop door and lurched inside the dingy musty narrow shadowed room.

The old guy stood exactly where he'd been the last time Eric walked inside here: hunched across a battered desk, a quarter-inch of cigarette between his yellowed fingers, scowling at a racing form. He even wore the same frayed sweater with the buttons missing. Cobweb hair, and sallow face.

The old man peered up from the racing form. "All sales are final. Can't you read the sign?"

Off balance from his burden, he gaped in disbelief. "You still remember me?"

"You bet I do. I can't forget that piece of trash. I told you I don't take returns."

"But that's not why I'm here."

"Then why'd you bring that damn thing back? Good God, it's ugly. I can't stand to look at it."

"It's broken."

"Yeah, it figures."

"I can't get it fixed. The serviceman won't touch it. He's afraid he'll break it even more."

"So throw it in the garbage. Sell it as scrap metal. Sure, it weighs enough. You'll maybe get a couple of dollars."

"But I like it!"

"I don't know." The old man shook his head. "Some people's taste."

"The serviceman suggested the guy who built it might know how to fix it."

"And if cows had wings——"

"Look, tell me where you got it!"

"How much is the information worth to you?"

"A hundred bucks!"

The old man straightened. "I won't take a check."

"In cash! For God's sake, hurry!"

"Where's the money?"

The old man took several hours. Eric paced and smoked and sweated. Finally the old man groaned up from his basement with some scribbles on a scrap of paper.

234

"An estate," the old man said. "Out on Long Island. Some guy died. He drowned, I think. Let's see." The old man struggled to decipher what he'd scrawled across the scrap of paper. "Yeah, his name was Winston Davis."

Eric clutched the battered desk; his stomach dropped; his heart skipped several beats. "No, that can't be."

"You mean you know this guy?" the old man said. "This Winston Davis."

Eric tasted dust. "I've heard of him. He was a novelist." His voice sounded hoarse.

"I hope he didn't try to write his novels on that thing. It's like I told you when you bought it. I tried every way I knew to make them keep it. But the owners sold the dead guy's stuff in one big lump. They wouldn't split the package. Everything or nothing."

"On Long Island?"

"The address is on this paper."

Eric grabbed it, frantically picked up the heavy broken typewriter, and stumbled toward the door.

"Say, don't I know your face?" the old man asked behind him. "Weren't you on the Carson show last night?"

The sun had almost set as Eric found his destination. All the way across Long Island, he'd trembled fearfully. He realized now why so many readers had compared his work with that of Winston Davis. Davis once had owned this same machine. He'd typed his novels on it. The machine had done the actual composing. That's why Eric's work and Davis's were similar. Their novels had the same creator.

Just as Eric kept the secret, so had Davis, evidently never even telling his close friends or his family. When Davis died, the family had guessed that this old typewriter was nothing more than junk, and they'd sold it with some other junk around the house. If they'd known about the secret, surely they'd have kept this golden goose, this gold mine.

But it wasn't any gold mine now. It was a hunk of junk, a broken hulk of bolts and levers.

"Here's the mansion, sir," the totally confused chauffeur told Eric.

Frightened, he studied the big open gates, the wide smooth lawn, the huge black road that curved up to the massive house. It's like a castle, Eric thought. Apprehensively he told the driver, "Go up to the front."

Suppose there's no one home, he thought. Suppose they don't remember. What if someone else is living there?

He left his burden in the car. At once both hesitant and frantic, he walked up the marble front steps toward the large oak door. His fingers shook. He pressed a button, heard the echo of a bell inside, and was surprised when someone soon opened the door.

A gray-haired woman in her sixties. Kindly, well-dressed, pleasant-looking though wrinkled.

Smiling, with a feeble voice, she asked how she could help him.

He stammered, but the woman's gentle gaze encouraged him, and soon he spoke to her with ease, explaining he knew her husband's work and admired it.

"How good of you to remember," she said.

"I was in the neighborhood. I hoped you wouldn't mind if I stopped by. To tell you how I felt about his novels."

"Wouldn't mind? No, I'm delighted. So few readers take the time to care. Won't you come in?"

The mansion seemed like a mausoleum—cold and brittle. Sounds reverberated.

"Would you care to see my husband's study? Where he worked?" the aging woman asked.

They went along a chilly marble hall. The old woman pushed an ornate door and gestured toward the sacristy, the sanctum.

It was wonderful. A high wide spacious room with priceless paintings on the walls—and bookshelves, thick soft carpeting, big windows that faced toward the white-capped ocean where three sunset-tinted sailboats listed in the evening breeze.

But the attraction of the room was in its middle—a large gleaming teakwood desk, and, like a chalice on its center, an old Smith-Corona from the fifties.

"This is where my husband wrote his books," the old woman told him proudly. "Every morning—eight till noon. Then we'd have lunch, and we'd go shopping for our supper, or we'd swim and use the sailboat. In the winter, we took long walks by the water. Winston loved the ocean in the winter. He—— I'm babbling. Please forgive me."

236

"No, it's quite all right. I understand the way you feel. He used this Smith-Corona?"

"Every day."

"I ask, because I bought a clunky typewriter the other day. It looked so strange it appealed to me. The man who sold it told me your husband used to own it."

"No, I——"

His throat constricted him. His heart sank in despair.

"Wait, I remember now," the gray-haired woman said, and he held his breath.

"That awful ugly one," she said.

"Yes, that describes it," he blurted.

"Winston kept it in a closet. I kept telling him to throw it out, but Winston said his friend would never forgive him."

"Friend?" The word stuck like fishbone in Eric's throat.

"Yes, Stuart Donovan. He owns a typewriter store in the village. Winston spent a lot of time with Donovan. They often sailed together. One day Winston brought that strange machine home. 'It's antique,' he said. 'A present. Stuart gave it to me.' Well, it looked like junk to me. But friends are friends, and Winston kept it. When he died, though——" The old woman's voice changed pitch, sank deeper, seemed to crack. "Well, anyway, I sold it with some other things I didn't need."

He left the car. The sun had set. The dusk loomed thickly around him. He smelled salty sea-air in this quaint Long Island village. He stared at the sign above the shop's door: DONOVAN'S TYPEWRITERS— NEW AND USED—REBUILT, RESTORED. His plan had been to find the shop and then to come back in the morning when it opened. But amazingly a light glowed faintly through the drawn blind of the window. Though a card on the door said CLOSED, a shadow moved behind the shielded window.

Eric knocked. A figure shuffled close. An ancient gentleman pulled up the blind and squinted out toward Eric.

"Closed," the old man told him faintly through the window.

"No, I have to see you. It's important."

"Closed," the man repeated.

"Winston Davis."

Though the shadow had begun to turn, it stopped. Again pulling the blind, the ancient gentleman peered out.

"Did you say Winston Davis?"

"Please, I have to talk to you about him."

Eric heard the lock snick open. The door swung slowly inward. The old man frowned at him.

"Is your name Stuart Donovan?"

The old man nodded. "You knew Winston? We were friends for many years."

"That's why I have to see you."

"Then come in," the old man told him, puzzled. Short and frail, he leaned on a wooden cane. He wore a double-breasted suit, a thin silk tie. The collar of his shirt was too large for his shrunken neck. He smelled of peppermint.

"I have to show you something," Eric said. Hurrying back from the limousine, he lugged his ugly typewriter toward the shop.

"Why, that's——" the old man said, his eyes wide, surprised.

"I know. It was your gift to Winston."

"Where——?"

"I bought it in a junk shop."

Wearied by his grief, the old man groaned.

"It's broken," Eric said. "I've brought it here for you to fix."

"Then you know about——?"

"Its secret. Absolutely. Look, I need it. I'm in trouble if it isn't fixed."

"You sound like Winston." The old man's eyes blurred with memories of long ago. "A few times, when it broke, he came to me in total panic. 'Contracts. Royalties. I'm ruined if you can't repair it,' he'd say to me. I always fixed it, though." The old man laughed nostalgically.

"And will you do the same for me? I'll pay you anything."

"Oh, no, my rate's the same for everyone. I was about to leave. My wife has supper waiting. But this model was my masterpiece. I'll look at it. For Winston. Bring it over to the counter."

Eric set it down and rubbed his aching arms. "What I don't understand is why you didn't keep this thing. It's worth a fortune."

"I had others."

Eric stiffened with surpise.

238

"Then too," the old man said, "I've always had sufficient money. Rich folks have too many worries. Winston, for example. Toward the end, he was a nervous wreck, afraid it'd be stolen or would break beyond repair. It ruined him. I wish I hadn't given it to him. But he was good to me. He always gave me ten percent of everything he earned."

"I'll do the same for you. Please fix it. Help me."

"I'll see what the problem is."

The old man tinkered, hummed and hawed, and poked. He took off bolts and tested levers.

Eric bit his lips. He chewed his fingernails.

"I know what's wrong," the old man said.

"That brace is cracked."

"Oh, that's a minor problem. I have other braces. I can easily replace it."

Eric sighed with absolute relief. "Then if you wouldn't mind. . . ."

"The keys are stuck because the brace is cracked," the old man said. "Before the keys stuck, though, this model wasn't typing what you wanted. It wasn't composing."

Eric feared he'd throw up. He nodded palely.

"See, the trouble is," the old man said. "This typewriter ran out of words. It used up every word it had inside it."

Eric fought the urge to scream. This can't be happening, he told himself. "Then put more words inside it."

"Don't I wish I could. But once the words are gone, I can't put new ones in. I don't know why that happens, but I've tried repeatedly, and every time I've failed. I have to build a brand new model."

"Do it then, I'll pay you anything."

"I'm sorry, but I can't. I've lost the knack. I made five successful models. The sixth and seventh failed. The eighth was a complete disaster. I stopped trying."

"Try again."

"I can't. You don't know how it weakens me. The effort. Afterward, my brain feels empty. I need every word I've got."

"God dammit, try!"

The old man shook his head. "You have my sympathy."

Beyond the old man, past the counter, in the workshop, Eric saw another model. Knobs and levers, bolts.

"I'll pay a million dollars for that other one."

The old man slowly turned to look. "Oh, that one. No, I'm sorry. That's my own. I built it for my children. Now they're married. They have children of their own, and when they visit, my grandchildren like to play with it."

"I'll double what I offered."

Eric thought about his mansion on the Hudson, his estates in Bimini and Malibu, his yacht, his jet, his European trips, and his Ferrari.

"Hell, I'll triple what I offered."

Six more days, he thought. I've got to finish that new book by then. I'll just have time to do it. If I type every day and night.

"You've got to let me have it."

"I don't need the money. I'm an old man. What does money mean to me? I'm sorry."

Eric lost control. He scrambled past the counter, racing toward the workshop. He grabbed the other model. When the old man tried to take it from him, Eric pushed. The old man fell, clutching Eric's legs.

"It's mine!" the old man wailed. "I built it for my children! You can't have it!"

"Four! Four million dollars!" Eric shouted.

"Not for all the money in the world!"

The old man clung to Eric's legs, constricting, suffocating.

"Dammit!" Eric said. He set the model on the counter, grabbed the old man's cane, and struck him on the head. "I need it! Don't you understand!"

He struck again and again and again.

The old man shuddered. Blood dripped from his mangled forehead; blood dripped from the cane.

The shop was silent.

Eric stared at what he'd done. Stumbling back, he dropped the cane and put his hands up to his mouth.

And then he realized. "It's mine."

He wiped his fingerprints from everything he'd touched. He exchanged the models so his broken one sat on the workshop table. His chauffeur wouldn't know what had happened. It was likely he'd never learn. The murder of an old man in a tiny village on Long Island—there was little reason for publicity. True, Mrs. Davis might recall her evening visitor, but would she link this murder with her visitor? And anyway, she didn't know who Eric was.

He took his chance. He grabbed his prize, and, despite its weight, he ran.

His IBM Selectric sat on the desk in his study. For pure show. He never used it, but he needed it to fool his guests, to hide the way he actually composed. He dimly heard the limousine drive from the mansion toward the city. He turned on the lights. Hurrying toward his desk, he shoved the IBM away and set down his salvation. Six more days. Yes, he could do the job. A lot of bourbon and television. Stiff joints in his aching fingers after all the automatic typing. He could do it, though.

He poured a brimming glass of bourbon, needing it. He turned the Late Show on. He lit a cigarette, and as *The Body Snatcher*'s credits began, he desperately started typing.

He felt shaky, scared, and shocked by what had happened. But he had another model. He could keep his yacht, his jet, his three estates. The parties could continue. Now that Eric thought about it, he'd even saved the four million dollars he would have paid the old man for this model.

Curious, on impulse he glanced at what he'd typed so far.

And began to scream.

Because *The quick brown fox* was something different, as he'd expected. But not the gushy prose of *Parson's Grove*. Something far more different.

See Jane run. See Dick run. See Spot chase the ball.

("I built it for my children. Now they're married. They have children of their own, and when they visit, my grandchildren like to play with it.")

He screamed so loudly he couldn't hear the clatter as he typed.

See Spot run up the hill. See Jane run after Spot. See Dick run after Jane.

The neighbors half a mile away were wakened by his shrieks.

They feared he was being murdered, so they called Emergency, and when the State Police broke in the house, they found him typing, screaming.

They weren't sure which sight was worse—the man or the machine. But when they dragged him from the monstrous typewriter, one state policeman glanced down at the page.

See Jane climb up the tree. See Dick climb up the tree. See Spot bark at the cat.

Then further down—they soon discovered what it meant—*See Eric murder Mr. Donovan. See Eric club the old man with the cane. See Eric steal me. Now see Eric go to jail.*

Perhaps it was a trick of light, or maybe it was the consequence of the machine's peculiar keyboard. For whatever reason, the state policeman later swore—he only told his wife—the damned typewriter seemed to grin.

Nunc Dimittis

BY TANITH LEE

Tanith Lee is renowned for the gentleness of her prose, the care she takes with her characters and her settings; she is also known for her skill in taking the not-so-normal and rendering it seemingly normal, thereby heightening the chills she delivers when her readers realize what's been done to them without their knowing it. She is uncannily aware that all emotions—from love to hate—are double-edged, and more frightening than a well-aimed ax.

THE VAMPIRE was old, and no longer beautiful. In common with all living things, she had aged, though very slowly, like the tall trees in the park. Slender and gaunt and leafless, they stood out there, beyond the long windows, rain-dashed in the grey morning. While she sat in her high-backed chair in that corner of the room where the curtains of thick yellow lace and the wine-coloured blinds kept every drop of daylight out. In the glimmer of the ornate oil lamp, she had been reading. The lamp came from a Russian palace. The book had once graced the library of a corrupt pope named, in his temporal existence, Roderigo Borgia. Now the Vampire's dry hands had fallen upon the page. She sat in her black lace dress that was one hundred and eighty years of age, far younger than she herself, and looked at the old man, streaked by the shine of distant windows.

"You say you are tired, Vassu. I know how it is. To be so tired, and unable to rest. It is a terrible thing."

"But, Princess," said the old man quietly, "it is more than this. I am dying."

The Vampire stirred a little. The pale leaves of her hands rustled on the page. She stared, with an almost childlike wonder.

243

"Dying? Can this be? You are sure?"

The old man, very clean and neat in his dark clothing, nodded humbly.

"Yes, Princess."

"Oh, Vassu," she said, "are you glad?"

He seemed a little embarrassed. Finally he said:

"Forgive me, Princess, but I am very glad. Yes, very glad."

"I understand."

"Only," he said, "I am troubled for your sake."

"No, no," said the Vampire, with the fragile perfect courtesy of her class and kind. "No, it must not concern you. You have been a good servant. Far better than I might ever have hoped for. I am thankful, Vassu, for all your care of me. I shall miss you. But you have earned," she hesitated. She said, "You have more than earned your peace."

"But you," he said.

"I shall do very well. My requirements are small, now. The days when I was a huntress are gone, and the nights. Do you remember, Vassu?"

"I remember, Princess."

"When I was so hungry, and so relentless. And so lovely. My white face in a thousand ballroom mirrors. My silk slippers stained with dew. And my lovers waking in the cold morning, where I had left them. But now, I do not sleep, I am seldom hungry. I never lust. I never love. These are the comforts of old age. There is only one comfort that is denied to me. And who knows. One day, I too . . ." She smiled at him. Her teeth were beautiful, but almost even now, the exquisite points of the canines quite worn away. "Leave me when you must," she said. "I shall mourn you. I shall envy you. But I ask nothing more, my good and noble friend."

The old man bowed his head.

"I have," he said, "a few days, a handful of nights. There is something I wish to try to do in this time. I will try to find one who may take my place."

The Vampire stared at him again, now astonished. "But Vassu, my irreplaceable help—it is no longer possible."

"Yes. If I am swift."

"The world is not as it was," she said, with a grave and dreadful wisdom.

244

He lifted his head. More gravely, he answered:

"The world is as it has always been, Princess. Only our perceptions of it have grown more acute. Our knowledge less bearable."

She nodded.

"Yes, this must be so. How could the world have changed so terribly? It must be we who have changed."

He trimmed the lamp before he left her.

Outside, the rain dripped steadily from the trees.

The city, in the rain, was not unlike a forest. But the old man, who had been in many forests and many cities, had no special feeling for it. His feelings, his senses, were primed to other things.

Nevertheless, he was conscious of his bizarre and anachronistic effect, like that of a figure in some surrealist painting, walking the streets in clothes of a bygone era, aware he did not blend with his surroundings, nor render them homage of any kind. Yet even when, as sometimes happened, a gang of children or youths jeered and called after him the foul names he was familiar with in twenty languages, he neither cringed nor cared. He had no concern for such things. He had been so many places, seen so many sights; cities which burned or fell in ruin, the young who grew old, as he had, and who died, as now, at last, he too would die. This thought of death soothed him, comforted him, and brought with it a great sadness, a strange jealousy. He did not want to leave her. Of course he did not. The idea of her vulnerability in this harsh world, not new in its cruelty but ancient, though freshly recognised—it horrified him. This was the sadness. And the jealousy . . . that, because he must try to find another to take his place. And that other would come to be for her, as he had been.

The memories rose and sank in his brain like waking dreams all the time he moved about the streets. As he climbed the steps of museums and underpasses, he remembered other steps in other lands, of marble and fine stone. And looking out from high balconies, the city reduced to a map, he recollected the towers of cathedrals, the starswept points of mountains. And then at last, as if turning over the pages of a book backwards, he reached the beginning.

There she stood, between two tall white graves, the chateau grounds behind her, everything silvered in the dusk before the dawn. She wore a ball dress, and a long white cloak. And even then, her hair was dressed in the fashion of a century ago; dark hair, like black flowers.

He had known for a year before that he would serve her. The moment he had heard them talk of her in the town. They were not afraid of her, but in awe. She did not prey upon her own people, as some of her line had done.

When he could get up, he went to her. He had kneeled, and stammered something; he was only sixteen, and she not much older. But she had simply looked at him quietly and said: "I know. You are welcome." The words had been in a language they seldom spoke together now. Yet always, when he recalled that meeting, she said them in that tongue, and with the same gentle inflexion.

All about, in the small café where he had paused to sit and drink coffee, vague shapes came and went. Of no interest to him, no use to her. Throughout the morning, there had been nothing to alert him. He would know. He would know, as he had known it of himself.

He rose, and left the café, and the waking dream walked with him. A lean black car slid by, and he recaptured a carriage carving through white snow——

A step brushed the pavement, perhaps twenty feet behind him. The old man did not hesitate. He stepped on, and into an alleyway that ran between the high buildings. The steps followed him; he could not hear them all, only one in seven, or eight. A little wire of tension began to draw taut within him, but he gave no sign. Water trickled along the brickwork beside him, and the noise of the city was lost.

Abruptly, a hand was on the back of his neck, a capable hand, warm and sure, not harming him yet, almost the touch of a lover.

"That's right, old man. Keep still. I'm not going to hurt you, not if you do what I say."

He stood, the warm and vital hand on his neck, and waited.

"All right," said the voice, which was masculine and young and with some other elusive quality to it. "Now let me have your wallet."

The old man spoke in a faltering tone, very foreign, very fearful. "I have——no wallet."

The hand changed its nature, gripped him, bit.

"Don't lie. I can hurt you. I don't want to, but I can. Give me whatever money you have."

246

"Yes," he faltered, "yes—yes—"

And slipped from the sure and merciless grip like water, spinning, gripping in turn, flinging away—there was a whirl of movement.

The old man's attacker slammed against the wet grey wall and rolled down it. He lay on the rainy debris of the alley floor, and stared up, too surprised to look surprised.

This had happened many times before. Several had supposed the old man an easy mark, but he had all the steely power of what he was. Even now, even dying, he was terrible in his strength. And yet, though it had happened often, now it was different. The tension had not gone away.

Swiftly, deliberately, the old man studied the young one.

Something struck home instantly. Even sprawled, the adversary was peculiarly graceful, the grace of enormous physical co-ordination. The touch of the hand, also, impervious and certain—there was strength here, too. And now the eyes. Yes, the eyes were steady, intelligent, and with a curious lambency, an innocence——

"Get up," the old man said. He had waited upon an aristocrat. He had become one himself, and sounded it. "Up. I will not hit you again."

The young man grinned, aware of the irony. The humour flitted through his eyes. In the dull light of the alley, they were the colour of leopards not the eyes of leopards, but their *pelts*.

"Yes, and you could, couldn't you, granddad."

"My name," said the old man, "is Vasyelu Gorin. I am the father to none, and my nonexistent sons and daughters have no children. And you?"

"My name," said the young man, "is Snake."

The old man nodded. He did not really care about names, either.

"Get up, Snake. You attempted to rob me, because you are poor, having no work and no wish for work. I will buy you food, now."

The young man continued to lie, as if at ease, on the ground.

"Why?"

"Because I want something from you."

"What? You're right. I'll do almost anything, if you pay me enough. So you can tell me."

The old man looked at the young man called Snake, and knew that all he said was a fact. Knew that here was one who had stolen and whored, and stolen again when the slack bodies slept, both male and female, exhausted by the sexual vampirism he had practised on them, drawing their misguided souls out through their pores as later he would draw the notes from purse and pocket. Yes, a vampire. Maybe a murderer, too. Very probably a murderer.

"If you will do anything," said the old man, "I need not tell you beforehand. You will do it anyway."

"Almost anything, is what I said."

"Advise me then," said Vasyelu Gorin, the servant of the Vampire, "what you will not do. I shall then refrain from asking it of you."

The young man laughed. In one fluid movement he came to his feet. When the old man walked on, he followed.

Testing him, the old man took Snake to an expensive restaurant, far up on the white hills of the city, where the glass geography nearly scratched the sky. Ignoring the mud on his dilapidated leather jacket, Snake became a flawless image of decorum, became what is always ultimately respected, one who does not care. The old man, who also did not care, appreciated this act, but knew it was nothing more. Snake had learned how to be a prince. But he was a gigolo with a closet full of skins to put on. Now and then the speckled leopard eyes, searching, wary, would give him away.

After the good food and the excellent wine, the cognac, the cigarettes taken from the silver box—Snake had stolen three, but, stylishly overt, had left them sticking like porcupine quills from his breast pocket—they went out again into the rain.

The dark was gathering, and Snake solicitously took the old man's arm. Vasyelu Gorin dislodged him, offended by the cheapness of the gesture after the acceptable one with the cigarettes.

"Don't you like me any more?" said Snake. "I can go now, if you want. But you might pay for my wasted time."

"Stop that," said Vasyelu Gorin. "Come along."

Smiling, Snake came with him. They walked, between the glowing pyramids of stores, through shadowy tunnels, over the wet paving. When the thoroughfares folded away and the meadows of the great gardens began, Snake grew tense. The landscape was less familiar

248

to him, obviously. This part of the forest was unknown.

Trees hung down from the air to the sides of the road.

"I could kill you here," said Snake. "Take your money, and run."

"You could try," said the old man, but he was becoming weary. He was no longer certain, and yet, he was sufficiently certain that his jealousy had assumed a tinge of hatred. If the young man were stupid enough to set on him, how simple it would be to break the columnar neck, like pale amber, between his fleshless hands. But then, she would know. She would know he had found for her, and destroyed the finding. And she would be generous, and he would leave her, aware he had failed her, too.

When the huge gates appeared, Snake made no comment. He seemed, by then, to anticipate them. The old man went into the park, moving quickly now, in order to outdistance his own feelings. Snake loped at his side.

Three windows were alight, high in the house. Her windows. And as they came to the stair that led up, under its skeins of ivy, into the porch, her pencil-thin shadow passed over the lights above, like smoke, or a ghost.

"I thought you lived alone," said Snake. "I thought you were lonely."

The old man did not answer any more. He went up the stair and opened the door. Snake came in behind him, and stood quite still, until Vasyelu Gorin had found the lamp in the niche by the door, and lit it. Unnatural stained glass flared in the door panels, and the window-niches either side, owls and lotuses and far-off temples, scrolled and luminous, oddly aloof.

Vasyelu began to walk toward the inner stair.

"Just a minute," said Snake. Vasyelu halted, saying nothing. "I'd just like to know," said Snake, "how many of your friends are here, and just what your friends are figuring to do, and how I fit into their plans."

The old man sighed.

"There is one woman in the room above. I am taking you to see her. She is a Princess. Her name is Darejan Draculas." He began to ascend the stair.

Left in the dark, the visitor said softly:

"What?"

"You think you have heard the name. You are correct. But it is another branch."

He heard only the first step as it touched the carpeted stair. With a bound, the creature was upon him, the lamp was lifted from his had. Snake danced behind it, glittering and unreal.

"Dracula," he said.

"Draculas. Another branch."

"A vampire."

"Do you believe in such things?" said the old man. "You should, living as you do, preying as you do."

"I never," said Snake, "pray."

"Prey," said the old man. "Prey upon. You cannot even speak your own language. Give me the lamp, or shall I take it? The stair is steep. You may be damaged, this time. Which will not be good for any of your trades."

Snake made a little bow, and returned the lamp.

They continued up the carpeted hill of stair, and reached a landing and so a passage, and so her door.

The appurtenances of the house, even glimpsed in the erratic fleeting of the lamp, were very gracious. The old man was used to them, but Snake, perhaps, took note. Then again, like the size and importance of the park gates, the young thief might well have anticipated such elegance.

And there was no neglect, no dust, no air of decay, or, more tritely, of the grave. Women arrived regularly from the city to clean, under Vasyelu Gorin's stern command; flowers were even arranged in the salon for those occasions when the Princess came downstairs. Which was rarely, now. How tired she had grown. Not aged, but bored by life. The old man sighed again, and knocked upon her door.

Her response was given softly. Vasyelu Gorin saw, from the tail of his eye, the young man's reaction, his ears almost pricked, like a cat's.

"Wait here," Vasyelu said, and went into the room, shutting the door, leaving the other outside it in the dark.

The windows which had shone bright outside were black within. The candles burned, red and white as carnations.

The Vampire was seated before her little harpsichord. She had probably been playing it, its song so quiet it was seldom audible beyond her door. Long ago, nonetheless, he would have heard it. Long ago——

"Princess," he said, "I have brought someone with me."

He had not been sure what she would do, or say, confronted by the actuality. She might even remonstrate, grow angry, though he had not often seen her angry. But he saw now she had guessed, in some tangible way, that he would not return alone, and she had been preparing herself. As she rose to her feet, he beheld the red satin dress, the jewelled silver crucifix at her throat, the trickle of silver from her ears. On the thin hands, the great rings throbbed their sable colours. Her hair, which had never lost its blackness, abbreviated at her shoulders and waved in a fashion of only twenty years before, framed the starved bones of her face with a savage luxuriance. She was magnificent. Gaunt, elderly, her beauty lost, her heart dulled, yet—magnificent, wondrous.

He stared at her humbly, ready to weep because, for the half of one half moment, he had doubted.

"Yes," she said. She gave him the briefest smile, like a swift caress. "Then I will see him, Vassu."

Snake was seated cross-legged a short distance along the passage. He had discovered, in the dark, a slender Chinese vase of the *yang ts'ai* palette, and held it between his hands, his chin resting on the brim.

"Shall I break this?" he asked.

Vasyelu ignored the remark. He indicated the opened door.

"You may go in now."

"May I? How excited you're making me."

Snake flowed upright. Still holding the vase, he went through into the Vampire's apartment. The old man came into the room after him, placing his black-garbed body, like a shadow, by the door, which he left now standing wide. The old man watched Snake.

Circling slightly, perhaps unconsciously, he had approached a third of the chamber's length towards the woman. Seeing him from the back, Vasyelu Gorin was able to observe all the play of tautening muscles along the spine, like those of something readying itself

251

to spring, or to escape. Yet, not seeing the face, the eyes, was unsatisfactory. The old man shifted his position, edged shadow-like along the room's perimeter, until he had gained a better vantage.

"Good evening," the Vampire said to Snake. "Would you care to put down the vase? Or, if you prefer, smash it. Indecision can be distressing."

"Perhaps I'd prefer to keep the vase."

"Oh, then do so, by all means. But I suggest you allow Vasyelu to wrap it up for you, before you go. Or someone may rob you on the street."

Snake pivotted, lightly, like a dancer, and put the vase on a side-table. Turning again, he smiled at her.

"There are so many valuable things here. What shall I take? What about the silver cross you're wearing?"

The Vampire also smiled.

"An heirloom. I am rather fond of it. I do not recommend you should try to take that."

Snake's eyes enlarged. He was naive, amazed.

"But I thought, if I did what you wanted, if I made you happy— I could have whatever I liked. Wasn't that the bargain?"

"And how would you propose to make me happy?"

Snake went close to her; he prowled about her, very slowly. Disgusted, fascinated, the old man watched him. Snake stood behind her, leaning against her, his breath stirring the filaments of her hair. He slipped his left hand along her shoulder, sliding from the red satin to the dry uncoloured skin of her throat. Vasyelu remembered the touch of the hand, electric, and so sensitive, the fingers of an artist or a surgeon.

The Vampire never changed. She said:

"No. You will not make me happy, my child."

"Oh," Snake said into her ear. "You can't be certain. If you like, if you really like, I'll let you drink my blood."

The Vampire laughed. It was frightening. Something dormant yet intensely powerful seemed to come alive in her as she did so, like flame from a finished coal. The sound, the appalling life, shook the young man away from her. And for an instant, the old man saw fear in the leopard-yellow eyes, a fear as intrinsic to the being of Snake as to cause fear was intrinsic to the being of the Vampire.

252

And, still blazing with her power, she turned on him.

"What do you think I am?" she said, "some senile hag greedy to rub her scaley flesh against your smoothness; some hag you can, being yourself without sanity or fastidiousness, corrupt with the phantoms, the left-overs of pleasure, and then murder, tearing the gems from her fingers with your teeth? Or I am a perverted hag, wanting to lick up your youth with your juices. Am I that? Come now," she said, her fire lowering itself, crackling with its amusement, with everything she held in check, her voice a long, long pin, skewering what she spoke to against the farther wall. "Come now. How can I be such a fiend, and wear the crucifix on my breast? My ancient, withered, fallen, empty breast. Come now. What's in a name?"

As the pin of her voice came out of him, the young man pushed himself away from the wall. For an instant there was an air of panic about him. He was accustomed to the characteristics of the world. Old men creeping through rainy alleys could not strike mighty blows with their iron hands. Women were moths that burnt, but did not burn, tones of tinsel and pleading, not razor blades.

Snake shuddered all over. And then his panic went away. Instinctively, he told something from the aura of the room itself. Living as he did, generally he had come to trust his instincts.

He slunk back to the woman, not close, this time, no nearer than two yards.

"Your man over there," he said, "he took me to a fancy restaurant. He got me drunk. I say things when I'm drunk I shouldn't say. You see? I'm a lout. I shouldn't be here in your nice house. I don't know how to talk to people like you. To a lady. You see? But I haven't any money. None. Ask him. I explained it all. I'll do anything for money. And the way I talk. Some of them like it. You see? It makes me sound dangerous. They like that. But it's just an act." Fawning on her, bending on her the groundless glory of his eyes, he had also retreated, was almost at the door.

The Vampire made no move. Like a marvelous waxwork she dominated the room, red and white and black, and the old man was only a shadow in a corner.

Snake darted about and bolted. In the blind lightlessness, he skimmed the passage, leapt out in space upon the stairs, touched, leapt, touched, reached the open area beyond. Some glint of star-

253

shine revealed the stained glass panes in the door. As it crashed open, he knew quite well that he had been let go. Then it slammed behind him and he pelted through ivy and down the outer steps, and across the hollow plain of tall wet trees.

So much, infallibly, his instincts had told him. Strangely, even as he came out of the gates upon the vacant road, and raced towards the heart of the city, they did not tell him he was free.

"Do you recollect," said the Vampire, "you asked me, at the very beginning, about the crucifix."

"I do recollect, Princess. It seemed odd to me, then. I did not understand, of course."

"And you," she said. "How would you have it, after——" She waited. She said, "After you leave me."

He rejoiced that his death would cause her a momentary pain. He could not help that, now. He had seen the fire wake in her, flash and scald in her, as it had not done for half a century, ignited by the presence of the thief, the gigolo, the parasite.

"He," said the old man, "is young and strong, and can dig some pit for me."

"And no ceremony?" She had overlooked his petulance, of course, and her tact made him ashamed.

"Just to lie quiet will be enough," he said, "but thank you, Princess, for your care. I do not suppose it will matter. Either there is nothing, or there is something so different I shall be astonished by it."

"Ah, my friend. Then you do not imagine yourself damned?"

"No," he said. "No, no." And all at once there was passion in his voice, one last fire of his own to offer her. "In the life you gave me, I was blessed."

She closed her eyes, and Vasyelu Gorin perceived he had wounded her with his love. And, no longer peevishly, but in the way of a lover, he was glad.

Next day, a little before three in the afternoon, Snake returned.

A wind was blowing, and seemed to have blown him to the door in a scurry of old brown leaves. His hair was also blown, and bright, his face wind-slapped to a ridiculous freshness. His eyes, however, were heavy, encircled, dulled. The eyes showed, as did nothing else about him, that he had spent the night, the forenoon, engaged in his second line of commerce. They might have drawn thick curtains and blown out the lights, but that would not have helped him. The senses of Snake were doubly acute in the dark, and he could see in the dark, like a lynx.

"Yes?" said the old man, looking at him blankly, as if at a trades-man.

"Yes," said Snake, and came by him into the house.

Vasyelu did not stop him. Of course not. He allowed the young man, and all his blown gleamingness and his wretched roúe eyes, to stroll across to the doors of the salon, and walk through. Vasyelu followed.

The blinds, a sombre ivory colour, were down, and the lamps had been lit; on a polished table hothouse flowers foamed from a jade bowl. A second door stood open on the small library, the soft glow of the lamps trembling over gold-worked spines, up and up, a tor-rent of static, priceless books.

Snake went into and around the library, and came out.

"I didn't take anything."

"Can you even read?" snapped Vasyelu Gorin, remmbering when he could not, a wood-cutter's fifth son, an oaf and a sot, drinking his way or sleeping his way through a life without windows or vistas, a mere blackness of error and unrecognised boredom. Long ago. In that little town cobbled together under the forest. And the chateau with its starry lights, the carriages on the road, shining, the dark trees either side. And bowing in answer to a question, lifting a silver comfit box from a pocket as easily as he had lifted a coin the day before . . .

Snake sat down, leaning back relaxedly in the chair. He was not relaxed, the old man knew. What was he telling himself? That there was money here, eccentricity to be battened upon. That he could take her, the old woman, one way or another. There were always excuses that one could make to oneself.

When the Vampire entered the room, Snake, practised, a gigolo, came to his feet. And the Vampire was amused by him, gently now. She wore a bone-white frock that had been sent from Paris last year. She had never worn it before. Pinned at the neck was a black velvet rose with a single drop of dew shivering on a single petal: a pearl

255

that had come from the crown jewels of a czar. Her tact, her peerless tact. *Naturally*, the pearl was saying, *this is why you have come back. Naturally. There is nothing to fear.*

Vasyelu Gorin left them. He returned later with the decanters and glasses. The cold supper had been laid out by people from the city who handled such things, paté and lobster and chicken, lemon slices cut like flowers, orange slices like suns, tomatoes that were anemones, and oceans of green lettuce, and cold, glittering ice. He decanted the wines. He arranged the silver coffee service, the boxes of different cigarettes. The winter night had settled by then against the house, and, roused by the brilliantly lighted rooms, a moth was dashing itself between the candles and the coloured fruits. The old man caught it in a crystal goblet, took it away, let it go into the darkness. For a hundred years and more, he had never killed anything.

Sometimes, he heard them laugh. The young man's laughter was at first too eloquent, too beautiful, too unreal. But then, it became ragged, boisterous; it became genuine.

The wind blew stonily. Vasyelu Gorin imagined the frail moth beating its wings against the huge wings of the wind, falling spent to the ground. It would be good to rest.

In the last half hour before dawn, she came quietly from the salon, and up the stair. The old man knew she had seen him as he waited in the shadows. That she did not look at him or call to him was her attempt to spare him this sudden sheen that was upon her, its direct and pitiless glare. So he glimpsed it obliquely, no more. Her straight pale figure ascending, slim and limpid as a girl's. Her eyes were young, full of a primal refinding, full of utter newness.

In the salon, Snake slept under his jacket on the long white couch, its brocaded cushions beneath his cheek. Would he, on waking, carefully examine his throat in a mirror?

The old man watched the young man sleeping. She had taught Vasyelu Gorin how to speak five languages, and how to read three others. She had allowed him to discover music, and art, history and the stars; profundity, mercy. He had found the closed tomb of life opened out on every side into unbelievable, inexpressible landscapes. And yet, and yet. The journey must have its end. Worn out with ecstasy and experience, too tired any more to laugh with joy. To rest was everything. To be still. Only she could continue, for only

256

she could be eternally reborn. For Vasyelu, once had been enough.

He left the young man sleeping. Five hours later, Snake was noiselessly gone. He had taken all the cigarettes, but nothing else.

Snake sold the cigarettes quickly. At one of the cafés he sometimes frequented, he met with those who, sensing some change in his fortunes, urged him to boast. Snake did not, remaining irritatingly reticent, vague. It was another patron. An old man who liked to give him things. Where did the old man live? Oh, a fine apartment, the north side of the city.

Some of the day, he walked.

A hunter, he distrusted the open veldt of daylight. There was too little cover, and equally too great cover for the things he stalked. In the afternoon, he sat in the gardens of a museum. Students came and went, seriously alone, or in groups riotously. Snake observed them. They were scarcely younger than he himself, yet to him, another species. Now and then a girl, catching his eye, might smile, or make an attempt to linger, to interest him. Snake did not respond. With the economic contempt of what he had become, he dismissed all such sexual encounters. Their allure, their youth, these were commodities valueless in others. They would not pay him.

The old woman, however, he did not dismiss. How old was she? Sixty, perhaps—no, much older. Ninety was more likely. And yet, her face, her neck, her hands were curiously smooth, unlined. At times, she might only have been fifty. And the dyed hair, which should have made her seem raddled, somehow enhanced the illusion of a young woman.

Yes, she fascinated him. Probably she had been an actress. Foreign, theatrical—rich. If she was prepared to keep him, thinking him mistakenly her pet cat, then he was willing, for a while. He could steal from her when she began to cloy and he decided to leave.

Yet, something in the uncomplexity of these thoughts disturbed him. The first time he had run away, he was unsure now from what. Not the vampire name, certainly, a stage name—*Draculas*—what else? But from something—some awareness of fate for which idea his vocabulary had no word, and no explanation. Driven once away, driven thereafter to return, since it was foolish not to. And she had known how to treat him. Gracefully, graciously. She would be hon-

257

ourable, for her kind always were. Used to spending money for what
they wanted, they did not baulk at buying people, too. They had
never forgotten flesh, also, had a price, since their roots were firmly
locked in an era when there had been slaves.

But. But he would not, he told himself, go there tonight. No. It
would be good she should not be able to rely on him. He might go
tomorrow, or the next day, but not tonight.

The turning world lifted away from the sun, through a winter
sunset, into darkness. Snake was glad to see the ending of the light,
and false light instead spring up from the apartment blocks, the
cafés.

He moved out on to the wide pavement of a street, and a man
came and took his arm on the right side, another starting to walk by
him on the left.

"Yes, this is the one, the one calls himself Snake."

"Are you?" the man who walked beside him asked.

"Of course it is," said the first man, squeezing his arm. "Didn't we
have an exact description? Isn't he just the way he was described?"

"And the right place, too," agreed the other man, who did not
hold him. "The right area."

The men wore neat nondescript clothing. Their faces were sallow
and smiling, and fixed. This was a routine with which both were
familiar. Snake did not know them, but he knew the touch, the ac-
cent, the smiling fixture of their masks. He had tensed. Now he let
the tension melt away, so they should see and feel it had gone.

"What do you want?"

The man who held his arm only smiled.

The other man said, "Just to earn our living."

"Doing what?"

On either side the lighted street went by. Ahead, at the street's
corner, a vacant lot opened where a broken wall lunged away into
the shadows.

"It seems you upset someone," said the man who only walked.
"Upset them badly."

"I upset a lot of people," Snake said.

"I'm sure you do. But some of them won't stand for it."

"Who was this? Perhaps I should see them."

"No. They don't want that. They don't want you to see anybody."

The black turn was a few feet away.

"Perhaps I can put it right."

"No. That's what we've been paid to do."

"But if I don't know——" said Snake, and lurched against the man who held his arm, ramming his fist into the soft belly. The man let go of him and fell. Snake ran. He ran past the lot, into the brilliant glare of another street beyond, and was almost laughing when the thrown knife caught him in the back.

The lights turned over. Something hard and cold struck his chest, his face. Snake realized it was the pavement. There was a dim blurred noise, coming and going, perhaps a crowd gathering. Someone stood on his ribs and pulled the knife out of him and the pain began.

"Is that it?" a choked voice asked some way above him: the man he had punched in the stomach.

"It'll do nicely."

A new voice shouted. A car swam to the kerb and pulled up raucously. The car door slammed, and footsteps went over the cement. Behind him, Snake heard the two men walking briskly away.

Snake began to get up, and was surprised to find he was unable to.

"What happened?" someone asked, high, high above.

"I don't know."

A woman said softly, "Look, there's blood——"

Snake took no notice. After a moment he tried again to get up, and succeeded in getting to his knees. He had been hurt, that was all. He could feel the pain, no longer sharp, blurred, like the noise he could hear, coming and going. He opened his eyes. The light had faded, then came back in a long wave, then faded again. There seemed to be only five or six people standing around him. As he rose, the nearer shapes backed away.

"He shouldn't move," someone said urgently.

A hand touched his shoulder, fluttered off, like an insect.

The light faded into black, and the noise swept in like a tide, filling his ears, dazing him. Something supported him, and he shook it from him—a wall—

"Come back, son," a man called. The lights burned up again, reminiscent of a cinema. He would be all right in a moment. He walked away from the small crowd, not looking at them. Respectfully, in awe, they let him go, and noted his blood trailing behind him along the pavement.

The French clock chimed sweetly in the salon; it was seven. Beyond the window, the park was black. It had begun to rain again.

The old man had been watching from the downstairs window for rather more than an hour. Sometimes, he would step restlessly away, circle the room, straighten a picture, pick up a petal discarded by the dying flowers. Then go back to the window, looking out at the trees, the rain and the night.

Less than a minute after the chiming of the clock, a piece of the static darkness came away and began to move, very slowly, towards the house.

Vasyelu Gorin went out into the hall. As he did so, he glanced towards the stairway. The lamp at the stairhead was alight, and she stood there in its rays, her hands lying loosely at her sides, elegant as if weightless, her head raised.

"Princess?"

"Yes, I know. Please hurry, Vassu. I think there is scarcely any margin left."

The old man opened the door quickly. He sprang down the steps as lightly as a boy of eighteen. The black rain swept against his face, redolent of a thousand memories, and he ran through an orchard in Burgundy, across a hillside in Tuscany, along the path of a wild garden near St. Petersburg that was St. Petersburg no more, until he reached the body of a young man lying over the roots of a tree.

The old man bent down, and an eye opened palely in the dark and looked at him.

"Knifed me," said Snake. "Crawled all this way."

Vasyelu Gorin leaned in the rain to the grass of France, Italy and Russia, and lifted Snake in his arms. The body lolled, heavy, not helping him. But it did not matter. How strong he was, he might marvel at it, as he stood, holding the young man across his breast, and turning, ran back towards the house.

"I don't know," Snake muttered, "don't know who sent them. Plenty would like to—— How bad is it? I didn't think it was so bad."

The ivy drifted across Snake's face and he closed his eyes.

260

As Vasyelu entered the hall, the Vampire was already on the lowest stair. Vasyelu carried the dying man across to her, and laid him at her feet. Then Vasyelu turned to leave.

"Wait," she said.

"No, Princess. This is a private thing. Between the two of you, as once it was between us. I do not want to see it, Princess. I do not want to see it with another."

She looked at him, for a moment like a child, sorry to have distressed him, unwilling to give in. Then she nodded. "Go then, my dear."

He went away at once. So he did not witness it as she left the stair, and knelt beside Snake on the Turkish carpet newly coloured with blood. Yet, it seemed to him he heard the rustle her dress made, like thin crisp paper, and the whisper of the tiny dagger parting her flesh, and then the long still sigh.

He walked down through the house, into the clean and frigid modern kitchen full of electricity. There he sat, and remembered the forest above the town, the torches as the yelling aristocrats hunted him for his theft of the comfit box, the blows when they caught up with him. He remembered, with a painless unoppressed refinding, what it was like to begin to die in such a way, the confused anger, the coming and going of tangible things, long pulses of being alternating with deep valleys of non-being. And then the agonised impossible crawl, fingers in the earth itself, pulling him forward, legs sometimes able to assist, sometimes failing, passengers which must be dragged with the rest. In the graveyard at the edge of the estate, he ceased to move. He could go no farther. The soil was cold, and the white tombs, curious petrified vegetation over his head, seemed to suck the black sky into themselves, so they darkened, and the sky grew pale.

But as the sky was drained of its blood, the foretaste of day began to possess it. In less than an hour, the sun would rise.

He had heard her name, and known he would eventually come to serve her. The way in which he had known, both for himself and for the young man called Snake, had been in a presage of violent death.

All the while, searching through the city, there had been no one with that stigma upon them, that mark. Until, in the alley, the warm hand gripped his neck, until he looked into the leopard-coloured eyes. Then Vasyelu saw the mark, smelled the scent of it like singed bone.

How Snake, crippled by a mortal wound, bleeding and semi-aware, had brought himself such a distance, through the long streets hard as nails, through the mossy garden-land of the rich, through the colossal gates, over the watery, night-tuned plain, so far, dying, the old man did not require to ask, or to be puzzled by. He, too, had done such a thing, more than two centuries ago. And there she had found him, between the tall white graves. When he could focus his vision again, he had looked and seen her, the most beautiful thing he ever set eyes upon. She had given him her blood. He had drunk the blood of Darejan Draculas, a princess, a vampire. Unique elixir, it had saved him. All wounds had healed. Death had dropped from him like a torn skin, and everything he had been—scavenger, thief, brawler, drunkard, and, for a certain number of coins, *whore*—each of these things had crumbled away. Standing up, he had trodden on them, left them behind. He had gone to her, and kneeled down as, a short while before, she had kneeled by him, cradling him, giving him the life of her silver veins.

And this, all this, was now for the other. Even her blood, it seemed, did not bestow immortality, only longevity, at last coming to a stop for Vasyelu Gorin. And so, many many decades from this night the other, too, would come to the same hiatus. Snake, too, would remember the waking moment, conscious another now endured the stupefied thrill of it, and all that would begin thereafter.

Finally, with a sort of guiltiness, the old man left the hygienic kitchen and went back towards the glow of the upper floor, stealing out into the shadow at the light's edge.

He understood that she would sense him there, untroubled by his presence—had she not been prepared to let him remain?

It was done.

Her dress was spread like an open rose, the young man lying against her, his eyes wide, gazing up at her. And she would be the most beautiful thing that he had ever seen. All about, invisible, the shed skins of his life, husks he would presently scuff uncaringly underfoot. And she?

The Vampire's head inclined toward Snake. The dark hair fell softly. Her face, powdered by the lampshine, was young, was full of vitality, serene vivacity, loveliness. Everything had come back to her. She was reborn.

Perhaps it was only an illusion.

The old man bowed his head, there in the shadows. The jealousy, the regret were gone. In the end, his life with her had become only another skin that he must cast. He would have the peace that she might never have, and be glad of it. The young man would serve her, and she would be huntress once more, and dancer, a bright phantom gliding over the ballroom of the city, this city and others, and all the worlds of land and soul between.

Vasyelu Gorin stirred on the platform of his existence. He would depart now, or very soon; already he heard the murmur of the approaching train. It would be simple, this time, not like the other time at all. To go willingly, everything achieved, in order. Knowing she was safe.

There was even a faint colour in her cheeks, a blooming. Or maybe, that was just a trick of the lamp.

The old man waited until they had risen to their feet, and walked together quietly into the salon, before he came from the shadows and began to climb the stairs, hearing the silence, their silence, like that of new lovers.

At the head of the stair, beyond the lamp, the dark was gentle, soft as the Vampire's hair. Vasyelu walked forward into the dark without misgiving, tenderly.

How he had loved her.

Derelicts

BY STEVE RASNIC TEM

Every man and woman has an ambition, however humble, however vaulted. Each of us has an instinctive reaction when we see a panhandler on the street, a wino sleeping in a door-way, a beggar limping through the rain: we either feel re-pulsed by such a waste of humanity, turn away in embarrass-ment, bleed a little from the heart, or don't give a damn. What we all seem to forget, though, is that those men and women had ambitions just as we do now, and something hap-pened to kill them.

Simply saying it can't happen to me doesn't change the fact that it can.

Steve Rasnic Tem is a Colorado poet, short story writer, and editor. His dozens of stories have appeared throughout this country and abroad, their hallmark being the illumination of fears we don't like to admit we even recognize.

THEY always seemed to find him, the derelicts. They always seemed to know just where to look. He'd go into a store to buy cigarettes or beer, and when he came out there'd be several of them gathered around, waiting for him. Washed out eyes and dark stubble, frayed collars and cuffs. Hand always outstretched, that look of hunger in the face. They seemed convinced he would give them something; they were sure of him. They'd pass by far more likely prospects to hit on him. It was as if they had a network, passing the word around that he, the red-haired one, was the one to ask.

And yet he never gave them anything. He was polite enough about it, never rude, but still he never went into his pockets for them, never gave them money or offered to buy them food. He would walk past them, self-consciously holding his head erect. He would

265

not be intimidated by them; they had no right to intimidate him. And yet they continued to approach him: individually, in couples, even small groups.

He lived in an old part of Denver, an odd mixture of housing developments, antique houses, abandoned buildings and vacant lots. The shopping malls nearby were among the oldest in the city, every other store boarded up or rented out for warehouse space. Shops seemed to come and go, few lasting more than a couple of months. "Coming Soon To This Location" signs were much in evidence, and were removed frequently, often before the neighborhood had even been told the nature of the new business.

Tatters of poster overlaying poster made ragged murals on nearly half the buildings. Stripped away with but partial success, each succeeding layer blended and weathered until they made Rorschach arrangements of color. He had never seen so many posters and handbills anywhere; where did they all come from? He had never seen anyone actually putting them up. Circus posters and campaign posters, handbills promoting the Socialist Workers' Party, advertising community meetings, block parties, year-old garage sales. Always asking you to join, to belong to something. They suggested excessive activity, but he knew there had been little such activity in some time.

Abandoned stores, boarded-up houses, overgrown lots (wasn't there some sort of ordinance governing those?), structures crumbling dangerously into the streets, trash-filled alleys . . . if he really thought about it the sense of desolation was nearly overwhelming. Like a city in wartime, or a bad dream about the world after a nuclear attack. So few people out in the streets, especially this time of year. It was too unpleasant.

And where did all the trash come from, or the wind-blown grit that stung your eyes? Sometimes he had the fantasy it was manufactured outside the city, brought in on trucks or dropped from planes.

The number of derelicts in the area increased, even as the apparent wealth declined. He couldn't understand it. He theorized enough: perhaps the police had driven them out of other areas, perhaps they were local hotel dwellers with Social Security money—not wanting handouts so much as to make contact. Perhaps they were a club. He watched closely for hidden handshakes and meaningful looks. They seemed so well organized; he couldn't believe it had happened by accident.

He'd changed jobs twice the past year. Staying too long in one office had always made him uncomfortable. Both his employers had been surprised; they'd insisted he talk out any problems he might be having with them personally. They said he was a valuable man. They said they couldn't get along without him. Their insistence made him anxious, and in both cases he cleaned out his desk immediately, canceling his two weeks' notice.

He hadn't seen his wife and two kids in over three years. Last thing he'd heard they'd moved to Chicago. He felt sad about that, but not enough to write, not enough to make contact. He knew he should, but he just couldn't force himself. His attitude nagged him; he was aware of how cold, how inhuman it must seem to others. But he didn't have it in him to tie himself to a wife and children. It was somehow . . . wrong, for him. As if he were committing some moral wrong—he felt it that strongly.

He left the grocery store with bags in the crooks of both arms. Twice as much food as he needed, really, and he wasn't sure why he'd been so extravagant, except sometimes since he'd left his family he'd had a crazy urge to buy, to consume, to let the food spoil and then throw it out when it smelled too bad to tolerate. It released something in him to do that; it was relaxing.

They were waiting for him, a group of five or six, outside the grocery store. He couldn't get to his car without passing through them. They had no right. They had no . . .

They wouldn't move. He strode closer and closer to their little group, and still they wouldn't budge. The tallest one turned slightly as he approached, the derelict opened his mouth wide, and expelled a long, slow and rancid breath into his face. A smell of ancient appetites, things dying in the cavern of the mouth. He veered away from them, and two old women raised ragged hands, grease staining them in streaks, or was it blood, and dirt caked over to seal their wounds? It was a slow, dirty dance as they moved ever so slightly with his own movements, seeming to follow him with their thoughts, their smells, their dirt, the sluggish cells of their bodies following in kind.

He couldn't bear the thought of having those filthy, tattered clothes touch him, those torn and grimy fingers. And the eyes . . . he couldn't see them. The eyelids so dark and greasy . . . the eyes seemed lost.

He slid past, and, incredibly, they didn't touch him. They slipped by like oil. Dark and silent. He'd never be able to wash them off if they touched him.

They followed him to the car, two steps behind the whole way. He got in, pulled out, and would have run them over if they hadn't suddenly slid aside like a dark and stained curtain.

Driving home he suddenly realized he'd been thinking about his parents. Their faces had crept into his daydreaming, merely as additional faces in the crowd, and then they had stepped forward. When was the last time he had thought about them? He couldn't remember.

For a moment he couldn't remember what he had been thinking about them, and although that kind of lapse happened to him all the time he found it disconcerting. He knew it was something important. Then with a shock he realized he'd been trying to remember the day of their death, and the funeral that followed. What had he been doing? He couldn't remember. He couldn't even remember their death —but it did happen, he was sure it happened—but he suddenly couldn't remember anything about it. Where it occurred, when it occurred . . . it was all a blank.

It was quite remarkable really the way the derelicts worked things. Each derelict seemed assigned a specific streetcorner, but was ready to move, to regroup if it seemed necessary. There were always a few of them everywhere he went in the neighborhood: outside a movie theater, on the steps of the local branch library, sitting by the trees next to his bank, congregating in the parking lot of the insurance company where he worked. And it would always be a mixture of new and old faces. They must have squad leaders, he thought. He began noticing definite patterns. Many of the same faces showed up at his bank that also appeared at his grocery store, but none of those derelicts ever seemed to make an appearance at the library.

At the library they watched him return some long overdue books. At the grocery store they caught him overspending again, buying much more food than he needed. At the theater he bought a ticket to an X-rated movie under their watchful gaze. At the laundromat he sorted shirts he'd let go much too long without washing, and they were there just past his left shoulder, on the other side of the window, lounging on the sidewalk.

He could have done all his shopping outside the neighborhood, but he didn't want to do that. It wasn't loyalty to local commerce so much as an interest in watching how things went in the neighborhood, how things occurred. Observing the life of the neighborhood had become a kind of hobby for him. He watched it go downhill; he studied its decay. He performed a kind of accounting on each building he saw, day after day. He observed whether there were more tiles missing, more chips in the paint, more splits in the wood. He knew where all the broken windows were, and when a new one appeared. He saw the merchandise leave the shelves and noted the failure to reorder. He watched the weeds grow around the buildings and in the vacant lots.

On a Saturday he drove around the lake. There seemed more of the derelicts than he had ever seen before, hundreds of them, mixed in thoroughly with the usual Saturday lake crowd. Lounging about, picnicking, even playing basketball. Almost a convention of them. There were more of them than he had imagined, and he wondered if perhaps more of them were migrating here, to his neighborhood, from other parts of the city, or if it were just that large numbers of his neighbors were going over—their lives decaying as the neighborhood decayed.

He thought he saw his parents in the crowd, sunning themselves in tattered and greasy clothes with the other derelicts, and he spent some time driving around in that area, but he couldn't be sure, and he did not see them again.

On his way home that day he realized he didn't really know if his parents were alive or dead. He could not remember at all.

When he got home he sat out on the front porch a while. He realized he had been paying little attention to his own block of late. The house across the street was boarded up, weeds covering the sidewalk, the flower beds, most of a tricycle. The house just north of his had its shades pulled, several windows broken, and a few weeks' worth of mail spilling out of the mail box. All up and down the street:

dark and gray houses, empty driveways, a few cars abandoned on the street, their sides rusting, lights broken, windshields spiderwebbed with cracks. Trash and leaves covered the shallow curbs.

He wondered if it were possible. If he could be the last person living on his block.

He couldn't sleep that night. After dark he'd gone inside and sat on the couch, turning the radio up loud to fill the emptiness. He had things to do, he knew, but he could not remember what they were. He could not remember the names of his missing neighbors. He could not remember what was on TV that night. He could not remember if the mail had come. He could not remember if he had eaten. He repeated his own name over and over to himself, silently, his lips moving slightly. It made him feel better.

When he looked out his front window he thought he could see the tattered shadows on his porch, looking in on him, their eyes but slightly lighter in color than their soiled clothing. Varied shades of gray. But perhaps it was an effect of the lighting. He couldn't be sure, and he would not check.

The bright sun through his window woke him up early the next morning. He sat on the edge of the bed, feeling slightly startled with the morning. Everything seemed much too bright somehow . . . full of glare. But it made him feel better this morning than he had in some time. As if there were energy in the brightness he could use.

He drove to work and noticed that even the neighborhood seemed brighter somehow, full of sun, and full of promise despite the condition of the streets and buildings. There were no derelicts in sight. They did not stare out at him from street corners as they usually did.

Their absence made him vaguely uneasy, but he forced a smile. He wasn't going to let them spoil this bright morning.

In the parking lot outside the insurance building was a welcoming committee to greet him. Bright and shiny faces, arms outstretched to shake his hand, pull him into the crowd. Hundreds of them. He searched their faces for deceit, but he found none there.

They waved at him with their torn fingers and tattered clothes, smiled with their unshaven, greasy jowls. The women with dark eyes beckoned, the stoic men with their oily hair and heavy smell gestured invitingly. He recognized the lady who lived across the street from him, the man from two houses down.

He thought he saw his parents near the center of the crowd and slowly pushed into the mass of bodies, seeking them, wanting to talk to them. It had been a long time. He wanted to tell them how he was doing, share his thoughts, ask for advice. He needed them now.

The mass of bodies moved rhythmically as he pushed to its center, seeing his father's face here, the back of his mother's head over there, just out of reach. He was feeling better now, more satisfied. He felt certain he would get his own streetcorner. Surely they owed him that?

In Darkness, Angels

BY ERIC VAN LUSTBADER

Love is an emotion with which writers have a field day because of its complexities, its simplicity, and the joy and anguish it causes in any given person, on any given day, at any given moment—more often than not, both at the same time. There are, however, darker sides to this emotion, which cause it to produce more personal fears, more darknight terrors, than any other emotion.

Eric Van Lustbader is the author of the bestselling novels The Ninja *and* Sirens, *and his latest is* Black Heart. *He lives in New York City.*

IF I had known then what I know now.

How those words echo on and on inside my mind, like a rubber ball bouncing down an endless staircase. As if they had a life of their own. Which, I suppose, they do now.

I cannot sleep but is it any wonder? Outside, blue-white lightning forks like a giant's jagged claw and the thunder is so loud at times that I feel I must be trapped inside an immense bell, reverberations like memory unspooling in a reckless helix, making a mess at my feet.

If I had known then what I know now. And yet. . . .

And yet I return again and again to that windswept evening when the ferry deposited me at the east end of the island. It had once been, so I had been told by the rather garrulous captain, a swansneck peninsula. But over time, the water had gradually eaten away at the rocky soil until at last the land had succumbed to the ocean's cool tidal embrace, severing itself from the mainland a mile away.

Of course the captain had an entirely different version of what had

273

transpired. "It's them folks up there," he had said, jerking his sharp unshaven chin toward the castle high atop the island's central mount. "Didn't want no more interference from the other folks hereabouts." He gave a short barking laugh and spat over the boat's side. "Just as well, I say," he observed as he squinted heavily into the last of the dying sun's watery light. "Them rocks were awfully sharp." He shook his head as if weighed down by the memory. "Kids were always darin one another t'do their balancin act goin across, down that long spit o land." He turned the wheel hard over and spuming water rushed up the bow of the ferry. "Many's the night we'd come out with the searchlights, tryin to rescue some fool boy'd gone over."

For just a moment he swung us away from the island looming up on our starboard side, getting the most out of the crosswinds. "Never found em, though. Not a one." He spat again. "You go over the side around here, you're never seen again."

"The undertow," I offered.

He whipped his ruddy windburned face around, impaling me with one pale gray eye. "Undertow, you say?" His laugh was harsh now and unpleasant. "You gotta lot t'learn up there at Fuego del Aire, boyo. Oh, yes indeed!"

He left me on the quayside with no one around to mark my arrival. As the wide-beamed ferry tacked away, pushed by the strong sunset wind, I thought I saw the captain raise an arm in my direction.

I turned away from the sea. Great stands of pine, bristly and dark in the failing light, marched upward in majestic array toward the castle high above me. Their tops whipsawed, sending off an odd melancholy drone.

I felt utterly, irretrievably alone and for the first time since I had sent the letter I began to feel the queasy fluttering of reservations. An odd kind of inner darkness had settled about my shoulders like a vulture descending upon the flesh of the dead.

I took a deep breath and shook my head to clear it. The captain's stories were only words strung one after the other—all the legends just words and nothing more. Now I would see for myself. After all, that was what I wanted.

The last of the sunset torched the upper spires so that for a moment they looked like bloody spears. Imagination, that's all it was. A writer's imagination. I clutched at my battered weekender and

274

continued onward, puffing, for the way was steep. But I had arrived at just the right time of the day when the scorching sun was gone from the sky and night's deep chill had not yet settled over the land.

The air was rich with the scents of the sea, an agglomeration so fecund it took my breath away. Far off over the water, great gulls twisted and turned in lazy circles, skimming over the shining face of the ocean only to whirl high aloft, disappearing for long moments into the fleecy pink and yellow clouds.

From the outside, the castle seemed stupendous. It was immense, thrusting upward into the sky as if it were about to take off in flight. It was constructed—obviously many years ago—from massive blocks of granite laced with iridescent chips of mica that shone like diamonds, rubies and sapphires in the evening's light.

A fairy tale castle it surely looked with its shooting turrets and sharply angled spires, horned and horrific. However, on closer inspection, I saw that it had been put together with nothing more fantastic than mortar.

Below me, a mist was beginning to form, swiftly climbing the route I had taken moments before as if following me. Already the sight of the quay had been snuffed out and the cries of the gulls, filtered through the stuff, were eerie and vaguely disquieting.

I climbed the basalt steps to the front door of the castle. The span was fully large enough to drive a semi through. It was composed of a black substance that seemed to be neither stone nor metal. Cautiously, I ran my hand over its textured surface. It was petrified wood. In its center was a circular scrollwork knocker of black iron and this I used.

There was surprisingly little noise but almost immediately the door swung inward. At first I could see nothing. The creeping mist had curled itself around the twilight, plunging me into a dank and uncomfortable night.

"Yes?" It was a melodious voice, light and airy. A woman's voice. I told her my name.

"I am so sorry," she said. "We tend to lose track of time at Fuego del Aire. I am Marissa. Of course you were expected. My brother will be extremely angry that you were not met at the quay."

"It's all right," I said. "I thoroughly enjoyed the walk."

"Won't you come in."

I picked up my suitcase and crossed the threshold, felt her slim hand slip into mine. The hallway was as dark as the night outside. I did not hear the door swing shut but when I looked back the sky and the rolling mist were gone.

I heard the rustling of her just in front of me and I could smell a scent like a hillside of flowers at dusk. Her skin was as soft as velvet but the flesh beneath was firm and supple and I found myself suddenly curious to find out what she looked like. Did she resemble the image in my thoughts? A thin, pale waif-like creature, faint blue traceries of veins visible beneath her thin delicate skin, her long hair as black as a raven's wings.

After what seemed an interminable time, we emerged into a dimly lighted chamber from which all other rooms on this floor seemed to branch. Directly ahead of us, an enormous staircase wound upward. It was certainly wide enough for twenty people to ascend abreast.

Torches flickered and the smoky, perfumed air was thick with the scent of burning tallow and whale oil. Uncomfortable looking furniture lined the walls: bare, wooden stiff-backed benches and chairs one might find in a Methodist church. Huge, heavy banners hung limply but they were so high above my head and the light so poor I could not make out their designs.

Marissa turned to face me and I saw that she was not at all as I had imagined her.

True, she was beautiful enough. But her cheeks were ruddy, her eyes cornflower blue and her hair was the color of sun-dazzled honey, falling in thick, gentle waves from a thin tortoise-shell band that held it from her face, back over her head, across her shoulders, cascading all the way down to the small of her back.

Her coral lips pursed as if she could not help the smile that now brightened her face. "Yes," she said softly, musically, "you are truly surprised."

"I'm sorry," I said. "Am I staring?" I gave an unnatural laugh. Of course I was staring. I could not stop.

"Perhaps you are weary from your climb. Would you like some food now? A cool drink to refresh you?"

"I would like to meet Morodor," I said, breaking my eyes away from her gaze with a concerted effort. She seemed to possess an ability to draw emotion out of me, as if she held the key to channels in myself I did not know existed.

"In time," she said. "You must be patient. There are many pressing matters that need attending to. Only he can see to them. I am certain you understand."

Indeed I did not. To have come this far, to have waited so long . . . all I felt was frustration. Like a hurt little boy, I had wanted Morodor to greet me at the front door by way of apology for the discourtesy of the utter stillness at the quay when I arrived. But no. There were more important matters for him.

"When I wrote to your brother——"

Marissa had lifted her long pale palm. "Please," she said, smiling. "Be assured that my brother wishes to aid you. I suspect that is because he is a writer himself. There is much time here at Fuego del Aire and lately his contemplation has found this somewhat more physical outlet."

I thought of the grisly stories the ferryboat captain had heaped on me—and others, over time, that had come my way from other loquacious mouths—and felt a chill creeping through my bones at the idea of Morodor's physical outlets.

"It must be fascinating to be able to write novels," Marissa said. "I must confess that I was quite selfishly happy when I learned of your coming. Your writing has given me much pleasure." She touched the back of my hand as if I might be a sculpture of great artistry. "This extraordinary talent must make you very desirable in . . . your world."

"You mean literary circles . . . entertainment. . . ."

"Circles, yes. You are quite special. My brother doubtless divined this from your letter." She took her fingertips from me. "But now it is late and I am certain you are tired. May I show you to your room? Food and drink are waiting for you there."

That night there was no moon. Or rather no moon could be seen. Nor the stars nor even the sky itself. Peering out the window of my turret room, I could see nothing but the whiteness of the mist. It was as if the rest of the world had vanished.

Gripping the edge of the windowsill with my fingers, I leaned out

277

as far as I dared, peering into the night in an attempt to pick up any outline, any shape. But not even the tops of the enormous pines could poke their way through the pall.

I strained to hear the comforting hiss and suck of the ocean spending itself on the rocky shore so far below me. There was nothing of that, only the odd intermittent whistling of the wind through the stiff-fingered turrets of the castle.

At length I went back to bed, but for the longest time I could not fall asleep. I had waited so long for Morodor's reply to my letter, had traveled for so many days just to be here now, it seemed impossible to relax enough for sleep to overtake me.

I was itchy with anticipation. Oh more. I was burning. . . . In the days after I had received his affirmative answer, the thought of coming here, of talking to him, of learning his secrets had, more and more, come to stand for my own salvation.

It is perhaps difficult enough for any author to be blocked in his work. But for me . . . I lived to write. Without it, there seemed no reason at all to live, for I had found during this blocked time that the days and nights passed like months, years, centuries, as ponderous as old elephants. They had become my burden.

I had been like a machine, feverishly turning out one book after another—one a year—for . . . how many years now? Fifteen? Twenty? You see, the enfant terrible has lost count already. Mercifully.

Until this year when there was nothing, a desert of paper, and I grew increasingly desperate, sitting home like a hermit, traveling incessantly, bringing smiling girls home, abstaining, swinging from one extreme to the other like a human pendulum in an attempt to get the insides in working order again.

Nothing.

And then one drunken night I had heard the first of the stories about Fuego del Aire and, even through the vapors of my stupor, *something* had penetrated. An idea, perhaps or, more accurately at that point, the ghost of an idea. Of lost love, betrayal and the ultimate horror. As simple as that. And as complex. But I knew that imagination was no longer enough, that I would have to seek out this place myself. I had to find Morodor and somehow persuade him to see me. . . .

Sleep. I swear to you it finally came, although, oddly, it was like no slumber I had ever had, for I dreamed that I was awake and trying desperately to fall asleep. I knew that I was to see Morodor in the morning, that I had to be sharp and that, sleepless, I would fall far short of that.

In the dream I lay awake, clutching the bedspread up around my chest, staring at the ceiling with such intensity that I suspected at any minute I would be able to see right through it.

I opened my eyes. Or closed them and opened them again to find the dawnlight streaming through the tall narrow window. I had forgotten to close the curtains before going to bed.

For just an instant I had the strangest sensation in my body. It was as if my legs had gone dead, all the strength flowing out of my muscles and into the wooden floor of my room. But the paralysis had somehow freed my upper torso so that I felt an enormous outpouring of energy.

A brief stab of fear rustled through my chest and my heart fluttered. But as soon as I sat up, the sensation went away. I rose, washed, dressed and went down to breakfast.

Food was waiting in steaming array along the length of an immense wooden table. In fact, now that I had my first good look at Fuego del Aire in the light of day, I saw that everything was of wood: the paneled walls, the floor where you could see it between the series of dark-patterned carpets, the cathedral ceilings; door handles, windowsills, even the lighting fixtures. If I had not seen the outside of the castle myself, I would have sworn the place had been built entirely of wood.

Two formal settings were laid out, one at the head of the table and the other by its left side. Assuming the first was for Morodor, I settled into the side chair and began to help myself.

But it was not Morodor who came down the wide staircase; it was Marissa. She was, that morning, a sight to make the heart pound. It was as if the sun had detached itself from its prescribed route across the heavens and had descended to earth. She wore a sky-blue tunic, wrapped criss-cross between her breasts and around her narrow waist with a deep green satin sash. On her feet she wore rope sandals. I saw that one of her toes was girdled by a tiny gold ring.

Her smile as she approached had the warmth of summer itself.

279

And her hair! How can I adequately describe the way her hair shone in the daylight, sparking and glittering as if each strand were itself some mysterious source of light. Those waves of golden honey acted as if they had a life of their own.

"Good morning," she said easily. "Did you sleep well?"

"Yes," I lied. "Perfectly." I lifted a bowl of green figs. "Fruit?"

"Yes, please. Just a bit." But even with that she left more on her plate than she ate.

"I was hoping to find your brother already awake," I said, finishing up my meal.

She smiled sweetly. "Unfortunately, he is not an early riser. Be patient. All will be well." She rose. "If you are finished, I imagine you are quite curious about Fuego del Aire. There is much here to see."

We went out of the main hall, through corridors and chambers one after another, so filled, so disparate that I soon became dizzied with wonder. The place seemed to go on forever.

At length we emerged into a room that, judging by its accouterments, must once have been a scullery. We crossed it quickly and went through a small door I did not see until Marissa pulled it open.

The mist of last night had gone completely and above was only an enormous cerulean sky clear of cloud or bird. I could hear the distant sea hurling itself with ceaseless abandon at the jagged base of the mount. But lowering my gaze I saw only foliage.

"The garden," Marissa breathed, slipping her hand into mine. "Come on." She took me past a field of tiger lilies, rows of flowering woodbine; through a rose garden of such humbling perfection, it took my breath away.

Beyond, we came upon a long sculptured hedge half again as tall as I stand. There was a long narrow opening through which she led me and immediately we were surrounded by high walls of hedges. They were lushly verdant and immaculately groomed so that it was impossible to say where one left off and another began, seamless on and on and——

"What is this place?" I said.

But Marissa did not answer until, after many twistings and turnings, we were deep within. Then she faced me and said, "This is the

280

labyrinth. My brother had it constructed for me when I was just a child. Perhaps he thought it would keep me out of trouble."

"There *is* a way out," I said uneasily, looking around me at the dark-green screens looming up on every side.

"Oh yes." She laughed, a bell-like silvery tone. "It is up here." And tapped the side of her head with a slender forefinger. "This is where I come to think, when I am sad or distraught. It is so peaceful and still and no one can find me here if I choose to remain hidden, not even Morodor. This is my domain."

She began to lead me onward, through switchbacks, past cul-de-sacs, moving as unerringly as if she were a magnet being drawn toward the North Pole. And I followed her silently; I was already lost.

"My brother used to say to me, 'Marissa, this labyrinth is unique in all the world for I have made it from the blueprint of your mind. All these intricate convolutions . . . the pattern corresponds to the eddies and whorls of your own brain.' "

She stared at me with those huge mocking eyes, so blue it seemed as if the noonday sky were reflected there. The hint of a smile played at the corners of her lips. "But of course I was only a child then and always trying to do what he did . . . to be like him." She shrugged. "He was most likely trying to make me feel special . . . don't you think?"

"He wouldn't need this place to do that," I said. "How on earth do you find your way out of here?" Nothing she had said had lessened my uneasiness.

"The years," she said seriously, "have taken care of that."

She pulled at me and we sat, our torsos in the deep shade of the hedges, our stretched-out legs in the buttery warmth of the sunlight. Somewhere, close at hand, a bumblebee buzzed fatly, contentedly.

I put my head back and watched the play of light and shadow on the hedge opposite us. Ten thousand tiny leaves moved minutely in the soft breeze as if I were watching a distant crowd fluttering lifted handkerchiefs at the arrival of some visiting emperor. A kind of dreamy warmth stole over me and at once my uneasiness was gone.

"Yes," I told her. "It *is* peaceful here."

"I am glad," she said. "You feel it too. Perhaps that is because you are a writer. A writer feels things more deeply, is that not so?"

281

I smiled. "Maybe some, yes. We're always creating characters for our stories so we have to be adept at pulling apart the people we meet. We have to be able to get beyond the world and, like a surgeon, expose their workings."

"And you're never frightened of such things?"

"Frightened? Why?"

"Of what you'll find there."

"I've discovered many things there over the years. How could all of them be pleasant? Why should I want them to be? I sometimes think that many of my colleagues live off the *un*pleasant traits they find beneath the surface." I shrugged. "In any event, nothing seems to work well without the darkness of conflict. In life as well as in writing."

Her eyes opened and she looked at me sideways. "Am I wrong to think that knowledge is very important to you?"

"What could be more important to a writer? I sometimes think there is a finite amount of knowledge—not to be assimilated—but that can be used."

"And that is why you have come here."

"Yes."

She looked away. "You have never married. Why is that?"

I shrugged while I thought about that for a moment. "I imagine it's because I've never fallen in love."

She smiled at that. "Never ever. Not in all the time——"

I laughed. "Now wait a minute! I'm not that old. Thirty-seven is hardly ancient."

"Thirty-seven," she mouthed softly, as if she were repeating words alien to her. "Thirty-seven. Really?"

"Yes." I was puzzled. "How old are you?"

"As old as I look." She tossed her hair. "I told you last night. Time means very little here."

"Oh yes, day to day. But I mean you must——"

"No more talk now," she said, rising and pulling at my hand. "There is too much to see."

We left the labyrinth by a simple enough path, though, left to myself, I undoubtedly would have wandered around in there until someone had the decency to come and get me.

Presently we found ourselves at a stone parapet beyond which the peak dropped off so precipitously that it seemed as if we were standing on the verge of a rift in the world.

This was the western face of the island, one that I had not seen on my journey here. Far below us—certainly more than a thousand feet—the sea creamed and sucked at the jagged rocks, iced at their base by shining pale-gray barnacles. Three or four large lavender and white gulls dipped and wheeled through the foaming spray as they searched for food.

"Beautiful, isn't it?" Marissa said.

But I had already turned from the dark face of the sea to watch the planes and hollows of her own shining face, lit by the soft summer light, all rose and golden, radiating a warmth. . . .

It took me some time to understand the true nature of that heat. It stemmed from the same spot deep inside me from which had leaped that sharp momentary anger.

"Marissa," I breathed, saying her name as if it were a prayer.

And she turned to me, her cornflower blue eyes wide, her full lips slightly parted, shining. I leaned over her, coming closer inch by inch until I had to shut my eyes or cross them. Then I felt the brush of her lips against mine, so incredibly soft, at first cool and fragrant, then quickly warming to blood-heat.

"No," she said, her voice muffled by our flesh. "Oh, don't." But her lips opened under mine and I felt her hot tongue probing into my mouth.

My arms went around her, pulling her to me as gently as I would handle a stalk of wheat. I could feel the hard press of her breasts, the round softness of her stomach, and the heat. The heat rising. . . .

And with the lightning comes the rain. That's from an old poem my mother used to sing to me late at night when the storms woke me up. I cannot remember any more of it. Now it's just a fragment of truth, an artifact unearthed from the silty riverbed of my mind. And I the archeologist of this region as puzzled as everyone else at what I sometimes find. But that, after all, is what has kept me writing, year after year. An engine of creation.

The night is impenetrable with cloud and the hissing downpour. But still I stand at my open window, high up above the city, at the very edge of heaven.

I cannot see the streets below me—the one or two hurrying people beneath their trembling umbrellas or the lights of the cars, if indeed there are any out at this ungodly hour—just the spectral geometric patterns, charcoal-gray on black, of the buildings' tops closest to mine. But not as high. None of them is as high.

Nothing exists now but this tempest and its fury. The night is alive with it, juddering and crackling. Or am I wrong? Is the night alive with something else? I know. *I know.*

I hear the sound of them now. . . .

The days passed like the most intense of dreams. The kind where you can recall every single detail any time you wish, producing its emotions again and again with a conjurer's facility.

Being with Marissa, I forgot about my obsessive desire to seek out Morodor. I no longer asked her where he was or when I would get to see him. In fact, I hoped I never would, for, if there were any truth to the legends of Fuego del Aire, they most assuredly must stem from his dark soul and not from this creature of air and light who never left my side.

In the afternoons we strolled through the endless gardens—for she was ill at ease indoors—and holding her hand seemed infinitely more joyous than looking upon the castle's illimitable marvels. I fully believe that if we had chanced upon a griffin during one of those walks I would have taken no more notice of it than I would an alley cat.

However, no such fabled creature made its appearance, and as the time passed I became more and more convinced that there was no basis at all to the stories that had been told and re-told over the years. The only magical power Marissa possessed was the one that enabled her to cut to the very core of me with but one word or the merest touch of her flesh against mine.

"I lied to you," I told her one day. It was late afternoon. Thick dark sunlight slanted down on our shoulders and backs, as slow-running as honey. The cicadas wailed like beaten brass and butter-flies danced like living jewels in and out of the low bushes and the blossoms as if they were a flock of children playing tag.

"About what?"

"When I said that I had never been in love." I turned over on my

284

back, staring up at a fleecy cloud piled high, a castle in the sky. "I was. Once."

I took her hand, rubbed my thumb over the delicate bones ribbing the back. "It was when I was in college. We met in a child psychology class and fell in love without even knowing it."

For a moment there was a silence between us and I thought perhaps I had made a mistake in bringing it up.

"But you did not marry her."

"No."

"Why not?"

"We were from different . . . backgrounds." I turned to see her face peering at me, seeming as large as the sun in the sky. "I think it would be difficult to explain to you, Marissa. It had something to do with religion."

"Religion." Again she rolled a word off her tongue as if trying to get the taste of a new and exotic food. "I am not certain that I understand."

"We believed in different things—or, more accurately, she believed and I didn't."

"And there was no room for . . . compromise?"

"In this, no. But the ironic part of all of it is that now I have begun to believe, if just a little bit; and she, I think, has begun to disbelieve some of what she had always held sacred."

"How sad," Marissa said. "Will you go back to her?"

"Our time has long passed."

Something curious had come into her eyes. "Then you believe that love has a beginning and an end, always."

I could no longer bear to have those fantastic eyes riveting me. "I had thought so."

"Why do you look away?"

"I——" I watched the sky. The cloud-castle had metamorphosed into a great humpbacked bird. "I don't know."

Her eyes were very clear, piercing though the natural light was dusky. "We are explorers," she said, "at the very precipice of time." Something in her voice drew me. "Can there really be a love without end?"

Now she began to search my face in detail as if she were committing it to memory, as if she might never see me again. And that wild

285

thought brought me fully out of my peaceful dozing.

"Do you love me?"

"Yes," I whispered with someone else's voice. Like a dry wind through sere reeds. And pulled her down to me.

At night we seemed even closer. It was as if I had taken a bit of the sun to bed with me: she was as radiant at night as she was during the day, light and supple and so eager to be held, to be caressed. To be loved.

"Feel how I feel," she whispered, trembling, "when I am close to you." She stretched herself over me. "The mouth can lie with words but the body cannot. This heat is real. All love flows out through the body, do you know that?"

I was beyond being able to respond verbally.

She moved her fingertips on me, then the petal softness of her palms. "I feel your body. How you respond to me. Its depth. As if I were the moon and you the sea." Her lips were at my ear, her esses sibilant. "It is important. More important than you know."

"Why?" I sighed.

"Because only love can mend my heart."

I wondered at the scar there. I moved against her, opening her legs.

"Darling!"

I met Morodor on the first day of my second week at Fuego del Aire. And then it seemed quite by chance.

It was just after breakfast and Marissa had gone back to her room to change. I was strolling along the second floor balustrade when I came across a niche in the wall that I had missed before.

I went through it and found myself on a parapet along the jutting north side of the castle. It was like hanging in mid-air and I would have been utterly stunned by the vista had I not almost immediately run into a dark towering shape.

Hastily I backed up against the stone wall of the castle, thinking I had inadvertently run into another outcropping of this odd structure.

Then, quite literally, it seemed as if a shadow had come to life. It

286

detached itself from the edge of the parapet and now I could see that it was the figure of a man.

He must have been nearly seven feet tall and held about him a great ebon cape, thick and swirling, that rushed down his slender form so that it hissed against the stone floor when he moved.

He turned toward me and I gasped. His face was long and narrow, as bony as a corpse's, his skin fully as pale. His eyes, beneath darkly furred brows, were bits of bituminous matter as if put there to plug a pair of holes into his interior. His nose was long and thin to the point of severity but his lips were full and rubicund, providing the only bit of color to his otherwise deathly pallid face.

His lips opened infinitesimally and he spoke my name. Involuntarily, I shuddered and immediately saw something pass across his eyes: not anger or sorrow but rather a weary kind of resignation.

"How do you do."

The greeting was so formal that it startled me and I was tongue-tied. After all this time, he had faded from my mind and now I longed only to be with Marissa. I found myself annoyed with him for intruding upon us.

"Morodor," I said. I had the oddest impulse to tell him that what he needed most was a good dose of sunshine. That almost made me giggle. Almost.

"Pardon me for saying this but I thought . . . that is, to see you up and around, outside in the daylight——" I stopped, my cheeks burning, unable to go on. I had done it anyway. I cursed myself for the fool that I was.

But Morodor took no offense. He merely smiled—a perfectly ghastly sight—and inclined his head a fraction. "A rather common misconception," he said in his disturbing, rumbling voice. "It is in fact *direct* sunlight that is injurious to my health. I am like a fine old print." His dark hair brushed against his high forehead. "I quite enjoy the daytime, otherwise."

"But surely you must sleep sometime."

He shook his great head. "Sleep is unknown to me. If I slept, I would dream and this is not allowed me." He took a long hissing stride along the parapet. "Come," he said. "Let us walk." I looked

287

back the way I had come and he said, "Marissa knows we are together. Do not fear. She will be waiting for you when we are finished."

Together we walked along the narrow parapet. Apparently, it girdled the entire castle, for I saw no beginning to it and no end.

"You may wonder," Morodor said in his booming, vibratory voice, "why I granted you this interview." His great cape swept around him like the coils of a midnight sea so that it seemed as if he kept the night around him wherever he went. "I sensed in your writing a certain desperation." He turned to me. "And desperation is an emotion with which I can empathize."

"It was kind of you to see me."

"Kind, yes."

"But I must confess that things have . . . changed since I wrote that letter."

"Indeed." Was that a vibratory warning?

"Yes," I plunged onward. "In fact, since I came here, I——" I paused, not knowing how to continue. "The change has come since I arrived at Fuego del Aire."

Morodor said nothing and we continued our perambulation around the perimeter of the castle. Now I could accurately judge just how high up we were. Perhaps that mist I had seen the first night had been a cloud passing us as if across the face of the moon. And why not? All things seemed possible here. It struck me as ridiculous that just fifty miles from here there were supertankers and express trains, Learjets and paved streets lined with shops dispensing sleekly packaged products manufactured by multinational corporations. Surely all those modern artifacts were part of a fading dream I once had.

The sea was clear of sails for as far as the horizon. It was a flat and glittering pool there solely for the pleasure of this man.

"I'm in love with your sister." I had blurted it out and now I stood stunned, waiting, I suppose, for the full brunt of his wrath.

But instead, he stopped and stared at me. Then he threw his head back and laughed, a deep booming sound like thunder. Far off, a gull screeched, perhaps in alarm.

"My dear sir," he said. "You really are the limit!"

"And she's in love with me."

"Oh oh oh. I have no doubt that she is."

"I don't——"

His brows gathered darkly like stormclouds. "You believe your race to be run." He moved away. "But fear, not love, ends it." Through another niche, he slid back inside the castle. It was as if he had passed through the wall.

"If I had known that today was the day," Marissa said, "I would have prepared you."

"For what?"

We were sitting in a bower on a swing-chaise. Above our heads arched brilliant hyacinth and bougainvillea, wrapped around and around a white wooden trellis. It was near dusk and the garden was filled with a deep sapphire light that was almost luminescent. A westerly wind brought us the rich scent of the sea.

"For him. We are not . . . very much alike. At least, superficially."

"Marissa," I said, taking her hand, "are you certain that you *are* Morodor's sister?"

"Of course I am. What do you mean?"

"Well, it's obvious, isn't it?" But when she looked at me blankly, I was forced to go on. "What I mean is, he's precisely . . . what he's supposed to be. At least the way the legends describe . . . what he is."

Her eyes grew dark and she jerked her hand away. She gave me a basilisk stare. "I should have known." Her voice was filled with bitter contempt. "You're just like the rest. And why shouldn't you be?" She stood. "You think he's a monster. Yes, admit it. A monster!"

Her eyes welled up with tears. "And that makes me a monster too, doesn't it. Well, to hell with you!" And she whirled away.

"Marissa!" I cried in anguish. "That's not what I meant at all."

And I ran after her knowing that it was a lie, that it was what I had meant after all. Morodor was all the legends had said he should be. And more. My God but he was hideous. Pallid and cold as the dead. An engine of negative energy, incapable of any real feeling; of crying or true humor. Or love.

Only love can mend my heart.

I *had* meant it. How could this golden girl of air and sunlight bear any family ties to that great looming figure of darkness? Where was

289

the sense in it? The rationality? She had feelings. She laughed and cried, felt pleasure and pain. And she loved. She loved.

"Marissa!" I called again, running. "Marissa, come back!" But she had vanished into the labyrinth and I stood there on the threshold, the scent of roses strong in my nostrils, and peered within. I called out her name over and over again but she did not appear and, unguided, I could not bring myself to venture farther.

Instead, I stormed back to the castle, searching for Morodor. It was already dark and the lights had been lit. As if by magic. In just the same way that the food was prepared, the wine bottles uncorked, my bed turned down in the evening and made in the morning, my soiled clothes washed, pressed and laid out with the professional's precision. And all done without my seeing a soul.

I found Morodor in the library. It was a room as large as a gallery: at least three floors of books, rising upward until the neat rows were lost in the haze of distance. Narrow wooden walkways circled the library at various levels, connected by a complex network of wide wooden ladders.

He was crouched on one of these, three or four steps off the floor. It seemed an odd position for a man of his size.

He was studying a book as I came in but he quietly closed it when he heard me approach.

"What," I said, rather nastily, "no leather bindings?"

His hard ebon eyes regarded me without obvious emotion. "Leather," he said softly, "would mean the needless killing of animals."

"Oh, I see." My tone had turned acid. "It's only humans who need fear you."

He stood up and I backed away, abruptly fearful as he unfolded upward and upward until he stood over me in all his monstrous height.

"Humans," he said, "fear me only because they choose to fear me."

"You mean you haven't given them any cause to fear you?"

"Don't be absurd." He was as close to being annoyed as I had seen him. "I cannot help being what I am. Just as you cannot. We are both carnivores."

290

I closed my eyes and shuddered. "But with what a difference!"

"To some I have been a god."

"Such a dark god." My eyes flew open.

"There is a need for that, too." He put the book way. "Yet I am a man for all that."

"A man who can't sleep, who doesn't dream."

"Who cannot die."

"Not even if I drive a stake through your heart?" I did not know whether or not I was serious.

He went across the room to where a strip of the wooden paneling intervened between two bookshelves. His hand merged from the folds of his voluminous cape and for the first time I saw the long talon-like nails exposed. I shivered as I saw them dig into the wood with ferocious strength. But not in any hot animal way. The movement was as precise as a surgeon peeling back a patient's peritoneum.

Morodor returned with a shard of wood perhaps eighteen inches in length. It was slightly tapered at one end, not needle sharp but pointed enough to do its work. He thrust it into my hands. "Here," he said harshly. "Do it now."

For an instant, I intended to do just that. But then something inside me cooled. I threw the stake from me. "I'll do no such thing."

He actually seemed disappointed. "No matter. That part of the legend, as others, is incorrect." He went back to his perch on the ladder, his long legs drawn up tightly beneath the cape, the outline of his bony knees like a violent set of punctuation marks on a blank page.

"Legends," he said, "are like funerals. They both serve the same purpose. They give comfort without which the encroachment of terrifying entropy would snuff out man's desire—his absolute hunger—for life."

He looked from his long nails up into my face. "Legends are created to set up their own kind of terror. But it is a terror very carefully bounded by certain limitations: the werewolf can be killed by a silver bullet, the medusa by seeing her own reflection in a mirror.

"You see? Always there is a way out for the intrepid. It is a necessary safety valve venting the terror that lurks within all mankind—atavistic darkness, the unconscious. And death."

291

He rested his long arms in his lap. "How secure do you imagine mankind would feel if all of them out there knew the reality of it? That there is no escape for me. No stake through the heart."

"But you said direct sunlight——"

"Was injurious to me. Like the flu, nothing more." He smiled wanly. "A week or two in bed and I am fit again." He laughed sardonically.

"Assuming I believe you, why are you telling me this? By your own admission, mankind could not accept the knowledge."

"Then you won't tell them, will you?"

"But *I* know."

He took a deep breath and for the first time his eyes seemed to come to life, sparking and dancing within their deep fleshless sockets. "Why did you wish to come here, my friend?"

"Why, I told you in the letter. I was blocked, out of ideas."

"And now?"

I stared at him quizzically while it slowly began to wash over me. "I can tell them, can't I?"

He smiled sphinx-like. "You are a writer. You can tell them anything you wish."

"When I told you before that I was a man, I meant it."

I was sitting with Morodor high up in one of the castle's peaks, in what he called the cloud room. Like all the other chambers I had been in here, it was paneled in wood.

"I have a hunger to live just like all the rest of the masses." He leaned back in his chair, shifting about as if he were uncomfortable. To his left and right, enormous windows stood open to the starry field of the night. There were no shutters, no curtains; they could not be closed. A sharp, chill wind blew in, ruffling his dark hair but he seemed oblivious to the caress. "But do not mistake my words. I speak not as some plutocrat bloated on wealth. It is only that I am . . . special."

"What happened?"

His eyes flashed and he shifted again. "In each case, it is different. In mine . . . well, let us say that my hunger for life outweighed my caution." He smiled bleakly. "But then I have never believed that caution was a desirable trait."

292

"Won't you tell me more."

He looked at me in the most avuncular fashion. "I entered into a wager with . . . someone."

"And you won."

"No. I lost. But it was meant that I should lose. Otherwise, I would not be here now." His eyes had turned inward and in so doing had become almost wistful. "I threw the dice one time, up against a wall of green baize."

"You crapped out."

"No. I entered into life."

"And became *El Amor Brujo*. That's what you're sometimes called: the love sorcerer."

"Because of my . . . hypnotic effect on women." He moved minutely and his cape rustled all about him like a copse of trees stirred by a midnight wind. "A survival trait. Like seeing in the dark or having built-in radar."

"Then there's nothing magical——"

"There is," he said, "magic involved. One learns . . . many arts over the years. I have time for everything."

I shivered, pulled my leather jacket closer about me. He might not mind the chill, but I did. I pointed to the walls. "Tell me something. The outside of Fuego del Aire is pure stone. But here, inside, there is only wood. Why is that?"

"I prefer wood, my friend. I am not a creature of the earth and so stone insults me; its density inhibits me. I feel more secure with the wood." His hand lifted, fluttered, dropped back into his lap. "Trees." He said it almost as if it were a sacred word.

In the ensuing silence, I began to sweat despite the coldness. I knew what I at least was leading up to. I rubbed my palms down the fabric of my trousers. I cleared my throat.

"Morodor. . . ."

"Yes." His eyes were half-shut as if he were close to sleep.

"I really do love Marissa."

"I know that." But there seemed no kindness in his voice.

I took a deep breath. "We had a row. She thinks I see you as a monster."

He did not move, his eyes did not open any wider, for which I was profoundly grateful. "In a world where so many possibilities exist,

293

this is true. Yet I am also a man. And I am Marissa's brother. I am friend . . . foe; master . . . servant. It is all in the perception." Still he did not move. "What do *you* see, my friend?"

I wished he'd stop calling me that. I said nothing.

"If you are not truthful with me, I shall know it." His ruby lips seemed to curve upward at their corners. "Something else you may add to the new legend . . . if you choose to write about it."

"I've no wish to deceive you, Morodor. I'm merely trying to sort through my own feelings." I thought he nodded slightly.

"I confess . . . to finding your appearance . . . startling."

"I appreciate your candor."

"Oh, hell, I thought you were hideous."

"I see."

"You hate me now."

"Why should I hate you? Because you take the world view?"

"But that was at first. Already you've changed before my eyes. God knows I've tried but now I don't even find your appearance odd."

As if divining my thoughts, he said, "And this disturbs you."

"It does."

He nodded his head again. "Quite understandable. It will pass." He looked at me. "But you are afraid of that too."

"Yes," I said softly.

"Soon you shall meet my sister again."

I shook my head. "I don't understand."

"Of course you don't." Now his voice sounded softer. "Have patience, my friend. You are young enough still to rush headlong over the precipice merely to discover what is beyond it."

"That's why I came here."

"I know. But that time has passed. Now life has you by the throat and it will be a struggle to the end." His eyes flew open, seeming as hot as burning coals. "And who shall be the victor, my friend? When you have the answer to that, you shall understand it all."

I ate dinner alone that night. I had spent hours searching the castle for Marissa but it was as if she had vanished. Weary at last, I returned to the dining hall and availed myself of vast quantities of the hot food.

I was terrified and I thought that this would act as an inhibitor on my appetite. But, strangely, just the opposite was happening. I ate and ate as if this alone could assuage my fear.

It was Morodor I was terrified of, I knew that. But was it because I feared him or liked him?

Afterward, it was all I could do to drag myself up the staircase. I stumbled down the hallway and into bed without even removing my clothes.

I slept a deep dreamless sleep but when I opened my eyes it was still dark out. I turned over, about to return to sleep, when I heard a sound. I sat bolt upright, the short hairs at the back of my neck stiff and quivering.

Silence.

And out of the silence a weird, thin cry. I got off the bed about to open the door to the hallway when it came again and I turned. It was coming from outside in the blackness of the night.

I threw open the shutters wide and leaned out just as I had on my first night here. This time there was no mist. Stars shone intermittently through the gauzy cloud cover with a fierce cold light, blinking on and off as if they were silently appealing for help.

At first I saw nothing, hearing only the high soughing of the wind through the pines. Then, off to my left, so high up that I mistook it for another cloud, something moved.

I turned my head in that direction and saw a shape a good deal darker than a cloud. It blossomed with sickening speed, blacker even than the night. Wraith or dream, which was it? The noise of the flapping wings, leathery, horned and, what?, scabbed, conjured up in my mind the image of a giant bat.

Precariously, I leaned farther out, saw that it was heading for the open apertures of the cloud room. I hurled myself across the room and out the door, heading up the stairs in giant bounds.

Consequently, I was somewhat out of breath by the time I launched myself through the open doorway to the aerie and there found only Morodor.

He turned quickly from his apparent contemplation of the sky. "You should be asleep," he said. But something in his tone told me that I had been expected.

"Something woke me."

"Not a nightmare, I trust."

"A sound from the night. It was nothing to do with me."

"It is usually quite still here. What kind of sound?"

"It sounded like a scream . . . a terrible cry."

Morodor only stared at me, unblinking, until I was forced to go on.

"I went to the window and looked out. I . . . saw a shape I could not clearly identify; I heard the awful sound of bat wings."

"Oh," Morodor said, "that's quite impossible. We have none here, I've seen to that. Bats are boring, really. As with octopi, I'm afraid their ferocious reputation has been unjustly thrust upon them."

"Just what the hell did I see then?"

Morodor's hand lifted, fell, the arch of a great avian wing. "Whatever it was, it brought you up here."

"Then there *was* something there!" I said in triumph. "You admit it."

"I admit," said Morodor carefully, "that I wanted to see you. The fact is you are here."

"You and I," I said. "But what of Marissa? I have been looking for her all evening. I must see her."

"Do you think it wise to see her now, to . . . continue what has begun, knowing what you do about me?"

"But she is nothing like you. You two are the shadow and the light."

Morodor's gaze was unwavering. "Two sides of the coin, my friend. The same coin."

I was fed up with his oblique answers. "Perhaps," I said sharply, "it's just that you don't want me to see her. After all, I'm an outsider. I don't belong at Fuego del Aire. But if that's the case, let me warn you, I won't be balked!"

"That's the spirit!" His hand clenched into a fist. "Forget all about that which you saw from your bedroom window. It has nothing to do with you." His tone was mocking.

"A bird," I said uncertainly. "That's all it was."

"My friend," he said calmly, "there is no bird as large as the one you saw tonight."

And he reached out for the first time. I felt his chill touch as his long fingers gripped my shoulder with a power that made me wither inside. "Come," he commanded. "Over here at the windowledge."

I stood there, dazed with shock as he let go of me and leaped out into the night.

I screamed, reaching out to save him, thinking that, after all, his apparent melancholy signaled a wish to die. Then I saw his great ebon cape ballooning out like a sail, drawn upward by the cross-currents and, for the first time, I saw what had been hidden beneath its voluminous folds.

I had thought he wore the thing as an affectation, because it was part of the legend. But now I understood. What care had he for legends? He wore the cape for practical reasons.

For now from under it spread a pair of the most extraordinary wings I had ever seen. They were glossy and pitch black, as far away from bat's wings as you could get. For one thing, they were feathered or at least covered in long silky strips that had the appearance of feathers. For another, they were as supple as a hummingbird's and quite as beautiful. And made even more so by the thick, muscular tendons by which they were attached to his back. It was like seeing the most beautifully developed torso: hard muscle tone combined with sleek line. And yet. And yet there was more, in the most literal sense, because more musculature was required in order for those massive wings to support the weight of the rest of the body.

Those wings! Sharply angled and hard, delicate as brushstrokes, they beat at the air like heroic engines. They were a magnificent creation, nothing less than a crowning achievement, an evolutionary pinnacle of the Creator.

But out of the wonder came terror and I thought: Marissa! My God! My God! He means to turn her into this. *El Amor Brujo.*

Without a word, I turned and bolted from the room. Taking the steps three at a time, I returned to the second floor and there found Marissa asleep in her own bed.

My heart beating like a triphammer, I brought a light close to her face. But no. An exhalation hissed from my mouth. There was no change. But still I feared Morodor and what he could do to her.

"Marissa!" I whispered urgently. "Marissa! Wake up!" I shook her but she would not waken. Hurling the light aside, I bent and scooped her up in my arms. Turning, I kicked the door wide and hurried down the stairs. Where I thought to go at that moment remains a mystery to me still. All I know was that I had to get Marissa away from that place.

The way to the disused scullery I knew and this was the route I took. Outside, the wind ruffled my hair but Marissa remained asleep.

I carried her through the field of tiger lilies and the woodbine, down the center aisle of the vast rose garden, to the verge of the labyrinth. Without thinking, I took her inside.

It was dark there. Darker than the night with the high ebon walls, textured like stucco, looming up on every side. I stumbled down the narrow pathways, turning now left or right at random until I knew that I was truly lost. But at least Morodor could not find us and I had with me this place's only key.

Panting, my muscles aching, I knelt on the grass and set Marissa down beside me. I looked around. All I could hear was the faroff whistle of the wind as if diminished by time. Even the booming surf was beyond hearing now.

I sat back and wiped my brow, staring down at that golden face, so innocent in repose, so shockingly beautiful. I could not allow——

Marissa's eyes opened and I helped her to sit up.

"What has happened?"

"I was awakened by a strange sound," I told her. "I saw your brother outside the castle. I thought at first it was a bird but when I went to find out, I saw him."

She looked at me but said nothing.

I gripped her shoulders. I had begun sweating again. "Marissa," I said hoarsely. "He was flying."

Her eyes brightened and she leaned toward me, kissed me hard on the lips. "Then it's happened! The time is here."

"Time," I echoed her stupidly. "Time for what?"

"For the change," she said as if talking to a slow-witted child.

"Yes," I said. "I suspected as much. That's why I've brought you into the labyrinth. We're safe here."

Her brows furrowed. "Safe? Safe from what?"

"From Morodor," I said desperately. "He can't touch you here. Now he cannot change you. You'll stay like this forever. You'll never have to look like him."

For the first time, I saw fright in her eyes. "I don't understand." She shivered. "Didn't he tell you?"

298

"Tell me what?" I hung on to her. "I ran out of there as soon as I saw him——"

"Oh no!" she cried. "It's all destroyed now. All destroyed!" She put her face in her hands, weeping bitterly.

"Marissa," I said softly, holding her close. "Please don't cry. I can't bear it. I've saved you. Why are you crying?"

She shook me off and stared wide-eyed at me. Even tear-streaked she was exquisitely beautiful. It did not matter that she was filled with pain. No emotion could alter those features. Not even, it seemed, time itself. Only Morodor, her haunted brother.

"He was supposed to tell you. To prepare you," she said between sobs. "Now it has all gone wrong."

"Marissa," I said, stroking her, "don't you know I love you? I've said it and I meant it. Nothing can change that. As soon as we get out of here, we'll——"

"Tell me, how deep is your love for me?" She was abruptly icily calm.

"How deep can any emotion be? I don't think it can be measured."

"Do not be so certain of that," she whispered, "until you've heard me out." She put her hands up before her body, steepling them as if they were a church's spire. "It is not Morodor who will work the change. It is you."

"Me?"

"And it has already begun."

My head was whirling and I put the flat of my hand against the ground as if to balance myself. "What are you saying?"

"The change comes only when we are in love and that love is returned. When we find a mate. The emotion and its reflection releases some chemical catalyst hidden deep inside our DNA helices which has remained dormant until triggered."

Her fingers twined and untwined anxiously. "This is not a . . . state that can be borne alone; it is far too lonely. So this is how it is handled. An imperative of nature."

"No!" I cried. "No no no! What you're telling me is impossible. It's madness!"

"It is life, and life only."

"Your life! Not mine!"

I stood up, stumbled, but I could not escape the gaze of her lambent eyes. I stared at her in mounting horror. "Liar!" I cried. "Where is Morodor's mate if this is true?"

"Away," she said calmly. "Feeding."

"My God!" I whirled away. "My God!" And slammed into the prickly wall of a hedge.

"Can love hold so much terror for you?" she asked. "You have a responsibility. To yourself as well as to me. Isn't that what love is?"

But I could no longer think clearly. I only knew that I must get away from them both. *The change has already begun*, she had said. I did not think that I wanted to see the fruits of that terrible metamorphosis. Not after having known her and loved her like this, all air and sunlight.

Two sides of the coin. Wasn't that what I had said to Morodor? How he must have laughed at that. Yes. Two sides. But of the same coin.

"Don't you see?" I heard her voice but could no longer see her. "You have nothing to fear. It is your destiny——*our* destiny, together."

Howling, I clawed my way from her, staggering, tripping as I ran through the labyrinth. My only coherent thought was to somehow get to the sea and then to hurl myself into its rocking embrace.

To swim. To swim. And if I were lucky I would at last be thrown up onto the soft sand of some beach far, far away.

But the night had come alive with shadows drenched in my own terror. And, like a mirror, they threw up to me the ugly writhing apparitions from the very bottom of my soul, thrusting them rudely into the light for me to view.

And above me the sound of. . . .

Wings.

Even through the horrendous tattoo of the storm I can make out that sound. It's the same sound that reached down into my heavy slumber that night in Fuego del Aire and wrenched me awake. I did not know it then but I know it now.

But I know many things now that I did not then. I have had time to think. To think and to write. Sometimes they are one and the same. Like tonight.

Coming to terms. I have never been able to do that. I have never *wanted* to do that. My writing kept me fluid, moving in and out as the spirit took me. New York today, Capri the next. The world was my oyster.

But what of *me?*

The sound is louder now: that high keening whistle like the wind through the pines. It buzzes through my brain like a downed bottle of vintage champagne. I feel lightheaded but more than that. Light-bodied. Because I know. *I know.*

There is nothing but excitement inside me now. All the fear and the horror I felt in the labyrinth leached away from me. I have had six months to contemplate my destiny. Morodor was right: For each one, it is different. The doorway metamorphoses to suit the nature of the individual.

For me it is love. I denied that when Marissa confronted me with the process of her transmogrification. Such beauty! How could I lose that? I thought. It took me all of this time to understand that it was not her I feared losing but myself. Marissa will always be Marissa.

But what of me? Change is what we fear above all else and I am no different.

Was no different. I have already forgotten the golden creature of Fuego del Aire: she haunts my dreams still but I remember only her inner self. It is somehow like death, this acceptance of life. Perhaps this is where the legends began.

All around me the city sleeps on, safe and secure, wrapped in the arms of the myths of its own creation. Shhh! Don't bother to disturb it. No one would listen anyway.

The beating of the wings is very loud now, drowning out even the heavy pulsing of the rain. It reverberates in my mind like a heartbeat, dimming sight, taste, touch, smell. It dominates me in a way I thought only my writing could.

My shutters are open wide. I am drenched by the rain, buffeted by the chill wind. I am buoyed up by them both. I tremble at the thought. I love. *I love.* Those words a river of silver turning my bones hollow.

And now I lift my head to the place where last night the full moon rode calm and clear, a ghostly idiogram written upon the air, telling me that it is time for me to let go of all I know, to plunge inward toward the center of my heart. Six months have passed and it is time. *I know.* For now the enormous thrumming emanates from that spot. Beat-beat. Beat-beat. Beat-beat.

The heart-sound.

At last. There in the night, I see her face as she comes for me.

The Arrows

BY CHELSEA QUINN YARBRO

*It's a common enough (and true enough) belief that an artist
(of any stripe—painter, writer, actor, etc.) is more than a little different from the average citizen. Yet an artist has the
same feelings as anyone else, and definitely the same fears.
The basic difference is the reaction to those fears, the intensity
an artist experiences when those fears prove to be somewhat
overwhelming.*

*Chelsea Quinn Yarbro lives in California, is an avid music
devotee, and is the author of a quintology featuring Le Comte
St. Germain, a unique and extremely popular vampire; she
has also written science fiction, nonfiction, and mysteries.*

SLOWLY he took aim, concentrating on the target. His hand was
steady, his mind preternaturally clear. This time, this time he would
be right: he held his breath.

The brush moved, leaving a smear of raw umber beneath the
vermilion.

Witlin stood back, frowning at the canvas. "Shit," he muttered as
he glared at the results of his work. God, would it never be right?
He wiped the brush on an ancient rag already stiff with encrustations
of color, then poked it into an old coffee can half filled with turpentine that had absorbed so much paint that it was the color and con-
sistency of wet silt.

Afternoon sun slanted across the untidy room he called his studio,
turning it glaringly bright. He rubbed his face with both hands,
wishing he could afford another place, one with north light instead
of this western exposure. But such places were expensive and he was
almost out of money. Better this than doing charcoal sketches for the
tourists down at the waterfront, he told himself, as he had every day
for the last six weeks. Better this than doing lettering for the adver-

tising agency where he had slaved for three years before getting the courage to work on his own. And far better this than those wasted semesters at the community college, where all they taught were better ways to make messes in oils.

He wandered over to the window and looked down on the playground, three floors below. Children were playing there now that school was over for the day. They ran and shouted, making a racket that gave him a headache as he listened. He leaned his forehead against the glass and sighed. Another day shot, and the painting worse than ever. When he had asked for a six-month leave, it had seemed to be a luxurious, a voluptuous amount of time, but now he knew it was completely inadequate.

A baseball thunked against the side of the building and Witlin jumped at the sound of it. The world was full of aimed missiles, he thought. Baseballs, ICBMs, arrows; it made no difference. He turned away from the window, cursing the noise that erupted beneath him. They did not understand what he was doing, how important it was.

When Witlin had finished cleaning his brushes it was almost sunset and the children were gone from the playground. He studied his canvas as he prepared to go out for the cheapest meal he could find. It wasn't right, not yet. Some ineffable quality of reality and suffering continued to elude him. The canvas itself was big enough—almost eight feet high—and the figure slightly larger than life. That wasn't the problem. He brought out the sheaf of sketches that had guided him through his work for more than five months.

Brakes squealed in the street; horns clamored.

Cursing, he got to his knees to gather up the paper he had dropped. One of the sketches had torn: it was a study of heads and necks and the jagged division neatly decapitated the best of the heads he had done. Conscientiously he pressed the sketch back together though he knew it was a futile gesture. He would not be able to look at the sketch again without seeing the damage and feeling it had been compromised in his vision as well as ruined on paper.

Why was it so difficult? That question had plagued him for weeks, haunting him as he strove to bring his work to fruition. Why should the bound figure of a man transfixed with arrows torment him in this way? He had already done half a dozen iconographic drawings, but that had been early in his leave of absence, when his confidence had been high and nothing seemed beyond him. That had changed; oh, yes, it had changed.

The smell of frying foods drifted up from the floor below and Witlin felt his stomach tighten. Hamburgers had become as rich and exotic as Chateubriand in forcemeat had once been. Now he had to content himself with soup and hard rolls at the local cafeteria. On such a regimen he might eke out his funds for another two weeks. As it was, he barely had enough for the extra tube of thalo green that he needed; food would have to wait until he had the supplies he required.

A television blared, driving music and an announcer's voice proclaiming the superiority of a particular tire over all others.

"Scum." He was disgusted with it all, mostly with himself. He had been so sure that he would be able to paint the Saint Sebastian that he had done only the most cursory sketches of the subject. Doubt had come to him three months ago, when he had made his first attempt at the work. The canvas lay against the wall, the face turned away from him so that he would not have to look at it. That first effort had been small, as most of his work had been up to that point. When he was less than half finished with the underpainting, he knew that he had not allowed adequate scope to his ambition, and that a larger canvas would be needed. That had led to the second attempt which he had burned more than three weeks before. Now he was working on the fifth version, and knew it, too, had failed.

"It's not possible," he said to the canvas, defying it. "I'll do it. I swear I'll do it." He could not stand the thought that all his efforts had come to nothing. He scowled at his palette, as if seeking blame in the colors or the scent of the oils. He was using the highest grade of paint available, he had stretched, sized, sanded and sized the canvas again, taking care that the surface was right and the paint would not crack. "But the painting must have worth," he muttered as he scraped his palette clean, putting the used bits of paint into an old milk carton with the top cut off.

When at last he had cleaned the dismal attic room, he went out, taking great care to lock the door and pocket the key.

A week later he was in despair. He took his pocket knife and jabbed it at the painting, seeking those places where he had shown arrows entering the flesh of the saint. "There! There! Be wounded, damn you!" In his frenzy he kicked over the table where he kept his supplies; brushes, paint tubes, turpentine, linseed oil, gesso, all went flying and skittering and spreading over the bare wood floor. Witlin knelt down, weeping, hardly noticing the new stains on his faded clothing. "Damn you, damn you, damn you," he crooned in a rapture of defeat.

There was a sharp knock at the door. "Mister Witlin? Mister Witlin!" came his landlady's voice, querulous and timid at once.

It was a moment before Witlin came to himself enough to answer. Awkwardly he got to his feet and stumbled toward the sound. "Missus Argent?" he called after a moment of hesitation.

"What's going on in there, Mister Witlin?" the woman asked, trying to sound demanding and achieving only petulance.

He blinked at the shambles he had created. "I . . . tripped, Missus Argent."

"Are you all right, Mister Witlin?" It was more of an accusation than an expression of concern.

"I think so," he answered, wishing she would go away and leave him to deal with the wreckage around him.

"What's that smell?"

Witlin sighed. "I guess it's turpentine," he said, sounding like a chastised child. "It . . . spilled." He knew it was the wrong thing to say as soon as he had spoken.

"I think you'd better let me in, Mister Witlin," his landlady said in whining determination.

Reluctantly he opened the door and stood aside.

Missus Argent had a pointy, rodent's face, not endearing like a rabbit but pinched and mean, more like a rat. She held herself like a rat, too, he realized as he watched her survey the damage: her hands held up close to her chest, drooping, her head with its receding chin thrust forward. He could almost imagine her nose twitching. Belatedly he found something to say. "I was going to clean it up at once. I didn't know it would disturb you."

"Good gracious," was all she would say, but there was condemnation in every line of her. "What have you been doing up here, Mister Witlin?"

"Painting, as I told you when I rented the . . ." He almost said attic but stopped himself, since he knew she disliked having this room called that, though it was.

"Clean it up? But look at the floor. Does any of that horrible stuff come out? What if you've ruined it? Well, at least there isn't a carpet up here, but this . . . Mister Witlin, I don't know what to say. Yes, you will clean it up, and if there is any sign of staining or other . . . problems, we'll have to review your responsibility and make some financial adjustment." She folded her arms across her skinny chest.

Witlin was filled with anxiety. He did not have money enough to move, let alone pay for a new room. Recognition of this spurred him to a defense that he might not otherwise have used. "Look, Missus Argent, if there's any problem, any problem at all, I'll take care of it. If you don't think that the stains are out of the boards, well, I *am* a painter, and I can paint a floor as well as a picture. I'll do a good job, Missus Argent. You won't be disappointed. And it would be easier to take care of a painted surface than bare boards." He could not tell what she thought of this offer; her face suddenly puckered closed and she watched him closely.

"Mister Witlin, I won't have shoddy work in my house."

"No," he agreed at once. "Of course not." He thought of the bedraggled plants in the front garden, the frayed carpets on the stairs, the loose bannister supports, the cracked and peeling paint on the windowsills. "It would be a good job, Missus Argent. And," he added, inspired by his own fear, "I'd . . . pay for the paint myself."

Her face relaxed a bit. "I'd have to approve the quality and color of the paint," she said at once.

"Oh, yes. Well, yes." He could hear himself blither in relief, but it no longer mattered to him that she thought him an irresponsible fool. He was far more concerned about the cost of the enamel for the floor. He could manage it if he gave up lunch at the cafeteria and confined himself to one egg and toast in the morning.

"You come downstairs to get me when you've cleaned up here," Missus Argent said with decision. "I want to see what you've accomplished." She looked around the room disdainfully. "Those drawings of naked men . . . and you call yourself an artist!" She glared at him in triumph, and then slammed herself out of the room.

Witlin set to work restoring order to the attic; he could not get the memory of Missus Argent's expression of fascinated revulsion out of his mind.

Painting the floor took more than two days, and another day to dry. During that time Witlin spent as much time as he could in the nearby park, escaping the fumes which made him lightheaded. His eyes stung, and when he tried to draw, his vision wavered so that all he put down on paper were vague and awkward lines, not the sweeping gestures in his mind. Twice policemen told him to move on; when he protested that he lived in the neighborhood, they threatened to run him in for vagrancy or something worse. He had not dared to object, though it galled him to be mistaken for one of those derelicts who dozed on the park benches and pestered the more affluent strollers for quarters. Not, he had to admit, that he could not use a few quarters. He had not been able to afford new razor blades for more than a week and his face showed scrapes and stubble in proof of this. Perhaps, he thought, he ought simply to grow a beard. So many other artists did. There was nothing wrong with it—in fact, it was almost expected.

At such moments, he would think of Saint Sebastian, who was almost never shown bearded. Saint Sebastian, the youth, the archer killed by his own men, his body quilled with arrows. How it haunted him, that vision! So he continued to shave, and each day the results were a bit more crude.

Once the floor was dry and Missus Argent had grudgingly approved it, Witlin set to work again, this time choosing the highest grade of canvas and taking more time than usual to stretch it on the enormous frame he had made for it. His arms ached with the work. Twice he skipped breakfast and bought a chocolate bar instead, hoping that the rich candy would give him more energy for his task. When he was satisfied that the preparation was of archival quality, he took charcoal and began, once again, to sketch.

This time it went better, or so he told himself. The enormous scope of the painting, its sheer physical size promised an impact his previous efforts had lacked. No matter that the canvas itself had to be canted and braced in order to fit under the low ceiling, no matter that he had to stand on a drafting stool to reach the top of it, this time the work would be perfect: he would achieve his masterpiece.

Witlin stood back to look at the painting, which was almost complete now. It was better, definitely better, he thought, than any of his previous efforts. Yet it was not up to the quality of the image he had held in his mind for all these months. Working large had helped, no doubt of that. He had been able to show the torment of the saint, the arrows lodged deep in his body, his features at once resigned and agonized. That much he believed he could be proud of. But the rest . . . the rest was another matter. He wanted to show how heavy the body was, hanging from its bonds and the arrows, the languor of approaching death, the finality of it. That was still not on the canvas, for all his work and thought. He had been able to find it only in his mind.

The attic was stifling this afternoon in May. The sun pressed at the windows and made the air hard with heat. He felt lightly ill, but he was determined to ignore it, to persevere. He had to finish. At the end of the month he would have run out of money and would no longer be able to pay his rent; he knew better than to suppose Missus Argent would permit him to remain here if he could not give her the seventy-five dollars she demanded of him. So he had to be prepared to move, though where he would go now he could not imagine. He would think of it later, when he was through with Saint Sebastian.

He glared at the painting, trying to think of ways to correct the lifelessness of it that so dissatisfied him.

The wounds, that was it, he decided. They were not real. Anyone looking at them would know that what they saw was paint, not blood, and the holes made by the painted arrows appeared equally false. This was not holy flesh rent by metal and wood, it was pigment. "It's hopeless," he muttered, sitting down on the drafting stool and wiping at his eyes with the last comparatively clean corner of the rag he held. He could not think of what to do. He could not concentrate any more, no matter how he forced himself to clear his thoughts of everything but the painting.

Was it the color? Was that the problem? With the light so glaring and hot, had it changed his perceptions so that he could not see as clearly as he needed to? Was the glare from the windows so strong that he was no longer able to weigh the hue and value of his paints? Would a stronger shade of red have more impact? Did he have to make the flesh a pastier shade, suggesting Sebastian was in deep shock? Was that what was lacking? Had he been misled by the angle at which he had to paint so that he had unintentionally distorted the work? Or was it something deeper, something more profound? Was it a failure not of the canvas and paint, of the medium, but of himself as an artist? Did he shy away from the reality of the saint's suffering, and had that aversion found its way onto the canvas? He could not bring himself to examine his feelings too closely, for fear he would discover how much he was lacking.

He decided he would attempt to fix the colors first. That he could do with comparative ease. The rest he would have to consider later, when he was more prepared to examine the state of his soul.

Green for shadows in the skin, then, a mustard shade for where the direct rays of the setting sun struck it. Acidic orange to make the blood shine more—was it true that blood was more the color of rust than rubies?—and five kinds of brown for the shafts of the arrows. And white, great amounts of white, for the feathers, for highlights, to mix with other paint, to lend radiance to the canvas. If only oil-paints could be truly transparent, like stained glass, and still have the force of their opacity. Other painters had achieved it, that luminosity; why couldn't he? What prevented him from doing with his hand what his mind conceived so totally?

Sunset came, and with it the scattering colors that usually irritated him, but now he paid it no heed. He could not be distracted by the sunset, by alterations in the colors around him, by shifts in the light. Those were excuses, not valid reasons for his failure. Surely if he had the right to call himself an artist, he also had the obligation to put himself above those intrusions that had no part in his work.

When the night came, he continued to work, illuminating the cramped studio with two bare bulbs. He felt like an acolyte proving his calling at last.

"I'm sure I'm sorry, Mister Witlin," said Missus Argent in a tone that revealed she was nothing of the kind. "If I could, I'd keep you on a week or two. But there, it isn't as if you have a job. If you were looking for work, Mister Witlin, it might be another matter. But you're a . . . painter."

"And my work is important, Missus Argent," he said in a remote way. He no longer worried about how or where or if he would find a place to live. "Saint Sebastian is immortal. That's more than either you or I can say."

She gave him a puzzled glare. "Well, I'll have to ask you to be out by the end of the week unless you can pay the rent. And I won't have excuses."

"Of course not," he told her, thinking that it would take care of itself. "I'll tell you what I've decided to do by Wednesday."

Her expression grew sharper and a whine came into her voice. "And you'll have to clean this place proper. No more nonsense about painting the floor. The way it smells, I don't know who'd want to rent it. You'll have to set aside one day at least to scrubbing it."

"If that's necessary," Witlin agreed.

"It is," she insisted with a sniff. "You've been up here for months with those paints of yours. You may be used to it, but there are others who . . ." Her eyes traveled over the room, pausing accusingly at paintings and brushes as if identifying incriminating bits of evidence. "It's bad enough you wantng to paint things like that, but the smell is more than I can bear."

He drew breath to protest. then let it out in a sigh. He could not explain to anyone how he felt about the smell of paint, that was as rich as the scent of food to him, and in many ways more necessary. He only nodded. "I'll do my best, Missus Argent. And I'll try to get the money. I will."

"Well . . ." She stared at him dubiously. "You're not quite the sort of tenant I usually have, Mister Witlin. If there is another place you can go, it might be better if you . . ." She let the words dangle, as if asking him to spare her the necessity of saying anything more.

"Missus Argent, I don't want to move. I haven't the money. I haven't the time. Don't you see? I'm getting close to the work I want to turn out. I know it doesn't look like much yet, with only the underpainting and just a few of the colors, but this canvas is the best I've ever done. It is." He extended his hands toward the surface as if warming them at a fire.

311

The landlady sniffed. "It isn't the sort of picture I'm . . . used to." She gave it a grudging look. "And your face on it, too," was the only comment she was able to muster, saying it so condemningly that he dared not question her, though he did not agree at all with her observation.

"I'll talk to you tomorrow, Missus Argent. I . . . I want to work some more." He pointed toward the windows. "This isn't the best light for an artist, but I need to make the most of it. Especially if I have to find another place. It won't be as good." It was not an accusation because he was inwardly certain that would not happen; he would be here to finish his work.

"All right, Mister Witlin," she said, making no attempt to hide her disapproval. "I don't want any excuses if you can't find the money for this project of yours. Pay or leave." She stepped back, preparing to close the door. "And I don't want to have you working all night. It disturbs the rest of the household to have you do that."

"I don't work on this phase of the painting at night, Missus Argent," he told her with an austere glare. "You have to have clear light at this stage."

She sniffed once to show her doubt, then left the room.

Witlin hardly noticed her going; his mind was on the painting again, and there was nothing in his mind but the glorious suffering of Saint Sebastian.

His head ached, a combination of hunger and fumes gnawing at him from the inside. He had risen just after dawn and set to work, and now sunset was distorting the colors on his canvas. And what colors! Finally the glowing, pain-wracked figure was emerging from the flat surface, taking on the kind of reality he had only dreamed of having until now. Witlin was dizzy with it, and his pulse raced. He paused to squeeze out a little more paint onto his palette, thinking vaguely how appetizing it was, that thick, rich worm of color. It was enough to make him hunger for the taste of it, as if the hue carried a special savor all its own. He touched his brush to it, and felt a thrill go up his arm, as electric as a caress. The first pressure of the brush on the canvas made him tremble; he held the wooden shaft in eager, quivering fingers, almost afraid to move for fear of bringing the wonderful sensations to an end.

When he had worked for another hour, he drew back, seeing that the sky was already fading. It astonished him to discover how much he had accomplished, and how swiftly the day had gone. His thoughts were dizzied by what he saw, for at last he perceived some shadow of the vision he carried. Nothing could ever be as vivid, as overwhelming as the impressions that drove him to paint, but he saw that an approximation of that powerful gleam was within his grasp. He contemplated the twisted, lean features of the saint, wondering if Missus Argent had been right, and that he had somehow put his own likeness on that countenance. It had happened before, he reminded himself: Michelangelo had painted himslf in his "Last Judgement," Gaugain had included himself in his tropical groves, the likenesses of Rembrandt, Tintoretto, Cézanne, van Gogh, Botticelli, Giracault, and the rest of the illustrious roster blazed, frowned, smiled, peeked and stared out of their work. Witlin dared not number himself with the others, but he wished to be their equal in integrity if not immortality. He would have to study his face more closely the next time he attempted to shave.

Because he knew he had to see his face more clearly, Witlin began to search through trashcans in the night, hoping to find bits of discarded food and once-used razor blades that would tide him through his last few days. He knew that he was becoming gaunt from his hunger, but that was no longer important to him—as the bones showed more distinctly in his long features he detected a definition of line he had not found there before, and it pleased him. If he was indeed using his own face as his model, it was now more worthy of that honor than it had been before, when indulgence had blurred and softened the angles and planes to a formlessness that could never serve Saint Sebastian in his travail.

Satisfied for the first time in more than a week at his appearance, he decided to bring a small mirror into the studio. Earlier he had disdained such methods, but with his time so short and the painting so near to completion, he took a chance that this intrusion would not interfere with what he had accomplished already. It took him the better part of an hour—and he begrudged every second—to place the mirror so that he could see himself without throwing unwanted light onto the canvas by reflection. He set to work feverishly when

313

he had accomplished this, for he did not want to waste another instant on such considerations. The odors of paint and turpentine were like drugs to him now, the fumes filling his senses more intensely than wine ever had.

He was so caught up in his work that he was not aware of the knocking on his door until it became a pounding. He stepped back, one hand to his forehead to clear his mind enough to respond.

"Mister *Witlin*!" Missus Argent shouted, using both fists now.

He reeled back from the canvas, reaching out for a sloping beam to steady himself. "Yes, Missus Argent!" he called back. "I was . . . napping."

"Open this door at once!" There was nothing tentative about her, none of the whining hesitancy he had come to expect, and it jarred him a bit to realize that she was truly angry with him.

"I'll be here in a moment," he told her, fumbling toward the door. "Just a moment."

"*Now*, Mister Witlin," she ordered him, and poked her flushed, pinched face at him the instant he had the door wide enough to permit her to do so. "I have to speak with you, Mister Witlin."

"Come in," he mumbled, setting his brush aside. "I've been working and . . ."

"I know you've been up here," she said, refusing to use the word work for what he did. We can hear you all over the house, with your muttering and climbing and moving."

"It's necessary," he said, trying to find a way to get rid of her. She distracted him, with her greedy eyes and rapacious little hands. "I don't mean to disturb you when I . . ."

"That's all very well," she interrupted, her hands going to her hips. "But there are complaints. Do you understand that? I can't run this house if everyone is complaining to me about my tenant in the attic."

"Missus Argent . . ." he began, but could think of nothing to say to her that she would understand or accept.

"Well?"

"I have work to do. I'm almost finished." He could hardly hear his own voice, and knew from the way she looked at him that she was not paying any attention to what he said.

"This place stinks!" she announced with more irritation than she had shown so far. "What have you been doing up here, Mister Witlin?" She cast an eye around the room. "You haven't cleaned the floor, have you? You told me that you'd attend to cleaning up this place before you move . . ."

"Missus Argent," he cut in, goaded to protest by her behavior, "I will clean the room, such as it is, the moment I'm finished with this painting. To do so before then would be a fruitless waste of time. Don't you see? I have only a little bit of work to do, and it will be . . ." He indicated the canvas. "Look at it, Missus Argent. I want you to see what I'm doing. You've got to understand what it means to me."

Once again the landlady glared around the attic. "I see the painting. But daubs and smears of paint . . . Well, I don't know anything about art. I'm too busy taking care of the people in this house, Mister Witlin. I haven't time for art. Or whatever that thing is."

He did not hear most of this; his mind had caught on one particular phrase. "Daubs of paint!" he demanded of her. "You think this is nothing but daubs of paint? Don't you see . . . no, of course you don't. People like you throw eggs at the 'Mona Lisa.' You tear down a Rivera mural to make way for a glass box full of offices. You think you have a right to ignore me because I don't go off to a regular job. You think that makes me nothing but a bum and a sponger! But that's not true." He turned away from her, convinced that she would never comprehend him, no matter what he said or how he strove to explain himself and his work to her.

"You're crazy," Missus Argent whispered, drawing back from Witlin, one arm up as if to brace herself against him. "You're just crazy."

Witlin sighed. "I suppose I am, to you."

"You're dangerous," she went on, not hearing him.

"Missus Argent, don't talk . . ."

"I want you out of here. Never mind the rent. I want you out of my house tomorrow night." Her eyes had turned glassy, her face was fixed in a ghastly smile. "You've got to leave."

He scowled. "I have a few days more, and I've already promised I'll pay my rent." He could feel a headache forming in his skull, driving out the sense and the comfort he had felt only a few minutes before. "I have to finish the painting, Missus Argent."

"Sure. You finish it here. But not in my house." It was her final word, every detail of her posture, expression and tone of voice emphasized it. She stalked to the door, angular and cautious as an insect. Witlin was reminded of a mantis or other delicate and predatory creature waiting to devour hapless victims.

"You'll get your rent," he said in what he wanted to be a reasonable tone.

"I don't want it. I want you out of here." If anything, she was more determined as she slammed the door.

Witlin stared at the knob, wishing he could think of the whole encounter as a dream. He resisted the urge to follow her down onto the lower floors where she undoubtedly was regaling the others with lurid tales of what he was doing in the attic. His work was more important than her petty lies, more important than money or time or anything else.

He waited in silence for hours, watching the light disappear and the eerie shadows of night claim the attic, bleaching first and then covering Saint Sebastian with an indigo gauze. The air was very still, so that he thought that the motes were endlessly suspended like little planets in the heavy air. Night engulfed him, leaving him feeling empty and without form. He could not say what he was any more, with the color gone from him and his world sunk into darkness. Idly he felt for his pulse, and was mildly surprised to feel it beat. Under his hand his chest rose for breath; he was still alive, but he no longer believed it, not when there was so much night around him.

Around midnight he left the attic, stealing softly down the stairs, freezing at the faintest noise. He let himself out of the house and trudged off through the streets toward the liquor store where he could get day-old sandwiches at half price. Testing the bristles on his face, he wondered if he had nerve enough to steal a packet of razor blades. He wanted to be neat when he finished the painting.

In the end he barricaded himself in the attic, all his old, unsatisfactory work serving now as a jamb against the doorknob. He had no intention of leaving now, when Saint Sebastian hovered so tantalizing near fruition. Twice he had heard a voice, loud and blustering, on the other side of the door, but now he had been left in peace to do the work he had to do.

316

He was almost out of paints, and that should have troubled him, yet it did not. There would be enough. Saint Sebastian would not let him down. Only the reds were precariously low, the tubes giving up mere dollops of color. He touched his finger to the rosy nipple of pigment he had put on the palette. The act consumed him with a pure sensuality that left him breathless. If he had dared to waste the paint, he would have pressed the paint flat and felt it squidge out around his finger, more yielding than flesh ever was.

Witlin hesitated. That was the trouble with paint, he realized, and the recognition shot through him hideously. It was soft and pliant, malleable, a substance without strength beyond the power of chroma and hue. With a cry he dropped his brush and brought his hands to his face to shut out the enormity of his failure. Saint Sebastian was not real, would never be real. He could not finish it. Anything he put on that canvas, though each work was bigger and of brighter colors and more emphatic shades, would always be nothing more than a pale, timid reflection of the might of his vision.

His hand slammed down into the paint, smearing all the colors into a blur as he deliberately twisted his hand. The paint had failed him, would always fail him and would betray his talent in every conceivable way. He had sold himself to a fraud!

He made an effort to stop sobbing, but there was no way to keep from that anguish and after a little time he no longer tried. His body shook and trembled, his hands turned to talons, weapons to eradicate the travesty he had seduced himself into creating. He went from palette to the painting itself, clawing at the paint, smudging the surface with other pigments now the color and texture of mud. It was a Pyrrhic satisfaction, but the only one left to him. There was no way he could avenge himself adequately. He had brought himself and Saint Sebastian to ruin because of the bright promise of chemicals suspended in oils. How many others had been similarly undone! The idea staggered him and he howled with the pain of it. And how many of those realized before they died how they had been compromised?

Suddenly he stood upright, the grief stilled in him. There was a way, there was still a way. He would show what art was, not this insignificant imitation that had masqueraded as art for so long. Yes, there was one way, and what was needed was a little resolution.

Surely that was easier to face than this ultimate despair. He wiped his face with the edge of his paint-fouled sleeve, paying no heed to the reds and yellows that were left behind on his skin. That was nothing, less than nothing.

He had to search for the better part of an hour, but at last he found his pocket knife under some discarded rags. He seized upon it with urgency, then went to find his brushes, his eyes filled with anticipation. Those who never tested themselves never learned the terrible joy of dedication, and over the lonely months he had felt his devotion grow from ill-defined hope to profound certainty. Only his focus had been misguided, and he would now remedy that and vindicate himself. He began to carve the ends of the handles of his brushes, taking great care to make them symmetrical and sharp before going for the packet of razor blades he had taken from the liquor store, remembering to reserve one or two for cutting the lying, deceitful canvas into strips.

When the door was finally broken in, Witlin could barely lift his head. It was not possible for him to see who was there, for the room had already faded into dusk. He heard a shocked exclamation and appalled swearing, which disturbed him. He had not done this to disgust them, but for art.

"Oh, my God," Missus Argent burst out before stumbling out of the room to keep from retching at what she saw.

"No," Witlin protested, but he had not enough voice left to be heard. Besides, when he breathed, the arrows sunk deep in his flesh hurt him. They had been excruciating at first, when he had thrust them, like the arrows of Saint Sebastian, into his thigh, his shoulder, his arm, his side, his abdomen while he hung in the hastily constructed canvas bonds. Then he spasmed once, twice, pulling his canvas restraints from the beam. But no matter; he had used only his longest and best brushes for his arrows and it pleased him to think that he had achieved something of merit at last.

Talent

BY THEODORE STURGEON

It's a given that children are not normal human beings. They haven't been taught the niceties of living, such as morals and honesty and truth and the shades of gray that wind about them all; nor have they been tainted with adulthood, so we blithely call them innocent and wish we were young again. But kids aren't always nice, especially to each other, and when they aren't normal in any respectable sense of the word, there isn't much one can do but look for a place to hide.

Theodore Sturgeon writes mostly, and beautifully, about love in all its forms, and though he generally confines himself to the genre of science fiction, he has occasionally broken out into Dark Fantasy to prove to his readers that he isn't always the kind and gentle man they like to think he is.

MRS. BRENT and Precious were sitting on the farmhouse porch when little Jokey sidled out from behind the barn and came catfooting up to them. Precious, who had ringlets and was seven years old and very clean, stopped swinging on the glider and watched him. Mrs. Brent was reading a magazine. Jokey stopped at the foot of the steps.

"MOM!" he rasped.

Mrs. Brent started violently, rocked too far back, bumped her knobby hairdo against the clapboards, and said, "Good heavens, you little br—— darling, you frightened me!"

Jokey smiled.

Precious said, "Snaggletooth."

"If you want your mother" said Mrs. Brent reasonably, "why don't you go inside and speak to her?"

Disgustedly, Jokey vetoed the suggestion with "Ah-h-h . . ." He faced the house. "MOM!" he shrieked, in a tone that spoke of death and disaster.

There was a crash from the kitchen, and light footsteps. Jokey's mother, whose name was Mrs. Purney, came out, pushing back a wisp of hair from frightened eyes.

"Oh, the sweet," she cooed. She flew out and fell on her knees beside Jokey. "Did it hurt its little, thn? Aw, did it was . . ."

Jokey said, "Gimme a nickel!"

"Please," suggested Precious.

"Of course, darling," fluttered Mrs. Purney. "My word, yes. Just as soon as ever we go into town, you shall have a nickel. Two, if you're good."

"Gimme a nickel," said Jokey ominously.

"But, darling, what for? What will you do with a nickel out here?"

Jokey thrust out his hand. "I'll hold my breath."

Mrs. Purney rose, panicked. "Oh, dear, don't. Oh, please don't. Where's my reticule?"

"On top of the bookcase, out of my reach," said Precious, without rancor.

"Oh, yes, so it is. Now, Jokey, you wait right here and I'll just . . ." and her twittering faded into the house.

Mrs. Brent cast her eyes upward and said nothing.

"You're a little stinker," said Precious.

Jokey looked at her with dignity. "Mom," he called imperiously.

Mrs. Purney came to heel on the instant, bearing a nickel.

Jokey, pointing with the same movement with which he acquired the coin, reported, "She called me a little stinker."

"Really!" breathed Mrs. Purney, bridling. "I think, Mrs. Brent, that your child could have better manners."

"She has, Mrs. Purney, and uses them when they seem called for."

Mrs. Purney looked at her curiously, decided, apparently, that Mrs. Brent meant nothing by the statement (in which she was wrong) and turned to her son, who was walking briskly back to the barn.

"Don't hurt yourself, Puddles," she called.

She elicited no response whatever, and, smiling vaguely at Mrs. Brent and daughter, went back to her kitchen.

"Puddles," said Precious ruminatively. "I bet I know why she calls him that. Remember Gladys's puppy that——"

"Precious," said Mrs. Brent, "you shouldn't have called Joachim a word like that."

"I s'pose not," Precious agreed thoughtfully. "He's really a——"

Mrs. Brent, watching the carven pink lips, said warningly, "Precious!" She shook her head. "I've asked you not to say that."

"Daddy——"

"Daddy caught his thumb in the hinge of the car-trunk. That was different."

"Oh, no," corrected Precious. "You're thinking of the time he opened on'y the bottom half of the Dutch door in the dark. When he pinched his thumb, he said——"

"Would you like to see my magazine?"

Precious rose and stretched delicately. "No, thank you, Mummy. I'm going out to the barn to see what Jokey's going to do with that nickel."

"Precious . . ."

"Yes, Mummy."

"Oh——nothing. I suppose it's all right. Don't quarrel with Jokey, now."

"Not 'less he quarrels with me," she replied, smiling charmingly.

Precious had new patent-leather shoes with hard heels and broad ankle-straps. They looked neat and very shiny against her yellow socks. She walked carefully in the path, avoiding the moist grasses that nodded over the edges, stepping sedately over a small muddy patch.

Jokey was not in the barn. Precious walked through, smelling with pleasure the mixed, warm smells of chaffdust, dry hay and manure. Just outside, by the wagondoor, was the pigpen. Jokey was standing by the rail fence. At his feet was a small pile of green apples. He picked one up and hurled it with all his might at the brown sow. It went *putt!* on her withers, and she went *ergh!*

"Hey!" said Precious.

Putt-ergh! Then he looked up at Precious, snarled silently, and picked up another apple. *Putt-ergh!*

"Why are you doing that for?"

Putt-ergh!

"Hear that? My mom done just like that when I hit her in the stummick."

"She did?"

"Now this," said Jokey, holding up an apple, "is a stone. Listen." He hurled it. *Thunk-e-e-e-ergh!*

Precious was impressed. Her eyes widened, and she stepped back a pace.

"Hey, look out where you're goin', stoopid!"

He ran to her and grasped her left biceps roughly, throwing her up against the railings. She yelped and stood rubbing her arm—rubbing off grime, and far deeper in indignation than she was in fright.

Jokey paid her no attention. "You an' your shiny feet," he growled. He was down on one knee, feeling for two twigs stuck in the ground about eight inches apart "Y'might've squashed 'em!"

Precious, her attention brought to her new shoes, stood turning one of them, glancing light from the toecaps, from the burnished sides, while complacency flowed back into her.

"What?"

With the sticks, Jokey scratched aside the loose earth and, one by one, uncovered the five tiny, naked, blind creatures which lay buried there. They were only about three-quarters of an inch long, with little withered limbs and twitching noses. They writhed. There were ants, too. Very busy ants.

"What are they?"

"Mice, stoopid," said Jokey. "Baby mice. I found 'em in the barn."

"How did they get there?"

"I put 'em there."

"How long have they been there?"

" 'Bout four days," said Jokey, covering them up again. "They last a long time."

"Does your mother know those mice are out here?"

"No, and you better not say nothin', ya hear?"

"Would your mother whip you?"

"*Her?*" The syllable came out as an incredulous jeer.

"What about your father?"

"Aw, I guess he'd like to lick me. But he ain't got a chance. Mom'd have a fit."

"You mean she'd get mad at him?"

"No, stoopid. A fit. You know, scrabbles at the air and get suds on her mouth, and all. Falls down and twitches." He chuckled.

"But——why?"

"Well, it's about the on'y way she can handle Pop, I guess. He's always wanting to do something about me. She won't let 'um, so I c'n do anything I want."

"What do you do?"

"You're sorta nosy."

"I don't believe you can do anything, stinky."

"Oh, I can't?" Jokey's face was reddening.

"No, you can't! You talk a lot, but you can't really do anything."

Jokey walked up close to her and breathed in her face the way the man with the grizzly beard does to the clean-cut cowboy who is tied up to the dynamite kegs in the movies on Saturday.

"I can't, huh?"

She stood her ground. "All right, if you're so smart, let's see what you were going to do with that nickel!"

Surprisingly, he looked abashed. "You'd laugh," he said.

"No, I wouldn't," she said guilelessly. She stepped forward, opened her eyes very wide, shook her head so that her gold ringlets swayed, and said very gently, "Truly I wouldn't, Jokey . . ."

"Well——" he said, and turned to the pigpen. The brindled sow was rubbing her shoulder against the railing, grunting softly to herself. She vouchsafed them one small red-rimmed glance, and returned to her thoughts.

Jokey and Precious stood up on the lower rail and looked down on the pig's broad back.

"You're not goin' to tell anybody?" he asked.

" 'Course not."

"Well, awright. Now lookit. You ever see a china piggy bank?"

"Sure I have," said Precious.

"How big?"

"Well, I got one about this big."

"Aw, that's nothin'."

"And my girl-friend Gladys has one *this* big."

"Phooey."

"Well," said Precious, "in town, in a big drugstore, I saw one

323

THIS big," and she put out her hands about thirty inches apart.

"That's pretty big," admitted Jokey. "Now I'll show you *something*." To the brindled sow, he said sternly, "You are a piggy bank."

The sow stopped rubbing herself against the rails. She stood quite still. Her bristles merged into her hide. She was hard and shiny—as shiny as the little girls hard shoes. In the middle of the broad back, a slot appeared—or had been there all along, as far as Precious could tell. Jokey produced a warm sweaty nickel and dropped it into the slot.

There was a distant, vitreous, hollow bouncing click from inside the sow.

Mrs. Purney came out on the porch and creaked into a wicker chair with a tired sigh.

"They are a handful, aren't they?" said Mrs. Brent.

"You just don't know," moaned Mrs. Purney.

Mrs. Brent's eyebrows went up. "Precious is a model. Her teacher says so. That wasn't too easy to do."

"Yes, she's a very good little girl. But my Joachim is——talented, you know. That makes it very hard."

"How is he talented? What can he do?"

"He can do anything," said Mrs. Purney after a slight hesitation.

Mrs. Brent glanced at her, saw that her tired eyes were closed, and shrugged. It made her feel better. Why must mothers always insist that their children are better than all others?

"Now, my Precious," she said, "—and mind you, I'm not saying this because she's my child—my Precious plays the piano very well for a child her age. Why, she's already in her third book and she's not eight yet."

Mrs. Purney said, without opening her eyes, "Jokey doesn't play. I'm sure he could if he wanted to."

Mrs. Brent saw what an inclusive boast this might be, and wisely refrained from further itemization. She took another tack. "Don't you find, Mrs. Purney, that it is easy to make a child obedient and polite by being firm?"

Mrs. Purney opened her eyes at last, and looked troubledly at Mrs. Brent. "A child should love its parents."

"Oh, of course!" smiled Mrs. Brent. "But these modern ideas of surrounding a child with love and freedom to an extent where it becomes a tyrant—well! I just can't see that! Of course I don't mean Joachim," she added quickly, sweetly. "He's a *dear* child, really . . ."

"He's got to be given everything he wants," murmured Mrs. Purney in a strange tone. It was fierce and it was by rote. "He's *got* to be kept happy."

"You must love him very much," snapped Mrs. Brent viciously, suddenly determined to get some reaction out of this weak, indulgent creature. She got it.

"I hate him," said Mrs. Purney.

Her eyes were closed again, and now she almost smiled, as if the release of those words had been a yearned-for thing. Then she sat abruptly erect, her pale eyes round, and she grasped her lower lip and pulled it absurdly down and to the side.

"I didn't mean that," she gasped. She flung herself down before Mrs. Brent, and gabbled, "I didn't mean it! Don't tell him! He'll do things to us. He'll loosen the housebeams while we're sleeping. He'll turn the breakfast to snakes and frogs, and make that big toothy mouth again out of the oven door. Don't tell him! Don't tell him!"

Mrs. Brent, profoundly shocked, and not comprehending a word of this, instinctively put out her arms and gathered the other woman close.

"I can do lots of things," Jokey said. "I can do anything."

"Gee," breathed Precious, looking at the china pig. "What are you going to do with it now?"

"I dunno. I'll let it be a pig again, I guess."

"Can you change it back into a pig?"

"I don't hafta, stoopid. It'll be a pig by itself. Soon's I forget about it."

"Does that always happen?"

"No. If I busted that ol' china pig, it'd take longer, an' the pig would be all busted up when it changed back. All guts and blood," he added, sniggering. "I done that with a calf once."

"Gee," said Precious, still wide-eyed. "When you grow up you'll be able to do anything you want."

"Yeah." Jokey looked pleased. "But I can do anything I want

now." He frowned. "I just sometimes don't know what to do next."

"You'll know when you grow up," she said confidently.

"Oh, sure. I'll live in a big house in town, and look out of the windows, and bust up people and change 'em to ducks and snakes and things. I'll make flies as big as chickenhawks, or maybe as big as horses, and put 'em in the schools. I'll knock down the big buildings an' squash people."

He picked up a green apple and hurled it accurately at the brown sow.

"Gosh, and you won't have to practice piano, or listen to any old teachers," said Precious, warming to the possibilities. "Why, you won't even have to——*oh*!"

"What'sa matter?"

"That beetle. I hate them."

"Thass just a stag beetle," said Jokey with superiority. "Lookit here. I'll show you something."

He took out a book of matches and struck one. He held the beetle down with a dirty forefinger, and put the flame in its head. Precious watched attentively until the creature stopped scrabbling.

"Those things scare me," she said when he stood up.

"You're a sissy."

"I am not."

"Yes you are. *All* girls are sissies."

"You're dirty and you're a stinker," said Precious.

He promptly went to the pigpen and, from beside the trough, scooped up a heavy handful of filth. From his crouch, Jokey hurled it at her with a wide overhand sweep, so that it splattered her from the shoulder down, across the front of her dress, with a great wet gob for the toe of her left shiny shoe.

"Now who's dirty? Now who stinks?" he sang.

Precious lifted her skirt and looked at it in horror and loathing. Her eyes filled with angry tears. Sobbing, she rushed at him. She slapped him with little-girl clumsiness, hand-over-shoulder fashion. She slapped him again.

"Hey! Who are you hitting?" he cried in amazement. He backed off and suddenly grinned. "I'll fix you," he said, and disappeared without another word.

326

Whimpering with fury and revulsion, Precious pulled a handful of grass and began wiping her shoe.

Something moved into her field of vision. She glanced at it, squealed, and moved back. It was an enormous stag beetle, three times life-size, and it was scuttling toward her.

Another beetle—or the same one—met her at the corner.

With her hard black shiny shoes, she stepped on this one, so hard that the calf of her leg ached and tingled for the next half-hour.

The men were back when she returned to the house. Mr. Brent had been surveying Mr. Purney's fence-lines. Jokey was not missed before they left. Mrs. Purney looked drawn and frightened, and seemed glad that Mrs. Brent was leaving before Jokey came in for his supper.

Precious said nothing when asked about the dirt on her dress, and, under the circumstances, Mrs. Brent thought better of questioning her too closely.

In the car, Mrs. Brent told her husband that she thought Jokey was driving Mrs. Purney crazy.

It was her turn to be driven very nearly mad, the next morning, when Jokey turned up. Most of him.

Surprising, really, how much beetle had stuck to the hard black shoe, and, when it was time, turned into what they found under their daughter's bed.

Aim for the Heart

BY CRAIG SHAW GARDNER

People have always believed that there is nothing they cannot do if they put their mind to it, especially when it comes to seeking, and finding, Truth. The hard part is convincing others that you have indeed found what they've been looking for . . . or running from.

Craig Shaw Gardner is among the best of the younger generation of horror writers, and his stories have appeared in nearly every major market for Dark Fantasy.

THEY didn't always open their eyes. That's one place the movies had it wrong. But if their eyes did open, you had to pound the stake in good and fast, before they could scream and wake the others.

The movies always simplify matters. That's one of the first things I learned, after I learned about vampires. Real vampires, not shadows on film, but real beings, part of a world of smog and stop signs and all-night grocery stores. I almost said real "flesh and blood." I had to catch myself. Vampires are anything but that.

Veronica's eyes, or the eyes of the thing that had once been Veronica, shot open as I placed the pointed wood in the space between her breasts. She was a powerful one; I'd known that all along. I slammed the stake with my iron mallet, driving it through the breast bone to the heart before she could resist. Before she could return me to her power. She had no time to scream. Her eyes showed horror, her mouth opened in a gasp to show her sharply pointed teeth. Then it was over. The wood pierced the heart. Veronica shuddered once and was still.

I took the machete from my tool chest and cut the head from the body, so Veronica could never become a vampire again. As a final measure, I stuffed the mouth with garlic. It always pays to be safe in these matters.

I placed the mallet, the machete, and what garlic I hadn't used back into the tool box, and snapped the lid tight. I returned to the window through which I had entered. By now I had done this so many times it might almost become routine. But I could never allow myself to grow careless again. I had been careless twice before, and the vampires had almost overwhelmed me.

I was paying for it still. They had sent Veronica to me. They are far too clever. I almost became one of them. They learned of me through my first mistake. I had shown pity, and hesitated when I should have killed. Word of my mission spread through their community, sent by the vampire I let live one night too long.

They knew about me' then. They knew how I would feel about Veronica, and that she would enter my life when I needed her most.

You heard me talk about the movies. That's how I think about Veronica, like I met her in a movie. I saw her first in a restaurant, weaving her way between the tables. She walked toward me like Ingrid Bergman stepping out of *Casablanca*.

It was after dark, of course. I prefer crowded places after dark. Crowds, I had always thought, protected me from them. I was eating alone. She wore a black dress, a simply cut thing that somehow made her figure fascinating. Her long hair was dark brown, and her face looked pale beneath it. I found it impossible to look away from the face. First it was the fullness of her lips that caught me, then the angle of her cheekbones, then, at last, the color of her eyes. She had green eyes, green with flecks of blue.

When I saw her I knew I had to talk to her. She looked at me for an instant, then past me. I felt my first moment of fear. I would do anything rather than have her walk out of my life.

But she looked at me again, and didn't see the waiter. The tray caught her shoulder. The waiter deftly rebalanced the tray, but Veronica stumbled against a chair.

I was on my feet as it happened. She had steadied herself by the time I reached her. I asked if she was all right. She smiled and said she was.

"If only I weren't so single-minded about things." She laughed. "All this difficulty because I ran out of cigarettes."

I offered her one of mine. She accepted and asked if I minded if she sat for a minute. She thought she had twisted her ankle a bit.

If she walked like Ingrid Bergman, she smoked like Bette Davis; slow, deep breaths as she stared at her fingers. Then she looked up at me and smiled. She always smiled with her mouth closed.

Veronica told me she was waiting for someone who was hours overdue. An ex-lover, I guessed. She said she was nervous and was smoking too much. We spent the evening talking, and that night I took her home with me.

How the senses fool you when your mind won't see! She seemed so soft and warm and human to me the first time we made love. That was her power, of course. That was her design. True vampires can change your way of thinking, and hide from you their true, cold selves.

If your will is strong enough, sometimes you see through. I saw almost too late, as she secretly drew my blood night after night.

They had planned well, to lure me into her trap. Veronica and I were inseparable then. Unlike her other sisters of the night, they had given her a family, a mother and a sister, both human. Or so I thought then. She took me to meet them, in the daylight. That's another place the movies have it wrong. Stoker's *Dracula* had it right, though. Sometimes the strong ones can go out in daylight.

I was happy then, until the day she wanted to leave.

That was her mistake. She thought herself too much in control. It was not enough that I accepted her little criticisms without complaint. No, she had to take her power and twist it, make me squirm. Called me too possessive. My attentions were flattering, but . . .

I realized then how cold her face had become. It had been cold all along, really, it was only her power that kept me from seeing it. They always use their power to crush their victims. That's another thing the movies haven't caught on to; they try to steal not only your blood, but your soul.

But Veronica was too sure of herself, too greedy. I finally saw her pale, bloodless face for what it really was, and noticed the true sharpness of her teeth.

I was called upon to fulfill my duty again. As I had with Carolyn, and Sandra, and Karen, and Sally, the first one to make me careless. As I might have to with Veronica's mother and sister.

So again I climbed through the window, into the room, and saw Veronica's face, peaceful in sleep, pale beneath her dark hair. Her skin was dead white in the moonlight. She slept naked on her bed. Her full breasts rose and fell with her breathing, and it took me a moment to properly position the stake without yet touching the skin.

The stake and the mallet had to be positioned just so. You had to be careful in these matters. You had to strike swiftly and surely, before they had time to scream. And you always aimed for the heart.

Nona

BY STEPHEN KING

*When someone is in the thrall of a powerful emotion, he or
she tends to lose perspective, lose control—or, rather, hand
control over to someone else. But, despite the momentary
gratification of such an act, sooner or later there comes the
realization that the only thing a person truly owns—freedom
—has been given away, and the reaction ranges from self-
disgust to self-pity to horror . . . and beyond.*
*Stephen King's success is based less on the stories he tells
than on the fact that he cares for the people he's writing
about, and in caring makes them real, and in making them
real makes their stories real. Once that happens, there's no
escape, whether you want to or not.*

I DON'T know how to explain it, even now. I can't tell you why
I did those things. I couldn't do it at the trial, either. And there are
a lot of people here who ask me about it. There's a psychiatrist who
does. But I am silent. My lips are sealed. Except here in my cell.
Here I am not silent. I wake up screaming.

In the dream I see her walking toward me. She is wearing a white
gown, almost transparent, and her expression is one of mingled desire and triumph. She comes to me across a dark room with a stone
floor and I smell dry October roses. Her arms are held open and I
go to her with mine out to enfold her.

I feel dread, revulsion . . . and unutterable longing. Dread and
revulsion because I know what this place is, and longing because I
love her. I will always love her. There are times when I wish there
were still a death penalty. A short walk down a dim corridor, a
straight-backed chair fitted with a steel skullcap, clamps . . . then one
quick jolt and I would be with her.

As we come together in the dream my fear grows, but it is impossible for me to draw back from her. My hands press against the smooth plane of her back, her skin near under silk. She smiles with those deep, black eyes. Her head tilts up to mine and her lips part, ready to be kissed.

That's when she changes, shrivels. Her hair grows coarse and matted, melting from black to an ugly brown that spills down over the creamy whiteness of her cheeks. The eyes shrink and go beady. The whites disappear and she is glaring at me with tiny eyes like two polished pieces of jet. The mouth becomes a maw through which crooked yellow teeth protrude.

I try to scream, I try to wake up.

I can't. I'm caught again. I'll always be caught.

I am in the grip of a huge, noisome graveyard rat. Lights sway in front of my eyes. October roses. Somewhere a dead bell is chanting.

"Mine," this thing whispers. "Mine, mine, mine." The smell of roses is its breath as it swoops toward me, dead flowers in a charnel house.

Then I do scream, and I am awake.

They think what we did together has driven me crazy. But my mind is still working in some way or other, and I've never stopped looking for the answers. I still want to know how it was . . . and what it was. . . .

They've let me have paper and a pen with a felt tip. And I'm going to write everything down. I'll answer all their questions and maybe while I'm doing that I can answer some of my own. And when I'm done, there's something else. Something they didn't let me have. Something I took. It's here, under my mattress. A knife from the prison dining hall.

I'll have to start by telling you about Augusta.

As I write this it is night, a fine August night poked through with blazing stars. I can see them through the mesh of my window, which overlooks the exercise yard and a slice of sky I can block out with two fingers. It's hot, and I'm naked except for my shorts. I can hear the soft summer sound of frogs and crickets. But I can bring back winter just by closing my eyes. The bitter cold of that night, the bleakness, the hard, unfriendly lights of a city that was not my city. It was the fourteenth of February. See, I remember everything.

Look at my arms—covered with sweat, they've pulled into goose-flesh.

Augusta . . .

When I got to Augusta I was more dead than alive, it was that cold. I had picked a fine day to say good-bye to the college scene and hitchhike West; it looked like I might freeze to death before I got out of the state.

A cop had kicked me off the interstate ramp and threatened to bust me if he caught me thumbing there again. I was almost tempted to wisemouth him and let him do it. The flat, four-lane stretch of highway had been like an airport landing strip, the wind whooping and pushing membranes of powdery snow skirling along the concrete. And to the anonymous Them behind their Saf-T-Glas windshields, everyone standing in the breakdown lane on a dark night is either a rapist or a murderer, and if he's got long hair you can throw in child molester and faggot on top.

I tried it awhile on the access road, but it was no good. And along about a quarter of eight I realized that if I didn't get someplace warm quick, I was going to pass out.

I walked a mile and a half before I found a combination diner and diesel stop on 202 just inside the city limits. JOE'S GOOD EATS, the neon said. There were three big rigs parked in the crushed-stone parking lot, and one new sedan. There was a wilted Christmas wreath on the door that nobody had bothered to take down, and next to it a thermometer showing just five degrees of mercury above the zero mark. I had nothing to cover my ears but my hair, and my rawhide gloves were falling apart. The tips of my fingers felt like pieces of furniture.

I opened the door and went in.

The heat was the first thing that struck me, warm and good. Next a hillbilly song on the juke, the unmistakable voice of Merle Haggard: *"We don't let our hair grow long and shaggy, like the hippies out in San Francisco do."*

The third thing that struck me was The Eye. You know about The Eye once you let your hair get down below the lobes of your ears. Right then people know you don't belong to the Lions, Elks, or the VFW. You know about The Eye, but you never get used to it.

Right now the people giving me The Eye were four truckers in one booth, two more at the counter, a pair of old ladies wearing cheap fur coats and blue rinses, the short-order cook, and a gawky kid with soapsuds on his hands. There was a girl sitting at the far end of the counter, but all she was looking at was the bottom of her coffee cup.

She was the fourth thing that struck me.

We're both old enough to know there's no such thing as love at first sight. It's just something Rogers and Hammerstein thought up one day to rhyme with moon and June. It's for kids holding hands at the Junior Prom, right?

But looking at her made me feel something. You can laugh, but you wouldn't have if you'd seen her. She was almost unbearably beautiful. I knew without a doubt that everybody else in Joe's knew that the same as me. Just like I knew she had been getting The Eye before I came in. She had coal-colored hair, so black that it seemed nearly blue under the fluorescents. It fell freely over the shoulders of her scuffed tan coat. Her skin was cream-white, with just the faintest blooded touch lingering beneath the skin—the cold she had brought in with her. Dark, sooty lashes. Solemn eyes that slanted up the tiniest bit at the corners. A full and mobile mouth below a straight, patrician nose. I couldn't tell what her body looked like. I didn't care. You wouldn't have, either. All she needed was that face, that hair, that *look*. She was exquisite. That's the only word we have for her in English.

Nona.

I sat two stools down from her, and the short-order cook came over and looked at me. "What?"

"Black coffee, please."

He went to get it. From behind me someone said: "Looks just like Jesus Christ, don't he?"

The gawky dishwasher laughed, a quick yuk-yuk sound. The truckers at the counter joined in.

The short-order cook brought me my coffee back, jarred it down on the counter and spilled some on the thawing meat of my hand. I jerked it back.

"Sorry," he said indifferently.

"He's gonna heal it himself," one of the truckers in the booth called over.

The blue-rinse twins paid their checks and hurried out. One of the knights of the road sauntered over to the juke and put another dime in. Johnny Cash began to sing "A Boy Named Sue." I blew on my coffee.

Someone tugged on my sleeve. I turned my head and there she was—she'd moved over to the empty stool. Looking at that face close up was almost blinding. I spilled some more of my coffee.

"I'm sorry." Her voice was low, almost atonal.

"My fault. I can't feel what I'm doing yet."

"I——"

She stopped, seemingly at a loss. I suddenly realized that she was scared. I felt my first reaction to her swim over me again—to protect her and take care of her, make her not afraid. "I need a ride," she finished in a rush. "I didn't dare ask any of them." She made a barely perceptible gesture toward the truckers in the booth.

How can I make you understand that I would have given anything —anything—to be able to tell her, *Sure, finish your coffee, I'm parked right outside*. It sounds crazy to say I felt that way after half a dozen words out of her mouth, and the same number out of mine, but I did. I did. Looking at her was like looking at the "Mona Lisa" or the "Venus de Milo" come to breathing life. And there was another feeling: It was as if a sudden, powerful light had been turned on in the confused darkness of my mind. It would make it easier if I could say she was a pickup and I was a fast man with the ladies, quick with a funny line and lots of patter, but she wasn't and I wasn't. All I knew was I didn't have what she needed and it tore me up.

"I'm thumbing," I told her. "A cop kicked me off the interstate and I only came in here to get out of the cold. I'm sorry."

"Are you from the university?"

"Not anymore. I quit before they could fire me."

"Are you going home?"

"No home to go to. I was a state ward. I got to school on a scholarship. I blew it. Now I don't know where I'm going." My life story in five sentences. It made me feel depressed.

337

She laughed—the sound made me run hot and cold—and sipped her own coffee. "We're cats out of the same bag, I guess."

I was about to make my best conversational shot—something witty like "Is that so?"—when a hand came down on my shoulder.

I turned around. It was one of the truckers from the booth. He had blond stubble on his chin and there was a wooden kitchen match poking out of his mouth. He smelled of engine oil.

"I think you're done with that coffee," he said. His lips parted around the match in a grin. He had a lot of very white teeth.

"What?"

"You're stinking the place up, fella. You are a fella, aren't you? Kind of hard to tell."

"You aren't any rose yourself," I said. "You smell like a crankcase."

He gave me a hard palm across the side of my face. I saw little black dots.

"Don't fight in here," the short-order cook said. "If you're going to scramble him, do it outside."

"Come on, you goddamned Commie," the trucker said.

This is the spot where the girl is supposed to say something like "Unhand him" or "You brute." She wasn't saying anything. She was watching both of us with feverish intensity. It was scary. I think it was the first time I'd noticed how huge her eyes really were.

"Do I have to sock you again, fag?"

"No. Come on, shitheels."

I don't know how that jumped out of me. I don't like to fight. I'm not a good fighter. I'm an even worse name-caller. But I was angry, just then. It came up all at once and I wanted to hurt him, kill him.

Maybe he got a mental whiff of it. For just a second a shade of uncertainty flicked over his face, an unconscious wondering if maybe he hadn't picked the wrong hippie. Then it was gone. He wasn't going to back off from some long-haired elitist effeminite snob who used the flag to wipe his ass with—at least not in front of his buddies. Not a big truck-driving son-of-a-gun like him.

The anger pounded over me again. *Faggot? Faggot?* I felt out of control, and it was good to feel that way. My tongue was thick in my mouth. My stomach was a slab.

338

We walked across to the door, and my buddy's buddies almost broke their backs getting up to watch the fun.

Nona? I thought of her, but only in an absent, back-of-my-mind way. I knew Nona would be there, Nona would take care of me. I knew it the same way I knew it would be cold outside. It was strange to know that about a girl I had only met five minutes before. Strange, but I didn't think about that until later. My mind was taken up—no, almost blotted out—by the heavy cloud of rage. I felt homicidal.

The cold was so clear and so clean that it felt as if we were cutting it with our bodies like knives. The frosted gravel of the parking lot gritted harshly under his heavy boots and under my shoes. The moon, full and bloated, looked down on us with a vapid eye, faintly rheumed with a rime of high atmospheric moisture, from a sky as black as a night in hell. We left tiny dwarfed shadows behind our feet in the monochrome glare of a single sodium light set high on a pole beyond the parked rigs. Our breath plumed the air in short bursts. The trucker turned to me, his gloved fists balled.

"Okay, you son-of-a-bitch," he said.

I seemed to be swelling—my whole body seemed to be swelling. Somehow, numbly, I knew that my intellect was about to be eclipsed by some huge, invisible something that I had never suspected might be in me. It was terrifying—but at the same time I welcomed it, desired it, lusted for it. In that last instant of coherent thought it seemed that my body had become a stone pyramid of violence incarnate, or a rushing, murderous cyclone that could sweep everything in front of it like so many colored pick-up sticks. The trucker seemed small, puny, insignificant. I laughed at him. I laughed, and the sound was as black and as bleak as that moonstruck sky overhead.

He came at me swinging his fists. I batted down his right, took his left on the side of my face, and then kicked him in the guts. The air whoofed out of him in a white, steaming rush. He tried to back away, holding himself and coughing.

I ran around in back of him, still laughing like some farmer's dog barking at the moon, and I had pounded him three times before he could make even a quarter turn—the neck, the shoulder, and one red ear.

He made a yowling noise, and one of his flailing hands brushed

339

my nose. The fury that had taken me over mushroomed—*me! he tried to strike at me!*—and I kicked him again, bringing my foot up high and hard, like a punter. He screamed into the night and I heard a rib snap. He folded up and I jumped on him.

At the trial one of the other truck drivers testified I was like a wild animal. And I was. I can't remember much of it, but I can remember that, snarling and growling at him like a wild dog.

I straddled him, grabbed double handfuls of his greasy hair, and began to rub his face into the gravel. In the flat glare of the sodium light his blood seemed black, like beetle's blood.

"Jesus, stop it!" somebody yelled.

Hands grabbed my shoulders and pulled me off. I saw whirling faces and I struck at them.

The trucker was trying to creep away. His face was a staring mask of blood, and dazed eyes. I began to kick him, dodging away from the others, grunting with satisfaction each time I connected on him.

He was beyond fighting back. All he knew was to try to get away. Each time I kicked him his eyes would squeeze closed, like the eyes of a tortoise, and he would halt. Then he would start to crawl again. He looked stupid. I decided I was going to kill him. I was going to kick him to death. Then I would kill the rest of them, all but Nona.

I kicked him again and he flopped over on his back and looked up at me dazedly.

"Uncle," he croaked. "I cry uncle. Please. Please——"

I knelt down beside him, feeling the gravel bite into my knees through my thin jeans.

"Here you are, bastard," I whispered. "Here's uncle for you."

I hooked my hands onto his throat.

Three of them jumped me all at once and knocked me off him. I got up, still grinning, and started toward them. They backed away, three big men, all of them scared green.

And it clicked off.

Just like that it clicked off and it was just me, standing in the parking lot of Joe's Good Eats, breathing hard and feeling sick and horrified.

I turned and looked back toward the diner. The girl was there, her beautiful features were lit with triumph. She raised one fist to shoulder height in salute.

I turned back to the man on the ground. He was still trying to crawl away, and when I approached him his eyeballs rolled fearfully.

"Don't you touch him!" one of his friends cried.

I looked at them, confused. "I'm sorry . . . I didn't mean to . . . to hurt him so bad. Let me help——"

"You get out of here, that's what you do," the short-order cook said. He was standing in front of Nona at the foot of the steps, clutching a greasy spatula in one hand. "I'm calling the cops."

"Aren't you forgetting he was the guy who started it? He——"

"Don't give me any of your lip, you lousy queer," he said, backing up. "All I know is you started trouble and then just about killed that guy. I'm calling the cops!" He dashed and went back inside.

"Okay," I said to nobody in particular. "Okay, okay."

I had left my rawhide gloves inside, but it didn't seem like a good idea to go back in and get them. I put my hands in my pockets and started to walk back to the interstate access road. I figured my chances against a ride before the cops picked me up were about ten to one. My ears were freezing and I felt sick to my stomach. Some night.

"Wait! Hey, wait!"

I turned around. It was her, running to catch up with me, her hair flying out behind her.

"You were wonderful!" she said. "Wonderful!"

"I hurt him bad," I said dully. "I never did anything like that before."

"I wish you'd killed him!"

I blinked at her in the frosty light.

"I heard the things they were saying about me before you came in. Laughing in that big, brave, dirty way—haw, haw, lookit the little girl out so long after dark. Where you going, honey? Need a lift? I'll give you a ride if you'll give me a ride. *Damn!*"

She glared back over her shoulder as if she could strike them dead with a sudden bolt from her dark eyes. Then she turned them on me, and again it seemed like that searchlight had been turned on in my mind. "I'm coming with you."

"Where? To jail?" I tugged at my hair with both hands. "With this, the first guy that gave us a ride would be a state cop. That cook meant what he said about calling them."

341

"*I'll* hitch. You stand behind me. They'll stop for me."

I couldn't argue with her about that and didn't want to. Love at first sight? I doubt it. But it was something.

"Here," she said, "you forgot these." She held out my gloves.

She hadn't gone back inside, and that meant she'd had them all along. She'd known she was coming with me. It gave me an eerie feeling. I put on my gloves and we walked up the access road to the turnpike ramp.

She was right about the ride. We got one with the first car that swung onto the ramp. Before that happened I asked, "What's your name?"

"Nona," she said simply. She didn't offer any more, but that was all right. I was satisfied.

We didn't say anything else while we waited, but it seemed as if we did. I won't give you a load of bull about ESP and that stuff; there was none of that. But we didn't need it. You've felt it yourself if you've ever been with someone you were really close to, or if you've taken one of those drugs with initials for a name. You don't *have* to talk. Communication seems to shift over to some high-frequency emotional band. A twist of the hand does it all. You don't need the social amenities. But we were strangers. I only knew her first name and, now that I think back, I don't believe I ever told her mine at all. But we were doing it. It wasn't love. I hate to keep repeating that, but I feel I have to. I wouldn't dirty that word with whatever we had—not after what we did, not after Blainesville, not after the dreams.

A high, wailing shriek filled the cold silence of the night, rising and falling.

"That's an ambulance, I think," I said.

"Yes."

Silence again. The moon's light was fading behind a thickening membrane of cloud. I thought we would have snow before the night was over.

Lights poked over the hill.

I stood behind her without having to be told. She brushed her hair back and raised that beautiful face. As I watched the car signal for the entrance ramp I was swept with a feeling of unreality—it was unreal that this beautiful girl had elected to come with me, it was unreal that I had beaten a man to the point where an ambulance had to be called for him, it was unreal to think I might be in jail by morning. Unreal. I felt caught in a spiderweb. But who was the spider?

Nona put out her thumb. The car, a Chevrolet sedan, went by us and I thought it was going to keep right on going. Then the tail-lights flashed and Nona grabbed my hand. "Come on, we got a ride!" She grinned at me with childish delight and I grinned back at her.

The guy was reaching enthusiastically across the seat to open the door for her. When the dome light flashed on I could see him—a fairly big man in an expensive camel's hair coat, graying around the edges of his hat, prosperous features softened by years of good meals. A businessman or a salesman. Alone. When he saw me he did a double take, but it was a second or two too late to put the car back in gear and haul out of there. And it was easier for him this way. Later he could fib himself into believing he had seen both of us, that he was a truly good-hearted soul giving a young couple a break.

"Cold night," he said as Nona slid in beside him and I got in beside her.

"It certainly is," Nona said sweetly. "Thank you!"

"Yeah," I said. "Thanks."

"Don't mention it." And we were off, leaving sirens, busted-up truckers, and Joe's Good Eats behind us.

I had gotten kicked off the interstate at seven-thirty. It was only eight-thirty now. It's amazing how much you can do in a short time, or how much can be done to you.

We were approaching the yellow flashing lights that signal the Augusta toll station.

"How far you going?" the driver asked.

That was a stumper. I had been hoping to make it as far as Kittery and crash with an acquaintance who was teaching school there. It still seemed as good an answer as any and I was opening my mouth to give it when Nona said:

"We're going to Blainesville. It's a small town just south of Lewiston-Auburn."

Blainesville. That made me feel strange. Once upon a time I had

been on pretty good terms with Blainesville. But that was before
Ace Carmody messed me up.

He brought his car to a stop, took a toll ticket, and then we were
on our way again.

"I'm only going as far as Gardner, myself," he said, lying
smoothly. "One exit up. But that's a start for you."

"It certainly is," Nona said, just as sweetly as before. "It was nice
of you to stop on such a cold night." And while she was saying it I
was getting her anger on that high emotional wavelength, naked and
full of venom. It scared me, the way ticking from a wrapped package might scare me.

"My name's Blanchette," he said. "Norman Blanchette." He
waved his hand in our direction to be shaken.

"Cheryl Craig," Nona said, taking it daintily.

I took her cue and gave him a false name. "Pleasure," I mumbled.
His hand was soft and flabby. It felt like a hot-water bottle in the
shape of a hand; the thought sickened me. It sickened me that we
had been forced to beg a ride with this patronizing man who thought
he had seen a chance to pick up a pretty girl hitching all by herself,
a girl who might or might not agree to an hour spent in a motel
room in return for enough cash to buy a bus ticket. It sickened me to
know that if I had been alone this man who had just offered me his
flabby, hot hand would have zipped by without a second look. It
sickened me to know he would drop us at the Gardner exit and then
dart right back on down the southbound ramp, congratulating himself on how smoothly he had solved an annoying situation. Everything about him sickened me. The porky droop of his jowls, the
slicked-back wings of his hair, the smell of his cologne.

And what right did he have? What right?

The sickness curdled, and the flowers of rage began to bloom
again. The headlights of his prosperous Impala sedan cut the night
with smooth ease, and my rage wanted to reach out and strangle
everything that he was set in among—the kind of music I knew he
would listen to as he lay back in his La-Z-Boy recliner with the evening paper in his hot-water-bottle hands, the blue rinse his wife
would use in her hair, the kids always sent off to the movies or off
to school or off to camp—as long as they were off somewhere—his

344

snobbish friends and the drunken parties they would attend with them.

But maybe his cologne was the worst. It seemed to fill the car with the sweet, sickish stench of his hypocrisy. It smelled like the perfumed disinfectant they use in a slaughterhouse at the end of each shift.

The car ripped through the night with Norman Blanchette holding the wheel in his bloated hands. His manicured nails gleamed softly in the lights from the instrument panel. I wanted to crack a wing window and get away from that cloying smell. No, more—I wanted to crank the whole window down and stick my head out into the cold, purifying air of the night, wallow in its chilled freshness— but I was frozen, frozen in the dumb maw of my wordless, inexpressible hate.

That was when Nona put the nail file into my hand.

When I was three I got a bad case of the flu and had to go to the hospital. While I was there, my dad fell asleep smoking in bed and the house burned down with them and my older brother Drake in it. I have their pictures. They look like actors in an old 1958 American-International horror movie, faces you don't know like those of the big stars, more like Elisha Cook, Jr., and Mara Corday and some child actor you can't quite remember . . . Brandon DeWilde, maybe.

I had no relatives to go to and so I was sent to a home in Portland for five years. Then I became a state ward. That means a family takes you in and the state pays them thirty dollars a month for your keep. I don't think there was ever a state ward who acquired a taste for lobster. Usually a couple will take two or three wards as a hardheaded business investment. If a kid is fed up he can earn his keep doing chores around the place and that hard thirty turns into gravy.

My folks were named Hollis and they lived in Falmouth. Not the fancy part near the country club or the yacht club but farther out toward the Blainesville town line. They had a three-story farmhouse with fourteen rooms. There was coal heat in the kitchen that got upstairs any way it could, and in January you went to bed with three quilts on you and still weren't sure if your feet were there when you woke up in the morning until you put them out on the floor where you could look at them. Mrs. Hollis was fat. Mr. Hollis was dour, rarely spoke, and wore a red-and-black checked hunting cap all year round. The house was a helter-skelter mess of white-elephant furniture, rummage-sale stuff, moldy mattresses, dogs, cats, and automotive parts laid on newspaper. I had three "brothers," all of them wards. We had a nodding acquaintance, like co-travelers on a three-day bus trip.

I made good grades in school and went out for spring baseball when I was a high school sophomore. Hollis was yapping after me to quit, but I stuck with it until the thing with Ace Carmody happened. Then I didn't want to go anymore, not with my face all puffed and cut, not with the stories Betsy Dirisko was telling around. So I quit the team, and Hollis got me a job in the local drugstore.

In February of my junior year I took the College Boards, paying for them with twelve bucks I had socked away in my mattress. I got accepted at the university with a small scholarship and a good work-study job in the library. The expression on the Hollises' faces when I showed them the financial-aid papers is the best memory of my life.

One of my "brothers," Curt, ran away. I couldn't have done that. I was too passive to take a step like that. I would have been back after two hours on the road. School was the only way out for me, and I took it.

The last thing Mrs. Hollis said when I left was, "You write, hear me? And send us something when you can." I never saw either of them again. I made good grades my freshman year and got a job that summer working full-time in the library. I sent them a Christmas card that first year, but that was the only one.

In the first semester of my sophomore year I fell in love. It was the biggest thing that had ever happened to me. Pretty? She would have knocked you back two steps. To this day I have no idea what she saw in me. I don't even know if she loved me or not. I think she did at first. After that I was just a habit that's hard to break, like smoking or driving with your elbow poked out the window. She held me for a while, maybe not wanting to break the habit. Maybe she held me for wonder, or maybe it was just her vanity. Good boy, roll over, sit up, fetch the paper. Here's a kiss good night. It doesn't matter. For a while it was love, then it was like love, then it was over.

I had slept with her twice, both times after other things had taken over for love. That fed the habit for a little while. Then she came back from the Thanksgiving break and said she was in love with a guy from Delta Tau Delta, a guy who also came from her hometown. I tried to get her back and almost made it once, but she had something she hadn't had before—perspective. It didn't work and when the Christmas vacation was over they were pinned.

Whatever I had been building up, all those years since the fire wiped out the B-movie actors who had once been my family, that broke it down. That pin on her blouse.

And after that, I was on again–off again with the three or four girls who were willing. I could blame it on my childhood, say I never had good sexual models, but that wasn't it. I'd never had any trouble with the girl. Only now the girl was gone.

I started being afraid of girls, a little. And it wasn't so much the ones I was impotent with as the ones I wasn't, the ones I could make it with. They made me uneasy. I kept asking myself where they were hiding whatever axes they liked to grind and when they were going to let me have it. I'm not so strange at that. You show me a married man or a man with a steady woman, and I'll show you someone who is asking himself (maybe only in the early hours of the morning or on Friday afternoon when she's off buying groceries), *What is she doing when I'm not around? What does she really think of me?* And maybe most of all, *How much of me has she got? How much is left?* Once I started thinking about those things, I thought about them all the time.

I started to drink and my grades took a nose dive. During semester break I got a letter saying that if they didn't improve in six weeks, my second-semester scholarship check would be withheld. I and some guys I hung around with got drunk and stayed drunk for the whole holiday. On the last day we went to a whorehouse and I operated just fine. It was too dark to see faces.

My grades stayed about the same. I called the girl once and cried over the telephone. She cried too, and in a way I think that pleased her. I didn't hate her then and I don't now. But she scared me plenty.

On February 9 I got a letter from the dean of Arts and Sciences saying I was flunking two of three courses in my major field. On

February 13 I got a hesitant sort of letter from the girl. She wanted everything to be all right between us. She was planning to marry the guy from Delta Tau Delta in July or August, and I could be invited if I wanted to be. That was almost funny. What could I give her for a wedding gift? My penis with a red ribbon tied around the fore-skin?

On the fourteenth, Valentine's Day, I decided it was time for a change of scene. Nona came next, but you know about that.

You have to understand how she was to me if this is to do any good at all. She was more beautiful than the girl, but that wasn't it. Good looks are cheap in a wealthy country. It was the her inside. There was sex, but the sex that came from her was like that of a vine—blind sex, a kind of clinging, not-to-be-denied sex that is not so important because it is as instinctual as photosynthesis. Not like an animal—that implies lust—but like a plant. I knew we would make love, that we would make it as men and women do, but that our joining would be as blunt and remote and meaningless as ivy clutching its way up a trellis in the August sun.

The sex was important only because it was unimportant.

I think—no, I'm sure—that violence was the real motive force. The violence was real and not just a dream. The violence of Joe's Good Eats, the violence of Norman Blanchette. And there was even something blind and vegetative about that. Maybe she was only a clinging vine after all, because the Venus flytrap is a species of vine, but that plant is carnivorous and will make animal motion when a fly or a bit of raw meat is placed in its jaws. And it was all *real*. The sporulating vine may only dream that it fornicates, but I am sure the Venus flytrap tastes that fly, relishes its diminishing struggles as its jaws close around it.

The last part was my own passivity. I could not fill up the hole in my life. Not the hole left by the girl when she said good-bye—I don't want to lay this at her door—but the hole that had always been there, the dark, confused swirling that never stopped down in the middle of me. Nona filled that hole. She made me her arm. She made me move and act.

She made me noble.

Now maybe you understand a little of it. Why I dream of her. Why the fascination remains in spite of the remorse and the revulsion. Why I hate her. Why I fear her. And why even now I still love her.

It was eight miles from the Augusta ramp to Gardner and we did it in a few short minutes. I grasped the nail file woodenly at my side and watched the green reflectorized sign—KEEP RIGHT FOR EXIT 14—twinkle up out of the night. The moon was gone and it had begun to spit snow.

"Wish I were going farther," Blanchette said.

"That's all right," Nona said warmly, and I could feel her fury buzzing and burrowing into the meat under my skull like a drill bit. "Just drop us at the top of the ramp."

He drove up, observing the ramp speed of thirty miles an hour. I knew what I was going to do. It felt as if my legs had turned to warm lead.

The top of the ramp was lit by one overhead light. To the left I could see the lights of Gardner against the thickening cloud cover. To the right, nothing but blackness. There was no traffic coming either way along the access road.

I got out. Nona slid across the seat, giving Norman Blanchette a final smile. I wasn't worried. She was quarterbacking the play.

Blanchette was smiling an infuriating porky smile, relieved at being almost rid of us. "Well, good ni——"

"Oh my purse! Don't drive off with my purse!"

"I'll get it," I told her. I leaned back into the car. Blanchette saw what I had in my hand, and the porky smile on his face froze solid.

Now lights showed on the hill, but it was too late to stop. Nothing could have stopped me. I picked up Nona's purse with my left hand. With my right I plunged the steel nail file into Blanchette's throat. He bleated once.

I got out of the car. Nona was waving the oncoming vehicle down. I couldn't see what it was in the dark and snow; all I could make out were the two bright circles of its headlamps. I crouched behind Blanchette's car, peeking through the back windows.

The voices were almost lost in the filling throat of the wind.

". . . trouble, lady?"

". . . father . . ." wind ". . . had a heart attack! Will you . . ."

I scurried around the trunk of Norman Blanchette's Impala, bent over. I could see them now, Nona's slender silhouette and a taller form. They appeared to be standing by a pickup truck. They turned and approached the driver's-side window of the Chevy, where Norman Blanchette was slumped over the wheel with Nona's file in his throat. The driver of the pickup was a young kid in what looked like an Air Force parka. He leaned inside. I came up behind him.

"Jesus, lady!" he said. "There's blood on this guy! What——"

I hooked my right elbow around his throat and grabbed my right wrist with my left hand. I pulled him up hard. His head connected with the top of my door and made a hollow *thock*! He went limp in my arms.

I could have stopped then. He hadn't gotten a good look at Nona, hadn't seen me at all. I could have stopped. But he was a busybody, a meddler, somebody else in our way, trying to hurt us. I was tired of being hurt. I strangled him.

When it was done I looked up and saw Nona spotlighted in the conflicting lights of the car and truck, her face a grotesque rictus of hate, love, triumph, and joy. She held her arms out to me and I went into them. We kissed. Her mouth was cold but her tongue was warm. I plunged both hands into the secret hollows of her hair, and the wind screamed around us.

"Now fix it," she said. "Before someone else comes."

I fixed it. It was a slipshod job, but I knew that was all we needed. A little more time. After that it wouldn't matter. We would be safe.

The kid's body was light. I picked him up in both arms, carried him across the road, and threw him into the gully beyond the guard-rails. His body tumbled loosely all the way to the bottom, head over heels, like the ragbag man Mr. Hollis had me put out in the corn-field every July. I went back to get Blanchette.

He was heavier, and bleeding like a stuck pig to boot. I tried to pick him up, staggered three steps backward, and then he slipped out of my arms and fell onto the road. I turned him over. The new snow had stuck to his face, turning it into a hideous skier's mask.

I bent over, grabbed him under the arms, and dragged him to the gully. His feet left trailing grooves behind him. I threw him over and watched him slide down the embankment on his back, his arms up over his head. His eyes were wide open, staring raptly at the snowflakes falling into them. If the snow kept coming, they would both be just two vague humps by the time the plows came by.

I went back across the road. Nona had already climbed into the pickup truck without having to be told. I could see the pallid smear of her face, the dark holes of her eyes, but that was all. I got into Blanchette's car, sitting in the streaks of his blood that had gathered on the nubby vinyl seat cover, and drove it onto the shoulder. I turned off the headlights, put on the four-way flashers, and got out. To anyone passing by, it would look like a motorist who had engine trouble and then walked into town to find a garage. Simple but workable. I was very pleased with my improvisation. It was as if I had been murdering people all my life. I trotted back to the idling truck, got in behind the wheel, and pointed it toward the turnpike entrance ramp.

She sat next to me, not touching but close. When she moved I could sometimes feel a strand of her hair on my neck. It was like being touched with a tiny electrode. Once I had to put my hand out and feel her leg, to make sure she was real. She laughed quietly. It was all real. The wind howled around the windows, driving snow in great, flapping gusts.

We ran South.

Just across the bridge from Gretna, as you go up 126 toward Freeport, you come up on a huge renovated farm that goes under the laughable title of the Blainesville Youth League. They have twelve lanes of candlepin bowling with cranky automatic pinsetters that usually take the last three days of the week off, a few ancient pinball machines, a juke featuring the greatest hits of 1957, three Brunswick pool tables, and a Coke-and-chips counter where you also rent bowling shoes that look like they might have just come off the feet of dead winos. The name of the place is laughable because most of the Blainesville youth head up to the drive-in at Gretna Hill at night or go to the stock-car races at Oxford Plains. The people who do hang out there are mostly toughies from Gretna, Falmouth, Freeport, Yarmouth. The average is one fight per evening in the parking lot.

I started hanging out there when I was a high school sophomore. One of my friends, Chris Kennedy, was working there three nights a week and if there was nobody waiting for a table he'd let me shoot some pool for free. It wasn't much, but it was better than going back to the Hollises' house.

That's where I met Ace Carmody. He was from Gretna, and nobody much doubted that he was the toughest guy in three towns. He
drove a chopped and channeled '51 Ford, and it was rumored that he
could push it all the way to 130 if he had to. He'd come in like a
king, his hair greased back and glistening in a perfect duck's-ass
pompadour, shoot a few games of double-bank for a dime a ball
(Was he good? You guess.), buy Shelley a Coke when she came in,
and then they'd leave. You could almost hear a reluctant sigh of relief from those present when the scarred front door wheezed shut.
Nobody ever went out in the parking lot with Ace Carmody.

Nobody, that is, but me.

Shelley Roberson was his girl, the prettiest girl in Blainesville, I
guess. I don't think she was terrifically bright, but that didn't matter
when you got a look at her. She had the most flawless complexion I
had ever seen, and it didn't come out of a cosmetics bottle, either.
Hair as black as coal, dark eyes, generous mouth, a body that just
wouldn't quit—and she didn't mind showing it off. Who was going
to drag her out back and try to stoke her locomotive while Ace was
around? Nobody sane, that's who.

I fell hard for her. Not like the girl and not like Nona, even
though Shelley did look like a younger version of her, but it was just
as desperate and just as serious in its way. If you've ever had the
worst case of puppy love going around, you know how I felt. She
was seventeen, two years older than I.

I started going down there more and more often, even nights
when Chris wasn't on, just to catch a glimpse of her. I felt like a
bird watcher, except it was a desperate kind of game for me. I'd go
back home, lie to the Hollises about where I'd been, and climb up to
my room. I'd write long, passionate letters to her, telling her everything I'd like to do to her, then tear them up. Study halls at school
I'd dream about asking her to marry me so we could run away to
Mexico together.

She must have tumbled to what was happening, and it must have
flattered her a little, because she was nice to me when Ace wasn't
around. She'd come over and talk to me, let me buy her a Coke, sit
on a stool, and kind of rub her leg against mine. It drove me crazy.

One night in early November I was just mooning around, shooting a little pool with Chris, waiting for her to come in. The place

was deserted because it wasn't even eight o'clock yet, and a lonesome wind was snuffling around outside, threatening winter.

"You better lay off," Chris said, shooting the nine straight into the corner.

"Lay off what?"

"You know."

"No I don't." I scratched and Chris added a ball to the table. He ran six and while he was running them I went over and put a dime in the juke.

"Shelley Roberson." He lined up the one carefully and sent it walking up the rail. "Jimmy Donner was telling Ace about the way you been sniffing around her. Jimmy thought it was really funny, her being older and all, but Ace wasn't laughing."

"She's nothing to me," I said through paper lips.

"She better not be," Chris said, and then a couple of guys came in and he went over to the counter and gave them a cue ball.

Ace came in around nine and he was alone. He'd never taken any notice of me before, and I'd just about forgotten what Chris said. When you're invisible you get to thinking you're invulnerable. I was playing pinball and I was pretty involved. I didn't even notice the place get quiet as people stopped bowling or shooting pool. The next thing I knew, somebody had thrown me right across the pinball machine. I landed on the floor in a heap. I got up feeling scared and sick. He had tilted the machine, wiping out my three replays. He was standing there and looking at me with not a strand of hair out of place, his garrison jacket half unzipped.

"You stop messing around," he said softly, "or I'm going to change your face."

He went out. Everybody was looking at me and I wanted to sink right down through the floor until I saw there was a kind of grudging admiration on most of their faces. So I brushed myself off, unconcerned, and put another dime in the pinball machine. The TILT light went out. A couple of guys came over and clapped me on the back before they went out, not saying anything.

At eleven, when the place closed, Chris offered me a ride home.

"You're going to take a fall if you don't watch out."

"Don't worry about me," I said.

He didn't answer.

353

Two or three nights later Shelley came in by herself around seven. There was one other guy there, a porky kid named John Dano, but I hardly noticed him. He was even more invisible than I was.

She came right over to where I was shooting, close enough so I could smell the clean-soap smell on her skin. It made me feel dizzy. "I heard about what Ace did to you," she said. "I'm not supposed to talk to you anymore and I'm not going to, but I've got something to make it all better." She kissed me. Then she went out, before I could even get my tongue down from the roof of my mouth. I went back to my game in a daze. I didn't even see John Dano when he went out to spread the word. I couldn't see anything but her dark, dark eyes.

So that night I ended up in the parking lot with Ace Carmody, and he beat the living Jesus out of me. It was cold, bitterly cold, and at the end I began to sob, not caring who was watching or listening, which was everybody. The single sodium arc lamp looked down on all of it mercilessly. I hadn't even landed a punch on him.

"Okay," he said, squatting down next to me. He wasn't even breathing hard. He took a switchblade out of his pocket and pressed the chrome button. Seven inches of moon-drenched silver sprang into the world. "This is what you get next time. I'll carve my name on your balls." Then he got up, gave me one last kick, and left. I just lay there for maybe ten minutes, shivering on the hard-packed dirt. No one came to help me up or pat me on the back, not even Chris. Shelley didn't show up to make it all better.

Finally I got up by myself and hitchhiked home. I told Mrs. Hollis I'd hitched a ride with a drunk and he drove off the road. I never went back to the bowling alley again.

Ace got killed two years later when he drove his fancy '51 Ford into a road-repair dumptruck while passing on a hill. I understand that he had dropped Shelley by then and that she had really gone downhill, picking up a case of clap on the way. Chris said he saw her one night in the Manoir up in Lewiston, hustling guys for drinks. She had lost most of her teeth, and her nose had been broken somewhere along the line, he said. He said I would never recognize her. By then I didn't much care one way or the other.

The pickup had no snow tires, and before we got to the Lewiston exit I had begun to skid around in the new powder. It took us over forty-five minutes to make the twenty-two miles.

The man at the Lewiston exit point took my toll card and my sixty cents. "Slippery traveling?"

Neither of us answered him. We were getting close to where we wanted to go now. If I hadn't had that odd kind of wordless contact with her, I would have been able to tell just by the way she sat on the dusty seat of the pickup, her hands folded tightly in her lap, those eyes fixed straight ahead on the road with fierce intensity. I felt a shudder work through me.

We took Route 136. There weren't many cars on the road; the wind was freshening and the snow was coming down harder than ever. On the other side of Gretna Village we passed a big Buick Riviera that had slued around sideways and climbed the curb. Its four-way flashers were going and I had a ghostly double image of Norman Blanchette's Impala. It would be drifted in with snow now, nothing but a ghostly hump in the darkness.

The Buick's driver tried to flag me down but I went by him without slowing, spraying him with slush. My wipers were clogging with snow and I reached out and snapped at the one on my side. Some of the snow loosened and I could see a little better.

Gretna was a ghost town, everything dark and closed. I signaled right to go over the bridge into Blainesville. The rear wheels wanted to slide out from under me, but I handled the skid. Up ahead and across the river I could see the dark shadow that was the Blainesville Youth League building. It looked shut up and lonely. I felt suddenly sorry, sorry that there had been so much pain. And death. That was when Nona spoke for the first time since the Gardner exit.

"There's a policeman behind you."

"Is he——?"

"No. His flasher is off."

But it made me nervous and maybe that's why it happened. Route 136 makes a ninety-degree turn on the Gretna side of the river and then it's straight across the bridge and into Blainesville. I made the first turn, but there was ice on the Blainesville side.

"*Damn*——"

The rear end of the truck flirted around and before I could steer clear, it had smashed into one of the heavy steel bridge stanchions.

355

We went sliding all the way around like kids on a Flexible Flyer, and the next thing I saw was the bright headlights of the police car that was behind us. He put on his brakes—I could see the red reflections in the falling snow—but the ice got him, too. He plowed right into us. There was a grinding, jarring shock as we went into the supporting girders again. I was jolted into Nona's lap, and even in that confused split second I had time to relish the smooth firmness of her thigh. Then everything stopped. Now the cop had his flasher on. It sent blue, revolving shadows chasing across the hood of the truck and the snowy steel crosswork of the Gretna-Blainesville bridge. The dome light inside the cruiser came on as the cop got out.

If he hadn't been behind us it wouldn't have happened. That thought was playing over and over in my mind, like a phonograph needle stuck in a single, flawed groove. I was grinning a strained, frozen grin into the dark as I groped on the floor of the truck's cab for something to hit him with.

There was an open toolbox. I came up with a socket wrench and laid it on the seat between Nona and me. The cop leaned in the window, his face changing like a devil's in the light from the flasher.

"Traveling a little fast for the conditions, weren't you, guy?"

"Following a little close, weren't you?" I asked. "For the conditions?"

He might have flushed. It was hard to tell in the flickering light. "Are you lipping me, son?"

"I am if you're trying to pin the dents in your cruiser on me."

"Let's see your driver's license and your registration."

I got out my wallet and handed him my license.

"Registration?"

"It's my brother's truck. The registration is in his wallet."

"That right?" He looked at me hard, trying to stare me down. When he saw it would take a while, he looked past me at Nona. I could have ripped his eyes out for what I saw in them. "What's your name?"

"Cheryl Craig, sir."

"What are you doing riding around in his brother's pickup in the middle of a snowstorm, Cheryl?"

"We're going to see my uncle."

"In Blainesville?"

"Yes."

"I don't know any Craigs in Blainesville."

"His name is Barlow. On Bowen Hill."

"That right?" He walked around to the back of the truck to look at the plate. I opened the door and leaned out. He was writing it down.

He came back while I was still leaning out, spotlighted from the waist up in the glare of his headlights. "I'm going to . . . What's that all over you, boy?"

I didn't have to look down to know what was all over me. It was all over Nona, too. I had smeared it on her tan coat when I kissed her. I used to think that leaning out like that was just absent-mindedness, but writing all of this has changed my mind. I don't think it was absent-minded at all. I think I wanted him to see it. I held onto the socket wrench.

"What do you mean?"

He came two steps closer. "You're hurt——cut yourself, looks like. Better——"

I swung at him. His hat had been knocked off in the crash and his head was bare. I hit him head on, just above the forehead. I've never forgotten the sound that made, like a pound of butter falling onto a hard floor.

"Hurry," Nona said. She put a calm hand on my neck. It was very cool, like air in a root cellar. My foster mother, Mrs. Hollis . . . she had a root cellar. . . .

Funny I should remember that. She sent me down there for vegetables in the winter. She canned them herself. Not in real cans, of course, but in thick Mason jars with those rubber sealers that go under the lid.

I went down there one day to get a jar of waxed beans for our supper. The preserves were all in boxes, neatly marked in Mrs. Hollis's hand. I remember that she always misspelled raspberry, and that used to fill me with a secret superiority.

On this day I went past the boxes marked "razberrys" and into the corner where she kept the beans. It was cool and dark. The walls were plain dark earth and in wet weather they exuded moisture in trickling, crooked streams. The smell was a secret, dark effluvium composed of living things and earth and stored vegetables, a smell remarkably like that of a woman's private parts. There was an old, shattered printing press in one corner that had been there ever since I came, and sometimes I used to play with it and pretend I could get it going again. I loved the root cellar. In those days—I was nine or ten—the root cellar was my favorite place. Mrs. Hollis refused to set foot in it, and it was against her husband's dignity to go down and fetch up vegetables. So I went there and smelled that peculiar secret earthy smell and enjoyed the privacy of its womblike confinement. It was lit by one cobwebby bulb that Mr. Hollis had strung, probably before the Boer War. Sometimes I wiggled my hands and made huge, elongated rabbits on the wall.

I got the beans and was about to go back when I heard a rustling movement under one of the old boxes. I went over and lifted it up.

There was a brown rat beneath it, lying on its side. It rolled its head up at me and stared. Its sides were heaving violently and it bared its teeth. It was the biggest rat I had ever seen, and I leaned closer. It was in the act of giving birth. Two of its young, hairless and blind, were already nursing at its belly. Another was halfway into the world.

The mother glared at me helplessly, ready to bite. I wanted to kill it, kill all of them, squash them, but I couldn't. It was the most horrible thing I'd ever seen. As I watched, a small brown spider—a daddy longlegs, I think—crawled rapidly across the floor. The mother snatched it up and ate it.

I fled. Halfway up the stairs I fell and broke the jar of beans. Mrs. Hollis thrashed me, and I never went into the root cellar again unless I had to.

I stood looking down at the cop, remembering.

"Hurry," Nona said again.

He was much lighter than Norman Blanchette had been, or perhaps my adrenalin was just flowing more freely. I gathered him up in both arms and carried him over to the edge of the bridge. I could barely make out the Gretna Falls downstream, and upstream the GS&WM railroad trestle was only a gaunt shadow, like a scaffold. The night wind whooped and screamed, and the snow beat against my face. For a moment I held the cop against my chest like a sleeping newborn child, and then I remembered what he really was and threw him over the side and down into darkness.

We went back to the truck and got in, but it wouldn't start. I cranked the engine until I could smell the sweetish aroma of gas from the flooded carb, and then stopped.

"Come on," I said.

We went to the cruiser. The front seat was littered with violation tags, forms, two clipboards. The shortwave under the dash crackled and spluttered.

"Unit Four, come in, Four. Do you copy?"

I reached under and turned it off, banging my knuckles on something as I searched for the right toggle switch. It was a shotgun, pump action. Probably the cop's personal property. I unclipped it and handed it to Nona. She put it on her lap. I backed the cruiser up. It was dented but otherwise not hurt. It had snow tires and they bit nicely once we got over the ice that had done the damage.

Then we were in Blainesville. The houses, except for an occasional shanty trailer set back from the road, had disappeared. The road itself hadn't been plowed yet and there were no tracks except the ones we were leaving behind us. Monolithic fir trees, weighted with snow, towered all around us, and they made me feel tiny and insignificant, just some tiny morsel caught in the giant throat of this night. It was now after ten o'clock.

I didn't see much of college social life during my freshman year at the university. I studied hard and worked in the library shelving books and repairing bindings and learning how to catalogue. In the spring there was jayvee baseball.

Near the end of the academic year, just before finals, there was a dance at the gym. I was at loose ends, studied up for my first two tests, and I wandered down. I had the buck admission, so I went in.

It was dark and crowded and sweaty and frantic as only a college social before the ax of finals can be. There was sex in the air. You didn't have to smell it; you could almost reach out and grab it in both hands, like a wet piece of heavy cloth. You knew that love was going to be made later on, or what passes for love. People were going to make it under bleachers and in the steam plant parking lot and in apartments and dormitory rooms. It was going to be made by

359

desperate man/boys with the draft one step behind them and by pretty coeds who were going to drop out this year and go home and start a family. It would be made with tears and laughter, drunk and sober, stiffly and with no inhibition. But mostly it would be made quickly.

There were a few stags, but not many. It wasn't a night you needed to go anyplace stag. I drifted down by the raised bandstand. As I got closer to the sound, the beat, the music got to be a palpable thing. The group had a half circle of five-foot amplifiers behind them, and you could feel your eardrums flapping in and out with the bass signature.

I leaned up against the wall and watched. The dancers moved in prescribed patterns (as if they were trios instead of couples, the third invisible but between, being humped from the front and back), feet moving through the sawdust that had been sprinkled over the varnished floor. I didn't see anybody I knew and I began to feel lonely, but pleasantly so. I was at that stage of the evening where you fantasize that everyone is looking at you, the romantic stranger, out of the corners of their eyes.

About a half hour later I went out and got a Coke in the lobby. When I went back in somebody had started a circle dance and I was pulled in, my arms around the shoulders of two girls I had never seen before. We went around and around. There were maybe two hundred people in the circle and it covered half the gym floor. Then part of it collapsed and twenty or thirty people formed another circle in the middle of the first and started to go around the other way. It made me feel dizzy. I saw a girl who looked like Shelley Roberson, but I knew that was a fantasy. When I looked for her again I couldn't see her or anyone who looked like her.

When the thing finally broke up I felt weak and not well. I went back over by the bleachers and sat down. The music was too loud, the air too greasy. I could hear my heartbeat in my head, the way you do after you threw the biggest drunk of your life.

I used to think what happened next happened because I was tired and a little nauseated from going around and around, but, as I said before, all this writing has brought everything into sharper focus. I can't believe that anymore.

I looked up at them again, all the beautiful, hurrying people in the semidarkness. It seemed to me that all the men looked terrified, their faces elongating into grotesque, slow-motion masks. It was understandable. The women—coeds in their sweaters, short skirts, their bellbottoms—were all turning into rats. At first it didn't frighten me. I even chuckled. I knew what I was seeing was some kind of hallucination, and for a while I could watch it almost clinically.

Then some girl stood on tiptoe to kiss her fellow, and that was too much. Hairy, twisted face with its black buckshot eyes reaching up, mouth spreading to reveal teeth . . .

I left.

I stood in the lobby for a moment, half distracted. There was a bathroom down the hall, but I went past it and up the stairs.

The locker room was on the third floor and I had to run the last flight. I pulled the door open and ran for one of the bathroom stalls. I threw up amid the mixed smells of liniment, sweaty uniforms, oiled leather. The music was far away down there, the silence up here virginal. I felt comforted.

We had come to a stop sign at Southwest Bend. The memory of the dance had left me excited for a reason I didn't understand. I began to shake.

She looked at me, smiling with her dark eyes. "Now?"

I couldn't answer her. I was shaking too badly for that. She nodded slowly.

I drove onto a spur of Route 7 that must have been a logging road in the summertime. I didn't drive in too deeply because I was afraid of getting stuck. I popped off the headlights and flecks of snow began to gather silently on the windshield. Some kind of sound was escaping me, being dragged out of me. I think it must have been a close oral counterpart to the thoughts of a rabbit caught in a snare.

"Here," she said. "Right here."

It was ecstasy.

We almost didn't get back onto the main road. The snowplow had gone by, orange lights winking and flashing in the night, throwing up a huge wall of snow in our way.

There was a shovel in the trunk of the police car. It took me half an hour to dig out, and by then it was almost midnight. She turned on the police radio while I was doing it, and it told us what we had to know. The bodies of Blanchette and the kid from the pickup truck had been found. They suspected that we had taken the cruiser. The cop's name had been Essegian, and that's a funny name. There used to be a major-league ballplayer named Essegian—I think he played for the Dodgers. Maybe I had killed one of his relatives. It didn't bother me to know the cop's name. He had been following too close and he had gotten in our way.

We drove back onto the main road.

I could feel her excitement, high and hot and burning. I stopped long enough to clear the windshield with my arm and then we were going again.

We went through West Blainesville and I knew without having to be told where to turn. A snow-crusted sign said it was Stackpole Road.

The plow had not been here, but one vehicle had been through before us. The tracks of its tires were still freshly cut in the blowing, restless snow.

A mile, then less than a mile. Her fierce eagerness, her need, came to me and I began to feel jumpy again. We came around a curve and there was the power truck, bright orange body and warning flashers pulsing the color of blood. It was blocking the road.

You can't imagine her rage—our rage, really—because now, after what happened, we were really one. You can't imagine the sweeping feeling of intense paranoia, the conviction that every hand was out to cut us down.

There were two of them. One was a bending shadow in the darkness ahead. The other was holding a flashlight. He came toward us, his light bobbing like a lurid eye. And there was more than hate. There was fear—fear that it was all going to be snatched away from us at the last moment.

He was yelling, and I cranked down my window.

"You can't get through here! Go on back by the Bowen Road! We got a live line down here! You can't——"

I got out of the car, lifted the shotgun, and gave him both barrels. He was flung forcibly back against the orange truck and I staggered

362

back against the cruiser. He slipped down an inch at a time, staring at me incredulously, and then he fell into the snow.

"Are there more shells?" I asked Nona.

"Yes." She gave them to me. I broke the shotgun, ejected the spent cartridges, and put in new ones.

The guy's buddy had straightened up and was watching incredulously. He shouted something at me that was lost in the wind. It sounded like a question but it didn't matter. I was going to kill him. I walked toward him and he just stood there, looking at me. He didn't move, even when I raised the shotgun. I don't think he had any conception of what was happening. I think he thought it was a dream.

I fired one barrel and was low. A great flurry of snow exploded up, coating him. Then he bellowed a great terrified scream and ran, taking one gigantic bound over the fallen power cable in the road. I fired the other barrel and missed again. Then he was gone into the dark and I could forget him. He wasn't in our way anymore. I went back to the cruiser.

"We'll have to walk," I said.

We walked past the fallen body, stepped over the spitting power line, and walked up the road, following the widely spaced tracks of the fleeing man. Some of the drifts were almost up to her knees, but she was always a little ahead of me. We were both panting.

We came over a hill and descended into a narrow dip. On one side was a leaning, deserted shed with glassless windows. She stopped and gripped my arm.

"There," she said, and pointed across to the other side. Her grip was strong and painful even through my coat. Her face was set in a glaring, triumphant rictus. "There. There."

It was a graveyard.

We slipped and stumbled up the banking and clambered over a snow-covered stone wall. I had been here too, of course. My real mother had come from Blainesville, and although she and my father had never lived there, this was where the family plot had been. It was a gift to my mother from her parents, who had lived and died in Blainesville. During the thing with Shelley Roberson I had come here often to read the poems of John Keats and Percy Shelley. I suppose you think that was a damned weird thing to do, but I don't. Not even now. I felt close to them, comforted. After Ace Carmody beat me up I never went there again. Not until Nona led me there.

I slipped and fell in the loose powder, twisting my ankle. I got up and walked on it, using the shotgun as a crutch. The silence was infinite and unbelievable. The snow fell in soft, straight lines, mounding atop the leaning stones and crosses, burying all but the tips of the corroded flagholders that would only hold flags on Memorial Day and Veterans Day. The silence was unholy in its immensity, and for the first time I felt terror.

She led me toward a stone building set into the whitened rise of the hill at the back of the cemetery. A vault. She had a key. I knew she would have a key, and she did.

She blew the snow away from the door's flange and found the keyhole. The sound the turning tumblers made seemed to stretch across the darkness. She leaned on the door and it swung inward.

The odor that came out at us was as cool as autumn, as cool as the air in the Hollis root cellar. I could see in only a little way. There were dead leaves on the stone floor. She entered, paused, looked back over her shoulder at me.

"No," I said.

She laughed at me.

I stood in the darkness, feeling everything begin to run together—past, present, future. I wanted to run, run screaming, run fast enough to take back everything I had done.

Nona stood there looking at me, the most beautiful girl in the world, the only thing that had ever been mine. She made a gesture with her hands on her body. I'm not going to tell you what it was. You would know it if you saw it.

I went in. She closed the door.

It was dark but I could see perfectly well. The place was alight with a slowly running green fire. It ran over the walls and snaked across the leaf-littered floor in writhing tongues. There was a bier in the center of the vault, but it was empty. The petals of withered roses were scattered across it. She beckoned to me, then pointed to the small door at the rear. Small, unmarked door. I dreaded it. I

364

think I knew then. She had used me and laughed at me. Now she would destroy me.

But I couldn't stop. I went to that door because I had to. That mental telegraph was still working at what I felt was glee—a terrible, insane glee—and triumph. My hand trembled toward the door. It was coated with green fire.

I opened the door and saw what was there.

It was the girl, my girl. Dead. Her eyes stared vacantly into that October vault, into my own eyes. She smelled of stolen kisses. She was naked and she had been ripped open from throat to crotch, her whole body turned into a sterile womb. And yet something lived in there. The rats. I could not see them but I could hear them, rustling around in there, inside her. I knew that in a moment her dry mouth would open and she would speak to me of love. I backed away, my whole body numb, my brain floating on a dark cloud of fear.

I turned to Nona. She was laughing, holding her arms out to me. And with a sudden blaze of understanding I knew, I knew, I knew. The last test had been passed. *I was free!*

I turned back to the doorway and of course it was nothing but an empty stone closet with dead leaves on the floor.

I went to Nona. I went to my life.

Her arms reached around my neck and I pulled her against me. That was when she began to change, to ripple and run like wax. The great dark eyes became small and beady. The hair coarsened, went brown. The nose shortened, the nostrils dilated. Her body lumped and hunched against me.

I was being embraced by a rat.

Her lipless mouth stretched upward for mine.

I didn't scream. There were no screams left. I doubt if I will ever scream again.

It's so hot in here.

I don't mind the heat, not really. I like to sweat if I can shower, I've always thought of sweat as a good, masculine thing, but sometimes there are bugs that bite—spiders, for instance. Did you know that female spiders sting and eat their mates? They do, right after copulation. Also, I've heard scurryings in the walls. I don't like that.

365

I've given myself writer's cramp, and the felt tip of the pen is all soft and mushy. But I'm done now. And things look different. It doesn't seem the same anymore at all.

Do you realize that for a while they almost had me believing that I did all those horrible things myself? Those men from the truck stop, the guy from the power truck who got away. They said I was alone. I was alone when they found me, almost frozen to death in that graveyard by the stones that mark my father, my mother, my brother Drake. But that only means she left, you can see that. Any fool could. But I'm glad she got away. Truly I am. But you must realize she was with me all the time, every step of the way.

I'm going to kill myself now. It will be much better. I'm tired of all the guilt and agony and bad dreams, and also I don't like the noises in the walls. Anybody could be in there. Or anything.

I'm not crazy. I know that and trust that you do, too. If you say you aren't, that's supposed to mean you are, but I am beyond all those little games. She was with me, she was real. I love her. True love will never die. That's how I signed all my letters to Shelley, the ones I tore up.

I didn't hurt any ladies, did I?

I never hurt any ladies.

She was the only one I ever really loved.

It's so hot in here. And I don't like the sounds in the walls.

True love will never die.